SF

P9-EMO-556

Monster #3

HERO

HERO

MICHAEL GRANT

KATHERINE TEGEN BOOKS

An Imprint of HarperCollins Publishers

Katherine Tegen Books is an imprint of HarperCollins Publishers.

Hero

Library of Congress Cataloging-in-Publication Data

Names: Grant, Michael, author.
Title: Hero / Michael Grant.
Description: First edition. | New York, NY : Katherine Tegen Books, an imprint of
  HarperCollins Publishers, [2019] | Summary: While the Rockborn Gang tries to
  outmaneuver a new supervillain created by meteorite shrapnel, Malik investigates
  the Dark Watchers and the possibility that their reality is advanced, elaborate
  simulation.
Identifiers: LCCN 2019000074 | ISBN 9780062467904 (hardcover)
Subjects: | CYAC: Superheroes—Fiction. | Supervillains—Fiction. | Good and
  evil—Fiction. | Science fiction.
Classification: LCC PZ7.G7671 He 2019 | DDC [Fic]—dc23 LC record available at
  https://lccn.loc.gov/2019000074

Typography by Joel Tippie
19 20 21 22 23   PC/LSCH   10 9 8 7 6 5 4 3 2 1

First Edition

To my two Katherines.

I lose sleep at night wondering whether we are intelligent enough to figure out the universe.

I don't know.

—Neil deGrasse Tyson

"The justifications of men who kill should always be heard with skepticism," said the monster.

—Patrick Ness, *A Monster Calls*

HERO

ASO-7

ANOMALOUS SPACE OBJECT Seven was being carefully tracked by Professor Martin Darby of Northwestern University, father of the famous and/or infamous Shade Darby. Shade's father had had his security clearance reinstated, despite the fact that his daughter had used his data to locate and steal one of the earlier ASOs and had then used the rock—its universal shorthand name—to become Rockborn, a mutant with a power—the power, in Shade's case, to move at speeds just over Mach 1.

ASO-7 had passed the orbit of the moon and was now spinning around the Earth in a decaying elliptical, an orbit that Professor Darby and counterparts at universities all over the world had calculated and recalculated with growing alarm.

ASO-7 was a large piece, roughly eighteen meters (fifty-nine feet) long and sixteen meters (fifty-two feet) wide. Estimated mass, assuming the composition matched earlier

ASOs, was 1,600 tons, about the weight of 550 Toyota Land Cruisers.

The size of the rock and the fact that it seemed to be moving erratically had left Professor Darby able to calculate only probabilities. He'd turned those probabilities into a simplified map, which he'd forwarded, along with his calculations, to Homeland Security, NASA, and the Department of Defense.

The map showed the likely strike zone as a pink cross-hatched area. That pink cross-hatching extended from just north of Elizabeth, New Jersey, to the Long Island Sound around Bayville.

But it was what occupied the middle of that strike zone that had sent alarm bells ringing throughout the US government. Because in the middle of that zone stood New York City.

The odds of a relatively safe splashdown in the water of Long Island Sound were 40 percent, which left smaller likelihoods of strikes near Elizabeth, or in Manhattan proper, which had only a 20 percent likelihood of being the bull's-eye.

But that was a one-in-five chance of utterly annihilating the greatest of American cities, because this much was certain: if ASO-7 hit land, it would release energy equivalent to thirty-five kilotons. The bomb that destroyed Hiroshima was fifteen kilotons. If ASO-7 was intact and hit, say, Rockefeller Center, it would obliterate sixty square blocks, and severely damage buildings and toss cars and buses around from Thirty-Ninth Street to Fifty-Seventh Street, and from Ninth Avenue almost to Lexington Avenue. If it landed on a weekday, the estimates were that it would kill as many as a million people instantly and another quarter million from fires and related injuries.

ASO-7 had the potential to be the greatest disaster ever to strike the United States.

Department of Homeland Security
Memo: 19-00475
Top Secret (HSTF-66)
Re: ASO-7

DoD, NASA, and university assessments suggest a likelihood that ASO-7 will impact in or near New York City. Likelihood 20 percent lowest estimate (Northwestern University), 40 percent highest estimate (Oxford University).

Potential Countermeasures:

THAAD *(Terminal High Altitude Area Defense). THAAD uses KKV technology (Kinetic Kill Vehicle) and would be ineffective.*

GMD *(Ground-Based Midcourse Defense). No units are within range.*

Aegis-capable ships. *Aegis RIM-161 Standard Missile 3 (SM-3) uses KKV technology and would be ineffective.*

DoD assesses likelihood of any of these systems being effective at 0 percent.

The only option we have to present at this time is to launch one or more ICBMs armed with nuclear warheads to intercept and either divert or break up the ASO. Such an application is theoretical and untested.

Preliminary estimates of effective destruction of ASO-7 by a single warhead are 5 percent. Preliminary estimates show a 30 percent likelihood of altering the ASO's course, with that new course being almost entirely unpredictable. The most likely result appears to be fracturing of ASO-7, resulting in multiple smaller meteorites with impact zones and damage impossible to predict.

Embassy of the People's Republic of China—Washington
ALERT
Top Secret

Ambassador Gao has been informed by US State Department that two ICBMs (Type: LGM-30) enhanced by additional solid-fuel boosters and carrying single warheads (Type: W87) with yields estimated at 475 kilotons will be launched from Vandenberg Air Force Base on an intercept course with ASO-7.

US Defense Department liaisons have offered reassurance as to angle and flight time. Recommend People's Army track but otherwise treat as nonhostile.

The Rachel Maddow Show—*Interview Transcript*

RACHEL MADDOW: I want to thank you for joining us by Skype from Las Vegas. It has been a very intense few weeks, and an especially intense forty-eight hours for all of you. So thank you for agreeing to this interview.

SHADE DARBY: You're welcome.

MADDOW: Would you mind . . . using Skype can be awkward . . . would you mind if we go around to each member of the group?

SHADE: No problem. Dekka?

DEKKA TALENT: I'm Dekka Talent.

MADDOW: You are a survivor of the Perdido Beach Anomaly—what you, I assume, call the FAYZ?

DEKKA: Yep.

MADDOW: How is this situation different from life in the PBA dome, in the FAYZ?

DEKKA: No dome. And the rock mutation is more physical. We change. Physically. Also we have food now, so that's different.

MADDOW: Is that transformation, that morphing, is that painful?

DEKKA: No. More creepy and disturbing than painful.

MADDOW: Can you give us a sense of how that feels? It must be just . . . well, let me just ask: What is it like? How does it feel?

DEKKA: (Shrugs.) You should probably ask Cruz or Shade or . . . (Pushes Cruz forward.)

CRUZ: Hi.

MADDOW: Cruz, you have become the face of the Rockborn Gang. In fact, we're going to put up the iconic photo of you carrying a baby away from the flames that engulfed hundreds of people in that just unspeakably awful moment in Las Vegas. I wonder if you see your new status as, well, like I said, the face of the Rockborn Gang, I wonder if you see this perhaps as an

*ironic twist, given that you are transgender and your ability,
your superpower, is to alter your appearance at will.*

CRUZ: *I guess. I mean, yeah, it's like, I don't know. Like the
rock has a weird sense of humor. Or else the media does. But I'm
not the hero here. It wasn't me that stopped Dillon Poe—*

MADDOW: *The so-called Charmer. Dillon Poe, who had
the power to compel absolute obedience with just the sound of
his voice.*

CRUZ: *Yeah, him. It wasn't me that stopped him. It was
Malik and Francis. I just happened to be in that picture.*

MADDOW: *The story is that you were recruited, in a way,
by Shade Darby, who was your friend from school. Is that
correct?*

CRUZ: *More or less. You should talk to Shade. Shade and
Dekka are sort of the . . . I don't know. I mean, I'm just this
chameleon person. Or talk to Malik, he's the one who . . .*

MADDOW: *Did you want to say something more about
Malik?*

CRUZ: *Malik, come here, your turn.*

MALIK TENERIFE: *Good evening, Ms. Maddow.*

MADDOW: *Welcome to the show, and thanks for coming
on. Your story is perhaps the most tragic. You were very badly
burned in the battle that took place at the Port of Los Angeles.*

MALIK: *Yes.*

MADDOW: *Doctors did not expect you to survive. Is it
true, as some reports have it, that the Malik you are now, the
person we are seeing, is actually a morph?*

MALIK: *Yes, that's true. I am in morph now. If I de-morph,
I revert back to the condition I was in the hospital. Which, as*

you said, is . . . intolerable.

MADDOW: *And the power you have is the ability to essentially project that pain onto others. That's how you prepared the ground for the raid on the so-called Ranch, the Homeland Security facility people are comparing to Dr. Mengele's Auschwitz.*

MALIK: *Yes. That is my power. The ability to project excruciating pain. It's not . . . It's not something I wanted.*

MADDOW: *Survivors from the Ranch, survivors—and there were very few—say the pain you projected was so awful that in some cases they attempted suicide rather than endure it.*

MALIK: *(Nods.)*

MADDOW: *And Dillon Poe did in fact kill himself rather than endure it.*

MALIK: *Yes.*

MADDOW: *Does it concern you at all that this power is in the hands of . . . well, in your hands and in the hands of the others in the group? And then I wonder if you would talk about how you see all of this playing out.*

MALIK: *Does it concern me? (Laughs.) Of course it concerns me. We have six people here who have extreme power. No one elected us. No one said, 'Let's give all this power to these kids.' The problem is that the rock gives power to the good and the bad alike, people like Justin DeVeere—*

MADDOW: *Knightmare.*

MALIK: *Yeah, him. And Tom Peaks—*

MADDOW: *Napalm or Dragon, as people are calling him.*

MALIK: *And Dillon Poe, yeah. The only thing the people in charge could do to stop Poe was send a tank brigade into the city,* *and, I'm sorry, but that wasn't going to stop him, either. Look, I don't want to be doing this; none of us wants to be doing this. But Dillon Poe had to die; there's no question about that. He had to die. He was a mass murderer. He killed—*

MADDOW: *The official death toll is currently 3,102 people. And may rise as more bodies are found.*

MALIK: *Yeah, he had to be stopped, and the only way to do it was by killing him. But that doesn't mean I wanted to be the one who . . . None of us likes doing this, Ms. Maddow. You know?*

MADDOW: *Shade Darby? Is that true for all of you? I ask because—and please correct me if any of this is wrong—but you actually chose this path. You actually obtained a piece of the rock and became a mutant deliberately.*

SHADE: *Yes. And I have to live with that. Not just what I did to myself, that's on me, but I dragged Cruz into it, and Malik. You could say I chose this for myself, although . . . Did I know this was how it would turn out? No, of course not.*

MADDOW: *I don't want to put words in your mouth, but I sense, and again, correct me, but I sense that you feel some guilt.*

SHADE: *Some guilt? (Laughs.) I saw my father thrown to the ground and arrested for something I did. I convinced Cruz to help me, and now she's in the middle of all this, living this life. And Malik . . . Do I feel guilty that someone I care about is haunted night and day by voices in his head? That he's defined by pain? People are calling him M-Pain and Screamer and, you know, Malik is the smartest, kindest . . . Yeah. Yes, Rachel, I feel guilt.*

MADDOW: *Is Aristotle Adamo there with you?*

ARMO: *Call me Armo.*

MADDOW: *I want to run a piece of tape we have obtained. I'll warn the audience that it is shaky and poor quality and . . . well, I was going to say it may disturb some viewers, but given what everyone has seen in recent days and weeks . . . Let's roll the tape. That is you, in morph, attacking an Apache helicopter, a military helicopter, as it hovers over the ground.*

ARMO: *Huh. Cool, I actually haven't seen that before.*

MADDOW: *You were a prisoner at the Ranch where—*

ARMO: *Can you run that tape again? That was way cool.*

MADDOW: *Actually, if you could answer my question and—*

ARMO: *Nah, first run the tape.*

MADDOW: *(Pause.) All right, ummmmm, control room?*

CHAPTER 1
Sex, Pastries, and the Laws of Physics

"GOTTA ADMIT: THIS is nice. I guess." Dekka Talent sounded unhappy about it as she rubbed a bedsheet between thumb and forefinger. "It's all so smooth and soft."

"Beats my old sleeping bag," Francis Specter said, yawning, ruffling her red hair, and throwing back the covers of her own bed. "Do you mind if I . . ." She gestured toward the bathroom.

"It's your bathroom as much as mine, kid."

They'd shared the bedroom, each with her own queen-sized bed, night-light, side table, bottle of spring water, TV remote, and pillow mints. Dekka was the elder of the two, of voting if not yet drinking age, and had about her a seriousness and physical presence that made her seem older.

Francis Specter was a new person in Dekka's life, and in the life of the rest of their group as well, an underfed white girl of fourteen, with wary, suspicious eyes.

Both girls had pasts full of pain and trauma. Dekka had

survived the FAYZ, usually called the Perdido Beach Anomaly or PBA, the bizarre twenty-mile-in-diameter, impenetrable, opaque dome that had imprisoned 332 kids under the age of fifteen. 332 kids at the start . . . far fewer by the end.

Following the collapse of the FAYZ dome, Dekka had had four years of relative normalcy, doing her best to sink back into obscurity as a cashier at a Bay Area Safeway. That obscurity had ended when it was learned that more of the rock—the same alien mutagenic virus-infected celestial debris that had caused the FAYZ—was heading for Earth.

A secret government group, Homeland Security Task Force 66, had brought Dekka to the Ranch and there had tried to use the rock to give her some of the powers she'd had in the FAYZ. HSTF-66's plan had worked, partially. Dekka had gained powers, but not the powers she'd once held in the FAYZ. Things had changed. Outside the confines of the dome, rock mutations yielded more terrifying powers that were accompanied by physical changes, often quite extreme. In Dekka's case, the rock had grabbed a bit of cat DNA and some imagery from Dekka's own mind, played its inscrutable game, and yielded a morph with poisonous snakes where her dreads were, and a body covered in fur.

And Dekka's old power of canceling gravity had been replaced by an ability to shred anything—or anyone—in her path. Like she was a human blender, a human chain saw. She'd learned to focus this power, but it was still horrifically destructive. In the course of too many battles, Dekka had turned walls and floors and ceilings to mulch. And human beings—bad guys, to be sure, but still human beings—had been reduced to bloody gobbets. By Dekka. By her will.

Dekka was not happy about the soft sheets because Dekka had zero reason to believe that life would continue to allow her to survive, let alone survive in luxury. She was also not happy about the four and a half bathrooms, each a wonder of marble and mirrors and glass, with deep tubs and showers that could have been used to hose off a whole rugby team, outfitted with towels so thick and soft Dekka could have slept comfortably on one of them, let alone the bed.

Luxury, in Dekka's opinion, made you soft. And the future did not feel soft.

But the sheets sure do.

Also, she admitted privately, it was a bit intimidating. She was not a rich kid like her sidekick, Armo, who took it all in stride. Armo's path to the Rockborn Gang had started when he wrecked his 600-horsepower, $90,000 Viper in Malibu. Dekka could not have afforded to pay a month's insurance on such a vehicle.

As for Francis Specter, Dekka knew that she had endured a very different sort of hardship, living with her mother as her mother descended into drug addiction and a depraved life with a racist biker gang at a bare-bones compound in the Mojave Desert.

Francis was also Rockborn, but while Dekka had a straight-forwardly destructive power, Francis had a stranger, deeper, harder-to-understand ability. Francis could pass through solid objects. Or at least that's how it looked to people. In reality, Francis moved into a fourth spatial dimension, and rather than go *through*, she went . . . *around*.

If Francis was "the kid" of the Rockborn Gang, then Dekka was what passed for a responsible adult, not a role Dekka relished. In addition to Dekka and Francis, the Rockborn Gang consisted of Shade Darby, Malik Tenerife, Cruz (neé Hugo Cruz Rojas), and Armo, who no longer used his birth name of Aristotle Adamo because it was too long and too open to mockery. Armo was not, perhaps, the guy to go through life wearing a great philosopher's name.

Armo was a white boy—a very large, strong, very handsome, rather sweet, not overly bright boy with Oppositional Defiant Disorder (ODD), which made it very, very hard for him to ever do as he was told.

Armo also had a morph, a creature not unlike a polar bear with various disturbing human features. In that morph, Armo—as long as you asked him politely and did not attempt to order him around—would happily charge a tank.

The Rockborn Gang currently occupied a three-bedroom, four-and-a-half-bath suite in Caesars Palace in Las Vegas. The suite would have cost $10,000 a day had it not been offered to them by the grateful management of Caesars Palace with the enthusiastic support of the Las Vegas Convention and Visitors Authority. The powers that be in Las Vegas knew how to show gratitude, and the Rockborn Gang had been given the lion's share of the credit for saving Las Vegas from the mind-controlling Rockborn psycho named Dillon Poe, the self-styled Charmer, and then from the army's brutal overreaction.

Had the Rockborn Gang not stopped Poe, it was very likely that Las Vegas would have been utterly destroyed.

Of course Las Vegas also knew the advantage for tourism in having the most Facebooked, Instagrammed, tweeted, YouTubed, reported, loved, hated, praised, reviled group of people on Planet Earth in residence. Just two days after what was being called the #CasinoWar, #MadMaxVegas, and #Vegapocalypse, among many other names, flights and room reservations were already coming back strong after having been shut down entirely.

The Rockborn Gang had saved Las Vegas billions of dollars, and now their presence was bringing the gamblers back. There was already serious talk of erecting a statue, which was fine, Dekka supposed, and certainly better than being hated and hunted, but it all made her nervous. A black, lesbian FAYZ survivor would never be able to relax as completely as Armo, who, upon exiting the bedroom, Dekka found sprawled across a couch and a coffee table wearing pajama bottoms, with a bagel resting on his bare left pectoral and a little tub of cream cheese balanced on the right side.

"Unh," Dekka said to Armo, the limits of her pre-coffee small talk.

"There's coffee in that carafe," Armo said, pointing with his cream cheese–smeared knife.

Cruz sat off to one side of the fabulously luxurious room with her battered purple Moleskine open on her lap, a pen in her hand, making notes and casting subtle glances at the ever-oblivious Armo.

Dekka poured. Dekka drank.

"Holy Communion in the Church of Caffeine?" Cruz teased.

Dekka nodded. "Damn right." There was an expectant air that made Dekka frown. "What? What are you two waiting for?"

"We're kind of . . ." Cruz tilted her head, hearing something, and held up a hand. "Never mind, you'll see."

Shade Darby, a white girl with blunt-cut dark hair—she'd hacked away at it herself—and the kind of eyes that drilled holes into you, opened the door to her bedroom, stepped through wearing a Caesars bathrobe, closed the door casually behind her, and said, "Any coffee left?"

"See, Dekka, what we're doing," Cruz said as though continuing a conversation, "is waiting to see how much time Shade and Malik have decided to allow before *he* comes out."

"Out?" Dekka looked at Armo, who shrugged, causing his cream cheese to tumble down his chest.

Cruz answered with a significant nod toward the door Shade had just closed.

"Huh? Oh. Ahhh," Dekka said. "I assumed you and Shade would share a room."

"She got a better offer," Cruz said.

"No, no, no. Just stop, right now," Shade warned.

Dekka was not a jovial person, not much given to banter or teasing, but this was too easy to pass up. In a mock-severe voice she said, "You know, Cruz, just because Shade and Malik shared a room, that doesn't mean anything, you know . . .

happened. You shouldn't jump to conclusions."

"Well, *something* happened," Armo said. "I know Malik's power is causing people pain, but the noises I heard last night didn't sound like pain."

"Oh it's going to be like this, is it?" Shade said, shaking her head. "You realize if I morph I'm fast enough to smack the shit out of all four of you, right?"

At which point Malik came out of the bedroom and Cruz said, "Hah! Three minutes on the dot."

"Good morning," Malik said. Malik was African American, a college freshman with adorable ringleted hair, sleepy eyes, and a scary IQ. He and Shade had dated long ago, and broken up because . . . well, because by Shade's own account she had been obsessive and driven and not above manipulating friends.

Or as Dekka put it: a ruthless bitch.

The person Dekka and the others now spoke to was in some ways not Malik. It was Malik's morph of himself. The real Malik, the Malik who would emerge if he ever left morph, was a boy who'd been burned so badly doctors had been about to put him in a medically induced coma and allow him to die. The rock had saved him, but at a terrible price. Each of them—with the fascinating exception of Francis—felt the intrusive, overbearing presence of the unseen Dark Watchers whenever they were in morph. Malik lived with that twenty-four/seven so long as he was in morph—and leaving morph would mean an excruciating death.

But at the moment, Malik looked unusually cheerful. So

uncharacteristically, stupidly happy that Cruz giggled out loud and the others could not help but grin. It wasn't prurient leering, Dekka told herself . . . well, okay, in part maybe it was . . . but each of them liked Malik, admired him, and each of them knew that of them all, he was the one who had suffered the most terrible harm. Seeing Malik smile was . . .

Like watching the sun rise.

Malik made a point of saying "Good morning" to Shade in an overly formal way, as though they hadn't seen each other since yesterday.

"Plausible," Cruz commented, dryly. "Totally plausible. I know I believed it."

Dekka drank her coffee and went to the floor-to-ceiling window to look out, and to hide the sadness that had welled up inside her. She was nothing but pleased to see Malik happy, and frankly she enjoyed seeing the eternally cool and self-possessed Shade looking abashed and embarrassed. Served her right. But it inevitably brought personal memories to the surface, memories of her own doomed, lost, one-way love for a girl named Brianna. The Breeze, she'd called herself. Crazy, fearless, reckless Breeze.

Crazy, fearless, and reckless one too many times, my love. One too many times.

Cruz, the girl whose rescue of a baby had become the iconic photo of #ArmageddonVegas, had spent the night alone because the alternative would have been sharing with Armo, and that was not on the agenda, though Dekka had spotted more than one longing look from Cruz directed at the boy who could pass as the fourth Hemsworth brother.

It made Dekka sad seeing Cruz crushing on Armo. Dekka had detected no nastiness or hate in Armo, but that did not mean he would fall for a six-foot-tall transgender Latina. Dekka's own life had been shadowed by lost love, and she didn't wish that ache on anyone.

Francis came in, hair wet and face alight with wonder. "There's like . . . like . . . in the shower," she began.

"Yeah, yeah, it's nice," Dekka muttered.

But Francis was not put off by Dekka's puritanical gloom in the face of luxury. "There's, like, six showerheads! Six! There's this big wide one in the ceiling and then there are . . ."

Dekka tuned her out as the description of the wonders of the shower went on. Truth was, it actually was an amazing shower. It was the shower Dekka might have expected when she got to heaven. She was momentarily distracted by the notion of Saint Peter, like some real-estate guy on HGTV, saying, *And wait till you see the shower!*

Armo stood up, adjusted his pajama bottoms, and announced, "It's already ten thirty, and unlike you people I've been up since eight. I'm going down to the pool. Who's with me?"

No one was interested aside from Cruz. Dekka saw her dark eyes zeroing in on a dab of cream cheese clinging to Armo's chest and thought, *You poor kid.*

Finding no takers, Armo disappeared into a bathroom and re-emerged in a bathing suit. "Call me if something happens."

"Cruz, I thought you liked sunbathing," Shade said once Armo was gone.

Cruz shrugged. "I don't know what to wear. It's a problem."

"Oh, right." Shade winced.

"You could always do what I do," Dekka suggested. "T-shirt and shorts. That's kind of gender nonspecific."

Cruz looked uncomfortable, and Dekka hoped she hadn't said anything stupid. She'd had years of people assuming various things just because she was gay, or because she was black, and even the innocently curious inquiries got to be tedious after a while. Or in Dekka's case, instantly.

"I don't want to look like . . . ," Cruz began, then veered away into a low, abashed mutter concluding with, "I don't want him to think I'm stalking him, geez."

Dekka sat down opposite her in the place Armo had vacated and leaned forward to keep her conversation with Cruz private. "Sweetheart, Armo is a good guy. Just whatever you do, don't ever try to order him around. Other than that, though? The boy is pure Malibu beach bum, mellow to the bone. Just, again, and I cannot stress this too much: don't tell him what to do."

Cruz grinned. "Yeah, I got that. He mentioned he was ODD. It took me a while to figure out he meant Oppositional Defiant Disorder."

Dekka smiled affectionately. "Oh, Armo's regular old *odd*, too, but he's good people. When things get hairy, you want Armo nearby."

Armo. *Crazy, fearless, and reckless. I have a type*, Dekka

thought dryly, *even if it isn't always a* romantic *type.*

She moved to the far end of the vast living room, where Shade was now in earnest conversation with Malik.

"Hey, Dekka," Shade said, waving her to a seat. "Malik is theorizing."

Of all the internal relationships within the Rockborn Gang, none was more emotionally loaded than Shade and Malik's. Shade had been present four years earlier when the FAYZ had at last come down, releasing its traumatized young inhabitants, Dekka among them. Shade had lost her mother that day, killed by Gaia, the monstrous alien in human form who had terrorized the last days of the FAYZ. That death had spawned an obsession in Shade, an obsession that had dragged Cruz and Malik into this new nightmare world with her.

Malik was what he now was because of Shade. He lived with the constant presence of the Dark Watchers because of Shade. They had been with him as he had spent the night with her, seeing what he saw, feeling his emotions.

What must that have been like for Malik? Dekka wondered. And the same phrase she'd applied to Cruz came to mind again: *you poor kid.*

"Once upon a time the most sophisticated computer game on earth was just a virtual tennis ball and two virtual rackets," Malik said, talking between bites of blueberry muffin. "We moved up to Pac-Man and Galaga. Then Mario and Donkey Kong. Then the Sims, where human players could create and control avatars meant to represent humans. That was the turning point, right there. That was the point when the gamer became a god. The gamer wasn't just a happy face gobbling up power dots and chasing ghosts; the gamer was creating virtual people and manipulating their world."

"Talking Dark Watchers?" Dekka asked in a low voice. Shade nodded.

"If you created a perfect sim, so perfect, so sophisticated that it encompassed millions, even billions of individual people," Malik went on, animated as he often was when prosing on about either science or great guitarists, "a simulation so advanced that each of those simulated people acted independently, so real that the game pieces, the avatars, experienced what felt like reality—"

Dekka held up a hand. "Is this going to involve math?"

Malik winked at her, and Dekka was caught off guard by the almost maternal feelings she had for him. Shade might be a manipulative brainiac, but the girl had excellent taste in men.

"I'll stick to English," Malik said.

"Proceed," Dekka said. Her gaze shifted to Shade and she thought, *If you break this boy's heart, I will personally administer a beat-down.*

"The point is that simulations can be reproduced like any other computer program. So if we suspect that there is a single simulation, we have to suspect that there could be millions. One reality and a potentially unlimited number of sims. Simulations might outnumber reality by billions to one. Which would mean statistically it's likely that we are not in an original, evolved reality, but in a sim."

Cruz returned from the bathroom and flopped down, spilling a bit of her coffee. "Oh, God, are we doing this again?"

"He promised no math," Dekka stage-whispered.

"Basically there would be no way to ever know if you are living in a sim or not. Unless something goes wrong. A glitch. Or maybe a hack."

"You think the Dark Watchers are the hackers?" Shade asked for the benefit of Dekka and Cruz, since she knew almost as much about it as Malik did, give or take a college-level physics course.

Malik shrugged. "I don't know. I don't know. Maybe we're a TV show. Maybe we're a game. Maybe we're something our three-dimensional brains can't even describe." He winced, closed his eyes as if in pain. Sometimes the attention of the Dark Watchers was so intrusive it felt like a kind of pain. After a moment Malik continued. "The question is: Francis."

"I can hear you," Francis said, coming back in, reaching for the overflowing platter of pastries, and pausing to ask, "Can anyone have these?"

"Francis, eat," Cruz said.

"You're an anomaly," Malik said, turning to address Francis. "Everyone else who has taken the rock has three things in common." He ticked them off on his fingers. "One: they've been changed physically, given a morph, sometimes vaguely animal, other times . . ." He shrugged. "Second: a power, an ability that defies conventional physics. And third: the Dark Watchers in your head anytime you're in morph."

"All except Francis," Shade said. "Morph? Yes, that whole prismatic, rainbowy thing she does. Power? Definitely. But no Watchers. Why?"

Malik sighed. "Well, babe . . ." He froze for a moment and shot a guilty look at Shade. "I mean, Shade, that just, um . . . slipped out."

Shade smiled, a rare occurrence, especially recently. "You know, *bunny*, I kind of don't think our secret is much of a secret."

"What?" Cruz erupted in mock surprise. "Shade and Malik?"

"I'm shocked," Dekka said in a perfectly flat voice.

"Anyway," Malik said, too loudly.

"Don't ever try to stop Malik once he's got his lecture on," Shade said.

"As I was saying—"

"So? How was it?" Cruz interrupted, batting her eyelashes.

Malik gaped at her in shock, his mouth open.

But Shade, in a low, marveling voice said, "Like you've fallen off a cliff and you're going to die and then, suddenly, a hand grabs you and hauls you back up." She made a face meant, belatedly, to make it seem like a joke.

Well, well, she's human.

"*So,*" Malik persisted, his voice a bit desperate, "The point is if we are living in a sim, then what we always saw as the immutable laws of physics are just so much software, the OS of this universe. And software can be rewritten. The fact is, none of this superpower stuff is possible, not under the laws of reality we've always accepted. Someone, some*thing*, has rewritten the program that defined those laws of physics."

Francis had kept well clear of the gentle teasing. Dekka knew she did not yet feel like she was really part of the group, and probably felt young besides.

"If we're just some program, then . . . well, what?" Francis asked.

Malik shrugged. "Nothing changes, really. We cannot help but feel real because we *are* real, subjectively. I think, therefore I am, as Descartes said."

"Who's day cart?" Francis wondered aloud.

"No, no," Shade said, shaking her head. "Whatever you do, don't get him off on a tangent."

"We experience real emotions, real pain, at least it's real to us," Malik went on, trying to float above the constant interruptions. "At one level it all doesn't change anything, real or sim. But . . ."

"But?" Dekka prompted, trying to resist a croissant and wondering if she could use the Caesars gym without being interrupted by people wanting to get a selfie with a Rockborn mutant freak.

"But Francis doesn't even conform to the 'new' rules. She doesn't feel the Dark Watchers. And more to the point, her power is not limited to our three dimensions. She can move into extra dimensions. Maybe," he said, with slow emphasis, "into *their* dimension."

They heard the door of the suite being unlocked, and Armo came back wearing a bathing suit, flip-flops, and a towel draped over his shoulders. "What are you guys talking about?"

"Extradimensional space and multiple universes," Malik said.

"So, I'm not missing anything. Anyway I just came back to get my shades. It's sunny and hot as hell, and they serve nachos at the pool. You guys should check it out. How about you, Cruz? Come on," he pleaded in a wheedling voice, "I need someone to hang out with and I've heard all of Dekka's stories at least twice."

Cruz's eyes went wide and a blush rose up her neck. "I don't have a bathing suit."

Armo waved that off. "Shorts and a T-shirt. Come on. They gave me one of those tent things, a cabana or whatever—I didn't even ask. It's got room for, like, six people. And they already brought me a massive fruit-and-cheese platter."

Cruz said, "Give me a minute and I'll find a picture I can morph into." She laughed, and it sounded just a bit hysterical. "You could be hanging out with Olivia Wilde or someone."

Armo made a face. "Yeah, see, I don't know who that is. Come on, Cruz, don't make me carry you."

"You wouldn't want that, Cruz," Shade said with a careful neutrality that Dekka recognized as knowing mockery, earning Shade a discreetly hidden upraised middle finger from Cruz.

"Okay, I'll change into shorts."

Armo flopped onto the sofa, nearly bouncing Shade off, and said, "That'll take a minute. So in sixty seconds or less, explain this whole space-alien-extra-universe thing."

Dekka looked around at them, seeing happy faces. Good. It was good to be happy. You never knew when it might be for the last time.

CHAPTER 2
Manhattan Mayhem

"FOOLS AND THEIR money are soon parted," Bob Markovic said to his daughter, Simone. "It's not illegal to profit from people's stupidity."

"No, just immoral," Simone snapped.

It was an argument they'd had more than once. A tired argument, but one still fed by powerful emotions on both sides. In some ways it was a proxy argument, Simone knew, a stand-in for a series of grudges between them, most especially Simone's decision to live with her mother and not her father following their divorce.

"Yes, well, morality and profit don't always walk hand in hand," Markovic muttered. "I live in the real world, not some college seminar." He stood leaning against the stone balustrade of his fourteenth-floor balcony and waved his hand to encompass New York City in late afternoon. Slanting light turned the buildings far across Central Park into dark silhouettes and dabbed the trees with yellow and orange.

"Different worlds, different realities."

Bob Markovic was in an expansive mood, which Simone knew meant that he'd had a good and profitable day. The payday loan company he owned, Markovic's Money Machine (offices all across the Northeast and upper Midwest), was doing gangbusters business. The whole country was on a mad panic-buying spree, grabbing up all the things they could never really afford, booking travel to places where people expected to be safe from the rolling apocalypse of the rock—New Zealand was very popular—and stocking cellars with emergency supplies and guns.

Guns, guns, guns, like that will keep them safe.

Simone Markovic had *not* had a productive day. She'd attended two classes at NYU—accounting and art appreciation. The accounting class had been a compromise to keep her father happy enough to continue paying tuition. The art class was her own choice. She didn't really enjoy either class, but she would be damned if she'd admit to her father that art per se was not going to be her thing. What she wanted to study was filmmaking, but that seemed so unlikely to be useful that she had a hard time fighting for it in the face of his (and even her mother's) skepticism. But for some time now, ever since she'd made the decision that film would be her thing, she'd seen the world around her in a frame, a series of shots.

Fade in: The arrogant tycoon is framed against a setting sun.

Simone had also put in a shift at an Italian restaurant, working as a hostess, a personal choice meant to give her some appreciation of what life was like for working people. The answer was: hard. The waitstaff messed with her because they knew she was a little rich girl, slumming. They cut her out of pooled tips, snapped at her every mistake, and never invited her for after-work drinks. Her manager would not stop hitting on her, despite a thirty-year age difference and her explanation that she liked girls, and even if she switched teams it would still not involve dating a married man in his late forties.

And then there was the matter of the general restaurant-going public. Simone tried to love humanity, but from the vantage point of the restaurant business, it wasn't easy.

So, all in all, Simone was in a bad mood and inclined to pick a fight. "You give them loans you know they can't pay back."

"That's the most profitable kind of loan," Markovic said with a laugh. "You don't want to loan a man a dollar and get a dollar and ten cents back the next day. You want to loan a man a dollar and have him pay you just the ten cents interest, but day after day, month after month after month. At the end of a few months you've made a dollar profit, and they still owe you the first dollar."

Cut to: A mother of three counts the money she's borrowed to buy Christmas presents, knowing she can never repay it.

Simone clenched her jaw. She was eighteen, white, a college freshman with blond hair she wore in a haystack bob, a cut meant to look casual, even indifferent, but which had cost three hundred dollars at her mother's favorite salon. From the ground up, she wore a pair of red Doc Martens, torn blue jeans, a green-and-black Hillbilly Moon Explosion T-shirt, and a black leather jacket. She wore silver rings in two lip piercings and three more in one ear. Simone's intention was not to look like a little rich girl, but she was self-aware enough to recognize that she just looked like a rich girl trying not to look like one.

Simone Markovic lived with her mother over on the West Side, and despite arguing with her, too, on a regular basis, they actually got along well enough. This was her weekend with Dad—who approved of very little about Simone except her last name. They had a contentious relationship, had since Simone had transitioned from girlhood to young woman-hood. They were two strong-willed people with very different worldviews. But had Simone been given truth serum, she'd have admitted that she loved her morally blind father and knew that he loved her in return.

Bob Markovic lived on the fourteenth floor of a prestigious building on Fifth Avenue, facing Central Park. The condo had four bedrooms, a separate office, and maid's quarters. It was decorated in what was almost a parody of masculin-ity of the aggressive, Hemingway variety. Markovic liked to hunt, and he liked to claim trophies, and he didn't much care whether a beast was endangered or not. The main room of the apartment was painted the green of a pool table's felt, with dark walnut molding. The walls were festooned with mounted animal heads: a water buffalo spread its gracefully curved horns nearly five feet; a polar bear looked startled; an entire eight-foot-long tiger had been stuffed and now stood menacingly in the corner by a floor-to-ceiling bookshelf.

Simone hated that room.

Slow pan of room reeking of sociopathy and masculine insecurity.

The apartment also had a long, narrow balcony opening onto a view of Central Park. It was on that balcony that Markovic and Simone sat nibbling on a plate of crudités and drinking a bottle of Tuscan red wine. Simone's father might be a rapacious businessman and a skirt-chasing hound who had cheated on Simone's mother repeatedly, but he was mellow where underage consumption of alcohol was concerned.

There were times Simone wondered how she would ever get through a weekend with him without being able to drink. Probably, she thought, he understood that and took the easy way out by keeping her glass filled.

Markovic made an effort to shift the conversation to less fraught grounds. "How are classes working out?"

"Fine." The all-purpose conversation-killer: fine.

Markovic frowned. He was a good-looking man. Back in the days when Simone still had friends over, they'd often made sotto voce comments on her "hot dad." But a full head of dark hair, broad shoulders, and fine features went only so far in distracting from dismissive brown eyes and what might be called "resting prick face."

"Hey, look!" Markovic pointed up to where dark blue seemed ready to smother the setting sun. He leaned forward against the carved, waist-high balustrade.

Simone joined him and saw a bright pinpoint of light, far to the southwest. At first she thought it might be a star, but the light . . . actually, now that she squinted it was *two* lights . . . while tiny, were piercing. The lights had appeared suddenly, grown, and blinked out. But now, from that same direction came trails, sparks of fast-moving brightness.

"Shooting stars?" Simone suggested.

Markovic shook his head. "Damned if I know."

Simone was just about to plead homework as an excuse to get away when it became suddenly, terrifyingly clear that the fast-moving sparks were not dimming or going away. In fact—

BOOOM!

A window-rattling concussion as the sound barrier was broken, and a heartbeat behind that, a shattering crash that literally shook the ground beneath Simone's feet.

"What the hell?" Markovic cried.

BOOOM! BOOOM!

Across the park, the Majestic, a luxury apartment building that rose in twin twenty-nine-story towers, exploded outward as a massive boulder blew through it like a baseball thrown through a Lego structure. The meteorite boulder tumbled across the park, annihilating anything in its path. Behind the boulder came tons of brick and steel and eviscerated bodies that fell on the street and into the park like a landslide, completely blocking Central Park West, crushing trees and burying the bridle path.

Neither Simone nor Markovic had time to move, time

even to react, when something like hail but infinitely faster hit them and knocked them flat. Simone had a flash of herself flying backward through the glass balcony door that had been blown out by the same hurtling shrapnel a millisecond before her head would have crashed into plate glass.

When she opened her eyes, the view was inexplicable. She was staring sideways at a dark fireplace at the far end of a stretch of carpet. There was a ringing in her ears and a pounding in her head so intense she half believed someone was beating her with a stick. Tiny pebbles, some barely larger than dust or sand, littered the floor.

Simone sat up and was overwhelmed by a feeling of nausea that nearly made her vomit. Then came the pain. Pain everywhere in her body; arms, chest, face, all hurt like she'd been battered. It felt as if every part of her was bruised.

Only then did she notice the blood.

Close-up on blood-smeared hands.

Simone stared in horror and realized that it was *her* blood, her own blood seeping from half a dozen punctures in the side of her left hand, more on the back of her right hand, more still up both arms, holes, most so tiny they could almost be insect bites that she'd scratched bloody. But other holes were bigger, like the hole an ice pick might make.

Blood seeped through her clothing, dots of red growing like poppies, and she felt a scream rising inside her. She scrabbled to her feet, nausea and pain making the world tilt and spin, and lurched on wobbly legs to the big, framed mirror over the mantel.

It was like a scene from *Carrie*. Her face was red with blood dribbling from half a dozen tiny holes, one within an inch of blowing out her right eye. It was like she'd been attacked by a porcupine. But this was Manhattan, for God's sake; there were no porcupines.

She tore off her T-shirt and gaped at similar puncture wounds across her shoulders and chest, down to her belly. Only her legs had been left untouched, protected by the stone balustrade.

"Dad? Daddy?" she cried in a wavering voice. "Daddy?"

She found him, unconscious, pierced as she was, bloody, and with his left hand hanging by veins and viscera. She screamed and fell to her knees beside him, looking for signs of life. His chest rose and fell; he was breathing, but the blood, the blood was gushing from his wrist. Simone pulled out her phone—it was pierced and dead. She ran for the landline and dialed 911 with trembling fingers and blurted out her fears to a harried operator. Then she ran back to her father, pulled off his belt, and used it as a tourniquet for his wrist.

She succeeded in slowing if not stopping the arterial flow, dragged an ottoman over, and elevated his feet as she'd learned in some half-forgotten first-aid course. Then she ran back to the balcony, thinking of shouting down to the street for help.

But one glance told her that help would be slow in coming.

The Majestic had only been the first building to be annihilated. The apartment building half a block south had been hit, and its wreckage now spilled across Fifth Avenue. Flames rose in huge columns, south near Rockefeller Center. Only then did she begin to realize the extent of the horror.

Mom! I have to call Mom!

But now the phone circuits were jammed. Manhattan had suffered the equivalent of a bombing attack.

Exterior. Upper East Side Manhattan. Evening. Like something out of a World War II movie, shattered buildings, fire and smoke.

If she was going to save her father's life, it would be up to her, alone. Step One: getting a man nearly twice her weight to the elevator, something she accomplished by hauling at the edge of the carpet he lay on.

Bob Markovic had two cars in the garage below street level, a black Mercedes S-Class roughly the size and weight of a small yacht, and a classic Triumph TR3 with a standard transmission. Simone found both keys in her father's pocket and chose the Mercedes. Markovic was not a small man, and cramming him, unconscious, into a tiny sports car was not going to work.

Simone dragged her father out of the elevator and out onto the concrete, leaving a slimy trail of blood. The car was a hundred feet away, and she sensibly decided to bring the car to him.

He was moaning and making slight movements, but was nowhere near being able to walk, and it took enormous effort to heft him into the back seat, made no easier by the pain rocketing around her own body, not to mention that her hands were slick with blood.

It had been a while since Simone's one and only driving lesson, and she moved at creeping speed up the ramp and out onto Fifth Avenue.

The emergency-room entrance to the hospital was jammed with cars, taxis, and ambulances, so Simone had to abandon the car a block away, but she found a helpful passerby who took one of her father's shoulders while she took the other. Inside the emergency room was chaos, orderlies, nurses, security guards all trying to cope with dozens of people marked by the same pinpricks, as well as some far more seriously hurt. One woman, hauled along unconscious by her two teenaged children, was missing the left side of her face. A woman cried and begged for attention as she cradled a blood-soaked mass of blankets swaddling a blessedly unseen baby.

Simone had no choice but to leave her father lying on the floor, where he risked being trampled, as she competed for the attention of besieged nurses.

After an interminable wait, during which time the numbers of patients doubled every few minutes, orderlies came to whisk Bob Markovic away on a gurney. Then Simone, too, was led to a line of curtained bays, all full to overflowing, and told to sit on the floor and wait. All around her a controlled panic of doctors and nurses dealt with burns, crush injuries from falling walls and roofs, terrible cuts from flying glass, panic-induced heart attacks, and quite a few with injuries like Simone's.

Simone waited and sat and oozed blood for hours, listening to cries of pain and screams of grief, forgotten in the mayhem. At one point she noticed that she was sitting in a pool of her own blood, that it had saturated the seat of her trousers. But her body was fighting back, deploying clotting factors, doing all that a billion years of evolved survival mechanisms could to keep the blood on the inside.

She managed to use a nurse's station line to call her mother, who was, thankfully, alive but unable to go anywhere since a piece of rock had blown right through the elevator in her building. Simone also called her current girlfriend, Mary, and snagged a few acetaminophen, which did almost nothing to dull the bruising pain in her body or the migraine building steam in her head.

After hours of waiting, after multiple unanswered questions about her father's condition, they put Simone through a full-body CT scan. A doctor had ordered an MRI, but that was before another victim had been placed in the machine. MRIs use superpowerful magnets, and no one had realized the shrapnel was magnetic. The first patient in the MRI had been ripped to hamburger by dozens of bits of the rock being drawn through the meat of her body.

Two hours after the CT scan, and far into the night, they were telling her nothing. But the staff—justifiably exhausted and haggard—looked more than just tired; they looked scared.

Explanation of what had happened came not from any of the doctors but from Mary, who'd had to walk twenty-three blocks through a city lit by police-vehicle light bars and accompanied by a soundtrack of sirens, car horns, and burglar alarms. The subway was shut down. Cabbies had all headed for cover. Buses were being used as emergency treatment facilities.

Mary's first words were not helpful. "Oh, my God, Simone! Oh, my God!"

Simone tried to smile, but her face was stiff from impact bruises, and a dozen bandages dotted her body. "Yeah, I know, sweetheart, it's gruesome. And I think my dad is worse off; they won't even tell me what's happening with him." Simone was not prone to hysteria, but she heard the edge of it in her own voice.

"Don't worry. It will be okay." Mary's tone carried no conviction, and her face was a mask of disgust. She kept moving her hands as if about to reach out to Simone, but then kept pulling away, as if she was frightened.

"I don't even know what happened," Simone said.

"Haven't you seen the news?"

"What do you mean?"

"It was one of those rocks. You know, like the ones that turn people into mutants or whatever?"

"Mary, what are you talking about?"

Mary shrugged. "I'm just saying what the news says. They said a big rock, a meteorite or asteroid or whatever, was heading toward Manhattan, so they nuked it."

The bright pinpoints of light: nuclear explosions going off at the edge of space.

"The nukes broke it up, I guess, but it still hit. There's buildings burning and all. I had to cross the park, and it's full of people all scared to death. People are saying it's worse than 9/11." Mary had started to cry, which angered Simone: Mary wasn't the one bleeding.

Still sitting on a floor no doubt crawling with exotic hospital germs, Simone looked past Mary and saw looming over her three people: one in NYPD uniform, two in jeans and blue windbreakers with large yellow letters across the back reading *ICE*, one male, one female.

A nurse was with them. She said, "This is one of them."

"All right," the female ICE agent said. She fixed Simone with a no-nonsense look, like a disappointed assistant principal who'd caught her ditching class, and pointed to a gold shield on her belt. "I'm with ICE, Immigration and Customs Enforcement, operating under emergency presidential decree."

"Wait, what?" Simone frowned and shook her head not so much to say no, but to try and clear her head. "ICE? But I'm a US citizen."

"Understood, miss. We've been deputized to act in this emergency. It's for your own safety."

Simone was confused, but not so confused that she didn't know bullshit when she heard it. And as a child of privilege, she knew what words to say. She climbed to her feet, wincing at pains that had become deep aches, fighting the resistance of bruised and stiffening muscles. She said, "I want a lawyer."

"We aren't arresting you, miss. This is for your own protection." The other ICE agent, a balding man with permanent worry lines around his eyes, tried out the same lie but was even less convincing.

"I want to see my father. And I want a lawyer. I'm not going anywhere until I—"

"Miss, you have to come with us."

Simone turned to the NYPD officer. "Are you standing there allowing these people to drag an American citizen, a New Yorker, out of a hospital?" The policeman winced, then looked away, clearly not happy with his role.

"We are the federal government," the plainclotheswoman said as if that would shut the conversation down. But this was tough New York, not nice Minnesota: New Yorkers were not by nature easy to shut up, and Simone was very much a New Yorker.

"Hey, Feds are the people who were doing that crazy stuff out in California. I'm not going anywhere with you people."

"Under the Special Emergency Decree, we can take you to a secure facility for—"

"Hey, you!" Simone snapped, pointing at the uniformed policeman again. "You're NYPD and I'm a New Yorker. Protect and freaking serve, man. Are you going to stand there and let these guys bully me? Where's the warrant?"

The policeman seemed to agree, but he shook his head ruefully and said, "I'm sorry, miss, but we have orders to cooperate with the Feds."

"I'm an American citizen in a goddamn hospital, I'm bleeding like a stuck pig, and I have done nothing wrong. You want me, you'll have to drag me. Mary! Are you taping?"

"On it," Mary said, holding her phone up.

"You need to put that phone down and wipe that recording," the male ICE agent demanded.

But Mary was also a New Yorker and answered, "It's live-streaming, and basically, screw you. I know my rights."

At which point the agent stepped in quickly and snatched the iPhone away as Mary and Simone both unleashed verbal tirades liberally punctuated with F-bombs.

In the end it took the NYPD officer plus both ICE agents to carry/drag Simone, while fending off Mary, and the five of them went kicking and yelling out through the emergency room and down a corridor to the parking garage, where a black SUV with darkened windows waited.

From the Purple Moleskine

FINDING IT HARDER and harder to think about writing fiction. Reality is too weird. I'm part of a group of superheroes, for God's sake. Best friend can run 800 mph. Malik can make people wish they were dead. Francis moves through walls. There are silent, unseen aliens in our heads when we morph. Just the fact that I can write words like "alien" and "morph" and have them be a real thing, WTF?

Times I think the Watchers have a sense of humor or irony. Gentle, thoughtful Malik can cause agony. Driven, obsessive Shade can outrun a 787—how perfect for someone always in a hurry.

Then there's me. How brilliantly cruel to give me the power I have. Let's take the trans girl just starting to figure out how to be who and what she is, and give her the ability to appear as anyone of any gender, age, race . . . Not complaining—it's so much better than what Malik got. Still.

Now I'm this famous person from an iconic photo. Millions

of people who don't know me have definite opinions about me. Expectations. I'm a hero to strangers and a mystery to myself. The personal is being obliterated. I'm in a war, and the war isn't about me or what I feel or what I need. I get that. I know I'm just one tiny part of something huge and terrifying. I get that people are scared to death and looking for a hero.

But I am still just this one person. Just me. Cruz.

Also I'm thinking way too much about Armo.

Warning to self: heartbreak ahead.

If I live that long.

CHAPTER 3
Boldly Going Where No 3-D Person Has Gone Before

"HOLD MY HAND," Francis Specter said.

Malik held her hand.

"Are you sure you want to do this?" Francis asked. "I'm worried you might get hurt or whatever and it would be my fault."

"You took me into the Triunfo to take down Dillon Poe," Malik said. "I was fine. Weirded out, but fine."

They were talking quietly in the separate dining room of the suite because a sunburned Armo and Cruz were watching a movie in the living room, and Shade was reading something on a laptop provided by the casino hotel's management. Dekka had gone down to replace a broken taillight on her precious motorcycle, involuntarily assisted by two starstruck guys from building maintenance.

Malik had not exactly cleared this experiment with the others. He worried that if they knew what he was up to, they'd come up with an endless list of objections, and he didn't want more delay. The others did not have the Dark Watchers constantly, *constantly* in their heads. *They* could watch a movie. *They* could read. Malik was straining just to avoid screaming half the time, not from physical pain but from the crushing humiliation and impotent anger that came from having alien consciousnesses poking through your mind, seeing the world through your eyes.

Using me. Violating me.

There were times when anger would almost suffocate him, and that was not a feeling Malik liked. Malik was about doing things, fixing things, and above all, understanding things. Passively raging at invisible creatures in his head was not good for him; it was toxic and foul. It made him feel weak.

It had been wonderful going to bed the night before with Shade. It had been her move. The assumption had been that the two guys, Malik and Armo, would share a room, but Shade had said, "I want you close so I can keep an eye on you."

Awkward had not begun to cover Malik's feelings. He'd thought of objecting but had not been able to come up with a good rationale. So he'd just nodded and excused himself to take a shower.

I was not hard to persuade.

Then Shade had joined Malik in the shower where they helped each other get very, very clean.

It was the closest Malik had come to being able to ignore the ongoing horror that was his true body now, and the loss of privacy and sanctity that twisted his mind. But even as they were making love, the Dark Watchers had been there,

making Malik feel that in some way he was betraying Shade
by exposing their intimacy to the voyeurs in the shadows.

Enough. Enough feeling bad. Time to do something.

"Okay, so something simple to start with," Malik suggested to Francis. "The hallway is on the other side of this
wall. Shall we?"

Malik squeezed her hand and smiled encouragingly at
Francis, whose eyes became swirling rainbows of color, a
rainbow that spread over her face.

There was a sudden feeling of the whole world tilting sideways, like Malik was looking at it through a prism. Colors
shifted toward ultraviolet, and then the world seemed to
unfold as if every object, the chairs, the bed, the walls, were
origami. They unfolded and refolded into impossible shapes,
nothing still, nothing permanent. He looked at Francis and
saw not a girl but a silhouette of light containing rainbows.

Then he chanced to look down and saw his own feet and
legs and nearly screamed, because the view was of the burned-
down-to-the-bone legs that were his de-morphed reality.

He quickly looked away and ordered himself to stay calm,
but by that point they were standing, still holding hands, in
the hallway outside, and reality was reassuringly 3-D again.

"Wow."

"Are you all right?" Francis asked anxiously.

"That is one serious roller coaster," Malik said.

"Yeah. Totally freaked me out the first time."

"I would imagine so," Malik said dryly. "Are you up for
another?"

Francis shrugged assent.

"Do you have any control over how fast we move?"

"I don't know. You want me to go slow?"

"Try, yes," Malik said. "How about we go from here down to the casino?"

They were still holding hands, and again the world tilted, shifted toward ultraviolet, and came apart as if all of reality was no more substantial than tissue paper. This time Malik carefully avoided looking at his own body, and instead found himself in a slow-moving tornado of things almost impossible to recognize. Was that the floor unfolded? Was that what a bed looked like from extradimensional space? He saw water pipes with water running not through them but beside them. He saw what were surely fiber-optic data lines, but they were writhing blue serpents surrounded by a hurricane of colorful dots.

He passed humans, men, women, a child, the inhabitants of the rooms between the suite and the casino floor far below, though up, down, above, and below had a very different meaning here. He saw people as paper-thin faces glued onto an explosion of gray matter; he saw their intestines sluggishly pumping food; he saw them as arms and legs spread out into a kind of diagram, with bone exposed and muscles twitching unattached, and arteries with blood both inside . . . and somehow not.

With his free hand, Malik reached toward a shimmering light seemingly made up of discrete, sparkling bits like so many fireflies, but there was nothing to touch. He tried again, reaching his hand to touch a deconstructed wall, and saw his fingers trace lines in dust but unable to go deeper into what he could see so clearly.

When he looked up and held his gaze steady, he found he could look through every floor above and see blue sky through a shifting forest of objects that obeyed none of the rules of three-dimensional euclidean geometry.

It was disorienting in the extreme, making his stomach churn and his balance fail. He stumbled, tried to stop himself, but fell through a wall and a floor and almost lost his grip on Francis's hand before he stopped falling for reasons he could not even guess at.

And then, all at once, they were on the casino floor in reassuring 3-D space being stared at, openmouthed, by a blackjack dealer who had just dropped a stack of chips on the floor upon seeing them materialize out of nothing.

"Sorry, we didn't mean to scare you," Francis said to the dealer.

"That was amazing," Malik said. "Incredible! I don't even . . ." He was breathless with excitement. He'd always liked his physics classes, and this was a wild master class in n-dimensional space, except that this wasn't a dry discussion of theory. He'd done in reality what in theory was impossible. He had passed through a dimension beyond normal 3-D space. He was a 3-D creature, with 3-D eyes and a 3-D brain, trying to make sense of his world as seen from a very different perspective.

"Amazing," Malik whispered again. "I . . . I mean . . . wow. Wow." He felt as if he'd just glimpsed the world like God—if such a creature existed—might see it. No other human being in the history of the world, aside from Francis, had seen what he'd just experienced.

"Yeah. Weird." Francis did not share Malik's pleasure; it was all just disorienting and unpleasant to her.

"Let's go back up. But even slower if you can."

Once more, with Francis's small hand held firmly in his, the world unfolded, opened up. Straight lines became curves, curves became curlicues, inside was out, and it was all madness, complete, swirling, colorful, impossible madness. Malik laughed in pure joy, his laughter a paisley fog in the air around him. He reminded himself sternly that he wasn't an extradimensional tourist: he was searching for answers. Searching for a way out.

Searching . . . for *them*.

He closed his eyes, trying to regain some sense of perspective, but it was no good: eyelids were just so 3-D. He focused his mind and "listened" for the Dark Watchers. They'd been there with him night and day since he'd been burned beyond saving. But now?

Where are you, my dark, invisible friends?

He could not feel them, which was a wonderful relief, but not the point. If he could not sense them, how could he find them?

The world around him was made entirely of bits and pieces: gypsum board walls, lumber, structural steel, the fabric of carpets, wires buzzing with electricity, which he saw as a pulsing green glow. Mixed in like croutons in a salad were humans, bulging water balloons of guts and muscle and blood that, when looked at from a certain angle, exploded outward in a disturbing vivisection, like something out of a Guillermo del Toro movie, strange and unsettling—and the more strange and unsettling for being recognizable.

But none of this was what he was looking for. He needed to look past all the debris. He needed, he told himself, to look in a *different* direction. But how was he to find that different direction, the direction where the Dark Watchers lurked?

He turned his head this way and that, and caught a glimpse of something. Not light—light was everywhere, seeming to shine right through everything in every direction but one, and in that one direction he saw a hole no bigger than a grapefruit. Inside that hole was not the black of total darkness, but something he could not describe, because inside that hole was nothingness, a pale gray, flat nothingness without surface or depth or feature.

"I want to go there," Malik said, and watched his technicolor words wrap themselves around the splayed gray mass that was Francis's brain. He saw the intricate muscles of her eyes contract and turn her gaze in the direction he'd indicated.

Francis moved toward the hole. If she was using her feet, Malik never saw them move. She just seemed to glide, smooth and slow, drawing him along, like he was Wendy to her Peter Pan.

Suddenly Malik felt an electric jolt, not painful, but alarming. And there! *There* he felt the presence of the Dark Watchers!

From the nothing hole something emerged, something

like an amoeba, but too big, and when he stared at it he did not see inside, did not see organs or viscera, just more of the same bland, featureless gray that shaped the rhythmically pulsating mass.

It's digital, not physical. Or whatever passes for digital in this universe.

The amoeba went straight for him, and all at once it had wrapped itself around his head, fast as a bullwhip. He cried out and tried to take hold of the thing, but his hands . . .

He had let go of Francis's hand!

He clawed frantically at the amoeba, but his hands would not touch it and just passed through with no resistance. He might as well have been batting at the air.

He twisted frantically, fear swelling inside him. He turned away from the nothing hole, and instantly the amoeba was gone.

Some kind of defense mechanism.

He tested his theory by looking back at the hole, and sure enough, the featureless amoeba went for him again.

He reversed direction, lost the amoeba, and called out in paisley swirls, "Francis! Francis!"

But his words did not reveal her. No answer came.

And now Malik was getting good and scared. Because the power to move between dimensions was Francis's, not his.

He was stuck.

CHAPTER 4
Psychopath Roll Call

DRAKE MERWIN HAD reassembled himself several times during his relatively short life. It was a process he neither understood nor controlled; he only knew that whatever was done to . . . *dis*assemble him, he came back together.

The latest such disassembly had been the result of a Hellfire missile launched from a Predator drone. The explosion had annihilated much of him, leaving bits and pieces, many burning, smeared all over a pile of rocks in the Mojave Desert. The largest bit of his head—left eye, a bit of nose cartilage, and his mouth—had landed on a cactus.

A few days had passed since then, and he now had a body capable of limited movement. His head was mostly complete, with the right side lacking only skin to cover exposed muscle and tendon. He had most of his left arm and all of his right arm, that being the ten-foot-long tentacle that was a legacy of the FAYZ. His right leg was minus a foot, and the left leg was scarcely better.

It was not an ideal body for crossing hundreds of miles
of desert. Before he could do anything he would need to be
more complete: hard to walk without two feet.

Drake experienced a moment of sadness and loss for the
excellent cave that had been collapsed by the explosion. He'd
spent years in that cave, torturing victims, savoring their
agony, laughing at their increasingly desperate pleas.

Often during the months and years of his desert exile,
Drake had passed the time by teasing Brittany Pig, the
homunculus that always reappeared, like a living bas relief
on his chest, complete with the protruding wire of her broken braces. Brittany had not yet re-emerged—that part of his
chest was still open to the ribs—but she would be back. Aside
from his victims, Brittany was the closest Drake ever came to
human contact. "Friends" would not be the right word, but
Drake had become accustomed to her.

Drake had foolishly allied himself with Tom Peaks, called
Dragon by some, Napalm by others, and damned near been
disassembled by various mutants at the Port of Los Angeles, including an old enemy, Dekka Talent. Dekka had been
Sam Temple's muscle, his enforcer, her and that brat Brianna.
Dekka had been dangerous enough then, and she was more
so now. But he could take her. Could and would.

In time. But not yet.

Peaks's cell-phone signal had led to the missile strike that
had wiped out Drake's excellent cave. They'd been trying to
kill Peaks, but he was gone by then, and Drake had borne the
brunt.

It was unfair, but Drake was not one to stew over life's unfairness. Anyway, now he had a mission. The world was coming apart, civilization was slowly crumbling, and the "new normal" was just abnormal enough that Drake thought he might have a chance at something he had wanted desperately for five years, from all the way back in the FAYZ: Astrid Ellison.

He didn't have an address, but he thought he knew how to find it. In the meantime he only had to wait for another foot to return, and then: Los Angeles.

He had come so close in the FAYZ. So close to making Astrid suffer. This time he would not fail.

Drake had learned patience down through the years, and he waited for hours more until he had two almost-complete legs. And then Drake marched . . . well, staggered . . . toward murder.

"I'm an artist, damn it!"

Justin DeVeere muttered those words to a cup of coffee at a Starbucks in McCarran International Airport.

Justin DeVeere, aka Knightmare and a few other less-flattering names, had escaped the massacre at the Ranch, the HSTF-66 facility, by running into the woods until he could run no more. He'd then managed to hitch a ride to Las Vegas, which turned out to be a very poor choice of destination. Only sheer, dumb luck had kept Justin from dying from a missile en route to Vegas.

After the explosion, he'd walked on toward Las Vegas until

he saw flames rising and explosions booming. Then he had sensibly turned around and walked in the other direction. He'd ended up spending the night shivering in the freezing desert and watching the flames of the distant battle.

It had sent his mind back onto half-forgotten tracks, back to when he was just a promising young artist. As he watched from a safe distance, he'd begun thinking about a multi-media art installation that would evoke the horror. And that led him to painful memories of his wealthy patron and girl-friend, Erin O'Day, who had been killed in an earlier battle.

The thing was, Justin admitted, he did not actually want to be Knightmare anymore. It had been exciting for a while, but had quickly become a bloody, violent, and very precarious existence. He'd been imprisoned at the Ranch before Shade Darby and her mutant friends had attacked and destroyed the place, freeing a freak show of mutants and cyborgs, things that were half-human, drones flown by the disembodied heads of infants, things . . . Bad things. Very bad things. And had any of the Rockborn Gang spotted him there, he'd almost certainly be dead now. He had experienced the blast of pain from Malik, and one thing was absolutely clear to Justin: he never, ever wanted to feel that again. It had been unendur-able, and it had shaken him down to his bones.

I'm an artist, dammit!

That phrase had become his rallying cry. He wasn't Knight-mare; he wasn't the creature who had destroyed a plane and burned its passengers alive. He wasn't the creature who had destroyed the Golden Gate Bridge. He was an artist.

Dammit!

It was this mantra that convinced him that he needed to get back to New York. Back to where people knew him for his art. Surely some art lover would grant him shelter until . . . until the madness descending on humanity was past.

The morning after the battle, he'd once again walked back toward Las Vegas, passed by an endless stream of National Guard troop transports and FEMA trucks carrying emergency relief.

Once there, unrecognized in his normal, human body, he'd overheard people talking about the Rockborn Gang, the heroes who had saved the city. And to his horror, he'd realized they were still there, still in Vegas.

One thing Justin was quite clear about: wherever the Rockborn Gang was, he wanted to be far away.

He had no wallet, no credit cards or phone. But a young man walking past a vast construction site in North Las Vegas, and who arguably looked a bit like Justin, had all that and more. Justin had not wanted to kill the young man, but necessity made its own rules. One more body for collection by the crews that were scouring the city for the dead. Justin took his victim's wallet and phone and caught a taxi to the airport. He'd bought the first available ticket to New York and now merely waited for the gate to be called.

Back to New York.

He would be safe in New York.

Tom Peaks had run from Las Vegas after the horror at the Triunfo, the hotel where Dillon Poe had made his unspeakably brutal last stand.

Peaks had arrived in Vegas as Napalm, the ten-story-tall reptile with the belly full of liquid fire, believing he was there to take down Dekka, who he hated for what he still thought of as betrayal.

But when he'd arrived . . .

He had not known about Dillon Poe. He'd had no idea what Dillon was doing. He had not known that the hundreds of people gathered by the entrance of the Triunfo were slaves to Dillon's will, unable to flee.

He had definitely not known that the Charmer had sprayed that crowd with gasoline.

Now Peaks sat trembling in a booth at a diner in one of the multitude of identical shopping centers that ringed the city. His coffee was undrunk. The pancakes he'd ordered were untouched and now cold.

There had been so many horrors. So much destruction. The Ranch, his great creation, was exposed to the world and destroyed. What had once been his staff of carefully recruited scientists and techs and guards had been hunted down and murdered by vengeful mutants and cyborgs.

His family . . . He closed his eyes and tried to picture them, but each time he did he saw disgust and contempt on their faces. He could never go home to them, not now.

No job. No home. No family. No purpose in life. And for the rest of his life he would see the Triunfo fire over and over and over again. A fire he had unwittingly lit.

"Can I get you anything else, honey?" the waitress asked.

Peaks shook his head. He fished out a twenty-dollar bill

and laid it on the table, got up, went to the men's room, and vomited coffee and bile.

Peaks splashed water on his face and looked at himself in the dirty mirror. Looked at a face now known to every law-enforcement agency on earth.

There was no safety.

There was no escape.

There were only the screams of people burning.

Peaks stumbled out of the diner into brilliant sunlight. Across the vast parking lot was a Big 5 Sporting Goods store. He headed for it, spotted a liquor store, and bought himself a bottle of excellent scotch on the way.

"Damn good scotch," Peaks muttered, draining a quarter of the bottle as he maneuvered through parked cars.

The clerk at the liquor store had given him a strange look, a shrewd look of recognition. Would he call the police? More likely than not.

Time was running short. If they came for him, he could morph and fight them off. He had only to belch the dreadful napalm and they would burn. . . .

Innocent police officers just doing their duty. My God.

He set the scotch bottle, now half-empty, on the curb and went into the Big 5. He easily found the gun-sales area. He pointed to a 12-gauge shotgun in a rack.

"How much?"

"That model will set you back $899.99."

Peaks stuck a credit card into the reader. Denied. Tried another card. Denied.

"I know who you are," the clerk said suddenly. He looked at Peaks as if seeing the devil himself.

"I need a gun," Peaks rasped.

"You get nothing from me, you piece of shit," the man said. "Give you a gun? Why, so you can kill some more children? Get out of here! Security! Security!"

Peaks bowed his head, then walked around behind the counter. The clerk, terrified, tried to back away but Peaks grabbed him by the shirt front and said, "I need a shotgun. Short barrel. And one shell. Just one."

A minute later store security came hustling up just in time to see Peaks jack the 12-gauge shell into the chamber, place the barrel of the shotgun under his chin, and blow the top of his head all over the display case.

CHAPTER 5
How Do You Get to Carnegie Hall?

IN SURGERY THEY had reattached Bob Markovic's nearly severed hand. He was given painkillers. He was also given a sedative. And by the time he woke he was in a very surprising yet oddly familiar place. Consciousness returned to Markovic in the form of too-bright lights and a sea of red velour. He blinked, and then squinted against the light, and then, with rapidly mounting panic, recognized where he was.

Carnegie Hall?

Markovic's Money Machine had season tickets to Carnegie Hall, using them to reward especially productive senior employees and the occasional politician who needed some TLC. But, he realized, he was not in the corporate seats, which were up in the first balcony, stage left. He was in a seat toward the rear of the orchestra section.

And the people around him were definitely not regular patrons. Not even close. Carnegie Hall's Isaac Stern Auditorium held 2,804 people; less than a tenth of that number were in the hall now, but they were not there to watch a show. Many were in pajamas or robes. Many others—like Markovic himself—were in hospital robes. Some were in street clothes. But all were bloody to one degree or another. Some showed just a few blood-soaked bandages slowly drying from crimson to rust color, but others looked as if they'd been dipped in red paint.

Markovic's pain seemed to come out of nowhere, a series of pains, really, starting with the total-body bruising he quickly traced to what looked like dozens of pinpricks, or ice-pick stabs on his arms, his hands, his face. Then there was a deeper wound, a thick bandage on his chest that seeped blood and felt terrible. That wound suggested danger to life and limb. But it was the hand, wrapped in gauze and surgical webbing, that was the most troubling because he had no idea what had happened to it, or why he could not feel his fingers.

He opened his robe with his good hand and peeled back the thick bandage on his upper pectoral. This was no pinprick; this was a gash, maybe three centimeters long with a dozen black stitches holding it closed.

Have I been shot? Stabbed?

Some kind of terrorist attack?

And, given the pain and the wounds and the blood and the incessant pounding in his head, why in holy hell was he at Carnegie Hall?

He tried to stand and sat right back down, head swimming, thighs quivering, knees as firm as overcooked spaghetti. Markovic began tracing back through his memories. He'd been arguing with Simone, which was not unusual. She was an amazing kid, of course—after all, she was his daughter—but she was headstrong. Then there had been a strange light . . . no, two lights, each far more steady and intense than any star. Then . . .

Beyond that point, memory became disconnected flashes. A flash of an impact of some sort. A flash of his living room. A flash of Simone, face bloody, bending over him. Then . . . doctors? Nurses? He furrowed his brow, thinking. Cops?

The back seat of his Mercedes?

A linoleum floor?

And a gurney rolling fast down long corridors, he remembered that. And the next memory was coming fully conscious in the last place on earth he'd ever . . .

It must have been a mass casualty event. His brain was working now despite the pain everywhere. Mass casualties, and the first responders had decided to use Carnegie Hall as a temporary . . .

Temporary what? Hospital?

He squinted to focus and turned his stiff neck. Beside every door—and there were a dozen or so—beside each one was a national guardsman in green uniform, helmeted, and carrying an assault rifle.

Some hospital.

He fumbled for his phone, but he was in a hospital robe, underpants, and socks, which meant his street clothes and phone were back at whatever hospital had done whatever they'd done. . . .

"What is going on?" he muttered, getting no response. So he looked left and right and decided the best target for conversation would be the woman seated in the row behind and left.

"Excuse me," he said through a parched mouth. "Do you know what's going on?"

The woman had gray hair cut short, was small, compact, and full of nervous energy, like a clever sparrow. "The explosion," the woman said.

"What explosion?"

The woman glanced over her shoulder like they were in fifth grade and she was worried the teacher might hear her gossiping. "One of those meteors. The alien ones. I heard the major—I think he's in charge here—talking about it. One of those alien rocks was heading for the city, so they nuked it. I guess they saved the city by breaking it up, maybe, but we still got hit by a lot of stuff. Smaller pieces. I live on West Forty-Ninth and it's burning."

Markovic nodded. "Thanks."

"They said we're here for our own safety," the woman said, reluctant to relapse into silence.

But Markovic was already on to considering the possibilities. He could just get up and walk out. He was in pain, but the serious wound in his chest had been sutured and, well, whatever had been done with his hand. Presumably he was not in imminent danger of death. And he'd be a lot more comfortable at home than here.

But could he leave? That was the question. He took a

moment to observe, twisting painfully this way and that. He saw two different people attempt to exit, and both times be sent back to their seat by a guardsman.

So, not a hospital: a holding cell, a temporary jail. They were prisoners. More importantly, *he* was a prisoner.

"Why hold us prisoner?" he wondered aloud.

The answer was not long in coming to him. They had all been struck by shrapnel from the meteorite. And by now everyone knew the possible consequences of exposure to the rock.

"They're isolating us," he muttered under his breath.

"Dad?"

"Simone?" There she was, standing right before him. "Oh, God, baby, I'm so glad you're okay." The word "okay" died on his lips as he realized that she had been peppered with shrapnel as well, that her body was a series of leaking bandages. Her face looked like she'd tried to shave during an earthquake.

Simone made a half-hearted effort to hug him, but stopped when she realized the pain it would cause them both. She lowered herself gingerly into the seat beside him.

"What are they going to do with us?" Simone demanded.

Markovic shrugged and winced at the movement, which sent pain stabbing up his neck. "I don't know, but I'm calling Cowan." Cowan was Markovic's lawyer.

"They took everyone's phones. I don't think they'll let you call," Simone said.

"The hell they won't," Markovic snapped. He stood up, fighting crashing waves of headache and nausea, and steadied himself with a hand on Simone's shoulder. He looked around imperiously, decided he should go straight to the top, and weaved his tottering way up the aisle to the main doors where a National Guard major stood, surrounded by junior officers.

Simone followed him. She didn't approve of her father, but he was still her father, and the truth was he generally got his way: no one was better at bullying underlings than Bob Markovic.

"Major, a word," Markovic said.

The major was a middle-aged man with blond hair cut so short he appeared bald from a distance, a fleshy nose, and a body as fit as a fifty-year-old man whose real full-time job was managing a branch office for a mortgage broker was likely to be.

"Sir, you need to take a seat," the major said.

"Actually, Major, I don't take orders from you. See, you're a National Guard toy soldier, and I'm Bob Markovic. If that name doesn't mean anything to you, I assure you it means a great deal to the mayor, the governor, and all the congress-people and senators you could name. So—"

"Sir. I'm very busy. We have an emergency situation here. So please take your seat."

"I will not take my seat, you jumped-up doorman." Markovic stabbed a finger at the major's chest.

The major turned away, a look of distaste on his face. "Lieutenant, have this gentleman escorted back to his seat."

The lieutenant reached for Markovic's intact arm.

"Don't you lay hands on me!" Markovic yelled, and slapped

the lieutenant's hand away, and that was when a military police sergeant stepped in and jabbed a black rectangular object into Markovic's side.

Markovic heard the sparking of the stun gun. He jerked wildly, staggered back, and was saved from falling by the lieutenant and a sergeant.

"This man with you?" the lieutenant demanded of Simone.

"He's my father."

"Then you need to get him to calm down."

Simone said nothing but stepped in to wrap her stunned and quivering father's arm over her shoulder. He had been barely ambulatory. Now he was not just weak but confused, unable to control what direction he was going, and Simone led him back and deposited him in his seat.

"Fascist bastards!" Markovic said when the effects of the stun gun's charge had diminished.

"You got the rich-white-guy treatment," Simone said pitilessly. "I saw a black guy try it and he got handcuffs."

"Spare me your libtard crap, Simone!" Markovic raged. "This is illegal. It's unconstitutional! I have rights!"

There was a flurry of activity around the major. Civilians in suits had come in from outside and were arguing with the major. Evidently the major lost the argument, because one of the men in suits walked down the aisle and climbed nimbly onto the stage.

"Ladies and gentlemen, I am Carlos Malina from the Department of Homeland Security. An emergency has been declared, and an emergency decree has been issued."

All in passive voice, Markovic noted. Like he was just the messenger.

The audience erupted in shouted questions and demands.

Malina ignored the questions until the volume died down. "I know you all have questions. And they will all be answered. But first we have to transport you to a secure location. Buses are pulling up outside."

It was then that the worm of doubt woke within Markovic. *A secure location? Buses?*

"It's all about the rock. They think we're going to become mutants," Simone said. Then, slowly, dreamily, as if marveling at the craziness of the words she was uttering, Simone said, "They're going to kill us. Dad? I think they're going to *kill* us."

CHAPTER 6
Inside the Kaleidoscope

MALIK WAS SCARED. Good and scared. He was in a place impossible for his mind to understand or explain. It was in some sense like being buried inside a fantastic junkyard. All around him were things that should have been connected, should have been part of some recognizable structure, but all rationality was subverted. He could make out lengths of structural steel, big I-beams, but they hung in midair, attached to nothing . . . unless he changed the angle of view, in which case, like glass beads in a kaleidoscope, objects moved, touched, intersected, or alternately separated, even disappeared entirely.

Who needs hallucinogens when you can travel in n-dimensional space?

Malik was fairly sure that everything around him was part of the casino or the people in the casino and hotel—at least he hoped so. But he caught glimpses of things that he could not rationalize as being any part of 3-D space: at certain angles he thought he saw a sort of faint web, like one of those orange plastic fences they put up around construction sites, but more pink than orange. He thought more than once that he saw a solid object become fluid. He saw tendrils, like a squid's legs, dangling and withdrawn, curled up like a measuring tape only to disappear, so that he wasn't at all sure they were real and not figments.

Malik knew that the apparent randomness of everything around him was a problem inside his own head. He was a man of three spatial dimensions, up and down, left and right, forward and back. He was now in four—well, who knew how many—dimensional space, a place where there was at least one more "direction" that was none of the usual three. His eyes were eyes evolved for three dimensions; his brain was a brain that could not really even picture extra dimensions. What he was seeing around him was his brain's futile effort to make sense of what it could never hope to understand.

I'm an ant walking across a computer motherboard.

The worst came when he saw parts of himself seeming to stand apart. He saw inside his body, saw the burns, the exposed bone, saw through the superficial normality of the morph he was doomed to remain in. He saw his organs, his liver seething with blood. He saw his intestines slowly pulsating with chewed food, but at the same time saw startling glimpses of that very food in its original, intact form. A bagel. Fried eggs that were simultaneously in and out of their shells. He saw the inside of his own brain, a pink cauliflower in a bone cage. Tendrils of light seemed to reach out from his brain, twisting and poking, turning objects this way and that.

I'm seeing my own consciousness!

He cried out in shock when his own eyes floated before him, staring at him, meeting his own gaze before erupting like a stop-motion video of a flower blossoming. He peered closer and he saw his own iris contract, saw the thousands of muscle fibers straining and releasing.

It was literally sickening, and he might or might not have vomited; it was impossible to be sure.

I have no way out of here.

Panic swelled, and he could see it as a wave of swirling blue crystals that followed his arteries—arteries which, if he looked at them from the wrong angle, would separate, become sections of tubing, with blood seeming to cross from piece to piece.

Sensory overload.

He tried shutting his eyes again and even put his hands over his eyes, but even his hands were no more an impediment than a dirty windshield.

"Am I going to die here?" He spoke the words aloud, but the sound was distorted, alien, not human.

Why had he not snapped back to reality? Francis had moved him into this dimension, and he had assumed that only her power was keeping him here. But that wasn't the way it was working. Her power was the ability to cross the line between there and here, and once he was across that dimensional line, he had no power to escape.

The amoeba he'd seen earlier, the amoeba that had

panicked him, had not returned. But then again, he had not tried finding that . . . what to call it? Direction? If it was a direction, it was one that was neither up, down, left, or right.

Try again.

He focused his thoughts and actually saw a swirl of yellow paisley rise from a brain that had been exploded into separate gobbets of flesh awash in a pool of cerebral fluid.

There!

The instant he focused on the hole, an amoeba came rushing at him, and just like before wrapped itself around his head. But this time he did not panic, but tried to will himself toward that hole.

The amoeba evaporated, and Malik reassured himself that he had passed the defensive system. He felt himself moving toward the hole, which seemed to recede as he approached, growing ever so slightly larger, far too slowly, as if it was moving away almost as quickly as he advanced.

Suddenly there was another organism, a mass of organs and bits of bone, and things he did not even want to guess at. He stopped moving and began to pull back, but then, a slight shift of perspective, and he saw a face.

"Francis?"

Her answer was not a sound but a color. A color never represented in even the biggest Crayola box. He knew nevertheless that it was an affirmative.

She reached with a bony claw wreathed in pulsing veins. He held out his own hand, a hand as deconstructed as hers.

And all at once the two of them were back in the bedroom.

In three-dimensional space.

For what felt like a very long time Malik just stood there trembling, breathing hard, looking at Francis. The rainbow effect in her eyes faded and disappeared. Solid objects were solid again, their insides hidden from view.

"Are you okay?" Francis asked, and Malik realized it was for the third time.

"I think so," Malik said in a harsh whisper. Then, "Wow."

"I'm really sorry I let go of you," Francis said. "You must have been scared."

"Scared? I was terrified," Malik admitted. "It's . . . I don't even know how to make sense of it."

"Yeah, it's weird, huh?" Francis said.

"You have a gift for understatement. There are people who spend a lot of money on drugs and never see anything one-tenth as weird."

"Did you find what you were after?"

Malik considered. "Maybe," he allowed. "You know what didn't happen? I did not feel the Dark Watchers. Just like you don't. Whatever they are, the effect—the Watcher effect—is something in three dimensions that is gone or transformed in n-space."

Francis nodded politely, but Malik was pretty sure that she was not interested in the physics of it all, let alone the metaphysics. To Francis, it was a trick she could do. It was a power. But she didn't grasp just how great a power it was.

"They have defenses, those *things*, those amoeba-looking things," Malik said. "But I think that's sort of an automated system, and not very effective. I would guess they are system cleaners, subroutines designed to redirect any random bit of data that takes the wrong turn. But I'm not some random databit, I'm a whole system."

"So, no more of that, huh?" Francis said, already losing interest and edging toward the door.

"Well, not today, anyway. It's very . . . unsettling."

But did he intend to go back to find out what was through that blank hole of nothingness? To seek out whoever was behind this deconstruction of reality? To confront whoever or whatever was screwing with the software of the universe to allow the growth of monsters and destroy human civilization?

Hell yes, I'm going back.

But he wisely said none of that, and instead said, "Shall we go find the others, see what they're up to?"

CHAPTER 7
Malmedy in the Pine Barrens

"DAD. THEY'RE GOING to kill us."

"Now you're being paranoid," Markovic said. "They're probably going to put us in a hotel for the night."

Simone hoped he was right. She tried to push away a growing panic as they were moved by rows to a side door and marched down a hallway. A National Guard private stood there handing out bottles of water and granola bars, smiling, looking normal and sympathetic. It should have calmed Simone's nerves, but she kept hearing echoes of books she'd read, books about the Holocaust. The Nazis had lulled Jews into a false sense of security as they were sent to die in showers spewing nerve gas.

In the crush of bodies, she was separated from her father. As they reached cold night air, she was stopped from catching up to him and saw her father loaded onto a bus by armed men in black tactical gear bearing no identification patches or badges.

Simone looked desperately for an escape, but there was none. They were in an alleyway loading bay, soldiers to both sides. She in her turn was herded aboard a bus, a borrowed yellow bus with the words "New York School Bus Service" in blue script down the side.

Simone was seated with a woman who, like everyone on the bus, bore the telltale bloody bandages.

"I heard we're going to a Motel 6."

"Yeah? My dad seems to think they'll take us to a suite at the Four Seasons."

Peering ahead, Simone could see her father's bus ahead of them, led through panic traffic by black SUVs with lights and sirens going.

They dipped down into the luridly lit Lincoln Tunnel, heading toward New Jersey, and Simone felt the anxiety on the bus grow. As the ride went on and on, complaints grew louder, and demands for a bathroom stop intensified.

They were far from the city now, far from any city. They had left the interstate, and pine trees crowded the road on both sides, interrupted by stretches of marsh.

"The Pine Barrens," a voice whispered.

Then Simone saw the lead bus slow and turn onto a narrow, pockmarked and unpaved road that dived straight into the woods.

"They're going to kill us," Simone whispered. It might have been paranoia earlier, but now she could see it about to play out. It made sense to kill them all; that's what she'd seen back at Carnegie Hall, that the cold logic of the situation would lead the government to snuff them out fast, before any of them could become a serious problem. Now it was no longer theoretical. There was no other explanation.

"They're going to kill us!" Simone yelled, standing up. Her seat partner gaped at her in disbelief.

The armed guards—one at the front, one at the back—both bristled and brought their weapons to bear on her. For a moment Simone was too appalled to react: they were pointing guns at her. At *her*!

"Sit down, please," the guard at the front said. "We're just taking a bathroom stop at a park restroom facility."

That calmed most, and Simone heard nervous relief laughter, but she felt in her bones that it was a lie. What was she going to do? What *could* she do?

She sat back down, hands twisting on her lap, and tried to hold her head still so as not to restart the headache that was receding at last, replaced on her list of physical woes by the fiery, insistent itching of her many puncture wounds.

Ahead the bus pulled into a clearing, silvery and vague in the faint starlight, eerily bright where the headlights illuminated grass and mud. There were some picnic tables that looked as if they'd never been used, and, sure enough, there was a wooden building marked with bathroom signs. Simone felt the collective sigh of those around her, saw their scornful looks at her, the girl who had panicked and started yelling about being killed, ha, ha, ha.

"Okay, we are taking a break," the guard announced. "Everyone off, and line up. We'll bring you up in groups of six to use the restroom."

Simone, abashed but not reassured, filed off the bus with

the others and headed toward the restrooms. But a man in black tactical gear with a balaclava covering his face held up a hand and pointed them to a space yards away. "Line up there. Three rows."

Then Simone saw the camouflage-painted military truck parked beside the clearing, a dark green canvas cover over the back.

Simone tried to make her way to her father, but here there were still more men and women in black tactical gear holding assault rifles, insisting that everyone line up.

"Line up! Line up!" an authoritative voice shouted. They did. They lined up. Three rows of about thirty people per row.

And that's when the canvas cover of the army truck was raised.

Simone stared at the perforated black tube of a machine gun's barrel.

"No!" she screamed. "No! No!"

The machine gun opened fire, spitting tracer rounds that flew like rocket-powered fireflies in the darkness.

Bap-bap-bap-bap-bap-bap!

Screams. Screams from everywhere, including from Simone's own throat.

Simone turned and ran in blind panic—no reasoning, no plan, just run from the machine gun! *Run!* Something punched her hard in the back and she fell on her face, hands sinking into soft, wet soil. She heard her own voice whimpering. She tasted mud.

The machine gun roared on, relentless, the well-oiled steel

parts pushing rounds out of the belt, striking the percussion caps, exploding the gunpowder, propelling the thumbtip-sized slugs down the rifle barrel, then kicking out the used brass casing and pushing the next round into place, many times each second. Tracer rounds flitted inches above her back, so close she could feel the breeze.

Screams of terror came from all sides, screams and cries and pitiful demands to know, "Why? Why?" and the grunts of those who were beyond words and would soon be beyond all pain.

The machine gun stopped, and the still-living who could move ran or crawled. But now the black-clad guards, faces behind balaclavas, began shooting, a higher-pitched sound of assault rifles. Simone raised her head and saw a child shot in the back. His mother screamed and crawled to him and was shot in the neck.

A man fell on Simone, a big man, his weight so still, so inert she knew he must be dead. She felt his blood trickling down on the back of her neck. She smelled the stink of his voided bowels.

The machine gun, reloaded, started up again, sweeping the field, punching holes into the still-living and the already-dead. Simone felt the impact as bullets struck the dead man over her. Bullets that would have struck her, would have torn holes through her, but for the shelter the dead man provided.

Her terrified, panicky brain told her she was wounded, too, that the sudden blow to her back, the blow that had knocked her down, had come from the machine gun. But she felt no pain and suspected she'd simply been knocked down by another victim. Some person whose name she would never know had taken the bullet with her name on it.

The machine gun stopped again. Sudden silence. Then the sound of a woman weeping and seconds later a cry for mercy and two rounds of assault rifle fire and the cry stopped abruptly. Simone opened one eye narrowly, a sideways view that revealed men in black walking like wraiths through the steam rising from bloody corpses, shooting everyone, living or dead, two rounds in the head.

Bang! Bang!

If she waited, she *would* die.

She tried to move, but the dead man's weight was too great to free herself from. She had a sudden flash of the last *Lord of the Rings* movie, of King Théoden lying broken on the battlefield, trapped beneath his dead horse, saying, *My body is broken.*

Bang! Bang!

Helpless. She was helpless, and for a moment despair offered her an easy way out. Simply wait for death. Just lie there beneath a dead man and wait for the *bang . . . bang.* She would only hear the first shot. Maybe not even that. And all the fear and fury would be gone.

But despair had not won out yet; rather, the temptation of surrender poured fuel on the fire of her anger. How dare they do this? How dare they simply murder people this way? Her father might already be dead. *Why?* It wasn't her fault or her father's or the fault of any of these people, these poor, massacred people.

She struggled again to free herself and this time drew the attention of a man in black, who looked at her from a hundred feet away and said, "Don't worry, honey, I'll get to you."

Nonchalant. Like mass murder was a daily affair for him. Like her life was nothing.

She felt a sick, acid bile in her throat, felt her whole body tingling, still racked by pain, but this was something else, something different. Rage filled her, rage and impotence, a burning sense of injustice and of her own weakness.

Then the dead man rolled aside.

He had rolled aside because suddenly Simone was on her hands and knees and had shrugged him off. Impossible just seconds earlier; the man weighed twice what she did. Impossible!

The man in black who'd noticed her yelled over his shoulder, "Live one here!" He came striding toward her, fast, weapon at his shoulder, leveled on her.

At nearly point-blank range, he fired!

Simone saw him fire. Saw the muzzle flash. Heard the loud popping noises.

Saw it and heard it . . . from about fifty feet in the air.

"Shit!" the killer yelled, and raised his weapon to aim up at her. He fired and missed again, because now Simone was higher still, and moving through the air with no more difficulty than a trout in a mountain stream.

Tracer bullets from a half dozen guns chased her through the sky, like something from an old World War II movie where she was the brave fighter pilot. She was not fast enough to outrun bullets, but she was too fast for them to be able to keep sight of her in the deepening darkness.

The army truck switched on a small spotlight. Its beam swept around the sky, searching, but too slowly, like someone trying to spear a cockroach with a chopstick—it followed her but had no chance of catching up and keeping her illuminated.

Simone found she had only to think of moving, and she did. No time yet to ask what had happened to her, and no need to ask how: even in her frazzled, freaked-out state, she knew it was the rock. Dozens of particles no bigger than a grain of sand had pierced her. Had they been larger they might still have been moving at twenty-eight thousand miles an hour and blown right through her, like gamma rays, but small particles traveling through air are slowed by friction. So the rock had not simply blown through her; it had stayed within her. Like buckshot.

Simone's overriding thought was that she needed to find her father. He might not be her favorite human being, but however he treated the poor fools who took his loans, he'd always been good to her. And whatever else might happen, he was her father.

Below she saw a bizarre scene, a sort of drone camera pan over a battlefield, except that this was not a battle but a cold-blooded massacre. A hundred or more bodies lay in twisted poses, holes dripping urine and stomach contents and blood. The black-clad killers were still finishing off the wounded.

Bang! Bang!

But now a more mundane fear shivered through her, the fear of falling. She was in the air.

In the air!

Visions of Road Runner cartoons flashed, and she imagined being Wile E. Coyote as he looks down to see he's run past the edge of the cliff. But Simone did not fall. She had no idea how she was doing this. . . . And then Simone looked down at her legs. The jeans were gone, and her legs . . . She stifled a scream. Her legs were covered with what looked like iridescent scales, like a trout—but no, that wasn't right, either. Because these scales did not lie flat; they moved. They beat like tiny hummingbird wings. And it wasn't just her legs. Her entire body was covered, every square inch of it, with hundreds, no, thousands of tiny, iridescent bee wings. She raised a hand and looked in fascination at the furiously buzzing things all down the back of her hand, though not on her palms. She touched her face—no wings there, or on her throat, but her head, her shoulders, her sides were all winged, like some weird insectoid bedazzling.

And she was no longer the color of a white girl who lived in the shadow of tall buildings: beneath the iridescent wings was flesh the color of a faded Smurf toy left too long in the sun.

I can fly!

The rock. There was no doubt about that. Nor was there any doubt that the government had feared just this sort of thing and had tried to solve the problem with bullets.

Simone veered away as the searchlight's shaft swept nearby. She didn't have to do anything to fly, just think, *go there*, or *go that way*, or *faster!*

Her duty was to find her father, but the killing field below was dark, and all she saw were twisted bodies and armed men. She spotted a column of vehicles approaching, headlights moving slowly, led by an earthmover, along with two heavy dump trucks and three black SUVs.

Coming to bury the dead!

If she reduced altitude far enough to search faces, she would be shot, and while she could fly and had become significantly stronger, she had no reason to imagine that she could survive being shot.

Simone knew she would feel sadness, terrible sadness, and soon, but right now was all about staying alive. In the distance she heard the air-punching sound of military helicopters and suspected that she would be their main target.

Her mother. That's what she needed to do: get to her mother. Then she could cry for her dead father.

CHAPTER 8
Uncle Sam Wants You

THE PHONE IN the suite rang at 1:20 in the morning. Shade was the only one awake, and picked up the receiver from the set in the dining room where she'd been sitting in the dark, looking out at the flash and sparkle of the Las Vegas Strip at night, and thinking.

"Hello?"

"This is Jody Wilkes. I'm terribly sorry to bother you; we are blocking all calls to you . . ."

Wilkes was the head of casino security at Caesars and their main contact person. Shade knew from Wilkes's tone that there was a "but" coming, and knew it would be bad news.

". . . but this call came from Washington."

"This is Shade, Ms. Wilkes. Given what we've seen from those clowns, I don't think we want to talk to them."

"It isn't from the White House or anyone political. It's from a General Eliopoulos. The chairman of the Joint Chiefs."

Shade held the phone out and stared at it as if reassuring herself she was actually awake. The country's highest-ranking soldier wanted to talk to them? Urgently? At one in the morning? Of course it would be nearly dawn on the East Coast.

"Is he holding or what?"

"He asked me to put him through."

Shade said, "Okay. Give me ten minutes. And have him FaceTime my cell phone." She recited the number.

She went to the sideboard and began brewing coffee. She needed to wake the others, starting with Dekka and Malik, and she didn't intend to wake either without some ready caffeine.

Five minutes later, a scowling Dekka, a distracted Malik, and an oddly perky Cruz were assembled in the living room. Shade had made the executive decision to let Armo and Francis sleep.

"The chairman of the Joint Chiefs?" Malik said, frowned, and then winced as he felt renewed interest from the Dark Watchers.

"I figured you should all hear the call," Shade said.

"You assume we should *take* the call?" Cruz asked. The days of Cruz passively taking her lead from Shade were over. They were friends, even close friends, but Cruz no longer blindly believed her brilliant friend was always better able to make decisions. Shade was relieved by the change: the fewer people looking to her for solutions, the better.

"I think we should," Shade said.

"They want something." Dekka searched for the remote

and clicked on MSNBC, the first any of them had heard of the shrapnelized landing of ASO-7. They'd all been avoiding news broadcasts, which still tended to rerun video of horrible events they'd been part of, events none of them wanted to be reminded of. "Aaaaannd that would be it."

"Jesus," Cruz whispered. "New York."

The phone rang.

"I'll prop the phone here," Shade said, balancing it against a bowl of fruit. She tapped the button, and a picture formed. The man was in full uniform but looked as if he was wearing a size too large. He was a fiftyish white man with a receding buzzcut and glasses that exaggerated his brown eyes. It was a capable face, a confident face, but one marked with lines of exhaustion that made him seem less impressive than he must have looked on a parade ground.

"Hello. This is Shade Darby."

The voice was higher than she'd expected, but carried heavy worry in its tone. "This is General Andy Eliopoulos. Thank you for taking my call."

"I'm here with Dekka Talent, Malik Tenerife, and Cruz."

The general got right to it. "Have you seen the news out of New York?"

"Just turned it on." Then, belatedly, added, "General."

"Ms. Darby, and the rest of you, you have no reason to trust me or the US military."

"No. We don't," Dekka said in a low rumble. "I was at the Ranch."

"That was not a military operation," Eliopoulos said.

"The tank column that shot up the Vegas Strip sure as hell was," Dekka snapped.

"Yes." Eliopoulos made no effort to offer excuses, nor did he argue about responsibility. "The relevant commanders have been relieved of duty. And may I say on behalf of the US military, and myself personally, how grateful we are that you were able to take down Dillon Poe and save so many lives. Not least being my soldiers, many of whom might have been killed, and many more would have had to live a lifetime of regret."

That caught Shade by surprise. "We wish we could have done more."

"Well, more is exactly what I'm going to ask of you, Ms. Darby."

"I knew this was too good to last," Dekka said, looking bereft as she gazed around the room whose luxury had made her feel out of place but which she now looked on with great fondness.

"The situation in New York is critical. Some actions have already been taken that . . ." The general looked uncomfortable. "People are scared shitless, I don't mind telling you, and they're doing stupid things. Bad, stupid things." He leaned into the screen. "And there are insistent demands that we take certain actions that . . . that I do not countenance at this time."

The four of them exchanged looks. The general was leaving it to their imaginations, but in a world where the US government had already used drone attacks to take out suspected mutants, a world where military helicopters had been deployed to attack civilian vehicles, where a nuclear device aboard a submarine had somehow blown up in the waters off Georgia, where a full tank column had been sent into Las Vegas, they could imagine all too well.

"ASO-7 was potentially on a course to annihilate New York City, so a decision was made to try to destroy it as it entered the atmosphere. Unfortunately, while the nukes broke up the ASO, tons of the rock still impacted the city. And worse, a number of people have been, for lack of a better word, shot: penetrated by granules of the ASO."

The four of them all understood what that meant: New York City was about to become ground zero for Rockborn mutants. None of them was naive enough to welcome that— the rock transformed the decent and the bad alike. Some who developed powers used them for good, or at least didn't cause problems. Others, however . . .

"We have no way of predicting," the general continued, "how many people will develop powers. Nor how many will choose the path that psychopath in Las Vegas did."

"It doesn't take many super-villains to mess up your day," Malik said. "If Poe had been a little smarter and more mature he could have destroyed civilization as we know it."

The general nodded. "The thing is, you saw our response. The US military is the most powerful instrument of destruction in the history of the world. But tank battalions and F-35s are not much use in Manhattan. If any of the people from this event turn into . . . well, monsters, no offense intended to you . . . The police and first responders have all they can do to cope with the straight-up destruction in Manhattan right now. They've got dozens of burning buildings, people buried under rubble, looting, panic. . . . They are not in a position to cope with the likes of a Tom Peaks, let alone a Dillon Poe."

"I'm sure you're right," Shade said, "but why are you calling us?" She had guessed the answer—they all had—but she wanted the general to say it.

Eliopoulos let go a long sigh. "I have no power to deputize you or convey any official status on you. I can't even pay you. And frankly, if you screw up, the Pentagon will disavow you."

"Cool. Just like *Mission: Impossible*," Malik said under his breath.

But Eliopoulos heard him and nodded. "Exactly. I'm asking for your help, knowing I don't have the right, and knowing you have no reason to do any more than you've already done. And I won't lie: there are half a dozen local law enforcement agencies and twice that many federal agencies involved, and it's all a massive cluster——, so I cannot guarantee you won't get shot at by NYPD or FBI or ICE or even my own people."

"Gosh," Cruz said dryly, "it sounds just great when you put it like that."

The general managed a weary smile. "You're a bunch of kids who've been through hell. Neither I nor anyone else has a right to ask you for more. But I've been asking young men and young women in uniform, men and women who mostly earn about what they could make flipping burgers, to do more than any human should be asked to do for my whole career. It's what these stars on my shoulders are about—sending good young people into harm's way. So, I'm asking you. Will the Rockborn Gang come to New York? I have a jet waiting at the airport."

Shade was on the verge of saying yes when Dekka held up a cautioning hand.

"No offense, General, but all of us together on an Air Force jet? That'd make a tempting target. I hate to seem suspicious, but like I said, I was at the Ranch. And I've already gone one-on-one with Apache gunships."

The general bridled and glared thunder at them but then dipped his head and said, "I understand your caution."

"Here's what we'll do," Shade said, with a grateful glance at Dekka. "We'll discuss it. We'll make a decision. If we decide to go, we'll arrange our own transportation. And we won't let you know we're going until we're there. If we go at all."

Eliopoulos nodded. "Fair enough. But quickly, please."

They broke contact with Eliopoulos and woke Armo and Francis. Once those two were fully conscious, Malik laid out the proposition.

"Oh, I've always wanted to see New York," Francis said.

Armo's reaction was more practical. He looked at Dekka. "We're bringing our bikes, right?"

"Let's not be too glib," Dekka said. "We'd be going into a situation where there could be a whole army of dangerous mutants. We haven't had time to work out how we act as a team. There's no front line, there's no safe space, there's no knowing in advance what we're up against. I think we need to take a vote—a secret vote—and it has to be unanimous."

Dekka expected Shade to argue, but she nodded.

Malik said, "We need to ask ourselves what we are. We need to decide whether we're a group, or just six fools thrown together temporarily by fate. Not to sound too Stan Lee here, but are we some kind of comic book superheroes or not? Is that our future? Is that what we're committing to? We have great power; do we also have great responsibility?"

They tore up scraps of hotel stationery, wrote their votes, folded the ballots, and dropped them into an empty ice bucket. Cruz read the votes out, one by one.

"Go. Go. Hell yeah." Cruz shot a look at Armo, who winked in acknowledgment. "Go. Go. And . . . go."

Dekka called down to Wilkes, who had to be roused from sleep. "Ms. Wilkes, it looks like we're checking out. And we need transportation to the East Coast."

Two hours later, they took off from McCarran International aboard one of the casino company's private jets, an Embraer Lineage 1000, which came complete with lie-flat seats, a bar, two flight attendants, an onboard chef offering to whip up omelets or stir-fry, and a resourceful loadmaster who'd managed to get Dekka's and Armo's big motorcycles aboard. Francis, too, had arrived by motorcycle, but hers had belonged to the leader of the racist meth-dealing biker gang she'd escaped from, and she was not sentimental about it.

Anyway, Francis had other means to get around.

As they crossed the Rockies, Dekka motioned Shade to join her on one of the plush couches, away from Armo, who, to the surprise of no one, had managed to fall asleep within seconds of wheels-up, and the others, who were testing the chef's skills.

"We have a problem," Dekka said with no preamble, but keeping her voice low.

Shade sensed the purpose of this conversation, but let Dekka lay it out.

"We're six people with two different people in charge," Dekka said. "So far it hasn't mattered, and maybe it never will. But . . ."

Shade nodded. "But it may matter if we're in a fight. And we're not just six random people anymore, we're the Rockborn Gang; that's what the vote was about. We've chosen the superhero path, and the chairman of the Joint Chiefs just lit up the bat signal. Jesus," she added in an aside, "the superhero path? Sometimes I can't believe the words coming out of my mouth."

Dekka nodded in agreement. "I know! I'm arguing with the chairman of the Joint Chiefs! Me. A Safeway cash-register jockey with a decent memory for the produce codes. Red onions: 4082. Honeycrisp apples: 3283. But it is what it is, Shade, so here's how I see it. Cruz and Malik are loyal to you. You're smarter than me, and aside from Francis, you're the one with the most useful power. So, if we're being logical, you ought to be in charge."

"But?"

Dekka shook her head. "No 'but.' Tag: you're it."

"Mmmm . . . No," Shade said flatly. She shook her head

and rolled her eyes, amazed at what she was about to say. "You know I've read, like, everything about the FAYZ, right? So the thing is, Dekka, in a way I've known you for a long time. Maybe Astrid Ellison's book was wrong in some details, and maybe the other books and movies are wrong, so maybe I have it wrong, too, but Astrid was always smarter than Sam Temple, right? Yet Sam was the leader. Why? Because he never wanted to be, but he was one of those people that other people will follow. And trust. And believe in."

"And you don't think that's you?"

Shade made a wry, self-deprecating grin. "Well, Dekka, I don't know if you've noticed, but I'm not short on ego."

Dekka lowered her head to conceal a smile.

"But I've had humility shoved right down my throat since this all started. I've had a master class in my own limitations. Malik and Cruz are only in this because I dragged them into it, and not for any grand purpose, just my own obsession. My own arrogance." She glanced at Malik and had to wait a moment for a wave of emotion that threatened to choke her speech to pass. "But not you, Dekka. You volunteered; you stepped up. That's what a leader does. It's what *you* do. So, I would be honored if I could be for you what you were for Sam. I've learned some humility, but even so, I think I'd be a hell of a strong right arm."

"No question," Dekka said, her voice roughened by emotion. "But am I ready to be Sam?"

They sat in silence for a while, each contemplating their own weaknesses and strengths with a realism and focus that only comes to people who've really been in what the Vietnam vets dubbed "the shit." It was a specificity and realism not possible for spectators and armchair heroes.

"We don't say anything to the others," Dekka said after a while. "We don't make a thing of it. But okay, Shade Darby, I will do my best to be Sam."

"And I am whatever you need me to be."

Four hours later they ate fresh-baked biscuits and drank excellent coffee as the late morning sun outlined the spires of Manhattan in gold.

From the Purple Moleskine

I STARTED OUT thinking this Moleskine would help me become a fiction writer. Instead I'm becoming a diarist. I guess I shouldn't fight fate. Anyway, diary writing was good for Virginia Woolf and Anne Frank. Not really very encouraging examples, I guess. One killed herself; the other was murdered by Nazis.

I overheard something I wasn't meant to hear. Shade gave up playing boss and turned it over to Dekka. I almost can't believe it. Shade is growing up, adding wisdom to intelligence. I love that girl, but the truth is I'm relieved—Dekka's the closest thing we have to an experienced leader.

New York. Never been there. Hell of a first trip. I'm scared. I imagine everyone is. Scared. I don't want to die, and I don't want to see any of my friends die. I am sick at heart for all this madness. I would almost rather be home in Evanston listening to my father sneer about ladyboys and chicks with dicks and all the rest.

Almost.

I've spent some time Googling pictures of people who might be useful, people I could pass as if necessary. My "repertoire" now includes a couple dozen folks. It feels wrong just taking people's appearance and using it, but I tell myself it's necessary. This is war, isn't it?

I just crossed myself and said a prayer, something I haven't done in a long time. War. But like no war ever. This isn't against some foreign enemy, it's a war of us against us, all against all, and no one worth trusting besides ourselves, and no one to follow.

Except Dekka.

Earlier I hid in the bathroom and morphed into Armo, which was just plain creepy and stalkery, but I find myself thinking about him a lot, which I know will end with me in tears. I know I'm rushing straight into pain and sadness and loneliness, and it's not like I need to look for more pain. I know I'm becoming obsessed, and I know what obsession did to Shade. I'm not crazy; I know it will end in embarrassment and humiliation. Maybe that means I'm actually more crazy than Shade—she at least thought she had control, and I know I don't.

I'm walking into a punch that will leave me hollowed out. And I can't seem to stop myself.

CHAPTER 9
Down and Dirty

BOB MARKOVIC HAD risked running toward the tree line when the shooting started. He had jumped up and run, gasping for breath, staggering, clutching the bandaged hole in his chest where a fragment of ASO-7 still lodged and ignoring the throbbing pain in his hand.

The first of what was to be five .50-caliber machine-gun bullets, each with more destructive energy than a hunter's rifle bullet, struck him just as he reached the line of pine trees.

That first .50-caliber round blew a tunnel right through his back and out of his chest, taking about a third of his heart with it.

The second round struck him in the thigh, penetrated to and shattered his femur, which stopped his momentum and made him crash headfirst into a tall, shaggy pine-tree trunk.

He was dead before he slumped to the ground.

The third entered through his right cheek, smashed a row of molars like someone attacking a porcelain sink with a sledgehammer, and in one of those odd quirks of ballistics, blew out through the back of his neck, severing his spinal cord.

The remaining two slugs turned his intestines and stomach to broken sewage pipes.

No human being could survive those wounds. Markovic's blood drained into the mud and filled the gaps in the bark of the pine tree he lay crumpled against. His bladder and bowels emptied. His liver had no blood left to cleanse. His heart fell silent.

And yet, Bob Markovic knew who he was and where he was. He felt the cold mud beneath him. He heard the sounds of truck engines, of heavy boots, the grunts of men and women carrying bodies. He saw a night sky retreating before oncoming dawn.

Markovic looked out over the field, over dozens, maybe more than a hundred, men, women, and yes, children, lying in clumps or alone in distorted positions. The black-clad gunmen were now walking through the bodies, making sure they were dead, firing twice into each: one in the head, one in the throat.

Bang. Bang.

Walking behind the shooters was a second echelon carrying five-gallon jerricans of gasoline, which they hefted high and upended to slosh fuel on the bodies. And a big earthmover was coming up the road, ready to dig a hole and shove the human ashes into it.

Markovic knew that any moment they might spot him. He

wondered if Simone was among the dead and felt a pang at the thought, though God knew Simone was already on the path to an early death in Markovic's mind—her experimentation with drugs, her bad taste in boys followed by a decision to cast herself as a lesbian. Her radical politics.

Still, she was his daughter. And he knew he should be feeling more than he was. The effects of stress, shock?

The effect of being both dead and somehow alive?

He wondered if he could stand and run. But he knew he could never outrun the gunmen. Somehow they had failed to kill him, but that didn't mean they wouldn't find a way. He doubted being incinerated would be a good thing.

Run!

Markovic tried to stand, expecting it to be hard, but to his surprise he stood easily, and was so shocked by this that for a moment he forgot to run. He held up his hand and could not stop the shriek of horror that came from him. His hand was not his hand. It was shaped like his hand, there were four fingers and a thumb, but it was a hand entirely covered by a seething mass of what had to be insects. Thousands of them.

A scream of pure panic rose within him, a scream that somehow emerged as an agitated buzzing sound. Like the sound a hive of bees might make if you poked it with a stick.

He looked down at his own body, and all of him, every exposed inch, was covered in a thick carpeting of tiny creatures, creatures as small as ants, creatures as large as small beetles.

BAM! BAM! BAM!

Three rifle shots, all carefully aimed. All struck their

target . . . and passed harmlessly through Markovic.

"What the . . . ," a black-clad man yelled. "Shoot that thing!"

BAM! BAM! BAM!

Now half a dozen weapons opened fire, bullets passing through Markovic and digging into the tree behind him, leaving small holes in him that were instantly covered by the insect mass.

At the same time, he felt himself sinking, sliding down along the tree trunk, sliding down until the damp earth seemed to have swallowed his bottom half up.

"Get that gas can over here!" a voice yelled.

Two men ran with heavy steps toward him, carrying jerricans. Gasoline spilled from one of the tanks.

Fire! No, he did not like fire. *Down! Down!* a panicked voice cried soundlessly. *Down into the ground!*

He was just head and shoulders when the first splash of gasoline landed on him. Markovic held up a bug-covered hand as if to shield himself, but something else happened.

Hundreds of insects flew in a mass at the nearest man with a jerrican. Markovic stared stupidly at what he'd thought was his hand, a hand that had just flown off. Beneath what he'd thought was a coating of insects, there was nothing. He had no body. He was nothing but . . . he was just . . .

He fought against a wave of terror that would cripple him if he let it. He had no body now, nothing, because if he'd had a body his heart would be hammering and his flesh would be tingling and his throat would be widening to scream and scream and never stop.

Markovic did not scream, but someone did; Markovic

heard the inhuman cry as he disappeared from view beneath the soil.

He heard guns firing right above him, bullets thudding into the earth, but the sound was muffled by dirt. Irrelevant. Because now Markovic was in a hallucinogenic dream, a dream that he was not one man but millions. A dream that he swam through soil as easily as he might move through air.

His mind was overwhelmed with images, shattered visuals, all devoid of true light but somehow lit nevertheless, as though the soil itself glowed faintly. But there was no making sense of what he saw; nothing was right, nothing was real, at least not any kind of real he'd ever known. It was like seeing the world through a million eyes at once, and even as that tidal wave of dim, distorted, kaleidoscopic visuals was overwhelming his ability to process, there were other inputs as well. He felt scraping all over his body, like sandpaper. He smelled things he could not place, things he knew he'd never smelled before.

Down he went, dirt-swimming, flowing, not a great, solid human, but thousands of individual bits and pieces, all digging and squirming as if directed by one will.

And they are, he thought: *my will!*

Markovic then felt a swelling rush of power, of the realization of power, of the thrilling knowledge that the extent of his power was not even yet known.

I can't be killed with bullets!

He was on a speed high, reveling in the liquid swiftness with which he bored through solid ground, flowing around rocks, reassembling, unstoppable. Like a flood. Like a swarm of locusts.

He felt no fear now, which was odd. He should be feeling fear; he knew that. He should be feeling scared to death. But, then again, he should be dead. Maybe *was* dead by most conventional standards. Certainly he was not breathing, nor did he feel any urge to.

The pieces fell into place quickly: it was the rock. Clearly. *Obviously.* He'd been hit with dozens of tiny pieces of the meteorite as well as the larger one that had ripped his hand nearly off, and the pebble that had lodged in his chest.

I'm one of them. A mutant.

Rockborn!

Again his daughter's name floated up in his consciousness. *Simone.* Had she been killed? Probably easier that she . . . No, no, no, she was his daughter. He loved her. It's just that she was not relevant to his current situation. He would worry about Simone, and if it came to it, he would grieve for her. But right here and now he had very pressing issues. In point of fact he was deep underground and moving at speed, moving for the sheer joy of speed, moving for the thrill of dirt scraping his thousands of shells.

Like an ant colony, he thought. *I am many, but with one mind over all.*

But he was not alone. He felt a different consciousness, not a will, really, just a mind other than his own. A strange sensation, like he was being watched. Like he was a curiosity. Like he was a specimen under a scientist's microscope.

What have I become?

Markovic moved on, heedless, reckless, pushing doubt aside and reveling in this incredible ability. Then, all at once he was hit head-on by a wall of cold water. It flowed over and past him, through him, bringing icy cold.

The thousands of compound eyes he looked through were blinded by bright light. He felt a panic seize him—he was exposed! Vulnerable!

But slowly he felt his parts adjust, swimming with churning insect feet, assembling into a swirling mass in gloomy, chemical-green water pierced by slanting early-morning sun. His thousands of eyes adjusted to the light, and his panic subsided as slowly the picture of his surroundings became comprehensible. This was no river, nor a natural lake. The sides were too steeply vertical. And he saw ramps wide enough to accommodate big trucks, spiraling down the sides of those submerged cliffs, and knew what this was. He had dug his way right into what must have been a gravel mine, now filled with water to form a lifeless lake. Far below him, on the floor of the pond, were two vehicles, old cars that had probably been pushed in so the owners could claim insurance.

He brought himself together—like a consolidation, his business mind thought—and breached, a densely packed cloud of insects swimming so fast that Markovic came almost all the way up out of the water. Before he settled back again, he saw two young boys standing at the edge of the flooded quarry, tossing rocks. The boys yelped and pointed. One fled; the other drew out his phone to take a picture.

Markovic let him. Who cared? There might be people to fear, but the boy with the camera was not one of them. So Markovic used the sunshine to examine himself. He was multitudes seeing through thousands of eyes at once, seeing in every direction. It was overwhelming, too much, like trying to watch a hundred televisions at once. Again panic threatened, but he did not give in, would not give in. He was Bob Markovic, and he would not be terrified.

Gradually he realized that he could control his visual feed, that he could mute the cascade of sights and sounds, and narrow his focus to those things he needed to see. And the most pressing need was to see and understand himself.

This was a nightmare of images, insect faces swirling around like they were caught in a tornado. He was within that tornado, able to see inside what he now was. He saw nothing human, no slight shred of his body, nothing solid or fixed. Nothing but the swarm of mismatched insects, things like dragonflies but with bright-red wings, things like cockroaches but with wings like moths. Bugs crawling on other bugs, as if they were hitching a ride. There were centipedes, but each ending in a circular, gnashing mouth full of tiny, sharp teeth; there were things that looked like common houseflies, but seen at close range they had canine muzzles—tiny, winged dogs.

He knew he should be horrified, disgusted, panicked, and he felt some of that emotion, but the urge to surrender to fear was gone. He had never been one to overly concern himself with risk—not when there was also opportunity. Power was opportunity, by definition, and he was powerful. Powerful in a way that even money had never given him, a physical power, a real power. The power to be shot and yet be unhurt. The power to move through dirt like it was water, and water like it was air. And he had only just begun to explore the possibilities.

Besides, he knew enough about the so-called Rockborn that they could move easily from human to morph and back to human. This was not him, this was not Bob Markovic, his essential self remained. Somewhere. This was just a brand-new, absolutely amazing ability. He felt like he had when he'd bought a Bugatti Veyron and stepped on the gas on an empty stretch of the Long Island Expressway.

The power!

Bob Markovic had not become the man he was through whining and self-pity, let alone panic. He was curious, however, especially about whether his swarm could move on the surface of the land as easily as beneath it. He spotted a low bank, a grim gravel beach of sorts, where one of the ramps emerged from the water. To his relief, he had no difficulty at all gliding up onto the narrow gravel beach. After that it took a few tries to stand up like a man, or at least like a buzzing, vibrating, clicking facsimile of a man.

He had a sudden image of addressing his board of directors in this guise.

Hah! That'd shake them up!

The kid with the camera phone had run off, presumably to upload his video to YouTube.

What was that?

He felt the odd, back-of-the-neck tingle that warned someone was watching him, and not the strange observers he seemed to feel in his head. Sure enough, when he looked around—something he could do without moving his man-shape, merely by choosing to focus in that direction—he spotted three men in black tactical gear carrying assault rifles at port arms. They were on the far lip of the quarry, and they'd spotted him. They were pointing, their faces twisted by confusion and growing fear.

Could they kill him?

Hah. You can't shoot a swarm of insects.

But now a fourth man appeared, straining under the weight of big steel tanks on his back. A short hose connected the top of the tanks to a sort of nozzle, something like a fireman's hose.

Flamethrower!

Markovic was definitely not sure he would survive that.

He began to dig again, experience and growing confidence making him faster, but he had failed to see the true danger until a military helicopter swept in just above treetop level and wheeled around to bring its weapons to bear.

A tail of flame shot from the helicopter's weapons pod.

One missile fired. One missile struck, with a massive *ka-BLAM!*

Markovic felt a wave of searing heat, felt parts of him wither and crisp and die. No pain, just an awareness that some of his eyes had suddenly gone blind. The debris of the explosion fell like hail around him, but the falling gravel did him no harm.

Now when he raised eyes above the surface of the water, he saw the gunmen were much closer, coming around the quarry, running toward him, pell-mell down the ramp. The man with the tanks on his back huffed and puffed to keep up.

Rage took Markovic. This was unfair! He had done nothing wrong. He'd hurt no one. He was the victim! He hadn't asked to be hit by some space rock, nor had he volunteered to be shot down in a stinking field.

"I am the victim here!" Markovic shouted in a voice unlike his own, a voice like a thousand locusts shaping buzzes and the beating of wings into words. It was a staccato sound like a person talking directly into whirring fan blades, a rasping, inhuman sound.

The man with the flamethrower caught up as the gunmen slowed, all four now grown cautious, seeing that the missile had not killed Markovic.

Markovic's reedy whisper said, "Leave me alone! Go back or I'll kill you!"

It was an empty threat, Markovic thought: he had no weapon, he had no armed men on his side, he could barely even "stand." This was his own government—a government that had collected millions in taxes from Markovic's Money Machine—and it was trying to kill him! Madness!

Unfairness. Injustice.

"Tone, light him up, for Christ's sake!" one of the gunmen shouted.

Suddenly Tone, the man with the flamethrower, slapped at his face. Then slapped again.

"What the hell, Tone?"

But then the gunmen, too, found themselves besieged by flying insects diving with relentless intent into their eyes, crawling toward their ears, scooting over lips and into screaming mouths.

"What the hell?"

"What, what, oh, God, what's happening?"

"Ah, ah, ah! They're biting!"

"Help me!"

Guns fell from fingers. The flamethrower was shrugged from Tone's back. The four men writhed wildly, looking like marionettes whose puppeteer was having a seizure. It was almost comical, Markovic thought. But for the screams.

Markovic moved toward them, striding on swarm legs, stepping with massed insects in lieu of feet. He could do more than see the four men: he could smell them, taste them, take their temperature, hear their panicky heartbeats. He had eyes inside their mouths. He had close-up views of insect mouthparts and stingers stabbing into flesh.

It was at once utterly fascinating and profoundly disturbing. He was watching, smelling, feeling men afraid for their lives, men desperate to escape the swarm of insects around them. He tasted the adrenaline flooding their veins, veins now feeding hundreds if not thousands of insects.

One man broke and ran toward the water to jump in, but he tripped, and when he tried to rise to his hands and knees, he could not.

The other men tried the same thing, each seeing the water

as a way to escape. And, Markovic thought, it might have been. But they would never reach the water, of that he was sure, though it was mere feet away. None of the men seemed able to walk, to move a leg. Their waving, slapping, gesticulating arms slowed, growing heavy.

Markovic sensed a foul odor, a smell so strong and repugnant he instinctively reached to pinch the nose he no longer had. He knew the smell. Sickness. Rot. Decay. Oh, yes, he knew that smell. He'd been in the Navy in the Persian Gulf, and the destroyer he'd served aboard had come across a derelict sailboat, its sail in tatters, the wood bleached white by the relentless, pitiless sun. He had been part of the boarding party. Markovic, then Lieutenant Markovic and armed with a pistol, had pried up a hatch and shone a flashlight down into hell.

Two dozen humans, men and women and babies in arms, lay there. Half at least were dead, and the rest might soon be. They were refugees from the war in Yemen and had contracted cholera from infected water and food. The deck was awash in vomit and diarrhea, but the worst of the stink was decaying flesh. The decaying flesh of people who had been six days dead in 115-degree heat, with no one strong enough to throw them overboard.

This was that same unbearable stink. The odor of putrefaction. The odor of disease and death.

He thought of his insects all returning to him, and in four distinct clouds they rose from the men and flew back to rejoin the swarm.

Somehow Markovic had expected to see the men perhaps pocked with red bite marks. The reality was worse. So very much worse.

Well, Markovic thought grimly, *I guess that will be a lesson to anyone who messes with me.*

But that did not mean he wanted to stay and watch. He moved away, fast. He kept moving his "legs," but that was mere habit, for he moved not like a running man, but like a cloud on a stiff breeze, a buzzing mass of death-dealing insects.

Okay, enough, Markovic thought as he reached the relative cover of some pine woods. *Time to change back.*

He focused his thoughts on his true body, his true self.

Nothing happened.

He tried again, adding urgency to the attempt. By now everyone knew the Rockborn could morph and de-morph at will, but nothing was happening. He had a mental image of himself running into a wall, a tall cinder-block wall. This was not in any of the accounts he'd read or seen on TV. The Rockborn could change back *at will.* Everyone said so!

Now the fear came at full throttle, irresistible. He tried again, and once again it was like hitting a wall, a wall beyond which there was nothingness.

Death.

He remembered the machine-gun bullets, the ones that had ripped his then-flesh-and-blood body. He remembered thinking he had to be dead, could not possibly be alive and yet . . .

The truth was there, easy to see, yet so awful, so impossibly horrific. . . . Bob Markovic, who always accepted reality and made the most of it, could not bring himself to believe what with dawning terror he knew to be true: he could not change back. His old body, the original Bob Markovic, was dead.

CHAPTER 10
New York, New York

THE ROCKBORN GANG, in their borrowed jet, landed at Teterboro Airport, across the Hudson River from New York City, in New Jersey. The sun was out, though a weak, pale thing compared to the Las Vegas sun, and it was distinctly chilly, just cold enough to turn breath to steam.

"So much for sunbathing by the pool," Armo muttered as they stepped out onto the stairs. "I'll miss my cabana."

Half a dozen photographers and reporters were waiting for them, despite the secrecy they'd hoped to maintain. The shouted questions began the instant the cabin door opened.

"Has the president summoned you?"

"Are you here to save New York?"

"Can you please spell the names of everyone in the Rockborn Gang?"

"I'm just the flight attendant," Armo said to the assembled media. He moved nimbly aside at the bottom of the stairs, allowing Dekka to step out from behind him.

Better her than me, Armo thought. *She has more words.*

Dekka stopped on the bottom step and cast a sour look at the assembled media. "Long flight, bad mood, leave us alone." Then she marched on, aiming for the stretch SUV that was to pick them up, pushing through the crowd like an ocean liner plowing through a wave. The reporters shifted attention to the next person off the plane.

"Cruz! Smile! Look here, smile!"

"You're being called the hero of Las Vegas. Can you comment?"

"Can you clear up your gender issue for us?"

Cruz froze halfway down the stairs, but Shade squeezed past, grabbed Cruz's hand, and urged her along. Armo admired the smooth way Shade drew the reporters and cameras around herself. Very smart girl, that Shade. She and Malik, both, way too smart for him, which was a good thing. He knew he was not "academic smart"; he was not the person to be making decisions for other people. Just for himself.

"Shade Darby! How fast can you go?"

"Why have you come to New York?"

"Shade! Shade! Do you have a comment on the accusation that you started all this?"

"I'll take three questions," Shade said. "Go."

It was a high step up into the SUV, and Armo gave Cruz a hand. Francis, Malik, and Dekka all piled in, while Armo waited behind just in case Shade needed some support.

Which, when he considered it, brought a wry smile to his lips. On the power scale, Shade was way more dangerous than he was.

A woman with a pile of blond hair, who Armo vaguely thought he might recognize from TV, thrust a microphone at Shade. "Why are you here?"

Shade made a show of thinking it over and said, "We're here to see some Broadway shows. Next question?"

"Can you morph for us?" came a shouted question.

"I could, but then I'd have to answer questions in a high-pitched buzz. I'm told it's hard to understand."

Then Shade made eye contact with Armo and jerked her head. Meaning . . . What? And then it dawned on him. He climbed in, closed the door, and said, "Drive. Go! Now! Trust me."

The SUV started moving, and instinctively the reporters and their cameramen shifted attention to it, some breaking into a run to try and keep pace.

The driver looked in the rearview mirror and said, "What about your friend?"

"Shade? Oh, she'll be along. Drive on."

Just as they were reaching the gate, the SUV's back left door flew open and slammed shut so fast it only seemed to make a single sound. And Shade sat vibrating and resuming her normal human form.

"Sweet," Armo said.

Shade winked at him. "Enh, it's what I do."

Armo was in the seat next to Cruz, careful not to sprawl into her. He had a tendency to take up most of whatever seat he was in, and he didn't want her to think he was being "handsy."

"Paparazzi," Malik said with a droll grin. "We're the new Kardashians."

"Maybe I'll start a fashion line," Shade said. "Sell a Shade Darby perfume that evaporates superfast so you only have half a second to smell it."

"Smell me now 'cause you won't smell me later?" Cruz suggested, and Armo laughed appreciatively. He usually got Cruz's jokes, while he often had the sense that Shade had said something funny that he just didn't get.

The limo pulled onto a four-lane road and passed first a KFC and then a Taco Bell, reminding Armo that he was hungry. He'd slept most of the flight and not taken full advantage of the omelet bar. Then he spotted an IHOP sign and followed it longingly with his eyes.

"Waffles or pancakes?" Cruz asked him.

Armo gave it some thought. "Pancakes. Waffles are great, but only in, like the first minute after they come out of the griddle. Pancakes hold up better."

Cruz laughed, and Armo smiled in response. He remembered being on a movie set his father was stunt coordinator for, and overhearing Jim Carrey talking about how getting a laugh was the best drug ever. Armo hadn't meant his answer to be funny, in fact he'd been going for thoughtful, but that didn't make Cruz's grin any less infectious.

According to Malik's phone, the drive was normally forty-five minutes into Manhattan, but the bombardment had made a hash of the city's already impossible traffic, and the ride took three hours, the last hour and fifteen minutes with Armo in agony from needing to pee. He'd considered peeing into a water bottle and decided no, that was not going to go over well, especially with a young girl like Francis in the car.

Armo would have distracted himself by talking more to Cruz, but she was asleep now, with her head lolling back and forth with each turn, until he let her head come to rest on his shoulder. Now he couldn't move, had no one to talk to, and he still had to pee.

Stuff that never happens to the X-Men.

Finally they arrived at what Armo had heard Malik call a brownstone, a five-story brick townhouse on the Upper West Side. It belonged to the grandparents of the baby Cruz had rescued from fire in Las Vegas.

Cruz woke with a start, wiped drool from her mouth, and stared at Armo in horror. "Oh, my God, I slobbered on you!"

There were probably witty things to say in response to that, but all Armo came up with was, "No damage."

A maid let them into the brownstone. The grandparents were in Idaho with extended family, dealing with the tragedy that had cost them their daughter and son-in-law.

The gang were exploring the brownstone and choosing rooms when Francis, looking through the sheer curtains hanging over the front windows, yelled, "Something's happening!"

Armo leaned over Francis's shoulder and saw four black SUVs and a big SWAT truck screeching up in front. Dekka moved beside him.

"What the hell?" Dekka snarled.

"We've been sold out!" Armo shouted, and began to morph, white fur sprouting from his body, puffing up the legs of his jeans and the sleeves of his shirt.

A fight? It had been a while. So, okay, then!

Malik said, "Not necessarily," and Armo groaned inwardly. He was restless after hours on the plane and more hours in the limo. He kind of liked the idea of stretching out by bashing a few heads together.

"I really don't want to have to hurt cops who are just doing their job," Dekka said, but she, too, was morphing, preparing for battle. None of them thought they'd have too hard a time winning this fight, but no one really wanted it, not even Armo, not really. They were all tired, and this was not the enemy. Probably.

"I've got this," Malik said.

"I've got your bzzz zz zzz." Shade Darby was morphing in mid-speech, vibrating in place like a hyperactive greyhound on a short leash.

Malik opened the front door and stepped out just as a dozen people in tactical gear, helmets and assault rifles at the ready, came storming up.

"Please stop. I don't want to hurt you," Malik said, but the SWAT team was not used to listening to protests from the people they were arresting.

"Hands in the air! Hands in the air!" They rushed him, guns leveled. There was a burst of wind, a blur, and the first three SWAT members suddenly had no guns.

"Take him down!" the special agent in charge yelled into a bullhorn, but a split second later the bullhorn was gone, and the special agent in charge was no longer in charge of anything, but had been physically dragged thirty feet to be propped up in front of Malik like a human shield.

"No one shoot! Safe your weapons!" the SAIC yelled, seeing sense now that *he* was in the line of fire.

"Please!" Malik said insistently. "Listen to me. We do not want to hurt you, but you will not win this fight. Please believe me: I can cause you terrible pain, pain that would drive you mad. I don't want to have to do that."

A woman in the navy-blue business suit of a federal agent held up her FBI shield and said, "We have warrants for your arrest. Release Special Agent Borowitz now! Do not attempt to resist."

Then something strange happened: NYPD patrol cars raced down the block to come to tire-squealing halts, lights flashing. The street was soon completely blocked by NYPD forming a ring around the SWAT vehicle and the FBI's SUVs. Out of one NYPD car stepped a man in a dress uniform so stiff it could probably stand by itself. He was one of those men who looked as if they must sleep, shower, and even use the toilet while at full, straight-backed attention. He had a voice to match the look.

"I'm Chief Hale, and someone better explain to me right the hell now why the FBI is pulling this bullshit while my city is still dealing with multiple deaths, panic, and looting."

Shade released her hold on the FBI SAIC and pushed him

gently away. There followed a heated conversation between the FBI and the NYPD over whether or not the Rockborn Gang was welcome in the city. After ten minutes, the mayor showed up looking like she hadn't slept and was ready to explode at any minute.

"Get the hell off my streets!" she yelled at the federal agents. "Do you inflamed federal rectums even know what's happening in this goddamn city? These people are here to help, and they have my personal guarantee of safety. So unless you intend to shoot it out with my officers, get the hell out of here."

"On your head, Your Honor," Special Agent in Charge Borowitz snapped, straightening his rumpled jacket. "I will inform Washington of your actions."

"Yeah? You can tell Washington to go and—"

At which point Armo put his big paws over Francis's ears. "You're too young for language like that."

The federal forces pulled away, tires squealing again, angry and frustrated. The mayor, the chief, and a youngish male detective in plain clothes came inside.

"I'm Mayor Chaffetz. Call me Louise. Chief Bob Hale, and Detective Peter Williams."

They shook hands. They sat in the living room of the borrowed house, a house they'd scarcely explored.

"I'll get right to it," Mayor Louise Chaffetz said. "Something very bad has happened, and I don't just mean asteroid shrapnel killing a bunch of my people and starting a bunch of goddamn fires." She had bottle-blond hair, narrow brown eyes, a sharp nose, and a habit of drumming armrests with both hands at once, burning off nervous energy. She reminded Armo a bit of Shade.

The detective was white, under thirty, with a narrow face, thinning dark hair, and alert, watchful eyes. He did not sit but stood leaning against the wall. He looked like he was jonesing for a cigarette.

"Tell us," Dekka said. "We're not easily shocked."

"No, I don't suppose you are." The mayor sighed. She looked around the room as if searching for allies. Her gaze lingered over a sideboard bearing half a dozen bottles of liquor. "Last night one hundred and three people who'd been struck by meteorite fragments were arrested by federal agents—some ATF but some ICE sons of bitches, too, and people we think were private contractors hired by who the hell knows anymore. The people—hurt people, injured people, people dragged out of surgery, for Christ's sake, were driven to the Jersey Pine Barrens and . . ." Her weary but confident voice caught in her throat, and she backed up to start again. "They were taken to the Pine Barrens and machine-gunned. Shot down."

The silence that followed stretched on so long Armo thought it might never end. He checked the faces of the others, not believing his own ears, but from their appalled expressions, they'd heard the same impossible thing he had.

Finally Dekka said, "I was wrong. I guess we are still able to be shocked."

"It was a panic move," the mayor said. "And it seems to

have failed anyway. One hundred and three people were driven there to be gunned down and their bodies burned. But the thing is, Jersey State Police say there are only ninety-nine bodies. That means four people are unaccounted for. Not to mention that there are still hundreds of people in the city who were hit."

"American citizens were just, just gunned down in a field?" Cruz demanded. "My God, what is happening?"

"Fear. Panic," the mayor said. "And it's not without reason. We are pretty sure that at least one of those who survived has acquired powers."

"What makes you think that?" Shade asked.

Mayor Chaffetz sat back and let go of a long sigh. "You're going to need to see it. One or two of you, we have a helicopter with room for two passengers in addition to Detective Williams . . ."

"Why Detective Williams?" Shade asked.

"He'll be your liaison with me and the NYPD. He has full authority to keep the Feds off your backs and make sure you have any city resources you need."

"You won't be coming?" Cruz asked the mayor.

The mayor looked down. Her whole body signaled weariness, but this was more than that. Armo saw that she clasped her hands together to hide a shake. "I went earlier. I saw." Chaffetz shook her head, and when she spoke again her voice was low and quivered with emotion. "I don't need to see that again. I don't ever need to see that again."

CHAPTER 11
Kill Us

TEN MINUTES LATER, Dekka and Francis—chosen at Malik's suggestion—were in helicopter jump seats. Dekka sat in front beside the pilot; Francis and Detective Williams were just behind them. All wore can headphone sets with microphones curving around beside their mouths.

As they flew over the city, Dekka had a spectacular if depressing view that included scenes of devastation, buildings shattered, their makings and their forlorn contents blocking streets. Smoke hung over Central Park, and the still-billowing smoke of active fires could be seen all the way from downtown to Harlem.

Soon they were across the river, past miles of urban sprawl, and skimming at treetop level above a seemingly endless forest of identical pine trees, interrupted by marshes, by meandering streams, by small ponds reflecting a sun that failed to spread cheer over the gloomy scenery.

They came to a wide clearing that had been scorched black

and scarred by earthmoving equipment. They hovered there for a while, rotors churning the air above futile ambulances and fire trucks, New Jersey State Police vehicles, and the ubiquitous black SUVs.

Then the helicopter swiveled and advanced a few hundred feet to an eerie, chemical-green pond. Beams of slanting sunlight revealed the ramps and deep gouges of an abandoned gravel quarry.

They landed near the edge of the sickly-green quarry lake. They got out and the detective led the way down a long ramp still marked with the deep ruts made by heavy trucks. Dekka felt Williams's hand on her shoulder.

"Prepare yourself," he said. "It's not good."

Dekka was tempted to shrug off both his hand and his warning, but she recalled the stricken, gray face of the mayor and allowed that maybe there really was something she needed to be prepared for.

The narrow gravel beach had been cordoned off with yellow crime-scene tape, and three policemen stood a distance away, smoking and looking at the new arrivals, or at the pond, or nowhere at all, anything to not look at what Dekka thought looked like a tangle of burned bodies.

I've seen burned bodies. Unfortunately.

Williams's face was grim, his jaw clenching. Dekka had learned that he was a murder cop, a homicide detective, not a job that sheltered you from horror. Yet he was visibly steeling himself for something. Dekka followed him with Francis at her heels. Their feet crunched gravel, too loud in the silence that followed the helicopter powering down.

Dekka felt before she saw. A tingling on her arms and up her neck.

Not burned bodies.

Not corpses.

Dekka stopped. The stink was awful, and for a moment she told herself it was that the quarry lake, but no, this was not a chemical smell. This was the stink of putrefying flesh. She knew this smell too well. In the early days of the FAYZ it had taken them a while to realize that every home needed to be searched for . . . for what they eventually found: infants, abandoned by disappeared parents, trapped in cribs, unable to do anything at all, but cry and starve.

She breathed hard, inhalations like sobs.

"Oh, Jesus. Oh, Jesus, no."

"What is that?" Francis cried, and instinctively grabbed Dekka's arm for support.

Four men stood—at least, their feet were planted on the ground, like they were glued or nailed down—but they slumped and sagged, and one lay on his side, legs twisted at an impossible angle.

Their bodies were emaciated, thin, their black tactical gear in tatters, the exposed skin red and black, entirely corrupted. Rotten.

Swollen boils, pustules, weeping open sores, blood-red ulcerations covered every square inch of the four men. There were blood blisters, lacerations, and tumors as big as tangerines.

And all of it, every inch of the four men, *seethed*. It was like watching time-lapse video of a pizza in a hot oven, the cheese bubbling and browning, the bits of meat or vegetables drying and withering.

The stink was overpowering, and Dekka saw Francis struggling to stop herself from vomiting.

Then the eyes in one head moved and focused, and Francis screamed.

Williams said, "Ms. Talent, Ms. Specter, these are ICE agents Franklin, Wallberg, and Pedroncelli. And ATF agent Hernandez."

"Help us," one of the ICE agents moaned, and with renewed shock Dekka realized that somehow they could still speak. Dekka recoiled in horror, not conscious of moving but obeying a DNA-deep imperative to get away, to put distance between herself and . . . and something that should never exist. Francis hugged Dekka's arm tightly and buried her face against Dekka's chest.

"Best we can tell," Williams said, his voice flat from suppressed emotion, "they are showing signs of, well, just about every awful disease you can think of. The coroner took a look and gathered some samples, but his first guess is smallpox, black plague, and leprosy. Other things, too. Like a goddamn display of every awful disease you can have, and all accelerated."

"But they're still alive," Dekka said.

"Yeah," Williams said. "They're locked in place, can't move, and that's a good thing." He shook his head at the irony of using the word "good."

"Why good?"

"You want men carrying a dozen infectious diseases running around loose?"

"Ah," Dekka said.

"They should be dead. Coroner took temperatures, and the weird thing was, no fever," Williams said. "That means their immune system isn't working. Isn't there at all. They should be dead."

That the men were not dead was testified to by a continuous moan of pain, occasional sharp yelps, and desperate pleas all saying the same thing.

Please. Please. Kill me. Let me die.

People were coming down the ramp to the gravel beach, people in white hazmat suits, five of them, their faces invisible behind plastic shields, looking like lost astronauts.

"What are they doing?" Francis asked.

"They're going to shoot them full of more antibiotics, I'd guess," Williams said.

"Can we talk to them?" Dekka asked.

"We're not to get any closer. This is it. The risk of disease . . . the city does not need the black plague; we have plenty to deal with."

Dekka watched as the hazmat team advanced, knelt by the tortured men, unlimbered medical kits, and stabbed needles into flesh that would barely register a needle's pinprick.

"How soon before we see results?" Dekka asked. Williams could only shrug.

And then: the answer.

The seething, the sense that their very flesh was crawling

with bacteria, viruses, amoebas, and parasites, grew worse, much worse, and with shocking speed, until they looked more like marshmallows dropped into a fire, their skin erupted in boils six inches across, with obscenely swollen buboes growing as big as cantaloupes before bursting and draining green pus.

And the screams. The screams. The pitiful cries for death. *Kill me! Please, God, kill me!*

The hazmat crew withdrew quickly to a safe distance. The antibiotics had not just failed; they seemed to act like accelerants, like spraying lighter fluid on hot charcoal.

"Why don't they die?" Francis cried, nearly hysterical.

Dekka put a comforting hand on her shoulder, but she knew it was useless. She couldn't comfort herself, let alone Francis. She was powerless. Powerless, standing there, watching something from a nightmare, listening to the agony of men being tortured like heretics in a medieval dungeon.

"Have you ever seen anything . . . ?" Williams asked, not wanting to seem helpless, not wanting to cede authority to Dekka, but unable to keep the pity and the horror out of his voice.

"Nothing like this," Dekka whispered.

Dekka struggled to keep breath in her lungs. Every cell in her body screamed, *Run, run!* Whoever, *what*ever had done this to these men could do it to her next. Dekka had survived unspeakable horrors in the FAYZ, the worst of which had been insects the size of rats inside her own body, the solution to which had been . . . She pushed that memory down, down to where she could put it aside and focus instead on this new wickedness.

"I have to call someone," Dekka said. She turned away from the scene, took a deep breath, and dialed. "Malik. Listen, Malik, there's a situation . . ." Right, *situation*. Like this was some random squabble between neighbors or something. She described what she saw to Malik and sent him a photo.

She listened to Malik, and said, "Stay on the line, huh?" To Francis she said, "Malik has a suggestion." She winced, knowing that she was asking the young girl to do something insane. "Francis? Do you suppose you could, you know, take a look in the . . . whatever you call it?"

"Over There," Francis supplied.

Francis swallowed hard. She was a brave girl, but she was shaking. Yet Francis seemed determined not to look weak, and Dekka had the stomach-turning realization that Francis was unwilling to look weak to *her*, to Dekka. She could give Francis an excuse not to do this; she could let Francis off the hook. She could tell her to run straight back up to the helicopter and close her eyes until they were far away.

But she wouldn't. This was leadership. This was what Sam Temple had done times beyond counting: sending good people into danger, sending them into trauma and a lifetime of nightmares—if they survived at all. General Eliopoulos's words came back to her. *It's what these stars on my shoulders are about—sending good young people into harm's way.*

"Do your best," Dekka said, hating herself for it.

Francis swallowed hard and nodded.

Francis's eyes took on the oil-slick rainbow whirl that signaled the first stage of her morph. Then her body itself became not a rainbow, quite, but a whirl of colors and shapes, of things unrecognizable, and a second later she slid through the ground, simply sank into the dirt.

Minutes passed, minutes with Dekka's ears filled with the chorus of agony, nostrils full of the reek of decay, eyes unable to look away because to look away was to abandon these poor men. Francis popped back into 3-D reality and stood trembling, fists clenched, eyes squeezed as tightly as her jaw. Dekka waited impatiently, knowing she could not rush the girl. Francis would speak when she was ready.

"I can't do anything," Francis said at last, tears spilling from closed eyes.

"Tell me," Dekka urged quietly.

Francis opened her eyes, looked at and then away from the doomed men. "There's something connected to them. Not like the cable things we saw from the Watchers, something different, like . . . like roots. Like tree roots, kind of, but everything Over There is hard to make sense of, you know?"

"Can you cut these root things?" Dekka asked.

Francis shook her head. "I tried grabbing on, but they aren't always, you know, actual *things*. My hands just passed right through them."

Into the phone, Dekka said, "Did you get all that, Malik?"

Malik said, "Antibiotics won't work. No medicine will. This goes deeper, this is way deeper than just disease organisms. This is bad. Someone has a very, very dangerous power."

"Yeah, no kidding," Dekka replied and hung up. "We've got nothing."

Williams sagged. Dekka shook her head.

"Who did this to you?" Dekka called to the men.

"Bugs . . . ," one man managed to gasp. "A man made out of bugs."

To Williams's questioning look, Dekka snapped, "No, I don't happen to know anyone made out of bugs."

"Don't leave us like this. Kill us!"

"Are you in pain?" Dekka asked gently.

A strangled laugh became a cry, and a second man said, "You can't even begin . . . My God! Kill me! God in heaven, make it stop!"

"End it," the first man gasped. "Have mercy and kill us. Please, please, I'm begging you: Kill us!"

Detective Williams took Dekka's arm with some force and pulled her away. Dekka took Francis's arm in turn, and they fled for the safety of the helicopter.

Kill us. . . .

Kill us. . . .

CHAPTER 12
Rare Moments of Peace

MALIK PUT AWAY his phone.

"Bad?" Shade asked him.

Malik nodded. "I think Dekka was crying."

The utter improbability of that was disturbing all by itself. Dekka? Crying?

Dekka?

"When do we get a day off from this?" Shade muttered. She was frying eggs in the brownstone's designer kitchen surrounded by gleaming copper and shiny stainless steel and every known or unknown kitchen device. It was, Shade thought, a kitchen you could run a restaurant out of. But frying eggs was the limit of Shade's culinary skill, and she was pretty sure she was screwing even that up.

Malik sat perched on a barstool at the granite-topped kitchen island and kept his hands busy arranging a basket of fruit by size.

"You ever read Heinlein?" Malik asked. "*Something Wicked This Way Comes*?"

Shade's answer was a knowing, mirthless laugh.

Malik had heard the heralds of a great evil in the voices of
men begging for death. He had heard it in the hopelessness
of Francis's voice. Worst of all was the awed pity in the voices
of his friends and the policeman. They were seeing something unspeakable. Something *wicked*.

Something was coming that would obliterate this small
moment of normalcy with Shade. Any moment of peace, any
moment that was not a crisis, was precious to Malik now. His
head was full. He felt like a swollen water balloon that only
needed a few more drops to burst. He had not a moment of
freedom from the Watchers; if anything, it felt as if there were
more of them than ever. Part of him wondered if they had
become alarmed at his penetrations into Over There. He felt no
emotion from the Watchers, seldom did, and when he sensed
anything like an emotion, it was eagerness or impatience.

Malik wished he felt fear from the Watchers; that would
be a good sign. He wanted them to be afraid. He wanted to
be what they feared. But it was more important than ever
to be very careful about what he believed and what he did
not, to separate facts from wishes. Malik had never been one
to accept anything at face value; he always needed evidence,
and of Watcher panic he sensed none.

"Feeling the Watchers? You kind of went silent on me."

Malik snapped back to the present, seeing Shade's concern. "A bit." Then he forced a smile. "You know what we'd
do if we were smart?"

"What would we do if we were smart? Dammit! I broke
one of my eggs! I mean, one of *your* eggs."

"We would trademark the Rockborn Gang and license our name for merchandise. We could make millions for doing no work." He forced a smile. Soon Dekka and Francis would be back. Soon this small moment of peace would end.

Shade slid the eggs onto two plates, taking the broken one for herself. "Here. And no complaints: I am not a chef."

"Merch, movies, a lecture tour . . . ," Malik went on. "Salt?"

"Comic-Con. We could absolutely do Comic-Con. Salt's right there. The grinder." Shade took a stool beside him. "Yeah, millions, with which we would do what?"

Malik shrugged. "Run away to New Zealand?"

They ate for a while. Then Shade said, "Do you think it's upsetting the group dynamic, me and you, I mean?"

Malik smiled and laid his hand over hers on the counter. "It's done good things for my personal dynamic. I assume that was your goal."

"Mmm? My goal?"

"I mean, sure, you find me irresistible—who wouldn't?— but I know you, Shade. You never have just one thing in mind."

Shade put her fork down. "You think it was charity?"

Malik shrugged. "Call it a morale boost."

Shade sighed. "You too, huh? Shade Darby, always up to something. Always manipulating."

Malik's expression was affectionate but dubious. "And you're not?"

Malik had expected her to toss off a quip, but Shade considered as she seasoned her food. Malik was testing her, and of course she knew it. That was the upside of his being with Shade: whatever Malik said or even thought, Shade got it, understood. But that was also the downside.

"Did it ever occur to you that I'm human? That I just needed to be with you?" Shade asked.

Malik nodded. "It did occur to me, babe. It did." He tilted his head and looked at her appraisingly. "People can have more than one motive. And, well, you feel bad. Guilty. Which, by the way, two things: one, it's progress. The Shade I used to know didn't do guilt. And two, you'll notice I'm not complaining."

Shade grabbed a napkin and wiped a bit of egg from his mouth. Then she leaned into him and kissed him on the lips. He closed his eyes because he always did. He felt her mouth on his, her tongue teasing him, her exhalation on his cheeks, and felt the wonderful, careless weakness of surrender.

After all this time, after all he had seen and done, after all that had been done to him, as strong as he felt he had become, he had no power, never would have any power, to resist her.

"Yes, I feel guilty," Shade whispered. "And no, I'm not that person anymore. Or at least I'm less that person."

Malik nodded. "When we were together, I used to tell you I loved you."

"Past tense?" Shade asked, trying for lighthearted and achieving only a quivery uncertainty.

"Oh, I have to say it again?" he asked archly. "Okay. Shade, I never got over you. Of course I still love you. How could I not still love you?"

Shade's breath caught in her throat, and Malik saw to his absolute amazement that tears were spilling down her cheeks. Malik took her napkin and wiped one away with great tenderness, as though he thought her flesh might bruise.

"Oh, shit," Shade muttered, and now the tears were coming fast, and sobs seized her next few words. She swallowed hard, started to speak, stopped. Then, finally, in a low, strained voice said, "I love you too, bunny."

Malik laughed. "This is what it takes to get you to say those words? After all these years. All it takes is a total catastrophe that may destroy all of human civilization, and then you can say it?"

"Well," Shade said, smiling weakly, "I didn't want to seem easy."

Malik erupted in his absurd, embarrassing donkey laugh. "The word 'easy' will never be applied to you, babe. In the dictionary next to the term 'high maintenance,' there's an illustration of you."

"Mmm. You know, Dekka and Francis are still out. Cruz went with Armo to pick up some junk food. . . . I mean, these people are nice to lend us this house, but they are way too into health food—"

"And?" Malik interrupted her digression.

"And, well, we kind of have privacy." She laid a hand on his thigh.

A while later they lay side by side in the king-sized bed in the master bedroom, Shade with her head on his bare chest.

"Just so we're clear," Malik said, "was that guilt or good, honest lust? Don't get me wrong, I'm fine either way."

"Just *fine*?"

He kissed her. "You practically killed me just now, so it may have been attempted murder, actually, but again, I'm totally fine with that."

"Hey, Malik?" Shade raised her head and turned him to look at her. "I love you."

They were silent for a while, savoring, relaxing, ignoring the rest of the world.

"This is all unreal, isn't it?" Shade asked, looking up at the ceiling. "Us. We're not real."

"Of course we're real," Malik said. "Yes, maybe we're in a simulation. But we have no alternative to treating it as real because this is the only reality we have. The walls are solid. Gravity still works. Pain is real, as real as ever. Pleasure, too."

"It's a bit creepy knowing *they're* seeing everything."

"Yeah. A bit."

"Are we some kind of experiment? Or a movie? Or a game?"

"I hope to find out," Malik said. "When we have time, I'm going back. If Francis is cool with it."

"I worry about you doing that."

"Why?"

"It's dangerous, duh."

"No, but why do you worry about me, specifically?" He rolled toward her and reached under the blanket.

"Well, you're a valuable member of the team."

"Uh-huh. And?"

"Mmmmm. What? Oh, well, what you're doing . . . right now . . . that's part of it."

"And?"

"Really, Malik? I have to say it again?"

"Yes. You do."

"I love you, Malik. Even when I was pretending not to, I did."

"All right, then. I'm going to take a shower."

"Um, I don't think so. You started something, you finish it."

CHAPTER 13
Parenting Fails

"DADDY IS DEAD."

Simone, fully human again, limply accepted her mother's hug. Her mother, Annette Belevance—she'd reclaimed her maiden name—held her out at arm's length, searching her face.

"It's true," Simone said. "We were both hit by bits of the rock. They rounded up a bunch of us and drove us to the Pine Barrens. Then they shot us, Mom. They shot us down."

Simone's affect was blank, her mind doing all it could to protect her from what she had seen. She needed to keep the emotions tamped down, way down inside, because the reality was too big, too horrible to absorb. Her father had been gunned down. She had nearly been gunned down. Men and women and kids who'd done nothing wrong had been machine-gunned by people working for some part of their own government.

"But . . . but you're okay, you're not shot. Baby love, this last day has been so stressful and scary, it's no surprise you'd . . ."

Simone had started to morph. It was easier than wasting time trying to convince her mother. Her clothing receded, exposing flesh already turning the blue of a clear evening sky. Lines appeared as if drawn by an invisible pen, lines detailing a pattern of tiny diamond shapes covering every inch of her save for her face. Her skin roughened as the diamond pattern resolved into thousands of tiny wings.

Then Simone took a deep breath and silently commanded her wings to beat. She rose from the floor, floated up to the ceiling, then settled back down.

"I'm not having a stress reaction," Simone said flatly. "I'm one of those rock people. A mutant."

Her mother fainted, eyes rolling up, neck allowing her head to loll, knees buckling. Simone made a grab for her, mostly caught her, and managed to deposit her in a breakfast-nook chair. She brought water and dribbled a bit into her mother's mouth as she knelt beside her.

"Listen, Mom, I'm ninety percent sure Daddy is dead. I know you're divorced and hate each other, but, still . . ."

Her mother nodded, eyes welling with tears.

"And I guess . . ." Simone looked around the famil-iar kitchen, suddenly overwhelmed by what she'd told her mother, and what she had still to tell her. "Look, maybe noth-ing else will happen, but they have my name, and if they realize I'm not dead, they'll come here looking for me."

"I'm calling Shepp!"

Shepp was the family lawyer. "This is way beyond lawyers,

Mom. This is . . . Normal has been left-swiped. Normal is done. I can fly. None of this is anything a lawyer can help with. I have to hide. I have to disappear until we can get a grip on . . . on . . ." She waved her hand, encompassing the world. "I need money. Cash. I know Daddy has . . . had . . . some in his safe, so I'm heading there next before the cops take the place apart." She took her mother's hands. Annette Belevance had never been a strong woman, never forceful, very much unlike her ex-husband. Or her daughter. "Listen, I can't have a phone; they can track phones. If Mary calls . . . just tell her I love her."

Simone packed some things—clothing, toiletries, a book— in her backpack, then stood at the foot of her bed and looked around at walls and furnishings that now seemed alien.

"I'm never coming back here, am I?"

Her voice found no echo in the room. Her bed. Her desk. Her computer with some of the short films she'd made. It was painful to say goodbye to those original files. "Oh well, they're on YouTube," she told herself.

She went back into the kitchen and hugged her mother, forcing smiles and reassurances that she did not believe. Her mother still lived in a world of the expected, the predictable, the normal. Her mother had not heard the brutal chatter of machine guns. She had not seen men stripping bodies of wallets and watches and anything else that might identify them. She had not seen burning bodies.

She had not been soaked in a dying man's blood as she lay with her face in the dirt waiting for death to find her.

Simone went for the stairs, but instead of taking them down to the street, she walked up to the top floor, then climbed the metal staircase leading to the roof. A small wood-framed deck had been built atop the roof, and people often sunbathed there on good days. Today the roof was abandoned.

Simone walked to the edge and looked down at the tree-lined Sixty-Ninth Street nine floors down. Looking to her right she saw a strangely abandoned segment of Columbus Avenue with far less traffic than normal. New York City was traumatized and scared, but New Yorkers had been through bad times before, so there was no panicked evacuation of the city. On the other hand, few people felt like going out for a stroll. It was hunker-down time in the Big Apple.

Simone closed her eyes and focused. Morphing was easy once you'd done it. Convincing yourself you could fly was harder. Even after she'd morphed, even after she had risen three feet off the roof, it still took an effort of will to zoom away and see that the ground was now a dizzying hundred feet down.

But once she got past the fear of heights . . . well, then it was amazing. It felt unreal, like she was in a movie. Like the world was all a green screen and she was an actor being held up by wires. Unreal. A fantasy. And yet, she was in the air. *Flying!* She felt a chilly breeze, saw a starling go careening by at eye level, read the numbers on the tops of police cars, caught glimpses into apartment windows.

Simone genuinely laughed aloud as she discovered that she could hover in midair. And it was effortless! She knew intuitively that there was more at work here than the physical force of the wings—they couldn't possibly support her weight, let alone allow her to zoom over the rooftops. And she knew that her body, which was capable at its best of running two, maybe three miles, was in no way capable of generating the energy required for this.

And yet: flying!

Despite the horror that weighed on her soul, she might have played around, had some fun with this astonishing ability, but within seconds of her tiny wings appearing came the oppressive sense of being watched. More than watched: spied on. Probed. She wished she knew others of her kind; she'd have liked to ask them about this. It made her feel wrong. Made her feel violated.

Simone flew above Central Park, heading for her father's apartment, aided greatly by Manhattan's gridwork, which allowed her to navigate fairly easily, keeping track of numbered streets and named avenues. She landed on the very balcony where she'd stood with her father. She de-morphed and went inside.

"Simone, is that you?"

Simone screamed and backed away, nearly tripped on the carpet, and banged into an ottoman.

The thing before her had roughly the shape of a man, but with nothing solid about it and nothing that was still. It was like a tornado of insects trimmed into insect topiary, an insect cloud buzzing and chittering and whirling but keeping itself to a sketch of a human body.

That this bizarre thing spoke was astonishing. The voice was a breeze of insect noises modulated into speech. It sounded like a bad phone connection.

"Sweetheart, it's me. It's Dad!"

"Oh, God," Simone whispered, backing away. "Oh, God. Daddy? No! *Daddy?*"

The bug man spread vibrating arms wide and twirled as if showing off a new suit. "Look at me! I'm one now, a mutant! And so are you, I see. Ha, ha, ha!" Like it was an accomplishment. Like he was happy about it. Like he expected his daughter to say, *Well done, Dad!*

"Change back!"

Markovic frowned. "Don't be scared. If you knew what I can do now. I mean, wow! Watch this!"

Markovic floated upward and flattened himself against the ceiling, becoming a single layer of tiny creatures, like a silhouette of a man. Then he re-formed into a single thick line, maybe six inches across and seven or eight feet long, and this bug-spear went racing around the room in a circle, faster and faster until he was just a blur, and Simone actually felt a breeze.

"Dad, change back! Okay, just . . . just . . ."

Markovic re-formed himself into a human shape. "Can't do it, sweetie. I tried, but the thing is, the old me? I think he died. When I tried to change back, it was like a wall. Like I was trying to open a door that was locked tight."

"You can't change back?" Simone's voice shook and she made no effort to conceal her disgust or her pity.

"Hey, I'm not so gross, am I? I'm still your dad!"

"You're like some insane ad for an exterminator. You're . . . you're a cloud of bugs! What are you even talking about?"

"Actually," Markovic said, in a familiarly pedantic tone, "I'm still me, but . . ." He stopped talking and sounded discouraged.

"Are you crazy? You're still you? How . . . what the . . . you're still my dad? In what universe?"

"I guess it isn't exactly pretty," Markovic allowed, as all the while Simone peered at bugs she did not recognize, a cloud of them, coppery and black with, here and there, dabs of red or blue.

It reminded Simone of a time when she was walking in Central Park and saw what she thought was an injured dog. It had been a dead dog, its crushed head entirely covered in flies.

"I feel pretty good, actually, for a dead man," Markovic said cheerfully. "Can't wait for my first board meeting. Hah! Look at me now! And . . ." He inclined his "head" toward her, his featureless, mouthless, eyeless "head," and in a lower tone said, "And you would not believe what I can do to people who mess with me."

"Are you trying to tell me this is a good thing?"

I'm talking to a cloud of bugs!

He shrugged figurative shoulders. "What have I always taught you? Don't argue with facts; accept them, use them, profit from them."

"I'm . . . I'm getting a drink."

"Kind of early, isn't it?"

"Are you seriously giving me grief over drinking? My father is an infestation and I'm . . . something, I don't know what! I kind of think I should be able to have a drink!" She walked on wobbly legs to the sideboard, poured the first thing she saw into a glass, and swallowed it in a single, fiery gulp.

"You know I've always taken a very liberal approach to your drinking, but—"

"*Shut up!*" Simone roared. "Shut up! Are you out of your mind? What's next, you want to ask me why I'm getting a D in calculus?"

"You're getting a—"

"No! No! No! You don't get to pretend this is normal! This is not normal and it's not okay."

"I can see in 360 degrees," Markovic said. "Front, back, up, down, I see it all. The sense of power . . . just imagine what you and I could do together."

"Give people nightmares?" Simone shot back.

"You don't get it because all you ever do is listen to your wimp professors," Markovic said, somehow conveying real anger. "This is power, Simone! *Power!* They tried to kill me, but I got them first, and oh boy, did I ever get them."

Simone felt her stomach churn. Too much! Her breath came in shallow gasps. Her heart pounded in a thumping, irregular beat. "What have you *done*?"

Markovic laughed, a dry sound like corn husks rubbing together. "My little buggies are not exactly, um, sanitary. They seem to be carriers of some kind of disease, and man, you should see how fast it works! All I had to do was think: *Danger!* And they attack. Hah!"

Simone was speechless. Her mother had tried to pretend everything was normal. Now her father was actually trying to convince her it was a good thing that he was—permanently— a malicious disease vector. Had it all been less deadly serious, she might have laughed; it was such a perfect microcosm of her parents: a mother in denial, a father always looking out for himself.

"I came for cash," Simone said. "They'll come looking for me, for anyone who got away. I can't use a credit card."

"Don't be an idiot, Simone. You'll stay here with me. We'll work together. We'll be a team and take all the sons of bitches down! You're always talking trash about the powers that be— well, the powers that be just murdered us in a field."

Finally, an emotion she understood. He was angry. But Simone shook her head. "Dad, no. When I talk about people with wealth and power, I just want to see poor people not being screwed all the time. I'm not into hurting anyone. Do you even know me?"

Markovic's bug cloud buzzed. It was, Simone realized with a shudder of disgust, an expression of disappointment, even dismissal. He was actually annoyed at her! Annoyed that she did not instantly see all the wonderful possibilities in having a gross mutant for a father.

"Well, I have some thinking to do," Markovic said. "I'll be in my office when you're ready to talk sensibly. Now, go to your room."

"Go to my room?" Her mouth hung open in disbelief.

Go to my room?

Markovic stabbed a vague finger in the direction of the room she used when at her father's place. "Now, young lady. Go. To. Your. Room!"

Simone went to her room, slammed the door behind her, and just stood staring at her plush, queen-sized bed and her books and her desk with the Apple monitor glowing softly, open to a web page on the filmography of Edgar Wright.

I've gone crazy. I've lost my mind!

She thought of calling Mary. But what could she say? *Hi, Mary. Guess what? I can fly, and my father's a bunch of diseased bugs! Come on over, we'll order a pizza.*

She sat on the edge of her bed, feeling that this familiar place was no longer familiar. She knew each element of her surroundings, had chosen most of them herself, but they all belonged to someone else now. That Simone no longer existed; that Simone had died in the Pine Barrens, almost as surely as her father had died.

Simone cried a little, silent weeping. She cried for herself and for her father. No, she didn't approve of what he did for a living, or his politics, and yes they fought, but he was still her father and she was his daughter, and that could not just be dismissed. She'd never believed that the tensions between them would be permanent. Simone was honest enough to know that some of the issues she had with her father were at least partly her fault. She wasn't so simple as to see herself as an angel or her father as a devil. He was wrong—about so many things—but he was still Dad.

Or had been. She had lost him and yet he was still there, like a terrifying ghost of himself.

But Simone did not let herself wallow in misery; she knew this was not a time for self-pity. The world had turned suddenly. Life had changed and was not going to change back. Simone followed the news and current events; she had not been blind to the unraveling of the world around her. She had been as shocked as anyone by the earliest outbreaks of mutant violence. She'd seen Knightmare's destruction of the Golden Gate Bridge live on TV. She followed most of the known Rockborn who had accounts on social media. And she had belatedly watched the movie based on Astrid Ellison's riveting account of life in the FAYZ.

She had been fascinated as the news and social media exploded with video of an attack on the so-called Ranch, followed all too swiftly by the bloody massacre in Las Vegas. But Simone felt like most New Yorkers: what happened outside the city seemed safely distant.

Now it was here. Not just here in New York, but here in her life, in her father, in her own freakish mutant body. There was no more hiding behind denial, no more pretending that this was all just a passing phase and that life would return to normal and she could go on with her life, with her plans, with her love affairs.

No. All of that, all of her dreams . . . She sighed. How strange, she thought, that she'd read so many books, seen so many movies and TV shows about this or that vision of dystopia, but all those dire scenarios had been safely unrealistic. And now? This was it. This was the birth of dystopia, the beginning of the end of civilization as she had known it.

But, on the plus side . . . she could fly. There was that.

It remained true, though, that this apartment was no longer safe. No place she'd ever frequented would be safe. The government would be desperate to find her, and her father, and finish the job they'd botched in the Pine Barrens.

Maybe for once her father was right: there was no point arguing with reality; there was only adapting and surviving. Or, in Bob Markovic's case, looking for a way to profit.

Simone could not sneak out of her room without walking right past her father's office. But she could open a window, fly two windows across, and open the window to her father's bedroom. He never locked his window—who did, fourteen floors up?

Inside that darkly masculine space with its greens and browns, she went to the Francis Calcraft Turner painting of a traditional English fox hunt that hung over the fireplace. She swung the painting aside on its hinges. Behind it was a wall safe with a six-digit code Simone had long since memorized. Inside the safe were important documents, a handgun, and neat stacks of currency. Each bank-banded stack of hundred-dollar bills was half an inch thick and represented ten thousand dollars. She took five.

Then she contemplated the handgun, her other unacknowledged goal. She had never before had any interest in guns, but at the same time, given her father's paranoid-yet-giddy state of mind? Leaving him a gun could only make matters worse. And in this Looney-Tunes world, a gun seemed like a good idea.

Close-up on Simone's face. She's conflicted. She touches the gun cautiously, hesitates, turns away, then turns back, decisive.

Simone slipped the gun, the extra clips, and the money into her backpack. She was closing the safe when she heard her father approaching, a clicking, scraping, buzzing sound very unlike his usual purposeful stride.

Simone raced for the window, climbed onto the sill, took a deep breath, and zoomed effortlessly across Fifth Avenue.

CHAPTER 14
Astrid Does Amazon

"HEY, YOU'RE THAT girl."

Astrid Ellison was often recognized. She'd been the unofficial public voice of FAYZ survivors and had given numerous interviews over the last four years, starting with the famous interview where she'd first been reunited with Sam Temple. Then, too, she'd had a bestselling book that had spawned a hit movie. The whole country knew the name Astrid Ellison, and knew she was the girlfriend—now wife—of the hero of the FAYZ.

Astrid Ellison nodded at the UPS driver. "Yes, I am." The direct gaze of her blue eyes and the chill in her voice ended the chitchat. She signed for the delivery, a long cardboard box. In the box was a forty-nine-inch-long galvanized-steel tool box of the sort that fits in the back of a pickup truck. It was way too heavy for her to lift, so she dragged it to the elevator that led down to the basement of the apartment building.

Astrid rode down with the box while checking her

find-a-phone feature for Sam's whereabouts. Good, he was still at Costco. Using a box cutter, she stripped away the cardboard box and shoved it into a recycling bin. Each apartment had a storage space in the underground parking garage, chain-link enclosures lit by bare bulbs, half of them burned out. She wiped sweat from her brow, opened the lock of the storage cage, and pushed the box inside. Then she carefully covered it with plastic containers of mementos and cartons of her Perdido Beach book so that a casual glance wouldn't reveal it.

The steel box had come from Amazon, and she was sure the government was watching her, but it was just a box, after all, and might mean anything or nothing. Still, for caution's sake, she would buy the rest of her list at various stores, using cash, and leave no digital trace.

When she was done in the storage cage, she opened her Notes app and scanned her list. Six items left to obtain.

Chain
Locks
Chain saw
Machete
Heavy-duty plastic

If she spread her purchases around, they shouldn't attract too much attention from the government. The government was rather busy at that moment with various major disasters, after all.

The final item on her list was more concerning. There were not that many innocent places to obtain hydrofluoric acid. There were easier acids to find, but the beauty of hydrofluoric acid was that it did not eat plastic or most metals.

It did, however, dissolve flesh.

Drake would come for her soon; Astrid was convinced of it. Ever since she had learned that Drake was still alive—if you could call it life—she'd thought about how to prepare, how to defeat the unkillable, tentacle-armed sadist.

She now had a heavy steel box. She would soon have chains and locks. And a chain saw. And heavy plastic. And acid.

All of which was good, but nowhere near enough.

Astrid was studious by nature and had gleaned everything she could from a brief earlier meeting with an old ally, Dekka, as well as from news accounts. She had a fairly clear idea how these new and even more dangerous mutations worked, how it manifested—the physical transformations that accompanied the acquisition of powers. The FAYZ dome, she hypothesized, had acted in lieu of physical morphs, protecting what was inside from the laws of physics outside. She suspected the physical transformations that were now part of the development of superpowers did something similar—exempting the mutant from the ordinary laws of physics.

Or not. It was just a theory.

But her research could not tell her what would happen to *her*. If there was rhyme or reason to the effects of the rock, she had not discovered it.

She retrieved from its hiding place the FedEx envelope

Dekka had sent her. The baggie holding two ounces of powdered rock was still inside.

Astrid had never developed a power in the FAYZ. At one
point she'd thought she had, but no, she had remained merely
herself. She'd never regretted that fact; she had never wanted
any power beyond her own native intelligence and whatever
courage she could summon. The idea of seeking such a power
now was deeply unsettling. Astrid was happy being Astrid.
She had never wanted physical power.

But that was then, and this was now, and she no longer had
Sam's power to protect her. Her husband, brave, resourceful,
determined Sam, was a mere human now, and no kind of
match for Drake. Whatever Drake did to her, he would do
it where Sam would be forced to watch. It would break Sam.
The unbreakable boy was now a vulnerable man.

Dekka had addressed the package to Astrid, not to Sam.
But she had included two doses, despite the fact that Astrid
and Dekka shared a fervent desire to keep Sam out of this
new fight. Sam had done enough. Sam had suffered enough.
And Sam now had his PTSD-driven substance abuse under
control, sober for many months. The two women who loved
him in different ways both wanted to protect him.

But Dekka had seen the dark possibilities and had been
the one to give them the news about Drake. So she had sent
some of the rock to Astrid, knowing that no natural power
could stop Whip Hand.

And more than enough. Just in case.

Not for the first time, Astrid considered recruiting an ally.

Edilio? Quinn? But Quinn was weak, and Edilio was in Honduras, deported by immigration despite testimonials from virtually every living FAYZ survivor, an injustice that still burned inside Astrid. At least Albert had helped him out with money so Edilio wouldn't be destitute.

Albert.

There was an ally she could use. She pulled out her cell phone, scrolled through contacts, and dialed Albert's personal line.

"Astrid?" Albert answered, recognizing the number.

"Listen, Albert, I hate to do this."

"What do you need?"

"Drake is alive."

The silence on Albert's end lasted for a while. Then a long, low stream of curses.

"I think he may come after us."

"What do you need?" Albert asked again.

"I need to buy something. It's something that may set off whoever is still monitoring us. It's a big ask, Albert. And I would need you not to ask questions. So if—"

Albert cut her off. "Anything you want, any amount of money, anytime, Astrid."

Astrid felt her eyes filling with tears. In the FAYZ Albert had never been liked, let alone loved. But his tough-love business sense had kept people fed, and without him many more would have died. Still, she had not expected unquestioning support. Albert was not exactly known for throwing money away, one reason he'd done so well after the FAYZ, making deals with McDonald's and other companies to exploit his fame.

"Thanks, Albert. That's . . ."

"I watch the news, Astrid. I know what's going on. I also know the only reason I have what I have, including my life, is because of your husband. So, down to my last penny if you need it, Astrid."

She texted him the name of the product.

She had most of what she needed and would soon have the rest. There was only one thing left to do.

Astrid went to their small, tidy kitchen and poured herself a glass of orange juice. She weighed an ounce of the ground rock on her digital kitchen scale. Then she mixed the powder into the juice.

She heard the sound of a key at the front door. Sam.

"Here goes," Astrid said, and quickly drank the juice down.

CHAPTER 15
Over There

"IT'S TERRIFYING," DEKKA said. "I've seen bad things, way too many bad, bad things, but . . ." Words failed her. She shook her head.

Francis sat silent, as usual, watching the people she irrationally thought of as "the grown-ups." Or maybe it wasn't so irrational; after all, they were each more "adult" than the adults in the biker gang she and her mother had lived with.

Their borrowed brownstone had a small yard, and they all felt like they'd spent way too much time in casinos and hotels and planes. They were craving fresh air and sunlight, and at the moment the sun was peeking through clouds, so four of them sat on lawn furniture while Dekka paced back and forth across the brick patio and Armo did chin-ups on a child's rusting swing set.

"Social media is in a panic," Cruz reported, looking up from her phone.

"Over this Pine Barrens thing?" Dekka asked, frowning.

"Someone streamed video."

They all huddled together to watch a fifteen-second video play. It was nothing but wildly blurry images and screams, all set to the soundtrack of machine guns.

"Don't read the comments," Cruz warned. "Half the people are like, 'good, kill them all.'"

Shade said, "Not that I usually follow the stock market, but they had to close it down because people are freaking out and selling everything."

"It's worse in some places," Malik said. "There's video of something that looks like a slug three miles long slowly eating Shanghai. They're evacuating the city—twenty-four million people—because the Chinese may have to drop a nuke on their largest city to kill the thing. People in Afghanistan and Pakistan are being inverted, turned inside out, if they disobey some character who calls himself the Supreme Caliph of the Universe. They've stopped the London Tube because something—no one knows what—is down in the tunnels spraying sulfuric acid on anyone who comes within fifty feet. A bunch of countries have been taken over by their own armies, and Rockborn are being rounded up." He shook his head dolefully. "I don't see the endgame. I don't see how we ever get back to normal."

"Normal is dead," Shade said harshly.

Francis liked Malik. He was always very kind to her, always deferential when he wanted her to do something. Shade Darby was a different story—she was not mean or cruel, but neither was she exactly warm and cuddly.

"The rest of the world will have to take care of itself," Shade said with a dismissive wave of her hand. "We've got enough on our plates."

Cruz sighed. "People are saying there's someone up in Harlem who looks like some kind of human-rhinoceros hybrid who's just destroying storefronts for no reason. They're also saying there's some blue girl flying around, and a woman who grew thirty feet tall and started tearing open liquor stores and drinking gallons of booze. They say she's passed out drunk in front of the Flatiron Building. People are taking selfies."

She turned her phone around to show Francis a picture of a massive woman's head, easily six feet from chin to crown, eyes closed. On her forehead someone had used a thick Sharpie to write *Fee, Fie, Fo, Fum*. Someone else had plastered a bumper sticker over her upper lip so that it looked like a bad mustache. The bumper sticker read, *I was an honor student—I don't know what happened*. And those were some of the more polite ways passersby had amused themselves.

Francis was shocked, though she knew her reaction was silly. There were about a thousand more important things than worrying about a giant unconscious woman. But the sight of a woman passed out reminded her of her mother, and of her old life. Francis missed nothing about that old life, but she'd had no time to begin to cope with the reality of her mother's death. Her mother had once been loving and kind and concerned before the meth addiction had relentlessly stripped away so much of her humanity.

Not for the first time, but with special urgency now, Francis realized that she was alone in the world, but for the Rockborn Gang. She had nowhere else to go. No one else to be with. This gaggle of strangers was the closest thing she had to family.

Dekka said, "You know it'd be easier to think about playing superhero if people weren't such tools. But giant naked drunk women aren't our problem, at least not right now. We could probably take care of the crazed rhino, but the bug guy is on a different level."

Armo sauntered over from the swing set. "I got this Rhino dude. You want to come, Cruz?"

"Me?"

Armo shrugged. "I don't need to be here for the strategizing. I'd rather, you know, do some superheroing."

"And you don't think I'm really necessary for the strategizing part, either?" Cruz asked him archly, before nodding and admitting, "Actually, you may have a point."

With Armo and Cruz gone, Dekka and Shade both looked to Malik. Shade said, "Okay, Francis tried to look at bug man's victims Over There. There may be something to what she described, some kind of strange laser link or whatever."

Malik shook his head. "Over There is a jumbled world I can't make sense of with 3-D eyes and a 3-D brain, so whatever Francis saw we can't understand it. The truth is, it might all just be some kind of sensory distortion, an illusion."

"Great," Dekka muttered, still pacing in her slow, deliberate way, like she'd thought carefully about each step.

"But," Malik said with a sigh and a significant look to Francis, "I still want to explore more, if Francis is willing."

Francis had been momentarily distracted by a crow that had landed on the garden wall, but snapped back to awareness on hearing her name. "I'll do whatever you guys think I should do."

Dekka stopped, turned, and made a sideways karate chopping motion. "No, no, no, Francis. We each have to decide what our limits are. You have to stand up for yourself."

"Okay," Francis said doubtfully. "But I want to help."

"You have something in mind, Malik?" Shade asked.

He nodded. "Yeah. I want to go Over There while one of you is in morph. I want to see what that looks like from Over There. I saw Francis there, but she's some kind of outlier, an exception."

Shade shrugged. "No problem."

"Not yet." Malik took Francis's hand. "Once we disappear, morph."

Francis was more prepared for the sensory weirdness this time, but still it was like stepping inside a kaleidoscope filled with the contents of a hardware store instead of colored stones. Malik had some kind of theory, she knew, but to her it was like what she'd heard some of the bikers say about LSD: jumbled shapes and colors and things that made no sense.

But now she saw Shade in the disturbing 4-D way, a series of bits and pieces, sometimes forming a whole, sometimes a tangle of floating, inverted body parts.

"I should not have to see a deconstructed version of my ex-girlfriend's liver," Malik muttered in paisley balloons, while Francis wondered at the prefix "ex."

Back in the normal world Shade began to morph. The parts began to shift and move in no discernible pattern. Then, suddenly, like a Transformers toy snapping into place, Shade appeared as a coherent whole. But a very different whole—a human, yes, but wreathed in a kind of glowing field of fireflies or charged particles. Francis saw her chitin armor and her human flesh all as the same thing.

And then . . .

"Ah!" Malik cried.

Because out of nowhere, black cables shot into Shade's head.

Each was as thick as a thumb; there were dozens, and as Francis gazed along the length of the cables, she saw that they branched and split, like a bush, a tangled mass disappearing into distant haze.

"Take us out," Malik said, and a moment later Francis had moved them back to regular space. They appeared before a startled Dekka and a vibrating, morphed Shade.

"Shade!" Malik yelped in excitement. "Count to ten and run back and forth real fast." Then he reconsidered. "Wait, have Dekka count to ten, not you; your seconds are too short."

Francis once again moved them into the Over There.

Malik waited, and then Shade moved, as fast as she could within the confines of the backyard.

Malik held his arm out. The cables passed through his arm.

"Wow," Malik said, and asked Francis to bring them back.

Shade de-morphed and said, "So?"

"I saw them," Malik said. "I mean, not *them* them, but their connection. It manifests as a series of cables that go straight into your brain. And when you move, no matter how fast you move, they stay attached."

Shade unconsciously smoothed her hands over her head. "Cables?"

"They manifest that way, but I doubt they're what they look like to me," Malik added.

"Then what are they?" Dekka demanded.

Malik shrugged. "Wi-Fi?"

"Wi-Fi?" Dekka echoed skeptically.

"I just mean they have some kind of connection that probably isn't cables or wires but looks that way to a 3-D mind. I tried interrupting one but couldn't touch anything."

"You're thinking the cables are the Dark Watchers," Dekka said, and both Shade and Malik nodded. "And the cables only appeared once Shade was morphed. Okay. So, you two are the big brains: What does that tell us?"

Malik sighed and sat down in a lawn chair. He shook his head slowly, side to side, and almost pleading, said, "Shade?"

But Shade's face was just as bleak.

"What?" Dekka demanded.

"Look," Malik said, "you have to bear in mind my limitations Over There. Don't assume I'm right; all I have is a theory."

"I'll take a theory," Dekka shot back, irritated now.

"Well, let's just say that the possibility that we are living in a simulation, basically a computer program, a manufactured reality, is not just a possibility. It's now a probability."

CHAPTER 16
Superhero Chores, Part 1

DEALING WITH THE rhinoceros mutant was easier than either Armo or Cruz had imagined. They took a cab uptown and got out a few blocks away from the scene of the craziness. Not that they wanted to get out several blocks away, but the cab driver said, "I escape war in Syria. Too much bomb and killing peoples. No more war, me."

Which was hard to argue with.

Armo and Cruz trotted the several blocks to 116th Street and Frederick Douglass Boulevard and were recognized more than once.

"Hey, that's that trans girl! The one from Vegas!"

"Is that Berserker Bear with her?"

"Change into Beyoncé!"

"Hey! Yo! Turn into a bear!"

They both waved and kept moving, but then a gaggle of people started following them and crowding around them and generally getting in the way and slowing their pace.

Cruz's natural shyness made all the attention very unpleasant, though no one meant to be annoying. Probably. So she took the opportunity to morph into an elderly black woman she happened to spot. The crowd cheered, all but one who said, "Damn, Bey has let herself go!" But after a bit more milling they lost track of Cruz and focused on Armo, who ended up signing autographs until he finally could no longer move forward.

At that point Cruz became a police officer she'd previously added to her repertoire. It happened "he" was a California Highway Patrolman, but an authoritative "Back up there folks, let the man do his work" was enough to free Armo.

As they hustled away, Armo whispered, "Some woman back there offered me a thousand dollars if I would, you know . . ."

"No," Cruz said, deliberately playing dumb. "I don't know."

"You know," Armo insisted. "Do *it*."

"It?"

At that point Armo realized she was playing with him. "Oh, fine, you can just turn into someone else and get away from these people."

"Poor you, Armo, you're stuck just being gorgeous." Cruz had meant it as a tease, but Armo looked pained. "What?"

He shrugged. "Nothing. It's just . . . nothing."

"No, tell me," Cruz insisted.

"Okay, the thing is, that word. I've been hearing it my whole life. Gorgeous." He shuddered.

"And . . . ?"

"You know I'm a person, right?" Armo asked. "I know what I look like, but you know, I'm not just, you know . . . I mean, I have ideas and stuff. I have plans. Well, I used to. I'm just saying, I do have a brain and all. I'm not just nice pecs."

"And a washboard stomach," Cruz added, but when Armo didn't smile, she said, "Oh. Okay. I get it. And Armo, for the record, I know you're not just your looks."

In fact, she added, silently chiding herself, *if there's anyone on earth who ought to know better than to judge a person on their looks, it's a trans girl who can look like anyone.* She demorphed out of her CHP shape and became Cruz again.

"Yeah?" Armo prodded.

It came to Cruz that he was actually fishing for compliments. Six foot four inches of movie-star looks and the kind of body a Ryan Reynolds could only envy, and he was fishing for compliments. From *her.* The thought amazed her. He was . . . well, he was . . . *Armo.*

"Well, Armo, you are gorgeous, there's no better word for it. But you're also kind. And thoughtful. And you treat people with respect."

Armo nodded and with stiff dignity said, "Thanks."

"Everyone in the gang likes you."

He shrugged, but he was enjoying it.

"Dekka likes you a lot and she doesn't like all that many people," Cruz said. "In fact, I'm not a hundred percent sure she likes anyone *but* you."

He grinned, displaying perfect teeth. "I love Dekka." Then he frowned and added, "Not that way. I mean, she's into chicks. Women, I mean. How about you?"

Cruz nearly swallowed her own tongue and tripped. Armo caught her arm. His hand was so big his fingers completely encircled her bicep.

"Me?" Cruz asked in a way that was intended to sound nonchalant but that came out as an anxious squeak.

"Yeah, I mean, you know." He made a vague sort of hand gesture that sort of seemed to encompass Cruz's body and then swept outward to take in the crowds streaming behind them, now following at a discreet distance, cell-phone cameras held high.

"Oh, well," Cruz said. "I'm, you know." Now she was stammering like he had. She drew a deep breath and in an overly loud exhale said, "Boys. I like boys."

"Huh," Armo said, and Cruz had no opportunity to parse that monosyllable because they had both just heard the sound of shattering glass.

"I think we're there," Cruz said.

"There" turned out to be a Rite Aid with the front glass destroyed so thoroughly that they could both see right into the store. Surrounded by destruction in the form of shampoo bottles, tampons, hair coloring, and laxatives all scattered around, stood a massive beast.

It was as big as a rhinoceros, and its armored flesh was gray. It had four stout legs and no arms or hands. But beyond those superficial similarities it was not a rhino. Its head was human, albeit a human head blown up to three times normal size. And rather than a single rhino horn it had stubby antlers, three horns on each side, two of them evidently broken.

The face was that of an old man, African American, distorted, stretched horribly, but still recognizably an old man, with now-oversized, yellowing eyes and a mouth with great gaps between isolated teeth.

"I used to only see things like this in movies or nightmares," Cruz said.

How has my life come to the point where I'm nonchalant about a mutant beast with a human face?

A crowd of maybe two hundred occupied the other three corners where Fredrick Douglass Boulevard met 117th Street. An Italian restaurant with a closed-down outdoor cafe had waiters on the street selling coffee and bottled water. Police cars had blockaded the streets in every direction. In all, a dozen police officers crouched behind squad-car doors with weapons at the ready.

The beast, the old man, moaned in a loud, heartrending cry of pain and confusion.

"Does anyone know this man?" Cruz yelled.

No answer.

"Please, someone must know this man!"

A police officer yelled, "Hey, you two, get back!"

But someone in the crowd said, "No, Officer, that's Berserker Bear and the trans chick from Vegas!"

"That true?" the cop asked.

"I'm not crazy about 'Berserker Bear,'" Armo grumbled. "But yeah."

"Please, it's an old man," Cruz said. "Someone must know him."

The cop shook his head, but behind him a woman in the crowd waved to get Cruz's attention. "Yes, ma'am, what can you tell me?"

"His name is Alfred Gordon," the woman said. "He lives with his daughter and granddaughter."

"Thank you," Cruz said. "Do you know them, the family?"

The woman did not, but in response to Cruz's question she described the granddaughter: about twenty-five, a big woman. "Looked kind of like that girl, what's her name, the actress who was in that movie. What was it called? *Precious!* That was it. Such a sad movie."

"Gabourey," Cruz suggested. She used her phone to Google pictures of Gabourey as Armo stood by, bemused, keeping an eye on the panting, frightened man-beast. Face. Head. Body. Cruz could not find shots of Gabourey taken from behind, but as long as she faced the old man . . .

Cruz focused her thoughts, and as the crowd oohed and aahed, she became the actress, wearing a brown silk dress with a scoop neckline and a jeweled waist, the outfit Gabourey had worn to an *Essence* magazine function where the photo had been taken.

"You want me to go all Berserker Bear?" Armo asked.

"No, you just . . ." Cruz caught herself. "You do what you think is right, Armo. But I feel like maybe I can talk to this man."

Armo made a mock salute and took a step back. Cruz

advanced across the street, picking her way through the debris from the destroyed drugstore.

"Grandpa! Papa!" Cruz wasn't sure what he might be called, and she hoped his eyesight was bad.

The stretched yellow eyes, each the size of a saucer, turned toward her.

"It's me, your granddaughter," Cruz said, wishing she knew the young woman's name.

"That you, Tiana?"

"Yes, it's me. Tiana. Are you okay?"

All the while Cruz walked steadily forward, like she had every right to, like she was unafraid.

"I came for my pills," the rhino-man said in a strangled voice.

"Of course. Of course. Which pills, do you remember?"

"My pills?"

"Yes, do you recall what pills you were looking for?"

"I don't know the name," the beast-man said irascibly. "Donny's. Donazzas. Something."

Cruz looked pleadingly back at the crowd.

"I'm a nurse," a man said. "He may be talking about done-pezil." Then in a lower voice he added, "It's for Alzheimer's."

Cruz sighed. For weeks she'd been suppressing a growing anger at whoever or whatever was doing this to people. So much death. So much pain. Now a confused old man had been turned into a beast—a beast centered in half a dozen police-sniper gun sights. "Grandpa . . . Listen to me, you need to focus really hard on something."

"Focus?"

"On yourself. On who you are. You're Alfred Gordon, right?"

The eerie head nodded stiffly. "Al, mostly. You know that."

"Of course I do, Grandpa. I just want you to think about who you are. How you look. You need to think about yourself. About your life. Think about Al Gordon. Try to picture your own face, Al. Grandpa."

The beast blinked. Then slowly, slowly the creature began to shrink It took minutes longer than it took Cruz or Armo to morph, but finally an old man sat, confused and afraid, amid the wreckage.

"Easy," Cruz cautioned the police. "If he gets upset, he could morph back."

"What happened?" Al Gordon wondered. "What am I doing . . . ? Where are my slippers?"

Two NYPD women in plain clothes advanced, guns held low, voices soothing. The officer nodded at Cruz. "Thanks. We didn't want to have to shoot the thing."

Cruz de-morphed, resuming her own body. "Happy to help. Probably best to find his daughter and granddaughter. He could go rhino again at any time."

The crowds cheered—the second time in Cruz's life she'd been cheered wildly. She heard a name being chanted, a name she'd seen a couple of times on social media. "Trans-it! Trans-it! Trans-it!"

The crowd took up the chorus as Cruz waved and nodded bashfully, and she and Armo went in search of a taxi.

"Transit, huh?" Armo said.

"No," Cruz said, shaking her head firmly. "Absolutely not. I thought that nickname had died out."

"It's better than Berserker Bear."

"I don't know. I sort of like Berserker Bear."

Armo shrugged. "Well, that was easy. All I had to do was stand around and look gorgeous." He added a wry twist to that final word.

Something you do so very well, Cruz did not say.

By the time they'd found a taxi and reached the brownstone, the *New York Post* had its online headline: "Transit Strike: Heroes of Harlem," along with photos and embedded video showing Cruz morphing into a blank-backed Gabourey.

By the time Cruz and Armo had started the coffee machine, the actual Gabourey had tweeted that she was proud her image had helped Transit save the day.

And by the time the coffee was brewed and peanut butter and jelly sandwiches had been made, Shade strolled into the kitchen and said, "Hey, Armo," then, with a wink, "Hey, Transit."

Then the doorbell rang.

CHAPTER 17
Superhero Chores, Part 2

THE DOORBELL RANG.

There was no such thing as an innocent doorbell anymore, so Dekka nodded at Shade, who quickly morphed.

Then Dekka opened the door.

"Detective Williams," Dekka said. "It's okay, Shade."

The NYPD detective stepped in and closed the door behind him. He nodded approval. "Good, you were ready for trouble."

"Yeah, we've noticed how trouble keeps happening," Armo said.

"We think we know the name of the guy, Bug Man." Williams pulled out his phone and opened a photo. "His name is Robert Markovic. He owns a chain of payday loan companies. He's rich, as in billionaire-with-a-'b' rich. We have a team watching his apartment now, and we think he's at home."

"Well, that's why we're here," Dekka said.

"Is this where we say 'Avengers assemble'?" Malik snarked.

"How about, 'Rock on, Rockborn Gang'?" Shade proposed.

Dekka shook her head half in amusement, half in irritation, and said to Williams, "We're still kind of working on how to do this. How to *be* this."

Williams nodded. "Ms. Talent, we are all trying to figure things out. No part of this was taught at the police academy. However . . ."

"Mmmm?" Shade asked.

Williams said, "I'm sorry about this, but we need to do something for the sake of maintaining at least some pretense of legality. The mayor says we need to deputize all of you."

"Say what now?" Armo said, bristling.

"How do you do that?" Dekka asked.

Williams laughed. "No one seems to know. But the law seems to be that you can be deputized so long as you're not a member of the military. So, look, I know this sounds crazy—"

"The rule of law is not crazy," Malik said, quite serious. "I'm not sure if it's much use right now, but you can deputize me, Detective."

In the end all six of them agreed—Armo only after he made clear that deputy or not, he would do whatever the hell he decided to do—and they raised their hands and swore an oath Williams made up on the spot.

"Do we get badges, at least?" Cruz wondered.

"I was thinking 'paycheck,'" Dekka said, dryly. "But whatever. Let's go see about this Markovic creep, and maybe we can go home."

Home.

Like that was a real thing. Dekka pictured her apartment in the East Bay. It had been her third home after the fall of the FAYZ. There had been a brief stay with her parents, then a shared apartment with Lana Lazar in Oakland, which had lasted until Lana went off to college. Then the apartment in Pinole. No part of that had ever really felt like home, and Dekka realized the closest thing to a real home in her mind was Perdido Beach. A depressing realization.

They were driven in a police van normally used for transporting prisoners and stepped out on Fifth Avenue, which was teeming with cleanup crews.

"Fourteenth floor," Williams said, gazing up. "See that stone balustrade up there? That's it."

"Yep," Dekka said. "Okay, we go at it three ways. First, Shade? Get to the roof. You can go in through the building next door and hop down to . . ."

By the time Dekka was done explaining what Shade should do, Shade was waving down at them from the roof.

"I am never going to get used to that," Dekka said, shaking her head. "Okay, is there a doorman or someone Markovic might expect to show up at his door?"

Williams produced an elderly Hispanic man named Julio Cantera. Cruz introduced herself, and they exchanged a few words in Spanish. He had a smoker's weak voice, and Cruz tried it out a few times.

"Mr. Markovic. It's Julio. There is a water leak."

"Not bad," Armo said, patting her shoulder.

Dekka's mind was very much on other things, but she could not help but notice that there had been some subtle change in the relationship between Armo and Cruz.

Cruz walked around Julio like he was a side of beef and she was looking to make steaks. After a moment she nodded and began to become the man.

"Okay, this isn't our first fight, so here's the beats," Dekka said. "Cruz goes to the door. Knock knock, water leak. Armo? I'm thinking you and I are just outside the door, out of sight, in morph, and the second Markovic opens the door for Cruz, we go in. Does that work for you, Armo?"

"Yeah, but only if I get to go first. I've been like a bystander today."

Dekka nodded agreement and went on. "Shade jumps down to his balcony and comes in that way. Francis, you bring Malik straight into his apartment. He gets hit from three sides at once. If he's morphed . . ." She hesitated. "Detective Williams, would you give us some privacy?"

Williams bridled, but acquiesced.

"If Markovic is in morph, if he's this bug thing, then we have no choice," Dekka said. Her next words sounded wrong in her own ears. They were the logical move, the inevitable move. Yet that did little to soften Dekka's loathing of her new role. "If he's in morph, he has to be killed. Fast. Immediately. No hesitation. His power is . . ." She shook her head, memories of desperate voices begging for death, memories of the smell of every possible disease and corruption. "This man has to go down."

"If he's not in morph?" Malik asked.

"If he's not, then we pin him down, we let Detective Williams handcuff him, and we stay with him until Markovic is in a cell he can't escape from."

"There's an old saying," Malik muttered. "No battle plan ever survives contact with the enemy."

Dekka nodded. "Preaching to the choir, Malik."

Five minutes later, they were in place.

Cruz knocked. "Mr. Markovic, it's Julio. We have a water leak coming from your bathroom."

A raspy, feathery voice from inside said, "Well then, I have no choice but to let you in, do I?"

That was when Dekka knew.

"He's morphed and he's ready!" Dekka whispered. "No waiting. Armo?"

Armo launched his morphed self—almost nine hundred pounds of muscle, sinew, and fur—against the door, which did not just splinter but almost seemed to fly apart. He staggered forward under his own momentum and fell facedown.

Dekka bounded in, stepped on Armo's back, raised her hands, and prepared to shred whatever the hell the creature in front of her was.

Shade burst in through the already-shattered balcony door.

And with terrible timing, Malik and Francis popped into view inside the apartment but just behind Markovic, where Dekka risked shredding them.

Dekka held her fire and momentum carried her forward

into—then *through*—Markovic. The insect cloud parted and re-formed as Dekka smashed into a side table and sent a vase to shatter on the marble floor.

Armo was on his feet, fast for a creature his size, but then came a flash of movement, a bluish blur, and Armo had gained a living backpack.

A living backpack in the form of a blue girl entirely covered in what looked like tiny bee wings. She had an arm around Armo's thick furry neck, her legs curled around his chest, and a pistol pressed hard against his head.

"I know you're fast, Shade Darby," this new apparition shouted, "but so are bullets."

CHAPTER 18
Bug Fighters

SHADE FROZE. COULD she take the gun before the girl could squeeze the trigger?

Dekka's folly was instantly clear to Shade. They'd come after a guy made of insects, and what did they have as a weapon? Dekka had cleverly brought all her forces into the fight, but her forces were powerless and in each other's way.

And no one had anticipated some flying Na'vi with a nine-millimeter.

"I'm not going to let you kill him!" the blue girl said, her voice shrill.

"If he doesn't back the hell off right now, we'll bring this whole building down on him," Dekka threatened.

That bold statement came out at molasses speed from Shade's perspective, but it still surprised her. Dekka had quickly seen her error and shifted her threat. Bring this whole building down?

All right, Dekka!

"Do that and we all die," the blue girl said, "including Berserker Bear!"

"Really?" Armo complained. "I gotta die under that name?"

Shade was carefully watching the girl's hand, her trigger finger in particular, wondering how quickly the girl would react. It was one thing to disarm cops who didn't expect to have to cope with some speed demon; it was a different story when it was a Rockborn girl who knew all about Shade and was watching her with unblinking gaze. Plus, the girl had been quick. Not Shade-quick, not even close, but quicker than a normal human.

Shade concluded that she could disarm the girl, but she would need a distraction. She vibrated in place, ablur, a missile ready to launch at the first opening.

"Who the hell are you?" Dekka demanded.

"My name is—"

"She's my daughter, Simone, you pathetic fools!" Markovic crowed as his thousands of component parts whirled in a contained tornado. "My little girl!"

To the surprise of everyone, Markovic included, Simone said, "Dad, if you hurt anyone, I'll let them have you."

"Okay, no one move," Dekka said. "Listen, whoever you are, Simone, it's not going to work. Your father here either de-morphs and lets us take him in, or he dies. You may get Armo, but we'll get him. And you."

"Go away!" Simone yelled. "Leave us alone!"

"No," Dekka said with deceptive calm.

It was like a scene from some old western, Shade thought. Like Clint Eastwood in a saloon facing down six guys with guns. But this Clint—Simone—would not win a fight against the Rockborn Gang.

"Simone? My name is Malik." Malik moved slowly closer and drew Francis with him, out of Dekka's line of fire. "I don't know if you know this, but there are three kinds of supers—people with powers."

Simone heard him but kept her gaze firmly on Shade, always with her pistol hard against Armo's shaggy head.

"Monsters, villains, and heroes," Malik went on. "To some extent we're all of us monsters! I mean, look at comic book characters. The Hulk is a monster, right? He doesn't mean to do anything wrong, but he is what he is. Then there are villains. In comic books, that would be people like—"

Shade moved so fast no one saw her. She leaped, stuck her right index finger through the trigger guard, and yanked the weapon away. One second Simone held a gun, and the next instant she didn't.

Armo reached back over his shoulder and grabbed Simone's arm as she tried to go airborne. "Uh-uh-uh, no you don't." Simone tugged with surprising strength, but Armo's huge paw had wrapped two-inch-long black claws around her arm, and if Simone wanted to pull away, she would have to leave an arm behind.

"Markovic or Bug Man or whatever you are," Dekka said, "I'll count to three, and you'd better be trending human or I'll shred you."

"That would be unfortunate for your police officer," Markovic sneered.

"What?"

Detective Peter Williams came through the door, staggering. His face was bathed in sweat. His hands and neck erupted in boils, pustules forming and popping and oozing. Then it was as if his feet were nailed to the floor. He struggled to move but could not.

"I . . . ," Williams gasped. "Don't let him . . . Kill him!"

"See, if I die," Markovic said, "then your pet cop gets sicker and sicker and . . . and here's the cool thing, the thing that makes it so scary: he will get sicker and sicker and yet not die. Hah! He doesn't die until I decide he dies."

Williams, unable to walk farther, sank in a heap.

"He stays like that, on his knees, right here, with every kind of disease eating him alive until—"

"No, Dad," Simone said.

"Don't be an idiot, Simone, it's leverage," Markovic snapped.

Williams gasped, "Kill him! K—"

His words ended in a grunt of pain and a sound like someone choking on a bone. Then his tongue, swollen to three times its usual size and turning black, filled his mouth and rendered anything else unintelligible.

Shade, still in morph, watched with horrified fascination as every visible inch of Williams was effortlessly conquered by billions of microorganisms. Her vaunted speed was of no use now.

"I don't want a fight," Markovic said. "I really don't. See, I'm a businessman; I understand risk. Reasonable risk, unavoidable risk, potentially profitable risk. And the thing is, I know if this turns into a bloodbath, you may kill me. But that won't save your pet cop. And before I go down, I will turn each of you into . . . that." He turned his insect-cloud head toward Williams.

"Let him go," Dekka said, knowing her words were useless.

Markovic laughed. "Dekka Talent. Shade Darby, Malik Tenerife. Well, well. Here to commit murder for a good cause, are you? Playing hero? Saving the world?"

"No one will die if you—"

"Don't be naive," Markovic snapped. "None of us get out of this alive. They *have* to kill us. Do you imagine for one minute that Washington will allow the existence of a girl who can run straight past security and poke a sharp stick in the president and then disappear? Please. We're all on a hit list, and you must know it!"

What Markovic was saying in his slow-as-drying-paint way had some resonance with Shade. It would have resonance with anyone who'd been at the Ranch. And anyone who'd seen tanks blasting their way down the Las Vegas Strip.

"What makes all of you the heroes and me the villain? How many died at the Ranch because of you, Shade Darby, the self-appointed hero? Hmm? What about you, Malik? The pain you caused? You broke people's minds, there are people in psych wards thanks to you, *hero*."

Markovic saved his harshest venom for Dekka. "And then

we have Dekka Talent, FAYZ survivor. I read the book. Saw the movie. The actress who played you was good." He nodded. "All of you FAYZ people, you PBA crowd, you managed to sell yourselves as the good guys, but oh—my, my, you've taken lives, haven't you? You, Dekka: you've killed people. And were there perhaps a few innocents who died along the way? Eh? Hero or villain depends on who's telling the story, Malik; that's the problem with your three-part taxonomy."

Markovic moved toward Dekka. She held her ground. Shade tensed, ready to . . . to do what, exactly? Use her speed to crush thousands of insects?

A can of Raid might be useful.

"Here's my origin story," Markovic went on. "Minding my own business, got sprayed by asteroid fragments, the government grabs me, takes me to a field, and murders me. Now the government has sent a hit squad of mutants to kill me. You. The six of you. The Rockborn *Gang*, indeed."

Shade blurred away, yanked a duvet from the nearest bedroom, zipped back and threw the blanket over Markovic, and was gratified to hear Dekka slow-mo shouting, "Run! Run!"

Francis grabbed Malik and Armo by their hands and blinked out of the 3-D world.

Shade yelled, "Hold on!" which of course no one could hear as anything but a half-second buzz, threw herself at Dekka, hit her like a linebacker, and propelled Dekka and herself through the shattered glass door and over the balustrade.

Could Dekka survive a fourteen-story fall, even in morph?

Francis, Malik, and Armo snapped back into reality on the sidewalk below, and Shade saw that there was a real chance of

Dekka crushing one or all of them.

But as she and Dekka fell, Francis looked up and spread her arms wide. Dekka landed on Francis and the two of them seemed to disappear into the concrete of the sidewalk.

Shade landed hard—she had a body built to absorb shock, but fourteen floors was no joke. She hit the ground, heard the sound of chitin snapping, like someone clipping a toenail, fell on her back, and began to de-morph even as Francis and Dekka reappeared.

Safe. All but Detective Williams, whose voice followed them down, screaming in agony.

"Williams," Shade said.

"I know!" Dekka snarled.

"We can't leave him like that. You know what we have to do, Dekka. I would but . . . wrong power."

Dekka swallowed hard and shook her head. "There must be some other way, some other thing we can . . ."

Cruz said, "Shade, we can't just—"

"We can't just do nothing," Shade interrupted. "That man helped us; he doesn't deserve to be left to scream in hell!"

But Cruz just shook her head, and Armo fixed his gaze on the ground.

It was Malik who decided the issue. "Look, I've been there, I know about pain that will drive you mad and make you beg for death. None of you know, not really. I do."

"And?" Dekka asked.

"We have to be compassionate," Malik said. "We can't leave him like that."

Dekka's face was a frozen mask; she said nothing and did

nothing but breathe as everyone waited on her. Shade knew what the answer had to be. But you don't bully or rush someone into taking life.

Finally, Dekka looked at Francis and in a voice so deep and so low it was almost inaudible said, "Francis? Can you give me a lift to the hallway outside the apartment?"

They crossed out of 3-D space and a minute later they returned. The look on Dekka's face left no one asking questions.

CHAPTER 19
Losing Battles

"WE LOST. I mean, that's the reality: we lost." Shade Darby paced across the living room of the brownstone.

"We haven't exactly surrendered," Malik said mildly. "We just got outplayed in the first game of a series."

"We *lost*," Shade snapped. "We went to take this bug guy down, and we walked away leaving him alive. We lost. We left a man behind, and it all would have been a hell of a lot worse without Francis."

"How are you?" Malik asked Francis.

"Shaky," she admitted.

"So Markovic is still around, and Williams is . . ." Dekka sagged into an easy chair, gripped the arms, and hung her head. "I wasn't prepared. I led you guys into it, and I was not prepared. I won't let that happen again."

"What could we have done differently?" Cruz asked.

"I would have . . ." Shade glanced at Dekka. "We should have thought about what we were facing. We had no useful weapons to use against it."

"Yeah, well, I don't recall you making that suggestion earlier, when it might have helped." It was clear, even to Shade, that Dekka was containing her anger, but might not hold it in forever.

Shade stabbed a finger toward Dekka, who sat, immobile, as Shade moved restlessly. "Listen, Dekka, we need some basic ideas for how we're doing this. Priorities. And priority number one is take down the bad guys."

"By letting Armo take a bullet in the head?"

Armo raised a hand tentatively, like a schoolboy who thought he might have an answer but wasn't sure. He was ignored and lowered his hand.

"Yes, if that's the only way," Shade said. She was admittedly intimidated by Dekka sometimes, but intimidation didn't stick with Shade. In her mind, Dekka had screwed up. She'd held her fire and she'd let herself be slowed down by Markovic, and worst of all, her plan had only gone as far as getting them all in place. Some distant part of Shade whispered that she was being unjust, that she was taking her frustration out on Dekka. But that was only a whisper.

"So as soon as you don't like a decision I make, you figure it's time for you to take over, Shade? One mistake and done, right? You want us to start counting up your mistakes? Because I'll bet we'd all have some things to say on that topic."

"At least I don't forget my goal!"

Dekka stood. Self-pity time was over. "That's the one thing you never forget, Shade: you. You, you, you."

Armo sighed, stood up, and wedged himself between

the two women as they moved closer to each other. "Dudes. Come on. Chill."

"How many people are going to die because we weren't ready?" Shade demanded, and she saw from the way Dekka winced that the blow had landed.

"You think I'm happy about that?" Dekka erupted. "Listen, little rich girl, this isn't my first time making a decision that could turn to shit. But don't throw that hesitation thing at me. I don't sacrifice people's lives, in this case Armo's life."

"Good leaders make sacrifices," Shade said. "This is war, Dekka. This is a war to save human civilization. People are going to die. And if we're part of this war, we're going to kill. And sometimes we're going to sacrifice the innocent. Because if we lose, then the villains win."

"Your idea of a hero is someone who lets people die?"

"I don't give a damn about heroism; I don't like losing. My idea of a winner is someone who does whatever it takes to win. And as it happened, we didn't exactly save Williams, did we? While we were talking with some blue bumblebee, Markovic was sending his bugs to infest Williams!"

Dekka stood dangerously still and silent, and Shade knew she'd gone too far. She tried to come up with words to take it back, but it was too late.

Finally, Dekka, speaking in a low, terse growl, said, "I didn't exactly see you volunteering to take care of Williams, Shade. You were happy enough to leave that to me." She held up her hands and looked at her own palms as if they had betrayed her.

With the power in those hands, Shade knew, Dekka had killed a man. A doomed man. A man begging for the release of death. But a human being, a man who had done no wrong, nothing to deserve being shredded into chunks no bigger than a McNugget . . . The accusation stung: she could have done it, maybe not as easily as Dekka, but she could have done it. And as Dekka said, she had not exactly volunteered.

Shade felt the anger drain away to be replaced by guilt and sadness. "He seemed like a good guy. Detective Williams."

Dekka swallowed and nodded and could only say, "Yep."

"I'm sorry, Dekka," Shade said, hanging her head. "I just . . . It doesn't matter, I'm sorry."

Dekka sighed, and as Armo stepped aside she took Shade in an embrace. "It's hard, Shade. All of this. Violence. Hurting people, even if you have no choice. Seeing people hurt. Seeing people afraid or in pain. It just hurts, Shade." And Shade felt Dekka's body shake with suppressed sobs.

"I used to wonder why so many FAYZ survivors became drunks or druggies. Or suicides." Shade stepped back and brushed away tears. Cruz appeared with a box of tissues.

"This stuff, you want to just put it all in a box," Dekka said. "But it never fits. You can never quite close the lid on that box. All of a sudden, from nowhere, for no reason, it just hits you." She accepted a tissue with a nod to Cruz. "We had this girl, Mary? She was a saint—I mean, if I ever met a saint. Mother Mary, we called her . . . and she broke. All of it, the fear mostly, I guess, it broke her. I watched Mary lead a group of little kids off the edge of . . . That kind, sweet girl . . . She just came apart. And people always think, 'Oh, that won't happen to me; I'm tough.' But you'll be standing in a line at Starbucks or whatever, everything fine, and then it'll come back, and suddenly you have to sit down, you know? It knocks the wind out of you."

Armo said, "Look, as long as we don't know the game, we can be outplayed."

"It's not a game," Shade said, frowning. "This is people's lives."

"But it's still a game," Armo insisted, "and we don't know what the rules are. Do we sacrifice people? How many? Do we just kill any mutant who does something bad? I mean, what is it we're doing? What *are* we?"

Shade was about to say something dismissive, but she recognized that there was truth in what Armo was saying.

"Maybe Armo's right," Shade admitted, her voice sounding like she felt: defeated. "If we play by some set of rules we don't even understand or know, we'll lose going up against assholes who know exactly what they want."

Cruz started to speak but was ignored.

"I thought we were supposed to be the good guys," Dekka said. "What the hell is the point if we're as ruthless as they are? If we turn into them, how is that a win?"

Shade shook that off impatiently. "We need to cut out the false equivalence here. We aren't looking to hurt people. We aren't looking to enslave people. We're trying to stop all of that."

Cruz tried to speak again, but again was overridden, this

time by Armo. "Hey, it's not like we're giving up. We lost a round, just a round. Like Malik said. Round One, ding-ding-ding."

Cruz held up a hand and was ignored again, then said, "Ahem. Excuse me! If I could maybe say a word or two?"

"What?" Shade snapped.

"We're all here, all six of us, and yet I hear footsteps upstairs," Cruz said.

That stopped conversation dead. Shade was already morphing. But then someone appeared, walking down the stairs.

"Who the hell are you?" Dekka demanded. "You've got like three seconds."

"We've met," the girl said. "My name is Simone. Simone Markovic. Sometimes I'm blue."

"How did you get in here?"

Simone raised an eyebrow. "I fly, remember? I followed you and came in through a bedroom window. And I'm not here looking for a fight."

"Well, what do you think, Shade?" Dekka snarked, some of her anger coming back. "Should we just go ahead and kill her? You want me to shred her, or do you want to do it yourself?"

"Simone?" Malik stood and held out his hand. "We spoke briefly . . ."

"You mean you distracted me so Shade could throw a blanket over my father."

Malik tilted his head in acknowledgment. "Why don't you have a seat?"

Simone, cautious, edged past the glowering Dekka and the

bemused Armo and sat stiff and rigid. Cruz sat beside her, signaling her own choice to listen rather than attack.

"Are you here to beg for your father's life?" Shade asked.

"I guess in a way I am," Simone said. And with that the temperature in the room dropped a few degrees. There was a collective sigh.

"Understandable," Dekka allowed. "He is your father."

"Look, don't misunderstand," Simone said, holding both hands palm out as if ready to push away any misconceptions. "I know my father. He's power hungry, a control freak, and really doesn't have much idea of right or wrong."

Shade had the impression that Dekka was holding herself back from saying something like, *Hmmm, now who does that remind me of?* Which, Shade had to admit, would be fair.

"So, what is it you want?" Shade demanded.

"He needs to be stopped," Simone said. "But he's still my dad . . ."

"You want us to stop him, but not hurt him?" Cruz asked.

Simone sighed and hung her head. "Look, I'm new to this, all right? Yesterday I was being gunned down in a field. Then I could fly. Then my father turned into a cloud of bugs. Now I'm sitting here talking to the Rockborn Gang. I just walked into a room full of people who could kill me."

"How do we know you're not a spy for your father?" Shade demanded.

"Because I'm here to help you stop him. He has to be stopped. He can't . . ." She looked down. "I saw what he did to that policeman."

"Francis and I saw what he did to some other guys, too,"

Dekka said. "I've seen some very bad things. I've seen children burning. And this was worse. Your father is sending people into unending pain and horror. He's condemning people to a living hell."

"You have some brilliant idea for how to stop your father without killing him?" Shade asked.

Simone met her eye coolly, not seeming as overawed as Shade had hoped. "You need to go at him when he's off guard. Find a way to . . ." She sighed. "I don't know. Maybe some nonfatal bug spray? Then take him to a cell. A jail. Somewhere he can be held safely until this is all over."

Shade was ready with a mocking rejoinder, but Malik held up a hand, stopping her. "Simone, there is no 'all over.' This isn't a phase. Or even a FAYZ, F-A-Y-Z: this is life now."

Simone's eyes widened as she took that in. "I don't . . . how would you know that?"

Patiently, like he was giving bad news to a grieving mother, Malik explained. "There are tons of the rock. Each ton is thirty-two thousand one-ounce doses. Say that there is a total of just one ton, just to simplify. Say that governments around the world have control of two-thirds of that, okay? That means there are still more than ten thousand doses of the rock out in the world somewhere. That means a possible ten thousand random people who can become Rockborn. Just one, Justin DeVeere, so-called Knightmare, destroyed a passenger jet, brought down the Golden Gate Bridge, and wiped out a famous lighthouse—and guess what? He's still out there. It only took one Dillon Poe to nearly destroy an

entire city. And if he'd been a bit smarter, he might have literally taken over the country. *That's* reality now."

Dekka decided this would be a good time to sit again, so
Shade did as well, signaling the end of their emotional back-
and-forth. For now.

"The point is, just a handful of Rockborn, people no worse
than we've already seen, could do as much damage to civilization as nuclear war." Malik let that sink in. "And that's
assuming the government—anyone's government—doesn't
start up another Ranch and start creating their own superpowered soldiers."

"So . . . so what's your big plan?" Simone asked.

"We don't have one," Malik said softly.

"Whac-a-Mole," Shade said. "Bad guy causes trouble; we
take him down."

Simone said, "It took the six of you to not quite stop
Knightmare, and not really stop Napalm, and not stop that
starfish kid, who I guess is dead now, but you didn't kill him.
The six of you barely stopped Dillon Poe, and you had nothing when it came to dealing with my father."

Dekka nodded. Shade frowned and nodded, too. Then the
two of them exchanged a confused look.

"She's right," Shade acknowledged. "We don't have a plan.
All we have is Whac-a-Mole. And that is a losing strategy in
the end."

"So your enemies are every clown with a piece of the rock,
plus possibly every government on earth?" Simone looked
around and saw blank faces.

"Parts of the government, not all of it," Shade said, then added, "But you're right: too many of *them*, not enough of *us*."

"Right," Simone said. "So your plan is to play Whac-a-Mole until sooner or later you're all dead. And then the world belongs to the bad guys."

Cruz interjected, "We're not the only so-called good guys."

"Exactly," Simone said. "You need more people. You need more power. And you need to stand for something more than just killing bad guys."

"More people?" Armo guffawed. "Who'd be dumb enough to join us?"

"Well . . . ," Simone said. "For a start, me."

CHAPTER 20
The Brownstone Declaration

We, the Rockborn Gang, state the following principles:

Our goals are peace and freedom for all people, human or human-mutant.

We value human life and will always do everything in our power to avoid causing the death of any human, including human-mutants.

We believe in the rule of law and will work with any legitimate law enforcement agency committed to our goals of peace and freedom.

We will oppose any human-mutant who uses their power to dominate, control, intimidate, or kill innocent people.

We will also oppose any government or part of government that seeks to use the rock to dominate, control, intimidate, or kill innocent people.

Cruz made copies and handed them around.

"You're like our very own Thomas Jefferson," Dekka

said, smiling wearily at Cruz.

"Mmmm, shouldn't it be 'We will oppose any mutant who uses *his or her* power,' instead of 'their?'" Shade asked. Then, spotting Cruz's raised eyebrow, she said, "Oh. Okay, gender neutral it is."

They debated language back and forth, but Cruz had summarized their feelings pretty well in the document.

Cruz produced the original and laid it on the coffee table. She placed a fine-point Sharpie beside it. "Sadly we don't have parchment or quill pens."

Dekka turned to Francis. "Francis, you haven't said a word."

Francis shrugged. "I figured I'm the youngest . . ."

Dekka smiled. "How old do you think I was when the FAYZ happened? How old do you think Sam Temple was? Any of us?"

"Okay, well, yeah," Francis said. "But what about what Simone was saying, that there aren't enough of us. What do we do about that?"

Cruz nodded, retrieved the paper, and handwrote:

We welcome any Rockborn who agrees to live by our principles.

"Good amendment," Malik said. "But it will be hard to control, hard to manage. What if a dozen Rockborn show up? We're not going to know them. We're not going to know if we can trust them."

"We can have the NYPD at least run background checks, right? The mayor wants our help," Shade said.

"Okay, someone sign," Dekka said impatiently.

Shade said, "You sign first, Dekka. Just because I disagree with some of your decisions . . . Look, you're the one person here who everyone trusts."

"Not to stick my nose in here," Cruz said. "But we'll need someone to just, manage, you know? Like, nonmutant, not someone who has to fight. The six of us . . . seven, I guess now . . . we're the front line, but someone's got to organize stuff. We're going to need people we can trust who won't be on the front line."

"People we can trust?" Shade frowned. "Trust to be calmly dealing with daily chores while everything's going to hell?"

Dekka said, "As it happens, I decided that last night, and I have an idea."

With that cryptic remark, Dekka took the pen, held the document flat, and in a bold hand wrote *Dekka Talent* and the date.

One by one, they signed. Shade Darby. Cruz. Malik Tenerife. Aristotle Adamo and in parentheses Armo. Francis Specter. Simone Markovic.

Dekka handed the signed declaration back to Cruz. "There you go, Ms. Jefferson. Time to put it up online and show it to the world."

Two minutes later what was to be known as the Brownstone Declaration hit Facebook.

"Great, now what?" Armo said.

"Now," Dekka said, looking at Simone. "We figure out how to take down the bug man. Without killing him. And I make a phone call to the chairman of the Joint Chiefs. Because somehow that's my life now."

From the Purple Moleskine

SOME DAY IN the future, if there is a future, I am going to need a long period of serious therapy. We have all of us become almost casual about things and events that could destroy our minds if we stopped long enough to think about them. Dekka talked about it a little, the lasting effects, the trauma, and Dekka knows about it in ways I'm just coming to understand.

And it's not just the violence and the fear; the sheer weirdness makes you doubt everything. Malik and Francis pop into and back out of some impossible-to-imagine extra dimension. There's a supervillain made out of insects that carry hyped-up, accelerated versions of every disease on this planet. I saw Williams. Dekka and Francis saw the poor men at the Pine Barrens. Speaking of which, the US government is now deliberately murdering people. And Twitter says Tom Peaks blew his own brains out in a sporting-goods store. And some old man with Alzheimer's tore up a drugstore after turning into a

*massive beast. And, and, and, and, and, and each new "and"
is like a nail being hammered into my brain, and I'm thinking, huh, I don't feel it yet. But I know that you cannot keep
doing this to yourself, living this way, and not pay a terrible
price for it.*

*How many FAYZ survivors ended up drug-addicted, drunk,
or ended their pain through suicide? A lot. I'm not arrogant
enough to think I'll be spared.*

*There's no point mourning all we've lost. Our families.
Friends. Familiar places that were ours. A world we mostly sort
of understood. If I think about all that's gone now I'll just start
crying. Even the simple belief that we are real, that we are the
creations of a loving God or the results of billions of years of
evolution, is lost. We're someone's game. Someone's entertain-
ment. We've lost everything. Everything except each other.*

*We all signed that Brownstone Declaration. My prose was
not as elegant as Mr. Jefferson's; sorry, I didn't have a lot of
time. The names on that sheet of paper, those people, are all I
have now.*

*It's beginning to dawn on regular people, too, that we are
never, ever going to be able to find our way back to where we
were. That world is gone. I don't think I ever spent five minutes
thinking about the concept of civilization before; it was just a
word in a textbook. But that's what is falling apart around us
now: civilization. The whole network of systems that defined
our world is coming down as we lurch uncontrollably toward
some future dystopia.*

There's an old song I stumbled across on YouTube. I'm

probably misquoting the lyrics, but it was something about how you don't know what you have till it's gone.

Civilization? I'm sorry I never paid attention to you. If I had, I'd probably have had a bunch of things to criticize. But now I've caught a glimpse of the future and it's not good, Civilization. It's not as good as what we had with you. Sorry it took your death for me to see that.

CHAPTER 21
The Desk Clerk

LATER HE WOULD learn just how it had happened. He would learn that Dekka had placed a call to the general in command of the deadliest military force in the world, reminding him that he had pledged his full support.

The general had then called the general in charge of US Southern Command in Mayport, Florida, who in turn called the US embassy in Tegucigalpa. Half an hour later a helicopter was en route from Tegucigalpa, the capital of Honduras, to the country's third-largest city, La Ceiba, a lovely resort town.

But he would learn all of that later. The eighteen-year-old had a pleasant brown face and neatly trimmed black hair, and dark eyes that seemed so much older than the rest of his face. He was the first to see three Honduran National Police vehicles, extended-cab Toyota pickups painted white and blue, skidding to a dramatic stop in the parking lot of the Quinta Real Hotel and Convention Center.

But this was not necessarily alarming. The National Police loved drama, and twice in the young man's time working as a front desk clerk at the Quinta Real, police had come swooping in to make an arrest. So the desk clerk put on his pleasant talking-to-customers expression as five heavily armed men came stomping up to the front desk.

"Can I help you?"

They asked him to show his ID, so he did, frowning in puzzlement and beginning to worry.

"You are to come with us."

"What? Why? Am I under arrest?"

"The Americans want you."

He was not allowed to pack, just make a quick phone call to his mother to let her know that he would be out of town for a while. Then a helicopter landed right on the beach and took him on the hour-long flight to the airport, where he was hustled aboard a US Department of Defense Gulfstream C-37A.

Just under nine hours after he'd seen the first National Police vehicle, a confused, worried, bleary ex–desk clerk climbed down the airplane stairs at Teterboro and was hustled by two New Jersey state troopers to a waiting SUV.

An airman opened the door of the SUV and he climbed in.

"Well, hello there, Edilio."

A slow smile spread across Edilio's face. "Dekka," he said. "I thought it might be you behind this."

They hugged awkwardly but with deep affection.

"I'm sorry to do this to you, Edilio," Dekka said as the SUV sped back toward Manhattan. "But I—we—needed someone we could trust."

"Things must be bad," Edilio said, half joking. Then, "You look good, Dekka."

"Oh, so sad to see you've taken up lying. You used to be so honest."

Edilio laughed. "Seriously. Good to see you, Big D." He reached for and took her hand, and neither of them broke contact for many miles.

"You may not feel that way once you know why I've dragged you here." She gave him a rundown of the situation, gratified that Edilio didn't interrupt or protest. He just sat quietly absorbing facts, nodding, occasionally asking for some small clarification.

The four years they'd been in different worlds now seemed no more substantial than a quickly forgotten dream. Edilio had never been deported, never worked as a desk clerk; that was someone else. He was not Edilio of the Quinta Real, he was Edilio of Perdido Beach. Edilio of the FAYZ. He felt it as a physical weight settling on his shoulders, a weight made of responsibility, fear, regret, and determination. An elastic band of tension wrapped around his chest, crushing the air from his lungs, making his heart labor for each leaden beat. Even his vision changed, becoming predatory, eyes searching for threats, ready to trip the alarm that would dump the oh-so-familiar shot of adrenaline into his arteries.

Edilio of the FAYZ.

"So," he said, forcing an upbeat tone. "You want me to help

organize a group of superpowered vigilantes. Is that pretty much it?"

"Pretty much. It's not the kind of job where I can just call a temp service or advertise on Craigslist, you know?"

"And this group of superpowered vigilantes includes a supersmart but ruthless girl who can outrun a bullet, an equally smart guy who isn't entirely real and can project excruciating pain, a big guy who can turn into a sort of polar bear, a trans girl who can change her appearance at will, and a girl who can travel back and forth into some n-dimensional space."

"Don't forget Simone. She's blue, she can fly, and her father is the very supervillain we're after."

Edilio smiled. "You know, I was just getting used to the fact that I would never return to the States. And now you're asking me to be Agent Coulson."

"Huh?"

"Agent Coulson." Edilio shook his head in mock disapproval. "You know, Dekka, if you're going to be living in a comic book . . . Coulson was the character who sort of organized the Avengers. He was killed in a movie and came back to life for a TV series."

"If you say so," Dekka agreed dubiously. "You and Malik will get along. He's our comics guy."

Edilio fell silent, thinking, as they crossed the bridge into Manhattan. Then he said, "We need a place, we need money, and I need to know what allies and resources we have."

"The mayor of New York has our back," Dekka said.

"Simone has fifty grand—don't even ask. The chairman of the Joint Chiefs and I are practically on a first-name basis. And we have a brownstone."

"It's a start," Edilio allowed. "The other thing we need is weapons."

"Weapons? We *are* weapons."

Edilio shrugged. "You couldn't take down the bug man, because your powers are great, but not for fighting a cloud of insects. You needed poison. Or a flamethrower."

He became aware that Dekka was smiling at him, and Dekka smiling was a rare occurrence.

"What were you doing when we came barging into your life?" she asked.

"I was working the front desk of a hotel. I speak English, and a lot of the tourists are American."

"And here you are, already plotting and planning." More seriously she added, "Sorry, man. Really."

Edilio leaned close as if about to divulge a great secret. "You know, Dekka, I really wasn't all that crazy about being a desk clerk."

"There's a pretty good chance you get yourself killed doing this."

"Enh," he said with a shrug. "Lots of people have wanted me dead. Drake. Caine. Gaia herself. I'm not so easy to kill."

And silently to himself added, *Don't tempt fate, Edilio.*

CHAPTER 22
Normal Is No Longer with Us

THE LOCATION EDILIO obtained from the mayor was the Park Avenue Armory. The armory had long since ceased to be an actual depository for weapons and was now a collection of elaborately decorated reception rooms, spaces for art exhibitions, and a fantastically big "drill hall," an enclosed space that looked like it could be used for the reception after a royal wedding. From the outside, it was a massive redbrick structure fronting on Park Avenue, conveniently just a block from the nearest Starbucks on Sixty-Sixth Street.

Convenient, Cruz thought as she balanced a cardboard drinks carrier and a paper sack of muffins and set them in front of the serious young Honduran. He sat at an ornate walnut desk beneath oil portraits, looking like he might be playing an updated Bob Cratchit role in *A Christmas Carol*, a hunched, focused person with a phone wedged against one ear and a laptop open on the ancient desk.

"Weapons. Yes, weapons," Edilio said into the phone.

"Guns. Stun grenades." He was nodding as someone at the other end of the line read off a list. "No, no body armor. Tasers, sure. But what I really want are flamethrowers."

Every day it gets weirder, Cruz thought, and walked down the corridor and into the echoing drill hall where Malik sat at a long card table with a police officer at his side with her own laptop open, taking names and running criminal background checks. There was a short line, very short, six people. And only two bore the telltale marks of ASO-7.

Cruz handed Malik a latte and the police officer a chai latte.

"How's it going?" Cruz asked.

Malik rolled his eyes.

Word had gone out that the Rockborn Gang were talking to anyone who had acquired powers following the fall of ASO-7. So far, Cruz knew, Malik had interviewed eight aspiring supers, though only one had had actual power, and that power had been the ability to become translucent. Not invisible, just translucent.

Malik had gently suggested that the ability to show people your internal organs might not be quite what they were looking for.

Another had insisted he could freeze time, but it turned out all he could really do was stand still and hold his breath while time marched on.

"I saw *Macbeth* here." Simone had come up behind Cruz and accepted a hot tea. "It was good."

"Here in this giant space?" Cruz asked.

Simone nodded, and gazed up at the arched honeycomb ceiling. "It was impressive."

"The good old days," Cruz said sadly.

"Yeah. New York is a city full of survivors, but what's happening now . . . Do you mind if I ask you a question?"

"If you walk with me to find Dekka. I am not bringing that girl cold coffee."

They walked back across the endless floor, steps echoing.

"You're trans, right?"

"Yep." Cruz braced for something stupid and told herself not to overreact.

"And everyone's okay with that?"

"You aren't?"

"Oh, no, no, no," Simone said quickly. "No. I just was wondering how they'd react if I told them I was a lesbian."

Cruz laughed. "Simone, half of us are from Chicago, Armo's from Malibu, and Francis has been living with her meth-head mother and a biker gang out in the Mojave. We're none of us real judgmental. Not to mention Dekka."

"What do you mean about Dekka?"

Cruz heard something in Simone's voice that Simone probably did not intend on anyone noticing. A bit too much interest, concealed poorly by a bit too much nonchalance. She resisted the urge to smile and said, "Well, you know she's a lesbian, too, right?"

"Is she?"

That was a palpably false question, Cruz thought. "Yep."

They reached a stairwell and began to climb. "She's

impressive, isn't she?" Simone asked.

Cruz stopped mid-flight of stairs, turned, and said, "Dekka Talent is impressive in just about every way a human being can be." She started trudging back up and out of sheer mischief added, "Lonely, though, I think."

"Oh?"

Oh, *she says, like she doesn't really care?*

"Dekka is one of these people who had one great love in their life. The girl died in the FAYZ, and Dekka still carries her picture wherever she goes."

"One great love," Simone muttered under her breath.

"Yep. I don't think she'll ever get over it, either," Cruz said. "Although, I think if the right girl came along . . ."

Simone's answer was a grunt. Then she snapped her fingers and said, "I just remembered, I have a thing to do. Downstairs."

"Ah."

Simone fled down the steps, and after a bit more climbing, Cruz emerged on the walkway that circled most of the building, a walkway defined by the raised roof of the drill hall on one side, and the crenelated redbrick front wall on the other. Dekka was on the north tower roof, a rectangular space that looked down on Park Avenue and Sixty-Seventh Street.

"Here you go," Cruz said, and handed her a coffee.

"Thanks."

"Whatcha doing up here?"

Dekka let go a long sigh. "Trying to think of something brilliant."

"Might help to talk about it."

"What are you, the resident therapist now?" Dekka affected a growl, but by now Cruz knew when Dekka was really annoyed and when she was just playing tough chick.

"Three hundred bucks an hour," Cruz said.

Dekka was silent for a while, sipping her coffee. "I'm out of my depth," she said at last. "It's been what, like, twenty-four hours since we even decided we're a group? Now we've got a mission statement, and a headquarters—"

"I like to think of it as a lair."

"Uh-huh. And Malik is interviewing people like we're Macy's looking for some temps. Edilio's organizing and hunting for weapons. Shade is downtown taking care of some lunatic who morphs into the image of Jesus and says he's Jesus and he can heal the sick. Last I heard, he was offering to cure cancer for ten thousand dollars a pop."

"White, blond, blue-eyed Jesus?" Cruz asked.

Dekka gave her a wry look. "Of course. Swedish Jesus. Just like all the paintings. Crazy, but since he's a mutant, I guess he's our business."

"Where's Francis?"

"The Statue of Liberty. Her and Armo. They wanted to play tourist."

Cruz was immediately hurt that Armo had not asked her to go with them. Then again, she'd been running errands, and Armo was not known for his patience. If he'd decided to go, he would go. Immediately.

Still . . .

"The Jesus thing, it's all over social media," Cruz reported. "Not this particular guy, but several people who were sprayed by ASO-7 and think it's stigmata."

"Stig what a?"

"Stigmata. It's when people have markings that look like Jesus's crucified hands."

"Oh, good," Dekka said dryly, "because I was worried we might be running short of crazy people."

Cruz lingered, sensing that Dekka still wanted to talk, an event about as rare as Halley's Comet.

"The thing is, I don't know what we're doing," Dekka confessed. "We're six, well, seven people, with weird abilities, but it's like suddenly people are looking to us to fix things. I got news for those people: we aren't that strong. We do not have the power to save the world. We barely saved Vegas."

A long, thoughtful silence. Cruz let it build.

"Now we're talking about bringing in more mutants? I'm not a general; I'm not some big organizer who should be running this."

"What about this Edilio person?"

Dekka shrugged. "Edilio's great. I trust no one more than him. But his job is organization; he's not really a leader and he knows it. The thing is, even a natural leader like Sam . . . I mean, this isn't the 314 square miles of the FAYZ; this is the whole country. The whole planet." She turned for the first time to look at Cruz. "We're not going to win, Cruz. We can't."

"We can try," Cruz said.

"So we can be good little avatars in some alien's simulation?"

"Oh, that," Cruz said.

"Yeah: that. If that's what we are, a sim, a program, if all this is fake . . ." She waved a hand to encompass Central Park and the larger city. "Then why are we bothering?"

"Nothing's really changed," Cruz said. "Look, I believe we were created by God. If I find out God created some aliens who created us, well, okay, that's pretty weird. But we are still us. You know? The sun is in the sky, donuts taste good, and there's another *Star Wars* movie. You know?"

Dekka was silent again, shaking her head slowly, side to side. She heaved a heavy sigh and said, "The four guys at the Pine Barrens? They're still alive. The mayor updated me. Us. Texted me, anyway. They tried shooting them full of opioids to reduce the pain. Didn't work." She turned to make eye contact. "They just scream. It's hell. That's hell, right? Eternal torment without the escape of death?"

Cruz put her hand on Dekka's arm, the first time she could remember touching Dekka. "Sweetie, there is a whole lot of pain and horror coming from this. People all over the country. All over the world. It's awful. We can't help all those people. We can only do what we can do."

"It's never going to get put back together, is it? The world. The country. Our lives. This isn't the FAYZ; we're not trapped in some dome hoping to get out and thinking everything will be fine if only we can escape. It's never, ever going back to normal, is it?"

Cruz wanted to argue. She wanted to dismiss Dekka's despair and cheer her up. But when she thought of lying, she just didn't have the energy for it.

"No, it's not," Cruz said.

CHAPTER 23
Problems at Home

SAM TEMPLE HAD never been the sort of person to spy on others. He was certainly not the sort of person who would spy on his wife. What he had with Astrid was a relationship that had already endured more stress than a hundred normal marriages. They weren't just solid as a couple; they were chiseled out of granite.

And yet . . .

Sam was also not overly neat or particularly obsessed with keeping a clean kitchen, so he was not the sort of person to reorganize the dishwasher. But the thing was, he had a coffee cup he'd left out on the balcony for, oh, maybe a week, and it had grown a ring of something green and scummy. He wanted to get it cleaned before Astrid noticed it because Astrid *was* overly neat and quite obsessed with keeping a clean kitchen.

But the dishwasher was almost completely full. In order to wedge his cup in there he had to move a few things around and . . . and then he saw the glass. It had clearly been used for orange juice. But clinging to the bottom and sides of the glass, along with the innocent pulp, were grains of something gray and gritty.

Sam pulled the orange-juice glass out and looked at it from every angle. Then he ran his finger around the inside and worked the grit between his thumb and forefinger.

"Oh, Astrid," Sam whispered. "No, no, no, sweetheart."

Astrid was at a spin class or Pilates or whatever, he could never recall. The world was falling apart, but the exercise classes must never stop; this was LA, after all. He glanced at the clock on the microwave, which displayed the proper time because: Astrid. He had a solid half hour, minimum.

It took just five minutes to locate the FedEx envelope, still containing a baggie partly filled with powdered rock.

Sam sat on the edge of their bed and hung his head, over-whelmed by a tidal wave of memory, and with those memories came dread. Dread of a repeat. Dread of more and more and more. He felt sick inside. He wanted to cry.

He wanted a drink.

But this wasn't about him, or his feelings; it was about Astrid. There was no point in asking why she had done it, and no point in asking where the powder had come from. Two women who loved him in different ways were doing their best to protect him. He couldn't get angry over the deception; they'd done it because they were worried about him.

They think I'll crack. They think I'll drink.

And Sam knew that Astrid did not trust him to be able

to stop Drake. Which was fair enough because he *knew* he couldn't stop Drake. He'd had many battles with Whip Hand, back when Sam could still fire a killing beam of light capable of cutting through stone. He'd killed Drake, or so Sam had once thought. And when they got word that Drake was still alive, Sam had done . . . had done what?

Stuck my head in the sand and did nothing.

He raised his head and saw his own forlorn reflection in the mirrored closet doors. He looked at himself almost curiously, as if trying to understand what was going on inside his own head. He was no longer the serious, quiet young surfer dude. His hair was growing darker. His skin, too, since he did still love to paddle out and sit there off the beach, sit out there on his board with his legs freezing, waiting for a wave he could ride all the way in. The surf report website was still the last thing he checked at night and the first thing he checked on waking. He didn't get to the beach as often as he would have liked, but still he felt a need to know the surf conditions at Venice Beach, Zuma, Ventura. . . . Each time he checked, he told himself not to look at conditions for Perdido Beach, his old beach, the one where he and Quinn had surfed before the FAYZ had stilled the waters and made surfing impossible. But he always did.

Sam had not gone back to Perdido Beach. Every now and again he would start to text his old friend and surfing buddy Quinn and see whether he was up for a road trip north. But he'd never sent the text. Quinn had made a life for himself, living with his folks, attending community college, and

working as a deckhand on a sportfishing boat out of San
Pedro.

"You're scared," Sam told his reflection.

He had good reason to be scared. He was sober and wanted
to stay that way.

No, that's just your excuse.

That thought fired up resentment in him. Had he not done
enough? Seriously? Had he not suffered enough? Was he not
still awakened in the small hours of the morning by nightmares? Good God, what more could anyone demand of him?

But that anger fizzled and died. No one was asking anything from him. No one.

And that's the real problem, isn't it?

No one had said, *Come on, Sam, once more.* . . . And the
truth was he wanted . . . Wanted what? He had a brilliant,
gorgeous wife. He had money in the bank. And he had more
job offers than he could even consider. He could get paid just
to show up at new clubs where he was too young to drink
(legally) but had enough celebrity to draw a crowd. Or he
could be the advertising spokesman for Pyzel, the surfboard
manufacturer—they'd made the offer. Or he could write a
book. Or he could go to work for Albert, who'd offered him a
make-work job doing nothing but collecting a charity check.

Or, or, or.

Each possibility filled him with a mix of dread and the
anticipation of brain-numbing boredom. He didn't want to
be a rent-a-celeb. He didn't want to pimp surfboards. He certainly didn't want to write a book, or sit in an office all day

doing whatever pity work Albert sent his way. No.

"What do you want?" he asked himself, but of course he knew. He knew exactly what he wanted to do, who he wanted to be.

He wanted to be Sam Temple. *That* Sam Temple.

Astrid returned, sweaty and sexy in her bodysuit.

"You started the dishes," she said, nodding approvingly at the churning dishwasher.

"Every few weeks I like to do something useful around the apartment," he said.

"Or at least once a year," Astrid snarked.

"Mmm," Sam said. "Oh, and by the way: we're out of orange juice."

Any other woman would have thought nothing of it. An innocent reminder that they needed orange juice.

But Astrid was not any other woman. She had been walking away, but Sam saw her hesitate. Then stop. Then turn to look first at the dishwasher and then aim her penetrating gaze at him.

"Astrid?" Sam said. "We need to talk."

Justin DeVecre had made his way back to New York, home sweet home: skyscrapers, yellow cabs, noise, the whole thing. The Big Apple, and if you can make it there, you can make it anywhere.

With some differences. One difference was that none of the cabs at LaGuardia would take a passenger into Manhattan. The Bronx, Brooklyn, New Jersey, sure. Not Manhattan.

So he'd taken a cab to the east end of the Williamsburg Bridge. From there he had walked across the bridge—the subway was on a very sketchy schedule with a main tunnel collapsed by the ASO impact. It was the first time he'd stepped foot on a bridge since the Golden Gate, and terrible memories of that fight flooded his brain. As he walked the wide bike and pedestrian path past traffic all heading out of the city, he saw tendrils of smoke rising from downtown all the way north to the park. That was another difference.

Reaching the far side, he found himself in a city far quieter than he recalled. New York had held firm, but in the end the reality had begun to sink in: the city was in chaos, and it was a really good time to be somewhere else. Many shops that should have been open were closed, their steel security gates rolled down and padlocked. He even spotted available street parking, an exceedingly rare sight.

There was a bad feel to the city—not panic, quite; more like defeat. The faces he saw were blank and gloomy. There was debris in the streets, glass and bricks and random bits of office furniture. Big black plastic trash bags formed hills on sidewalks, many split open and spilling their contents. And no one was cleaning it up. There were cops everywhere, many in tactical gear, ready if necessary to shoot looters. Looking north up Second Avenue, Justin saw the lights of fire trucks. The dominant sound was of burglar alarms in cars and in buildings, loudly insisting that attention should be paid. No one seemed to care.

The next difference he discovered was that the door to his

apartment—the one rented by his now-dead girlfriend and sponsor, Erin, lovely, rich Erin—was draped in yellow crime-scene tape. There was a notice pasted to the door that warned against entry.

He doubted anyone in law enforcement had the time or energy to come around and check, so he tore down the tape, found the spare key he kept under the edge of the hallway carpet, and went in.

The place had been trashed, or at least searched by people not concerned to keep the search secret. Books were strewn on the floor; the sofa cushions had been sliced open, fluffy white stuffing everywhere, like the aftermath of an epic pillow fight. The refrigerator was wide open and still running. His desktop computer was gone. All of his paintings had been taken down off the walls, presumably so the cops or the FBI or whoever could search the backs. They were leaned against the back of an easy chair.

One by one, moving as if in a trance, he opened his kitchen cupboards. Cheerios but no milk. Dry pasta, both linguine and cavatappi. A half-empty box of Kind bars. He took one of those.

They had left his TVs, the one in the living room and the one in the bedroom, where he sat disconsolate on his sliced-up mattress. He turned on the set and waited for it to warm up as he chewed the granola bar.

"Knightmare eating a Kind bar amid the wreckage," he muttered. "Wonderful."

He was an artist, dammit. So he reminded himself. An

artist! Not a monster. Not some crazy killer like that lunatic in Las Vegas. All he'd ever wanted was to be left alone.
Everything he'd done had been self-defense, perfectly reasonable self-defense. The plane. The bridge. The lighthouse.
He hadn't wanted any of that to happen. It wasn't his fault.

You have canvas and you have paint, he reminded himself
sternly. *You should get to work. You should get back to your
life, your real life. The life where you didn't get Erin killed. The
life where no families screamed behind windshields as their
cars plunged twenty-five stories into the churning green water
of San Francisco Bay.*

All of that, the horror, the fear, the excitement, the
creepiness of finding yourself in a mutant body built for
mayhem—he had to find a way to capture it on canvas. If he
could paint it, he could control it. On the canvas he could
shape his memories, rearrange and revise them.

Yes, that was the thing to do. Never become Knightmare
again. Pray that the cops were too overwhelmed to put any
effort into little Justin DeVeere. There was so much happening, so much madness, surely he was already in law
enforcement's rearview mirror.

The TV came to life. It had been many hours, days even,
since he had seen or heard news. He'd overheard conversa-
tions about ASO-7's spectacular deconstruction of the city,
but of a creature calling himself Vector, he'd heard nothing.
Until now.

Vector had control of at least one local TV station, and it
was running a loop of a creature made entirely of insects over
and over again.

By the third repetition, Justin had forgotten about canvas and paint. A new world was coming, a world ruled by Vector or others like him. A world very unlikely to have much of a place for an artistic prodigy.

But a world where Knightmare would perhaps be right at home.

Drake Merwin quite liked his nice new trench coat. He'd received it as a "gift" from a man who'd had Drake's tentacle tightening around his throat. The coat gave him a way to muffle random blurts from Brittany Pig, who had re-emerged on his chest. And it helped to hide both his whip hand and the fact that parts of him were still regrowing.

His feet were all the way restored, and that was a relief. It would have been very hard to drive the car he'd stolen without feet. He was on the I-10 West, passing Cabazon and trying to decide just how to go about locating one Astrid Ellison. He knew she was in Southern California, but that didn't narrow it down by much.

Drake was not a computer person. Maybe the address was in some corner of the internet or the dark web, but he didn't know where to start with that. What he did know was that someone knew. *Someone.* But who?

The FBI. They would know.

Drake did not know computers and he did not have a phone, but the Infiniti he'd stolen had GPS, and he knew how to use that. He pulled off to the side of the freeway, and as big rigs went past, their slipstream rocking the car, he punched in "FBI." A blue dot showed an FBI office in Riverside.

"Hah! Straight ahead."

He took the state highway 60 exit off the I-10, then followed directions until he pulled up in the parking lot of a three-story, Spanish-style office building with a red tile roof. The building fronted on a blank, gray wall that marked the freeway.

If Drake had one virtue, it was patience. He hadn't always been patient, far from it, but Drake had been "killed" several times, had even been locked in a box and sunk in a lake, and he had become accustomed to long waits with nothing to do but indulge his fantasies.

He waited patiently until he saw a woman in a charcoal-gray blazer and black pants come out and walk to her car. The car was a newish Lexus, so the woman was not a mere clerk. She pulled out, and Drake followed her. He waited as she stopped at Ralphs to buy groceries, then followed her the rest of her way home.

There was a Slip 'n Slide on the front lawn of the pleasant two-story tract home, and My Little Pony decals in the front window.

"Kids. Perfect."

Drake waited some more, until he was sure the woman would be at ease in her home. Then he got out of the car, discreetly coiling his whip hand beneath his purloined trench coat, and headed up the walkway to her front door, with a smile on his face in case she was looking out. He tried the handle. Locked. It was a good, sturdy door and would make a lot of noise if he kicked it in. He did not want to have to deal

with some FBI SWAT showing up and was considering his
options when the front door was opened by a boy of maybe
six, who was on a mission of some sort and was surprised to
see the tall young man in the trench coat.

"Who are you?" the boy demanded.

"Me? I'm Whip Hand, kid. Want to see?" Drake opened
his coat, freeing the ten-foot-long tentacle. The boy's eyes
went wide and his mouth opened, ready to scream, so Drake
wrapped the end of his whip hand around the boy's throat
and squeezed off any sound.

He lifted the kicking, struggling, red-faced boy effortlessly
up to eye level and said, "Is your mommy home?"

The bulging eyes said yes, so Drake let the boy breathe and
shifted his hold to the child's torso, and carrying him like a
gasping, wheezing suitcase, entered the home.

"Is someone at the door?"

A woman's voice, coming from the kitchen. She had
changed out of her suit into sweatpants and a UCLA sweat-
shirt. She was taking things out of the refrigerator and placing
them on the work counter. A package of hamburger meat.
Mustard. Pickles.

"Just me, your friendly neighborhood Whip Hand," Drake
said cheerily.

The FBI agent yelped in shock, started to run, but stopped
herself seeing her son in Drake's power. Her dark eyes went
wide. Drake could practically see the connections being made.
The FBI knew about him, Tom Peaks had said as much. They
had begun to realize that he was the person behind a string of

gruesome, sadistic attacks from Palm Springs to the outskirts of Phoenix, Arizona.

"Aren't you going to ask who I am?" Drake said.

The FBI agent was pale, eyes scared, but she didn't panic. "I know who you are." She made no effort to hide her contempt. "Put my son down."

"Good, that makes it easier that you know who I am. You know what I've done. You know what I can do to your kid, here, and to you."

The agent's lip was trembling, but Drake had to almost admire her strength. Most people took one look at Drake and ran. They didn't get away, but they always tried. Not this woman.

Pity he had other things on his mind, or it would have been fun to break her slowly, over the course of days. Weak people were no challenge to break, but Drake sensed this woman would be.

He sighed inwardly. Business before pleasure.

"You're going to hop on your computer and get me an address."

She shook her head. "I can't access FBI files from home."

Drake smiled. He dropped the boy onto the floor, took a step back, and heard the agent scream as he brought his whip hand down hard on the boy's back. The howl of pain was delicious; the mother's scream of "No! No!" was even better.

Ten minutes later, Drake had the address.

Thirty minutes later he was back in his car.

Eventually someone, perhaps the husband if there was

one, or worried coworkers, would find a baby crying in her crib, and two mutilated dead bodies. He'd had no choice but to kill the woman—she would have warned Astrid. The boy he'd killed mostly because he wouldn't stop crying and yelling, "You're bad! You're bad!" Which had struck Drake as being almost an insult. *Bad? Bad? I'm not bad, I'm the living embodiment of evil, you little monster.*

"Coming for you, Astrid," Drake said, laughing. "Coming for you."

CHAPTER 24
Coup

A SWAT TEAM assembled out of ICE agents and a couple of New York state troopers had assaulted Bob Markovic's apartment at two in the morning. And now, with the sun rising in the east, Markovic was distracted and annoyed by incessant cries of pain and fear from seven black-clad, heavily armed men and women in the hallway outside his apartment, and three more inside. The cries for mercy, the pleas for death, made it very hard for Markovic to concentrate. He had to plan for the future, for this new and amazing future. And he had to do it with the incessant, looming presence of unseen, unheard creatures watching his every thought and action from inside his own head.

Not that he had a head, per se.

What was it, that sense of being observed all the time? Was it some aftereffect of becoming what he now saw as his enhanced, superior self? Small price to pay for power. Still, it was an irritant, and it made him feel vulnerable.

Markovic had quickly realized that his lifelong habit of pursuing profit, of accumulating great piles of money in various off-shore tax havens, was no longer the right game to be playing. Money was an artifact of civilization, and civilization was dying. Civilization had made power abstract by inventing money and government, but this was the Wild West now. And in the Wild West, what had mattered was actual, real, brutal *power.*

Markovic had that power. In fact, his power was growing. His component elements—the bugs—had tripled in number, and he had learned how to dispatch groups of them. He could send a hundred of his bugs across town and still see what they saw and hear what they heard. And he could control them. The only limitation he had discovered was that he could not dispatch single bugs; there seemed to be a need for his component parts to move in swarms of hundreds or thousands. But this wasn't much of a handicap. That, and cold definitely slowed him down. It didn't stop him, certainly didn't kill him, but out on the cold streets his bits felt slow and sluggish.

Good thing it's not winter.

The ability to send portions of himself out on missions was very like being a drone pilot. He could sit (well, hover) comfortably and safely in one location and reach out and destroy anyone, anywhere. Or at least anywhere within the city—he hadn't yet tried to go farther.

Markovic was one of a new breed of oligarchs, he decided, an oligarchy not of money but of raw power. In the time before his rebirth as Vector, he had measured himself annually by the *Forbes* list of richest people. He'd risen as high as number eighty-two. Mostly those people, the super-rich, had ignored him. Markovic wasn't "cool." What he did for a living made right-thinking people squeamish, like bankers were any better. And he wasn't part of the old-money establishment, either, so he was dissed by the old bluenoses and by the tech bros as well.

He had never been invited to the big annual ball for the Metropolitan Museum of Art. He'd even donated some money to cancer research and still had not been invited to the Memorial Sloan Kettering Spring Ball. He'd bought a mansion in Palm Beach and done a little better there at easing into "society," but still he had few friends and far too many people who thought they were better than he.

But now? Now he had something even better than money. The power to terrorize and destroy. Which was good, but it did not define a goal for him, really. He'd known how to measure success in the money game, but this was a different game. All he knew for sure was that this was an opportunity, and whatever the game was, he intended to win it.

Markovic knew Simone had gone to join the Rockborn Gang. Stupid girl no doubt thought she could keep them from killing him. What nonsense—sooner or later Markovic would destroy the Rockborn Gang, or they would destroy him; there was no avoiding that reality. He'd have sought them out and killed them off already but for a fading concern for Simone. But Simone's involvement with them meant that he might, sooner or later, have to deal with his daughter, and that was not a pleasant thought. He could never do to Simone what he'd done to the men and women screaming and begging for death in his entryway. Not *that*.

But, that said, he couldn't wait passively for the young mutant killers to come for him, could he? Next time they might just find a way to succeed.

He had built his strength. He had learned the many ways to use his new body. The time had come for a demonstration of his power. Time to lay down the law and make New York understand that the city was his now.

Mine. All of it. Mine!

At nine a.m., when the people still in the city who still had jobs they still showed up for would be at work, Markovic swarmed out of the broken sliding glass door, barely pausing to note that he was effortlessly flying through the air, a dense cloud of insects—well, something like insects, anyway—that sometimes formed itself into the shape of a man. He raced down Park Avenue, then took Madison Avenue to Broadway, always heading downtown, south. He could have flown above the buildings but he wanted to assess the state of the city.

The city had already changed. He saw half a dozen looted stores, the evidence of fires, trash strewn in the street. A burned-out taxi sat in front of a tapas restaurant. A water main had broken and no one had yet fixed it, so that half a block of Broadway was under six inches of water. Most of the traffic lights he passed were in emergency flashing mode, which would have made traffic impossible but for the fact that there were fewer than the usual number of cars or trucks on the streets, and what traffic there was all had a single direction: away.

Markovic zoomed on, quite enjoying himself, until he reached his goal.

New York's City Hall was an early nineteenth-century building in French Renaissance style, a grand old edifice. It was big, but dwarfed by the even larger Tweed Courthouse behind it, which housed the Department of Education for the city.

Should he? No, just City Hall. No need to ruin the day of educators. The time would come when he'd need people like that to teach his laws to a generation of children who would grow up knowing that Markovic—Vector—ruled their world.

Markovic swarmed right in the front door, flowed past the security detail, split himself into a main group and three smaller swarms, and spread out through the building.

Ten minutes later, most of New York City's government were screaming in agony, their bodies devoured and yet never to be consumed by disease. Only the mayor was missing, which was a disappointment, but he would get to her. People tried to run, but he was too swift. They barricaded themselves in offices and pushed furniture against the doors. Silly fools: there had never been a door an insect could not get past.

One Police Plaza was just a block away, an awful, putty-colored cube. In minutes the police chief, his aides, and hundreds of cops and clerical support were in agony.

One last target. The Javits Federal Building, which housed the FBI and Homeland Security, was conveniently in the same neighborhood. Markovic struck here with extra relish, in light of what the Feds had done at the Pine Barrens. *Try to kill me? Hah. Go to hell.*

Literally.

In just under an hour, Markovic had infected hundreds of federal employees and crippled the leadership of the city.

New York City was without any functional government.

It only remained for Markovic to publicly inform the citizens of New York that they were no longer citizens, but subjects. His subjects, to whom he would dole out protection or pain, depending on how willingly they submitted.

One small problem. If he meant to summon the media to witness his statement, he would need to be able to make a phone call, and he had no fingers. But he solved that problem by finding the Public Affairs office and the woman who presumably ran it. She was in her office, hiding under her desk, as yet untouched by his insect hitmen.

"If you obey me, I will not harm you," he said in his reedy voice.

"Don't hurt me! Don't hurt me! I have two little children!" She actually had the framed photo clutched to her chest and turned it toward him. She wept pitifully as snot ran down her lip.

"Obey me and live, you and your children."

He told her to call the *New York Times* and CNN. That would be enough to start the ball rolling. She made the calls, and Markovic left her unharmed. He was, after all, a man of his word.

An hour later Markovic "stood" on the steps of City Hall,

facing dozens of cameras and a press corps doing their best not to wet themselves in sheer terror. Everyone by now knew what Vector could do.

"I have a statement to make. I will not answer questions," Markovic said. "I am Vector. I was a successful businessman when the asteroid strike came. The government tried to kill me, along with many others similarly affected. That's not some whimsical exaggeration; they drove us to a field in New Jersey and gunned us down."

He let that sink in for a moment, though of course the whole world had seen video of the Pine Barrens by now.

"I died. But, because of the rock, I was reborn, as you see me. And today, on behalf of all who have been failed or harmed by government forces, I have incapacitated City Hall, One Police Plaza, and the Federal Building. The pain they inflicted on me and on innocent people is now inflicted on them. Justice, I call it. Justice!"

The reporters did not seem convinced, but no matter, the common people were credulous fools who would believe what they needed to believe. Bizarre as his claim was, there would be many prepared to believe that he had indeed doled out justice. "As of now, the *people* run this city . . . with me as their sovereign. Regular people minding their own business have nothing to fear from me. But let us be clear: New York City is *mine*. And if the government in Albany or in Washington, DC, comes after me, no one will be safe from Vector."

It was petty, Markovic knew, but he enjoyed the thought of the society toffs and the upstart new money all suddenly realizing that maybe, just maybe, they should have welcomed him into New York society instead of treating him as a joke or a pariah.

"And one other thing. I know that others have been affected by the rock. Some of you will have developed powers. You are not safe from the government, or their willing tools, the vigilante thugs of the so-called Rockborn Gang. Come to me. Join me! Join me now at Grand Central Terminal, and I will care for you. Your only safety lies in joining me."

Rockborn Gang? Meet Vector's Gang.

CHAPTER 25
Of Course It's a Trap

"WINDOWS AND DOORS still all shut tight," Cruz reported, somewhat breathless after having raced around the armory with the janitorial crew, double-checking that every way into the building was sealed.

"He knows we'll come after him," Shade said. "He's bigger and stronger than before, and he's crossed his Rubicon."

"His what?" Armo and Francis both asked simultaneously.

Malik started to provide a complete answer but saw that this was not the time and shortened it to, "It means he's crossed a point of no return."

"We have to hit him soon, and we have to kill him." Shade looked directly at Simone.

"There has to be some way . . . ," Simone protested.

Shade was about to light into her when Dekka raised a hand and said, "You don't have to be part of this, Simone."

Simone said nothing, just sat on the edge of one of the ornate carved chairs they'd assembled into a circle dwarfed by the echoing space around them. She looked overwhelmed, and part of Shade sympathized. Over the last day and a half, she'd come to know Simone a little, and liked her well enough. But Shade dismissed sympathy—this was not the time for weakness or half measures.

"Edilio has put together a pretty fair cache of weapons," Shade went on, nodding respect to Edilio, who she had quickly come to like for his modesty, directness, and efficiency. Shade had been obsessed with the FAYZ and had read every book, seen every interview or TV show or movie, but she had not until now realized how important the unassuming young man had been. "We have insecticide. We have flamethrowers. And if we just sit here, waiting for him to come to us, sooner or later he'll get us all."

Shade knew she was treading close to challenging Dekka, and she didn't mean to do that. But Dekka had to act. She had to act *now*. Vector had publicly announced himself and carried out a Pearl Harbor–style sneak attack on the powers that be. The Rockborn Gang would be Vector's next target.

"He won't get in through windows or doors," Cruz said. "But honestly there are probably ways. Insects have a way of getting around obstacles."

Dekka sighed and hung her head. "Some stories have it that he can move through the ground, so I imagine if he put his mind to it he could eat right through the walls. What are you seeing on social media, Cruz?"

"People are saying the roads out of the city are still moving slowly, but a lot of the people who could leave, have,"

Cruz reported. "9/11 didn't scare New Yorkers away, the ASO strike didn't scare them away, but this has done it. There's all kinds of disgusting, terrible video of the people at City Hall and the other places. People are scared to death. The top trending hashtag is #PrayForNYC."

"Yeah, prayer ought to do it," Shade said.

"Any word on Markovic's location? Is he actually at Grand Central?" Dekka wondered.

Cruz shrugged. "People are thinking every bug they see is him. Also . . ." She stopped herself.

"Also?" Dekka prompted.

"Well, also you've got lots of people saying the city will have to be nuked. #NukeAllMonsters is number three on Twitter."

Every eye turned to stare at Cruz. Then turned to Dekka. Shade watched the consensus form. She looked most closely at Simone, who seemed on the edge of tears, and thought, *I do not like potential traitors in our midst.*

Dekka's cell phone rang and everyone jumped.

"Yes?" Dekka answered, then fell silent, listening for a long time as Shade grew increasingly impatient. Finally, Dekka said, "Give us twenty-four hours." Another silence, then an exasperated, "Okay, twelve hours. Come on, General, this is insane."

Dekka hung up and just sat, head hanging. Finally she said, "Not a nuke. The Pentagon thinks they have a better way."

"Not another bunch of tanks," Cruz said.

"No. Nerve gas. They think they can drop nerve gas around Markovic and kill him, kill the bugs. They've positioned shells near the city. Sarin gas. They think regular insecticide sprayed from planes or helicopters would be too diluted to be effective."

Simone winced like she'd been struck.

Malik, voice dripping sarcasm, said, "And yet we've always claimed we didn't have nerve gas in this country anymore."

Shade waited, impatient but knowing she had to let Dekka reach the decision on her own. When Shade had agreed to let Dekka play boss, she'd imagined that it was an act of generosity. She'd also imagined that she could take back the leadership anytime she wanted. But that was no longer true and maybe never had been. The others trusted Dekka in a way that they did not trust her.

"Okay," Dekka said, "We have two choices. Attack or defend. We can sit right here and wait for him to come for us. Shade's right, he knows sooner or later he has to take us out. The problem with waiting for him is that all Markovic has to do is take a building full of people hostage, start infecting them, and demand we pull back. Anyone left in the city will turn against us out of self-interest, and we'll have no choice but to walk away. So. Unfortunately, we really have no choice but to attack." She made deliberate eye contact with Simone. "Again: you don't have to be a part of this. But if you are, you need to be straight in your head. I can't be worried about you when the shit hits the fan."

"He *is* at Grand Central!" Cruz interjected. She held up her phone and played shaky video of a dense swarm, now in the form of a man's head, but ten, twenty times normal size, like a seething, pulsating giant Wizard of Oz.

"You know it's a trap, right?" Malik asked Dekka.

Dekka nodded. "A good one, too. A huge space so our little bug bombs won't accomplish much; they're each just good for a room, a normal-sized room. Plus tons of shops and restaurants, and tunnels leading off in all directions."

Shade said, "Edilio? Malik? Any of the people you've interviewed so far ready to help us?"

Edilio shook his head, face grim. "None that I would trust to be a real plus. But I've got a couple people who might be helpful in defending this place in case Markovic strikes back at us here while you're going after him. Also, I have these." He fished seven smartphones out of a canvas bag and handed them around. "They're new, so no one has the numbers but me. I've installed an encrypted text app and input all the numbers, including mine."

"Of course you have," Dekka said, nodding at Edilio.

"In terms of weapons, mostly it's guns, which are useless against Markovic. But I have something else, if you all will follow me."

He led them across the drill hall to a table loaded with gear.

"Okay, so these big steel tanks that look like scuba tanks? They are, basically, scuba tanks, but full of jellied gasoline. Napalm. Just like the bad guy of the same name. And see the smaller tank here? That's CO_2. The CO_2 pressurizes the napalm." Three steel tanks had been fitted with harnesses so they could be worn as backpacks, and Edilio hefted one onto his own back, groaning under the weight. "I had some help with this from a veteran who came by to offer support. Basically, the first thing you do is light the pilot."

Edilio unlimbered a three-foot-long black hose ending in a nozzle. Beneath the nozzle was a much smaller nipple that ended just beneath the nozzle's outflow. He snapped a lighter, and the pilot light burned a small blue flame.

"You point, and you squeeze. Step back."

"Are you going to . . . ?" Cruz asked, but her question was answered when Edilio pointed the nozzle down the length of the drill room and squeezed.

A jet of orange flame flew thirty feet. Most burned off in the air, but a smear on the floor burned on. Shade felt the wave of heat and smelled the familiar stink of gasoline.

"We have just these three, and they're heavy. Too heavy for Francis, and probably too heavy for Simone to fly with."

"Oh, I got one of those," Armo said, almost drooling.

"I can handle one," Dekka said.

"Me too," Shade said.

"Well, Shade, there are special considerations for you. You move much faster than the flamethrower sprays. Be careful not to run into your own flame. And remember that a flame blowing past at Mach 1 isn't going to burn anything. For the rest of you, something less dramatic." He held up a spray can with only a white label. "I reached out to an exterminator. They mixed up these cans for us, which contain a blend of the nastiest insecticides. They won't kill a human, but at the same time, do try to avoid breathing them. They spray about ten feet."

Shade caught Dekka's eye and nodded, impressed. She'd at first thought Dekka was silly for bringing Edilio into things. *Not silly at all.*

"I'm seeing people joining with Vector. Markovic, I mean," Cruz said, frowning at her phone. "Some people are probably just scared and going to him for protection. But some look like bad guys, a lot of skinheads, some gangbangers, and some of them are armed. And there are people saying he's got other mutants with him, too."

Simone spoke for the first time during the grim meeting. "I will fight skinheads. I'll fight other mutants. But I . . . Look, I understand what you have to do. But not me. I'm not going to kill my own father."

Dekka said, "You have to follow your own conscience, Simone."

Now Edilio was handing out printouts of the floor plan of Grand Central Terminal. He also had a laptop open to a site that showed pictures of the interior of the station. "You should all study these."

"You have suggestions?" Shade asked Edilio.

Edilio shrugged. "Well, you could get down to the subway at Lexington." He tapped the map. "You'd have to walk down the tunnel for, like, ten blocks. You'd come in through the lower-level subway terminal of Grand Central."

Dekka nodded. "Vector's smart to go for a big space with

lots of escape routes, but not as smart as he thinks he is: every escape route out is a way in as well. Markovic has a lot to cover—the subway tunnels, the doors and windows . . . We know he seems to be able to detach bits of himself, so he may have a lot of openings covered, but hopefully not all of them."

They all stood around Edilio looking at the pictures, the maps, committing as much as possible to memory.

"Okay," Dekka said finally. "Armo, Simone, and me go through the subway tunnel. Shade? I want you on Forty-Second Street until it's time. Cruz: stall and distract. Malik and Francis, you pop in somewhere . . ." She looked at the map again. "This bathroom here. If you can pop in without being spotted, you can give us a heads-up on the phone. And Malik?"

"Yes?"

"Your power doesn't seem to affect Rockborn in morph, so it won't bother Markovic, but we need to keep any possible civilians or hostages from getting in the way. I'd say a ten-second blast as soon as H-Hour hits. H-Hour is in three hours, five p.m. Everyone be in place by then. As soon as your phone clock rolls over from 4:59 to 5:00, Malik hits the humans not in morph to remove them from the equation. Shade comes in through the front door, and Armo, Simone, and me, we come up from the tunnel below."

Edilio cleared his throat, deferentially, almost as if he thought he should raise his hand.

"Yes?" Dekka asked.

"I overheard someone talking earlier," Edilio said. "Am I

right that Malik was trapped in this Over There place when he lost his grip on Francis's hand?"

Malik said, "Yes. She can move between dimensions. She can carry someone with her, but only so long as there's physical contact." He cocked his head quizzically. "So?"

"So," Edilio said, sighing, clearly not liking what he was saying. "Has it occurred to you that this represents a powerful weapon? Anyone she touches . . . She can strand them."

From the blank looks, that had not occurred to any of them. Shade certainly hadn't thought of it. Eyes turned in near-perfect synchrony toward Francis.

"Could you do that?" Dekka asked. "And would you?" Shade heard a quiver in her voice.

She's asking a child if she'll drag people to limbo.

Francis didn't answer glibly. She seemed to be running it through her head, watching it happen.

Francis started nodding, just a little, then a quick up and down. "Yes. This is war, right? Yes."

Shade happened to meet Dekka's gaze, and there was a strange, frozen moment of a shared emotion. Shame.

This is war, right? The facile, all-purpose excuse for any horror committed in the name of victory.

She thought then of what Dekka had done to Detective Williams. What he had begged her to do, what everyone agreed was an act of mercy. It was. But Shade could sense it twisting and twisting inside Dekka.

Shade reached for Malik; his back was to her. She just wanted to put her hand on his shoulder, wanted to make some kind of contact. She saw in her imagination, in her memory, the real Malik, the ruined boy who'd have been safely back at Northwestern if not for his foolish taste in women.

And Cruz . . .

And now Francis.

Not the time. Not the time.

This is war, right?

Then she met Dekka's gaze again. The shame was gone. The doubt was gone. There was a feral snarl on Dekka's lips, and Shade felt something like a bolt of electricity pass between them. Dekka winked.

Then Dekka took in a deep breath, lowered her face, and shook her head just enough to send her dreads flying. And when she looked up, every eye was on her.

"Everyone scared? Good. Scared is good, but hesitation is not." She looked each person in the eye, and Shade would have sworn that each of them stood taller.

"This is important, what we're doing. This is the future of the world. And that's not bullshit. We've all by now been in one kind of fight or another, and this may be the worst. But it's also the most important. If we all do what we're supposed to, we'll be all right."

A lie, Shade thought. Every single one of them knew it was a lie. But it was a reassuring one. And having seen what Markovic could do, they all needed reassuring.

CHAPTER 26
Hello There, Drake

THE FIRST THING Drake noticed was that the doorknob to Astrid and Sam's apartment was misshapen. It looked crushed, like someone had put the aluminum knob into a vise. It troubled him at some obscure level. It was wrong. Out of place.

But whatever. So their apartment building was poorly maintained, so what? She was in there, Astrid, just beyond the door. He could hear a female voice humming.

He had a crowbar and stuffed the sharp edge between door and jamb, just above the knob and below a bolt lock. He leaned against it, testing.

"Knock, knock," Brittany said, and began laughing.

"Shut up, you idiot," Drake snapped.

He steadied himself and took a deep breath. He closed his eyes, savoring the moment. He had stopped at a hardware store, and in addition to the crowbar had taken a good hammer, some five-inch nails, nylon rope, duct tape, two small rubber balls, and a butane torch. Good enough for a start. His plan was to incapacitate Astrid and Sam as well, if he was home. If not, he would have some fun with Astrid while waiting for Sam. Then he would tie them up, ball-gag them, stuff them in the trunk of the car, and drive them to someplace more private. Someplace where he wouldn't be interrupted for days.

She'll start out reasonable, trying to convince me to let them go. I'll let that go on for a while until the fear builds, until she really understands that she is powerless. And then she'll scream.

He felt the sharp edge of anticipation as lovely pictures and lovelier sounds played out in his head. This was going to be amazing. This would be the highest moment of his very strange life.

I actually feel nervous. But such an excellent nervousness!

With a lunge he threw his weight against the crowbar. The jamb splintered, but the door did not give way until Drake had kicked it several times.

When at last it did open, he yelled the line he'd decided on after much consideration.

"Honey! I'm home!"

There she was! Right there in front of him: Astrid! The daydream had turned real. After so long, she was right there, right in front of him. A little older, still just as beautiful and cold and disdainful as ever. Astrid the Genius.

"You look good, Astrid," he said, and licked his lips outrageously, then laughed out of pure joy.

Astrid sat in an easy chair that had been turned to face the door. Just sat there. Sat there in yoga pants and a cropped spandex top, with her blond hair spilling down to her shoulders and her icy blue eyes appraising him.

Gorgeous. Vulnerable. Alone! And still with that smug, I'm-smarter-than-you look in her eyes.

"Hello there, Drake," Astrid said.

In a flash Drake knew that something was wrong, very wrong. No one ever, upon seeing Whip Hand with his tentacle arm curling in anticipation, said *Hello there.* No one. Ever. Certainly not Astrid Ellison. But he'd prepared another line, also taken from a movie, and he couldn't think of what else to say so he said, "Going so soon? I wouldn't hear of it. Why, my little party's just beginning!" It was from *The Wizard of Oz,* a line from the Wicked Witch of the West.

Of course he'd assumed she would bolt. And here she was just sitting. In fact, she seemed to be calmly flexing her muscles, which were actually kind of impressive for a girl who . . .

Then Astrid stood up, and something was very definitely wrong. Astrid had always been tall for a girl, but she now stood well over six feet. And she had been working out. A lot. And taking steroids. A lot. Because even as he stood there gaping, Drake saw her Thor arms still expanding, like someone was inflating them with an air hose. Her thighs were thick as tree trunks and growing thicker, until the spandex yoga pants threatened to tear. It was all made stranger still by the fact that Astrid's face, the face from so many of his fantasies, remained unchanged except for the way her whole head seemed to be surrounded by shoulders like boulders. Drake flashed all the way back to his childhood: Astrid reminded of him of nothing so much as his old He-Man action figure. But without the boots.

"Why, Drake," Astrid said in a mocking voice. "Did you think I would run away?" She leaned toward him—*toward!* "Are you disappointed? You like when people run, don't you? It's part of the fun, right?"

Drake licked his lips, and Brittany muttered, "Heh. Heh-heh," like she was fake-laughing at a joke. But this was no joke. Astrid was not afraid.

Astrid. Was. Not.

Afraid.

Drake shot a glance at the door behind him thinking the unthinkable, that maybe he should be the one running. Crazy!

Astrid saw the glance and said, "You forgot to shut the door, Drake." She took one step to her right, bent down and grabbed the edge of a solid-looking end table, and with a mere flick of her wrist threw it past Drake's head.

Bang!

Slam!

The table hit the door and smashed it closed.

And that was when Drake realized why the doorknob had bothered him. It wasn't bad maintenance: Astrid must have crushed it accidentally.

His head was swimming. This was madness. This was an

impossibility! Four long years of greedy anticipation leading to *this*? He tried to think of some quip, some quote, some anything, anything to say, but this was not a situation he had ever experienced before. No one faced Whip Hand without fear.

And there was something worse than the absence of fear. There was a hunger in those cold eyes, a blue glitter of anticipation. A slight, close-lipped smile tugged at one corner of Astrid's mouth. Her kielbasa-sized fingers flexed threateningly.

Now, Drake was scared.

He spun and leaped for the door but was jerked back by a hand the size of a ham grabbing his shoulder. Astrid pulled him to her and turned him around as easily as if she'd been moving a chess piece. His face was inches from hers.

"You've dreamed of this day, haven't you, Drake?"

He shook his head violently.

"Oh, sure you have. And me? I've dreaded it. Dreaded it!"

Quick as a snake, Drake whipped his tentacle arm at her. It was a well-aimed blow, and Astrid was too slow to react. *Hah! I'll still . . .*

Then he saw that she was smiling. The whip hand should have laid a bloody gash across her face but . . . nothing.

"Yes," Astrid said, nodding with some satisfaction. "It's fascinating, really, the way the rock works out here in the wider world beyond the FAYZ. It should be random is the thing; you should develop mutations that don't necessarily function well. Take Shade Darby for example. She could have developed speed but been burned by the heat of air-friction, but no, her mutation came with a sort of armor. And think about the subtle changes that have to take place inside the brain to be able to process visual images while moving at the speed of sound. Frankly, it suggests intentionality."

"You stalling for Sam to sneak up behind me?"

"Sam? No, he's away. He had other things to do. And I wanted this to be just for us, you and me, Drake. Our special time together."

Drake's eyes darted. Door: no. Window? He'd have to get past her first.

"In any event, along with the super strength I got pretty much invulnerable skin. Yes, indeed. So honestly, you won't need this old thing anymore."

She shoved her right hand under his left arm and lifted him effortlessly into the air as he kicked and cursed and tried to whip her. She let him flail, then caught his tentacle in her free hand. Still firmly holding his whip, she threw him across the room. Threw him like he was nothing, and as he flew backward through the air he saw her intent and shrieked in outrage.

She held his whip. Had she not he might have smashed into the wall, but she held his whip and it yanked at him. He fell onto a glass coffee table, shattering it.

"Well, that's a mess I'll have to clean up."

Then as Drake tried to get back on his feet, Astrid yanked his tentacle arm so hard he was thrown against the kitchen counter, then, like he was a yo-yo, she snapped him back the other direction so hard that his head left a dent in the wallboard.

With an impossible leap, Astrid was over him, astride him, looking down at him like he was a worm, the bitch, and she still had his whip arm, and now she had one foot on his pecs, holding him down effortlessly. With her massive left arm she began coiling his tentacle, like she was putting away a garden hose.

He felt the tension in his shoulder, and the horror of her intentions was clear now, and he roared, "No! No! No, you bitch, I'll make you suffer. I'll nail you to the floor and drop burning coals on your . . . No, no, nooooo! No! Nooooo!"

Astrid, with a foot on his shoulder, pulled with the strength the rock had given her, pulled and coiled as the whip stretched and then would stretch no more and began to tear as Drake screamed the vilest curses and threats.

And then, all at once, she was holding it, a limp python.

"You see the lack of internal structure, the absence of viscera, tendons, veins. This goes to the . . . I won't say supernatural because I believe that word to be an oxymoron, but let's say, the unusual origin of this appendage of yours. It might as well be Play-Doh inside."

"Let me go!"

"You know, Drake, you tempt me to sadism. But I refuse to take pleasure in this."

And yet, she was smiling. She started toward the door, dragging him now by his hair.

"Where are you taking me?" he cried, kicking and yelling

and trying to grab the doorsill, all of it futile.

"Down to the garage. Let's take the elevator, shall we?"

"Let me go or I'll kill everyone you love! You know I'll come back! You know I can't be killed!"

"Well, that may be true, Drake," Astrid allowed, now carrying him down the exterior walkway to the elevator as easily as Drake had carried the FBI agent's brat. "But you can certainly be slowed down, can't you?"

The elevator door opened. Astrid tossed him inside, and Drake saw that she had his precious whip arm looped around her neck like a scarf. He thrashed frantically but pointlessly, trying to claw with his remaining hand, as Astrid calmly pressed the *B* for basement.

The door opened on the second floor, revealing an elderly man in shorts and a Hawaiian shirt, carrying a cooler.

"Might want to catch the next one," Astrid said. "Sorry."

In the basement garage, Astrid dragged Drake by the foot, allowing him to flail away, to claw at the concrete, to stretch to try and get hold of anything solid, almost seeming to enjoy it.

She fumbled with fat fingers for a key to unlock the storage cage but decided just to rip the lock from the latch. The cage was half-filled with white cardboard boxes and a heavy steel box. Leaned against a box were a machete and a chain saw. He saw, too, a cardboard carton stamped with a set of black triangles and octagons labeled with skulls and crossbones and words like "corrosive" and "highly toxic."

Astrid lifted the hinged lid of the box and Drake saw that

it was lined with heavy-gauge plastic. Then she raised the chain saw.

Drake tried more threats. He tried more curses. In his desperation he tried guilt. "If you do this, you're no better than me, you hypocrite bitch!"

"Yes, it has its moral gray areas, doesn't it?" Astrid acknowledged. "Then again, you're a rapist, a torturer, and a murderer so I'm betting I won't have too many regrets."

She fired up the chain saw, the metal teeth whirring too fast for the eye to follow.

Drake bolted for the exit, but she blocked the only way out. Then she delivered a backhand slap that knocked him through the air to smash into the concrete wall. She grabbed him by his thigh, held him half-suspended in the air, and said, "Let's first deal with making sure you can't run."

And she lowered the chain saw and held it firm as it buzzed through his leg.

"It's convenient you not having blood. Imagine the mess otherwise."

Brittany said, "Gentle Jesus, meek and mild." Not a barb, just a random blurt.

In all, it took twenty minutes for Astrid to reduce Drake (and Brittany) to bits using first the chain saw and then the machete. All but Drake's head, which still saw and heard, but could no longer speak. Astrid disassembled him without a quiver of emotion, without a qualm, as calmly as if she was cutting up a chicken for dinner. She tossed each new bit of him into the box, and made sure that he saw his parts lying there, squirming, each with a life of its own, but with no means of escape.

She set his head in a corner where he could watch as she donned a breather mask and poured bottles of hydrofluoric acid into the plastic-lined box, covering his parts.

The acid seethed and bubbled, and noxious fumes rose in the air. And he watched. He could do nothing else. He watched as the powerful acid boiled. Like she was making a stew! Like she might be about to add salt and a bay leaf

Astrid then knelt before him, peering down at him. As he watched, helpless, she began to change. Her shoulders seemed to deflate. Her massive biceps diminished. And soon she was just a young woman with arms no bigger than baguettes.

"I wanted to do this last part as myself. As me. No morph. No superpowers. Just me."

With that Astrid lifted him by his hair. He had the sensation of flying, but not far. He came to a stop two feet above the roiling, poisonous pool of acid.

"I want you to recognize that I'm not lowering you slowly so that I can enjoy the look of terror in your eyes. Yes, *that* look! No, I get no enjoyment from this," she said, and undercut her statement by laughing. "Actually, now that I think of it, I'd better do it slowly. I don't want to splash any of that nasty acid on myself."

Drake no longer experienced pain, but he was not without sensation. He felt the instant his severed neck touched the surface of the acid. It felt like an electric shock. He mouthed a silent curse and then a plea but the acid was lapping at his lips so he was soon unable to mouth anything as it filled his mouth, eating away at his teeth and tongue, burning its way through his gaunt cheeks.

"This is for everyone you ever terrorized, you vile, despicable, evil piece of shit, and most of all, Drake, most of all, for Sam."

He felt her release his hair.

Felt himself sink . . .

Saw . . .

CHAPTER 27
Lesbokitty Represents

THERE WERE ADVANTAGES to having the mayor and the NYPD on your side. All subways to or from Grand Central had been stopped anyway, but the mechanics of finding the right entry point to the vast subway tunnels was handled for Dekka.

Dekka, Armo, and Simone arrived discreetly at the Fifty-First Street and Lexington subway station by three different cabs, just in case Markovic had eyes on the streets. A single plainclothes transit policewoman waited for them and tried to shoo them straight to the stairs down, but Armo had different priorities. He had spotted a hot-dog stand, still open and operating despite an almost total lack of pedestrian traffic.

"Seriously?" Dekka asked.

Armo shrugged. "I need energy if I'm going to get my berserk on." To the vendor he said, "Give me two. No, three. With everything."

Dekka was impatient, but she knew not to push Armo. So

as the transit cop led them down the gloomy stairwell, Armo
ate the three dogs in a total of six bites.

"Good?" Dekka asked.

"Enh. I prefer them grilled."

They marched down the grimy stairs, stepping carefully to
avoid being overbalanced by the heavy flamethrower tanks
Armo and Dekka carried. They came to an electronic turnstile.

"Our first crime of the day," Armo said, winking at the
policewoman. He tried to hop over very nonchalantly but that
was something not even he could manage with fifty pounds
of steel and napalm on his back. He and Dekka both made it,
eventually, but it was an extremely clumsy start to the pro-
ceedings. Simone, less burdened, easily hopped over. The
policewoman sensibly swiped her MetroCard and walked in
normally, adding to the comedy of the moment.

"It's kind of like D-Day but with less dignity," Dekka said
as she tried to pull her wedged-in leg free of the turnstile with
an assist from Armo.

The subway platform was old, with tile more yellow than
white, and a blue tile sign reading *51st Street*. And it was eerily
empty. A homeless man slept curled up against one wall. A
pigeon fluttered past, came to rest on a trash bin, and cocked
a curious eye at them.

"So, here's where it gets hairy," the cop said. She pointed.
"We have to walk the track that way for about ten blocks."

"The third rail is off, right?" Simone asked.

"It is. They've killed all but emergency lighting, and the

downside is that the tunnel will be even darker than usual. Just the same, maybe don't lick the third rail."

"Thank you, Officer," Dekka said. "But we'll go ahead on our own. We aren't exactly professionals at this, and we may end up getting you hurt for no good reason."

She demurred, but in the end the cop decided not to argue. Especially when Dekka, Armo, and Simone all began to morph. She did, however, supply them with two excellent flashlights. Simone took one and levitated away, scouting the tunnel ahead.

"You think she's solid?" Armo asked Dekka, nodding his big shaggy head in Simone's direction.

Dekka shook her head, and her now-living dreads seemed to decide on their own to stare at Armo. "I don't know. If it comes down to killing her father? I don't know. Could you do it? I mean, not necessarily yourself, because she's been clear on that. But could you stand by and watch someone else doing it?"

"Well, my dad's a stuntman, not a supervillain, so it's hard to say."

They hopped down easily from the platform to the greasy, gravel-paved track. In their morphs they were much stronger, and the flamethrowers were much easier to manage.

"It's really hard to stand on a train track and not think you're about to get run down," Dekka said, nervously looking in both directions. At that moment Simone came back, flying level, like Superman, her flashlight looking disturbingly like the headlight of an approaching train.

"It's clear for the next six blocks. I didn't want to go any closer in case my fa—" She stopped herself. "In case Vector has spies down in the tunnels."

"Good thinking." Had she switched from the familiar "father" to Vector as a signal to Dekka and Armo? If so, was she sincere? Or was she mentally distancing herself from her father, using the name Vector to draw a line?

You think she's solid?

"There's a little colony of mole people," Simone reported. "Like half a dozen around where Forty-Sixth Street would be."

"Mole people? Mutants?" Dekka asked, alarmed.

Simone laughed. "No, it's a not-very-nice nickname for homeless people who live in the tunnels."

"People are living down here? In a city as rich as this?" Dekka shook her head.

"A rich city with very expensive rents," Simone said. She remained in morph but now walked between them, her wings still and silent.

Not for the first time, a part of Dekka's mind marveled at just how weird her life was.

I'm walking down a subway tunnel with a bear creature and a flying blue girl on my way to kill a bug man.

Sure. Because that's my life.

They had to stay in morph from here on in—despite the infuriating, distracting, will-sapping presence of the Watchers—in case Malik had to emit one of his blasts of pain.

"Expensive rents and a lot of rich assholes who don't care,"

Dekka said, then realized this might seem like a diss when addressing a girl whose father, while a vicious villain, was also very rich.

But Simone readily agreed. "Yes, rich assholes who don't care. Like my father. Like Vector." She nodded emphatically to herself on the word "Vector." Like she was reminding herself not to forget it.

The tunnel was oppressive in the extreme, with long gaps between inadequate lights. It stank of waste oil and urine. The walls were black with layers of grime. A rat ran past and Armo yelped.

"Really, dude?" Dekka teased. "You're like nine feet tall and weigh the same as a Prius."

"I do not like rats," Armo muttered. "Especially huge rats."

"You thought that was a huge rat?" Simone mocked. "I've seen rats that rat could saddle up and ride. I heard there was a mounted cop who rode a rat for a week before he realized it wasn't a horse."

"So not interested in talking about rats," Armo said, while Dekka and Simone shared a shaky laugh.

"The homeless camp is just ahead. See where the wall opens up?"

"I doubt they'll be happy to see a giant bear and a giant kitty and the world's biggest and bluest bumblebee," Dekka said. She raised her voice. "Hey, up there in the tunnel. Don't be afraid, we're coming your way, and we're . . ." She stopped, baffled as to how exactly to explain just what they were.

Simone said, "You guys know about the Rockborn Gang?"

No answer from the darkness ahead. Then a child's voice said, "Uh-huh."

"Well, we are Berserker Bear, Lesbokitty, and, um, Blue-bee."

"Lesbokitty," Dekka muttered. "You too?"

Simone said, "You don't like the name? I hadn't even heard it till Cruz mentioned it. Then I assumed you were representing. I could try Lesbee but I don't think it quite works."

Dekka took two more steps then stopped. "You're gay?"

"Yep."

"Huh." Dekka was pretty sure she should say something else, but what? *Lesbians rule? Yay, us? Sisterhood is powerful? #Resist?*

The first of the homeless people leaned into view, a girl of maybe twelve, standing on an inset of the concrete shelf, blinking in the beam of Dekka's flashlight.

"Are you really Lesbokitty?" the girl asked.

Dekka repressed a sigh and said, "That's me. Lesbokitty. Who else would I be? You see a lot of chicks covered in cat fur and snake-dreads down here?"

The girl made a face that eloquently conveyed the fact that she'd seen quite a few strange things down here.

They came to the little encampment. It was on two levels, below and above a concrete support that formed a horizontal shelf four feet up and a dozen feet deep. The residents had erected tents, some actual tents, others homemade from blankets and cardboard boxes. There were wooden crates, clothing hung from a wash line, a plastic five-gallon jug of water, mostly empty. Dekka saw three men, two women, and standing behind the girl who'd spoken, a boy of about the same age.

"Are you guys going after the Bug Man?" the boy asked.

"Yeah," Dekka said. "Do you know anything about him?"

One of the men, surprisingly well-dressed in jeans, a T-shirt, and a yellow down vest, climbed down from the shelf and stood up, knees cracking audibly. He crossed his arms over his chest and said, "We don't need trouble with that dude."

"Yeah, well, he's trouble whether you want it or not," Dekka said. She stuck out her, well, paw, and the man took it like it was a hand. "Dekka Talent. These are Armo and Simone."

"I'm Jason. I'm more or less in charge."

"Less!" came a sardonic shout from the darkness.

"True enough," Jason said, unbothered. He seemed, remarkably, not to be surprised or upset on seeing three monsters emerging from the darkness. "Listen, all we ask is don't bring the trouble back here."

"We'll do our best," Simone said.

"Yeah, okay. You, uh, hungry?" Jason jerked his head back. "We've got some stew on the fire."

"Thank you, that's a kind offer," Simone answered. "But we're on a schedule."

They moved on, but his voice followed them. "I can tell you one thing."

They paused and looked back at him.

"The bug man likes sugar."

"Why do you say that?" Dekka asked.

Jason tilted his head back and forth and stuck his hands in his back pockets. "Well, I know a guy who sometimes gets into a certain bistro kitchen in the terminal after they close. This guy knows the combination to their door lock. He never takes enough to be noticed, just a little of this and a little of that. But this guy I know was in the kitchen when the bug man came in. I, my friend, this guy—"

"We're not the cops, Jason," Dekka interrupted. "We don't care if you take food."

"Well then, I am the guy, of course. I hid, right? Bug Man comes in and there's an open five-pound bag of sugar on the prep table, and he, you know, the bugs, dude, they went crazy for it."

"Interesting. Thanks."

"Got any spare change?"

"No pockets," Dekka pointed out.

They walked on, back into deeper, emptier darkness, and now they moved stealthily, saying nothing. Ahead the darkness became gray. Then, after a curve in the tracks they saw a square of light: the end of the tunnel. And on one side of the tunnel someone was smoking.

"Sentry," Simone whispered.

Dekka pointed at herself. Of the three of them she was the one most able to move without making a sound. Even so the sentry spotted her and yelled, "Who is that? Who's there?"

Dekka heard the unmistakable metallic sound of a pistol being cocked, and she hesitated. If the man started blasting

away down the tunnel he could easily hit one of them. Worse
yet, he might hit the tank she was carrying on her back, and
that would be very bad. She did not want to hurt him, certainly
did not want to kill him, but with the weapons available—her
powers, those of Armo and Simone, and the flamethrowers,
she had limited options.

"Come to me," Dekka said.

"Yeah, right."

"Look, man, I don't want to—"

BAM! BAM!

He fired two shots and Dekka reacted instantly. She raised
her hands. From deep in her throat came a feline growl
ascending to a whine. The man dissolved. Came apart. With
a wet sound like a meat cleaver wielded by Shade at top speed,
the sentry became chunks of bloody meat, half of which
landed on the platform, the rest fell onto the tracks.

"Goddammit," Dekka snarled. "Let's hope Vector didn't
hear the gunshots! Simone, text the group that we're moving!
I'm going in. Count to ten and follow me. That way anyone
with guns will have given themselves away."

A man lay like so much stew meat. She had done that.

Not the time.

As Dekka walked ahead, the tunnel's acoustics allowed
her to overhear Simone saying, "That girl is fierce!"

And Armo, with a laugh, answered, "Yeah, a little bit,
huh?"

CHAPTER 28
No Battle Plan . . .

FRANCIS AND MALIK were near the station, just a block away, lurking in the doorway, waiting for the appointed time. Each was nursing a Starbucks cup and trying to look inconspicuous—not easy on a street with no more than two pedestrians per block. The city was not dead; there were still businesses open, and even the occasional yellow cab.

"I was here—in Manhattan, I mean—when I was ten," Malik said. "My mom had a business thing here. I can't get over how empty it all seems. This whole area should be jammed with people all rushing one direction or the other. Heading to their car or their train, heading home."

"If I lived here, I'd sure get out," Francis said. Immediately she wished she'd kept quiet. She hadn't meant to engage Malik in conversation. Malik intimidated her. In the Over There she had seen the true, unmorphed Malik, and it had evoked horror and pity in equal measure. But still more intimidating to Francis was the fact that Malik was supersmart. Or at least

that's how he seemed to her, not that she'd ever had experience dealing with supersmart people. And, too, all the others
in the group seemed smart to her: smart and brave and good,
none of those being character traits she'd really witnessed in
her life before joining the Rockborn Gang.

Francis had nothing in common with Malik. He came
from Chicago North Shore money, she came from a biker
gang's desert compound. He was educated, a college freshman, and she . . . well, she'd attended school through most
of fifth grade, but for several years since then her mother
had insisted she was homeschooling Francis. Of course that
was total crap. She hadn't been taught math or social studies
or English. What she'd learned with the gang was that the
threat of violence, including rape, was a constant, and that
her mother offered only weak protection. Francis was pretty
sure that was not on any official school curriculum.

"Do you miss your mother?" Malik asked suddenly, and
Francis started guiltily, as if Malik had read her mind. But of
course it was a normal enough question for an older guy to
ask a kid.

Francis shook her head. "Not really. I mean, I'm sorry
she died. I'm not sorry the rest of them died, but she was my
mom, even though she wasn't very good at it."

Malik nodded. "I miss my family. I miss my room. I miss
my guitar collection. I miss going to classes." He took a sip
from his cup, then another. "I miss privacy most of all."

"They're in your head? Those Watcher things?"

"Always. Always, always, always." He said it with a sigh

and a grim smile. "I am never alone. I would give a lot to get them out of my head."

Francis sensed that Malik wasn't talking to her, so much as just talking to pass the time. And as much as she was intimidated by him, she had deeper worries.

"What do you think happens to people if they get left in the Over There?" Francis asked.

Malik met her gaze. "I don't know. But I do know that when I let go of your hand I was scared. Badly scared. As far as I know, you are the only way in and out of that n-dimensional space."

"So maybe they'd just be stuck there forever?"

"Possibly," Malik admitted.

"That's pretty harsh."

"It's hard to stop evil without doing evil yourself." His face registered wry disgust, disgust with himself. "Are you religious?"

She frowned, searching her memory. She'd never been to church, let alone Sunday school. And the only references to the divine she'd ever heard were blasphemous curses. "I don't think so."

"Me neither. It's almost a pity, because people who believe in God, they have someone to ask forgiveness from. If I do something . . . something evil . . . who do I go to to absolve me?"

"Yourself, I guess."

"Yeah. I wonder when this is all over, *if* it's ever all over, I will forgive myself." Then he seemed to shake off the gloomy mood, and in a harder, more decisive voice, said, "Today,

however, Francis, our friends are counting on us. Shade and
Armo and Dekka and Cruz may die unless we do our part."

"Just . . ."

"What?"

"Just don't let me be like those people the bug man hurt.
Don't let me be like that."

Malik stood silent, looking at her until she reluctantly
turned to look him in the eye. "Francis," Malik said in a serious tone, "you need to explain what you mean."

"I mean don't let me live like that. Promise me if that happens you'll, you know . . ."

"You're asking me to kill you?" He said it softly, not as an
accusation. "Jesus, Francis."

"Promise me or I quit," she said with sudden vehemence.
"I'm not a coward, but . . ."

"Of course you're not a coward," Malik said. "You're brave
as hell." He was silent then, but she could practically see
the wheels turning in his head. At last he said, "All right, I
promise."

They had another three minutes to wait—their cue was
two minutes before everyone else—and passed the time in
silence, Francis savoring the fact that Malik thought she was
brave. She'd received very few compliments in her life, none
in recent years unless you counted leers and vulgar suggestions from the bikers.

At last Malik said, "Thirty seconds."

Francis could not speak past a lump in her throat but held
out her hand. Malik took it.

"Now," he said.

The world of right angles and straight lines, the world of up, down, left, right, forward, and back disappeared to be replaced by a lunatic vision of concrete and pipes under the street and gas lines spewing vapor like clouds of red gnats.

And then, all at once, they were in a brightly lit public restroom. The floor was dark terrazzo, the walls white tile. They were between two rows of stainless-steel sinks crowned by round mirrors. Francis saw a thin, frightened-looking girl in the mirrors, and as she looked at her reflection she imagined her skin turning red and black, pustules, seething masses of creepy-crawlies . . . imagined the unspeakable pain. The despair. Imagined her own voice screaming, begging for death . . .

Fear took over then, like a sudden fever. Her mouth was dry. She needed to go to the bathroom. She needed to vomit.

With a thought she could be gone. She could be back out on the street, and from there, who knew how far she could go? A long, long way from here. Mountains, maybe. The Rockies she'd seen from the back of a motorcycle with her arms holding on to the fat waist of her mother's then-lover.

It was very clean up there in the high passes. Air so fresh and pure, freezing-cold water running in streams, ready to drink. How great were her powers? Could she actually blink out into the Over There and pop up by the side of some road in Wyoming? So very much of her wanted to try. Just an experiment—she would transport herself there and . . .

And be alone. No family. No friends. Nowhere to go. But also, no Vector. No possibility of being trapped in a living hell of pain.

Suddenly Francis realized they were not alone. There was a young man just emerging from a toilet stall.

"What the holy hell?" the man yelped.

"Sorry, didn't mean to . . ." Malik started to apologize. Then he and Francis both took a long second look, feeling they'd seen the face somewhere before.

The young man, a handsome boy, began to back toward the exit, but at the same time he was changing. Thick armor like a lobster's shell rippled over a body growing swiftly larger. One arm flattened, like it had been run over by a road leveler, and then stretched and extended. The other hand was forming a heavy pincer.

"Knightmare!" Malik gasped.

"You can't hurt Knightmare!" said Justin DeVeere. "I know your pain blasts don't work against Rockborn."

Francis had worried that when something terrible happened she would hesitate or even run away, had in fact been thinking seriously about it just seconds before. And in the old days she might have done either, hesitate or flee. But Francis had survived Las Vegas, she'd come face-to-face with the Charmer, she'd witnessed the horror at the Triunfo, and she was no longer the little mouse she had once been, at least in her own mind.

"Save me, Knightmare! Malik's hurting me!" Francis cried. She rushed at Knightmare and before the startled and confused Justin DeVeere could react, she had grabbed his hand.

Ten seconds later Francis popped back into 3-D reality.

She and Malik were now alone.

"I guess that works," she said.

"I guess it does."

Cruz was lurking under the Park Avenue overpass, just opposite one of the entrances to Grand Central, in the form of a homeless woman she'd seen. Nothing was less visible in a city than the homeless, who most people just sort of edited out of what they saw. Cruz had given careful thought to just how she would enter Grand Central. Through the door, obviously, but as whom? Looking like what sort of person? Her repertoire of guises was heavily weighted toward female pop stars, with a few policemen and even a passable version of Tom Peaks as Dragon.

But would being morphed protect her against Vector's insect air force? Malik couldn't cause pain to people in morph, but these new laws of physics were either very complex or just random, and either way, Cruz was not at all certain that she would be safe.

If she sashayed in as Beyoncé or Adele, Vector would know immediately that she was Rockborn. She needed a morph that would make Vector hesitate before attacking, and it occurred to her that she might just have an idea. She'd met the person in question, but her visual memory lacked detail, so she pulled out her phone and Googled images. Front. Close-up of face. From the side. And yes, in a crowd shot, there was the view from behind.

Cruz checked the time. She was to enter the station five minutes before H-Hour as they were calling it. Two minutes to morph and another two minutes to figure out how to act the part. Then . . . walk.

Her job was to move in at two minutes before H-Hour, distract Markovic while the others attacked. Distract for as long as she could. And then?

And then Bug Man finds you inside your illusion and you scream and scream and never stop . . .

Cruz bent over suddenly, hands on her knees, feeling as if she'd had the wind knocked out of her. She felt sick with fear. Dying was bad, but she had faced death. What Vector threatened was so much worse. Unendurable.

Walk in. Just walk right in. Into what they all knew was a trap. Just walk in and . . . distract. Keep Vector busy. Wait for the attack. And then?

And then run, Cruz, run.

Run and hide. Get out of the way of the fight that would be won or lost by the others. At least that was some small comfort: she only had to be brave until the fight started. After that she could contribute very little.

So there is an upside to this stupid power of mine.

The time ticked by, each second seeming to last an infinity. Then, she took a deep breath and walked with purposeful stride despite legs that wanted to wobble and collapse, toward the entrance.

The entrance was, strangely, beneath the overpass. She reached the bank of doors, pulled a door open, and stepped inside.

"Hey, you, stop right there!"

Cruz froze.

The challenge came from a pimply teen armed with a baseball bat. He had a partner, a small, angry-looking older woman who seemed to be doing mime, waving her hands either in a parody of martial arts movies or in the delusional belief that she had powers.

"I'm here to speak to Markovic," Cruz said, doing her best to sound like the mayor.

"His name is Vector," the boy said smugly. "And unless you got powers or at least some muscle, he ain't talking to nobody."

"Yeah? Well, you listen to me, you little toady, I am the mayor of this city. I want to speak face-to-face with Vector, and if you send me away he will be mightily pissed at you."

To Cruz's amazement, her improvisation worked. The boy took a step back and muttered, "Okay, but it's on you, lady. If you end up covered in sores screaming for your mommy, don't blame me."

Cruz fought down a wave of nausea and was rescued from collapse by the appearance of the Watchers in her head.

I won't give you the satisfaction!

The boy led the way, baseball bat on his shoulder at a jaunty angle, down a marble ramp beneath too-bright lights in the ceiling. A sort of bridge supporting offices crossed the ramp, and Cruz looked up to see engraved signs indicating the waiting area and pointing an arrow ahead to tracks eleven and twelve.

Walk like a boss, Cruz reminded herself. *You're the mayor.*

At the bottom of the ramp a broad arch opened on the right, marked as the way to the Dining Concourse, and the pull of that safe-sounding space nearly drew her in. There was a Chase Bank, all blue and shiny on her left, but with a plate-glass window starred and needing only another tap to collapse in shards. They passed an information kiosk with posters of shows that would never happen, and discounts on tickets to places she didn't recognize.

Ahead was openness, a sense of a vast space, and then she saw three gigantic windows, each perhaps a hundred feet tall. The setting sun turned many of the panes red or gold, an arrestingly lovely sight, and Cruz wished she could savor it. Cruz had seen the windows—indeed every part of the terminal—in the photos and maps they'd all studied in preparation, but they seemed so much bigger in person, bigger and somehow both beautiful and overawing.

She marched boldly out into the main concourse. To her right was a long row of unoccupied, beaux arts marble ticket windows topped by a long black tote board now filled with cancellations. The entire concourse was framed by massive square pillars, each seeming as tall as a ten-story building. The pillars rose to support a gorgeous arched ceiling painted blue-green and decorated with a schematic of the galaxy. At the far end, beneath the glorious windows, was a balcony grand enough to host a papal visit. It was the most magnificent building Cruz had ever seen.

There were maybe a hundred people scattered over the acres of marble floor, some with weapons ranging from crowbars to guns. All, presumably, in service to Vector.

And then she saw the information booth, a round, ornate gilt kiosk in the middle of the floor. It was topped by a four-sided analog clock, and it was there that Cruz's gaze stopped. For up there, roped to the clock, was a man . . . a woman . . . it was impossible to say. The person tied to the clock was covered in boils and open sores. Their flesh was like some fever dream of Satan, red lesions and putrefying green-and-purple-and-black flesh. A warning. A demonstration for the benefit of Vector's enemies but also, perhaps, his friends.

Someone had taken a cushion and duct-taped it over the victim's mouth so that their pleas and cries for mercy were muffled to groans. They writhed, the poor person, writhed and struggled and with each muffled cry reminded everyone of Vector's power. It was medieval, like some baron or king sticking severed heads on poles to remind anyone passing by who had the power. And who did not.

Then Cruz had a crawling sensation go up her spine. She turned and nearly cried out in shock. There was a matching balcony beneath identical windows just behind her. She had been looking in the wrong direction.

Markovic, *Vector*, had stationed himself on the balcony level at the top of a wide set of stairs that Cruz thought she recognized from the movie *The Untouchables*, so that even as she was trying to quell the panic within and trying to ignore the insistent Watchers, she also was picturing the baby carriage from the movie bouncing in slo-mo down the steps.

Vector hovered in the air far above Cruz, a swirl like all the wasps and flies and locusts in creation, swarming, twisting, separating, and coming back together.

He'll put me next to that poor person on the information booth. And I will scream, scream forever.

She did not have to try too hard to conceal her fear; the mayor would also have been afraid. There was no way to approach what amounted to a malicious, sentient bee swarm, a swarm with terrifying power to inflict unspeakable pain and despair, and not be afraid.

Holy Mary, mother of God . . .

As she walked with measured steps to the base of the stairs, she was watched. Every eye in the place followed her. In addition to the merely human, she saw three people in morphs, one with fantastically wide, completely impractical bat wings.

He probably thinks he's Batman now.

But she also saw two morphed Rockborn who looked more dangerous. One might have been Armo's evil cousin: a shaggy, seven-foot-tall monster with the teeth of a saber-toothed tiger. But it was the other one that worried Cruz more: a person small enough to be a child but whose entire body was covered in iridescent gray scales, so that she looked like a fish that had grown legs and arms. The scary thing was not the scales, but the way the creature hovered in midair as if gravity simply did not apply.

Cruz reached the bottom stair, and Vector said, "You can stop right there, your honor."

"Markovic?" Cruz asked, looking up at him and trying for defiant body language.

"You don't recognize me? I'm hurt. We've met three times that I can recall."

"I'm not here to talk about old times, Markovic." Cruz reminded herself to act tough, like a New York City mayor would. "I'm here to see what it will take to get you to stop."

"No pleasantries, straight into negotiation." Markovic mocked her. "So, what are you offering?"

"I'm not offering, I'm demanding." Her voice was thready, occluded, the words hard to get out. But all the better, it would explain perhaps why she didn't sound quite like the mayor.

Markovic had learned a new and unsettling trick. His component parts swirled together and formed into a rough oval shape. Then holes in the mass appeared where eyes on a face might be. And a slit of a mouth formed below.

"I'm still working on getting my 'lips' to move like I'm talking," Markovic said.

"Impressive," Cruz sneered. Impressive seemed like a mayoral kind of word. Markovic was a massive head floating in the air. He might almost have been a swirl of coins, copper and silver and gold, glittering in the dimming light from the great windows behind him. It was overwhelming, and something about the scene nearly triggered Cruz to cross herself. She was in the Cathedral of Vector, and Vector was playing his part to perfection.

"So, spit it out, your honor. Get the demands and the threats on the table so I can tell you to go pound sand."

"I want you out of my city, Markovic. And I want you to undo the horrors you've caused."

"No." He appeared to be trying to shake his "head" but the result temporarily obscured his "eyes." "Anything else?"

Cruz had a can of high-power insecticide stuck in the back of her trousers, invisible while she was in morph. She calculated the time it would take her to rush that stairwell, pull out her can, and spray.

Spray what? Maybe 5 percent of the bugs? No, that would be suicide to no purpose. The thing before her would not be terrified by a can of Raid. Anyway, she reminded herself, her job was distraction and delay.

Well, if it was about delay . . .

Like a boss, she reminded herself. *Like a boss.*

Cruz put her hands on her hips and took a wide stance. "I am prepared to negotiate."

CHAPTER 29
... Ever Survives Contact With ...

SHADE DARBY WAS already inside the terminal by the time Cruz arrived. So long as you were careful not to let anyone feel your wake, moving at just under Mach 1 made you damned near invisible. Of course, once you slowed down or stopped, you were quite visible, so she had raced up to the balcony opposite Markovic's stage. Markovic was bizarrely framed by an Apple store, all glittery and sleek beneath the huge windows.

From the balcony level Shade sprang up to a narrow walkway behind a stone balustrade, nearly missing her landing because of the weight of the flamethrower. The walkway was just below the edge of the Sistine Chapel of a ceiling and ran all the way down the long sides the concourse. From here she could look across to the pillars framing huge chandeliers above the various arched ramps to the platforms, and by leaning out could quite easily see Markovic.

Beautiful place to die, Shade thought mordantly. It would

look great if they ever made a movie of this day. Unfortunately moving along the high walkway was not easy; it was not
intended for anyone but maintenance workers, and these had
left a fair amount of debris behind. There was nowhere near
enough room or clearance to get up to practically invisible
speed, and at this level, too, there were half-moon windows
against which she did not want to be silhouetted. She had
to basically crawl and drag herself along the walkway, keeping her head below the balustrade, pulling the flamethrower
behind her. And it was thickly dusty, so she had to fight a
raging desire to sneeze.

This part won't look so cool in the movie.

Below and to her left now was the circular information
booth. Shade blinked and stared hard, not at first believing
what she was seeing. A person in agony, with a comically
wrong orange cushion held in place with gray duct tape
wrapped repeatedly around his head.

It will be a pleasure killing you, Vector. A pleasure.

From her position at least fifty feet above and to Vector's right, Shade could see everything, but the acoustics and
Markovic's reedy unnatural voice conspired to make him
inaudible. She had seen the "mayor" walk in and had to stop
herself from racing down to haul her away to safety, until she
remembered that, of course, it was Cruz.

Cruz walking into the jaws of death. She must be terrified.
Shade felt competing waves of emotion: pride in her friend's
courage. Guilt for having made that courage necessary.

Shade retrieved the flamethrower she had set down and

adjusted the straps, then flicked a Bic to light the pilot.

Then she pulled out her phone and waited.

Waited . . .

Until . . . *ding!*

Time.

"Time to light up," Shade said.

Dekka ran flat out up a set of steel steps and found herself in a bewildering maze of pillars wrapped in posters, stainless-steel turnstiles, and signs that told her nothing useful. She'd already become disoriented.

"Dammit!"

Armo caught up to her and stopped short, equally confused, but Simone had been here many times before and led them through ratcheting turnstiles, up another set of stairs, and suddenly they were in a capacious marble-walled hallway. Directly ahead was a posh women's clothing store that looked as if it had been looted. To Dekka's left: natural light. Outside! Outside where she could just keep going. And never stop. Find herself some place far away, a beach in Mexico, a jungle, a swamp, anywhere. Anywhere but here.

She turned her back on the light and followed Simone, who was aloft, gliding ahead just a few feet off the ground. They raced along the ramp, footsteps echoing, past shops with broken windows and scattered goods. Past an optometrist with an unbroken window tagged with a big orange "V" and beside it a cartoon drawing of a hornet with a big stinger and a malicious expression.

"Almost there!" Simone cried. "Left here!"

Dekka and Armo scrabbled to keep their footing on the slick floor, with claws not made for marble. Ahead there was an arch through which Dekka could see the main concourse. And between her and that concourse, two men, one in a military uniform, the other in an expensive business suit, both with submachine guns propped on their hips and expressions of smug superiority on their faces.

Dekka ran straight at them, hands raised. The barrels of the machine pistols rose. And suddenly both men shrieked and fell to their knees and writhed in pain.

Malik.

Thank God!

They burst into the vastness of the main concourse and Dekka spotted Vector—not difficult, he was the only insect cloud, after all—and veered right toward him. She raced past Cruz, headed straight up the steps in great, bounding strides, and without a word, let loose a howl and fired.

Shade saw the sudden incapacitation of every unmorphed human in the concourse below. They dropped and bellowed and writhed, and she could not help but see the similarity to what Vector had done to the poor man or woman roped atop the information kiosk.

But Malik's victims survive.

Mostly.

Shade kicked off from the balustrade and fell at normal gravity speed, almost like slow-motion to her morphed senses.

As she fell, knees bent to take the impact, she squeezed the trigger on her flamethrower and watched a jet of liquid fire stab at the monstrous swarm. Where the napalm reached, the bugs stopped, crisped, and fell like propeller seeds from a maple tree.

They burn! Hah! They burn!

Shade landed hard and staggered under the unusual weight, and barreled ahead trying to keep her feet as she ran beneath Oz the Great and Murderous. She tripped and fell and twisted onto one side so that she could, with some difficulty, fire straight up into Vector. Hot, dead insects rained down on her like ash from a volcano.

Every one of Markovic's human tools was out of commission. Dekka had swung the nozzle of her own flamethrower forward and was firing it with one hand while shredding with the other. Armo was beside her. Three flamethrowers now poured death into Markovic.

It was a massacre. The air stank of gasoline and incinerated insects. Three long light sabers of flame swept back and forth like they were hosing down a car, back and forth, the fiery streams intersecting and sweeping on, and many, many of Markovic's creatures died.

Dekka quickly took stock of her battlefield. Everywhere rose the screams of those Malik had hit. And he was keeping it up, not letting them even think about recovering. Cruz had sensibly backed away and now cringed beside a pillar, still in her mayoral guise.

Armo had reached the top step and aimed his flame straight at the center of the faux face, playing his flame left and right. The air was choking with a smell like burned hair as bugs died in the thousands.

But then Dekka saw Armo stagger. His flamethrower spray veered wildly, barely missing Dekka herself. He skidded down the marble steps on his back, blistering the air above him, but not hitting the small, iridescent, scaly-fleshed creature that had flown into him and jabbed two Tasers into the sides of his head.

Dekka, still flaming and shredding, took in the situation. Armo sprawled down the marble steps, feet higher than head, with the fish-looking creature beating at his face with a crowbar, spraying red blood over white fur. Armo was down, but he was not in real danger. Yet.

"Simone!" Dekka yelled. "On Armo!"

"On it!" came the reassuring shout.

Shade was up and moving, not at her full speed but still at a velocity a cheetah would envy, running in a blurring circle, directing her flame at the insect mass in the middle.

Simone flew to Armo's defense, body-slamming the hovering fish creature, who swung the crowbar at Simone but missed. Simone got a grip on the creature and hauled her away, her tiny wings buzzing furiously, and now those two, one armed with a crowbar and one not, were carrying on a bizarre midair wrestling match, punching and grabbing and grunting.

Armo got up, face and neck red with blood, and aimed

his flamethrower again, but it would not light. The pilot had gone out, and bear claws do not flick lighters.

"Shade!" Dekka roared. "Light Armo!"

Shade instantly saw the problem and zoomed past Armo, trailing her flame over the end of his flamethrower, lighting it again.

We're doing okay. We're doing okay!

Another mutant was charging into the fight, the shaggy monster with the improbable saber-toothed-tiger teeth. It chose Armo as its target and ran straight at him, charging like a bull. Armo stepped nimbly aside but the tiger had anticipated that and twisted to grab Armo and spun him around. Armo's feet got tangled, and he went down with the beast atop him. The creature's teeth should never have been useful; it couldn't possibly open its jaw wide enough . . . but Dekka saw that it had done just that, dislocating its jaw to bring its teeth into play.

Armo swung a frantic paw but missed and left the creature a perfectly exposed upper arm. The saber-toothed jaw widened and the teeth closed, two thick ivory tusks spearing Armo's flesh.

"What the hell?" Armo let out a roar, but he was on his back again, with something as big as he was lying athwart him and Armo's arm shish-kebabed.

They were too entwined for Dekka to take out the beast without hitting Armo. But now Francis was running flat out across the floor, arms pumping, sneakers squeaking, running straight at the beast. Running straight into danger.

Like a stab to the heart, Dekka knew where she'd seen something like that before: a wild, slender girl running heedlessly toward destruction.

Brianna.

All the while Vector burned. The bugs that made him up fell in a rain of shriveled bodies, bouncing like hailstones as they hit marble. And Vector did nothing. He did not threaten, he did not try to escape, he just hung there in the air as the flamethrowers burned on and on.

Shade's flamethrower was the first to run dry. The ring of flame she'd run around Vector sputtered and died.

Francis reached the saber-tooth, tripped and plowed into it, and fell hard, elbows and knees slamming the edges of the stairs. The tiger creature spun around, leaving Armo gushing blood, and reached for Francis. Crawling, then flipping over and scooting back on her rear end, Francis tried to grab the claw that raked inches from her face, but couldn't get a hold.

But the tiger had made a fatal mistake: in chasing Francis, it had exposed its rear.

Dekka aimed carefully for the creature's rear end, farthest from both Francis and Armo. There was a feline howl and a noise like a meat grinder, and the creature's back legs disintegrated. They looked like they'd been jammed into a blender. Flesh and fur, bone and sinew dissolved, fragmented into bloody bits, and now it was the saber-tooth who roared in agony as parts of it slopped down the steps.

The tiger creature crawled away, trying to dig its claws into waxed stone. Blood poured from the stumps of its legs, and it had not yet begun to de-morph, return to its human form.

It doesn't know!

Francis jumped up, her face a furious mask, and avoiding the desperate, flailing claws of the beast, got behind it and grabbed a handful of fur. Seconds later, she was gone, and so was the beast.

Simone was still having all she could handle with the hovering girl. Neither of them was a boxer or martial artist, and a fistfight in midair was by its very nature a hard way to land a serious blow. They careened together into the black tote board, splintering it.

Oh, God, we're winning!

Now, though, Dekka's flamethrower was weakening; the jet that had been a straight line of fire became a downward arc.

"Poison!" Dekka cried, shut down the flame, and shrugged out of her harness.

Cruz and Malik, too, now both armed with insecticide, came at a run, bounding up the stairs trailing clouds of poison from spray cans. Their feet crunched on the dead bugs, lying two inches deep, like the aftermath of a hail storm.

We're actually winning!

So why don't I feel . . .

And then, Dekka knew why she didn't feel victorious. Her folly, her blindness was suddenly horribly clear: Markovic wasn't trying to get away.

Vector had a plan.

CHAPTER 30
. . . The Enemy

SHADE HAD SEEN the same thing as Dekka and had come to the same queasy conclusion. She skidded to a halt and tried to slow her speech enough to be understood.

"Vector's not running!"

"I know," Dekka snapped. "He's not even fighting back!"

Shade spun, taking in the whole room. The downed humans. The fish girl who Simone now had backed against a pillar, thirty feet up. Armo bloody but on his feet again. Francis and Malik spraying aerosol cans like a pothead spraying Febreze before his parents come for a visit. Cruz hugging a pillar, no longer as the mayor but as herself again.

Something was wrong. Something was very wrong.

And then, Shade saw why Markovic had not fled. From inside the long rank of ticket windows they came: an insect horde. They spilled out of the change slots like copper and silver coins flowing from a slot machine jackpot.

Hundreds of thousands.

Millions.

A dozen rivers of insects. Many times what had formed Vector on the balcony.

Their flamethrowers were dry. Their insecticides would be soon. They had nothing left to throw against this wave.

And then, something just as bad. Because as Shade was gaping in shock at Vector's counterattack, something stopped directly before her.

A reflection. Of *herself.*

A perfectly clear reflection standing not ten feet away.

The only observable difference was that Shade had a flamethrower on her back, and her reflection did not. But the flamethrower was empty now, so Shade dropped it.

"Who are you?" Shade demanded, not needing for once to slow her speech.

Her doppelganger grinned and said, "I'm calling myself Mirror."

"Oh, good, another Rockborn nut with delusions of comic-book heroism."

"I sent in an application for a trademark," said the voice identical to Shade's own with an identically ironic tone. "It's going to be tough figuring out an action figure since I always mirror someone else, but, hey, small price to pay, amiright?"

"Why are you backing that piece of shit, Vector?"

"Because you can't bring it all crashing down. And he *can.*"

"And you think it's a good idea to bring everything crashing down?"

Mirror shrugged. "Why not? We could use a revolution."

"Read some history, dude. Revolutions almost never work out well."

"Working out fine for me, so far," Mirror said. "See, I look like you right now, Shade Darby, but I'm not you. I'm not some entitled, rich white girl looking for thrills. In real life I'm a middle-aged paraplegic vet with a hajji bullet lodged in my spine. I haven't walked in nine years. Then I'm in my apartment minding my own business, and bang: the rock!"

"Congratulations. But if you fight for Vector you're going down."

Mirror shrugged and smiled with Shade's own smile. "You can try."

The entire conversation had not lasted five seconds of real time. And from Shade's point of view, it wasn't going well.

In one fluid move Shade snagged the strap of her flame-thrower and whipped it at super speed at a target a few feet to Mirror's left. A normal person would not even have seen the big tank flying, but Mirror did and instinctively leaped away from it.

Just as Shade had expected. She made a single leap, intersected Mirror's path, and hit him like a football blocker, shoulder to gut, carrying all the irresistible momentum her speed afforded. She slammed him into and over the balcony's railing, and together they fell.

But they fell at normal speed, a fall that because it was at the speed set by gravity, would take less than two seconds in real time. Plenty of time for Mirror to punch Shade straight in the nose, sending blood droplets flying. Shade counterpunched almost simultaneously, catching Mirror in the neck. Mirror kicked; Shade shifted to avoid the blow and grabbed a handful of Mirror's hair to pull herself into direct contact with him. Shade grabbed at his throat, hoping to choke him, but she couldn't get purchase. Instead Mirror got his arm around Shade's neck and twisted her around to face away, ready to snap her neck.

They hit the floor. Hard. Hard enough to knock the wind out of Shade and make her head swim, but worse for Mirror, who had landed on the bottom so that he not only slammed into unyielding marble but was pistoned by Shade's momentum.

Shade was up before she could make her lungs work. She knew the smart move was attack, attack, and finish him. But she was feeling dizzy and weak and instead retreated, zooming away to the far side of the concourse.

Cruz saw nothing of Shade's struggle, but she had seen the oncoming swarm and she ran. This was not a fight she could contribute to, and if she stayed she would just be someone the others had to protect when they needed to be protecting themselves.

She ran, and as she ran the fear grew and she ran faster, heedless of where she was going, but suddenly she had a companion, Simone, flying beside her.

"Follow me, Cruz, I have an idea!"

Any idea was better than none, and any company was better than being alone, so Cruz followed the blue girl as they ran/flew beneath the eastern balcony and found themselves in something like a very upscale supermarket. There were stalls of food on both sides, seafood, coffee, gourmet stores with little jars of mustard and balsamic vinegar.

It had all been looted, thrown about, trampled, but Simone kept going until she stopped in midair and pointed.

"There!" Simone cried, pointing at a chocolate shop.

"You want chocolate? Now?"

"Come on! Get some shopping bags. Grab anything sweet."

This involved crawling around and using fingernails to pry stepped on chocolates off the floor.

"What the hell are we doing?" Cruz asked, but Simone had gone behind the smashed glass service counter into the back room. She emerged with two five-pound bags of sugar.

"Forget the chocolate, this will do it! There's more back there, grab it!" And Simone flew, right back toward the concourse.

Cruz, not knowing why but responding to the urgency in Simone's voice, raced past the counter and on a shelf found a third bag of sugar, powdered, as it happened. She ran after Simone, who was already back out in the main concourse.

The bugs came crawling, a tide of bugs. They came flying, like horizontal rain. And Dekka's heart died within her.

They had done nothing to hurt Vector.

Nothing. He had waited patiently until the only weapon that mattered—the flamethrowers—had become useless. He had waited patiently as they burned some small portion of him, and now . . .

A mass of the insects swirled into the air and again formed the "face" of Vector.

"Don't feel bad," Vector crowed. "You did well. You did very well. And I've learned something from this: Don't bother with humans. Malik can take them out too easily."

"Stop it, Markovic!" Dekka yelled, though her voice sounded weak in her ears. "Why are you doing this?"

"Why are you?' Markovic countered. "Join me. Serve me. We can rule the world!"

"Great, a garden-variety megalomaniac." This came from Malik.

The Vector face formed a hideous smile. "Ah, Malik. Do you know, Malik, that I can see through your morph? Eh? Do you know that I see what you really are? My God, the pain you've endured, young man. And for what? You're powerless against me."

"We're still standing, Vector," Malik said defiantly.

Vector moved his millions of wings and his millions of mouthparts and let go a long sigh that seemed to come from everywhere at once. "Last chance, Rockborn Gang. I could have exterminated you long before this, but I wanted to see what you had. I'm impressed. Really, I am. But it's decision time for you. Now or never. Join me, or die."

The insect army was coming on, but at a measured pace, threatening but not yet attacking. Dekka knew that the instant she refused Vector's demand, they would attack, and by sheer weight of numbers would find their way into eyes and ears and nostrils. Maybe their disease organisms would work against Rockborn, or maybe they wouldn't, but either way, they would lose.

The choices now were submit or flee.

And then Simone came zooming in at about ten feet above the floor, zoomed over and through the storm of bugs, holding two big bags and trailing white powder.

"Come on," Markovic said impatiently. "With me or against me? I could use the Rockborn Gang, truly I could."

"We don't get used," Dekka snapped.

There came a whispery laugh. "Then what is to follow is on you."

Then, Vector's insects attacked, swarmed with violent purpose—not in an attack on the Rockborn Gang but in a frenzy of sugar addiction.

"Run!" Simone shouted as she passed. "The sugar won't last long!"

Dekka didn't have to be asked twice. "Shade! Malik! Cruz! Francis! Retreat, retreat, retreat!"

Even now she knew she shouldn't order Armo, but he got the idea anyway, and together they pelted down the stairs. Shade zoomed past carrying Cruz in her arms as Cruz dribbled out another bag of sugar.

"This way!" Simone yelled.

They burst through the doors out onto Forty-Second Street, shaking, panting, all of them terrified. And they kept running until they had put many blocks between themselves and Grand Central Terminal.

It was a mile back to the armory, and they ran the first half of it before slowing down. Panic. There was no better word for it. Dekka was leading a panicked army in full retreat.

Defeat. *Again.*

Simone had caught a brief glance at Detective Williams in the early stages of Vector's terrible attack. She'd had a much closer view of the person roped atop the information booth.

Maybe she could have tried to excuse Williams as a panic move, an instant reaction by her father when he found himself surrounded and under attack. Maybe.

INT: Grand Central Terminal. Evening. Move in on a creature writhing in torment. Slowly we reveal that this is a human being.

But there was no possible rationalization to explain doing horrifying things and then putting them on display. It was barbaric. It was inhuman. No, that wasn't right, it was very human, the worst of humanity. It was very human cruelty. It was human vanity and human contempt and very human greed for power.

It was very human evil.

She flew along now, not wanting to be down with the others where she had to interact, where she had to hear their careful efforts not to offend her by saying something harsh about her father.

Her father: a monster.

Simone felt as if her body was filled with a poison, as if she were contaminated, as if she were one of those touched by Vector's revenge. His acts had rubbed off on her. How could they not? It was his DNA as well as her mother's that had designed and built Simone in utero. She was his child. She was the child of a man she had once admired, relied on . . . loved. She had known her father was a predator, but had assumed that his greed extended only to money. But now . . .

Her strength failed, and she had to drop to her feet and lean against a stoplight post as stifling rage built inside her.

Montage: life events where Markovic had been present. Cut to Simone crying.

Simone was breathing in sobs, sharp noises on each inhalation, the opening notes in a symphony of despair and self-loathing. She felt a hand on her arm, and through eyes she only now realized had filled with tears, she saw Dekka.

Simone tried to talk, but the words were strangled in her throat.

"It's hard," Dekka said. "You have to give it time."

"Hard?" Simone managed to ask, her mouth in an ugly sneer.

"Yes. It's hard seeing bad things. It's in your head, and there's nothing you can do to stop it being engraved on your memory."

"Jesus Christ, he's my father! *He's my father!* That . . . that . . . filthy, murdering . . . he's my father! What he did . . ." A sound came from her that was almost a laugh, a tumble of words tinged with hysteria. "That bastard! How did I . . . God damn him, I hope there's a God, I hope that's real, I hope hell is real, I hope he burns. . . ."

Without willing it, Simone found herself wrapped in

strong arms. Human arms: Dekka de-morphed, a big black girl who had never struck Simone as a hugger. And to her own amazement, Simone buried her face in the crook of Dekka's neck and heaved sobs.

After a while Dekka gently disengaged and started Simone moving again. "We have to keep moving. He may come after us."

"Ask me again," Simone said, her voice like gravel.

"I don't know what—"

"Ask me again," Simone said, voice now savage. "Ask me again if I'll kill him. Go on, ask me again!"

Dekka did not.

Fade to black.

CHAPTER 31
Run Away! Run Away!

BY THE TIME they reached the armory, Dekka had already begun to plan, but this was a plan for defeat, for withdrawal. They could get away from New York. They could find some distant place, some cabin in some faraway, frozen wilderness. Maybe they could regroup there. Maybe they could attract more Rockborn. Maybe somehow they and the government together . . .

She had comforted Simone as a way of comforting herself. She had lost. They'd been beaten, and badly. She, Dekka Talent, had led them to a second defeat.

They filed into the armory, and Dekka began handing out orders. "Shade? Check the doors and windows, would you? And where's Edilio?"

A door opened and Edilio appeared as if by magic. There was someone with him.

Someone . . .

Dekka's heart stopped.

"Sam?"

"Afraid so," Sam said, smiling.

Dekka felt the last of her strength dissolve. Her knees almost buckled, and then Sam was there with his arms around her, as she had embraced Simone.

"Oh, God, Sam." She pulled away, brushing furiously at tears. "Sam, this is Cruz, and Malik. Francis. You know Armo. And Shade . . ." She looked around, momentarily forgetting that she'd sent Shade off on an errand. "And this is Simone Mar—"

"Simone," the girl interrupted. "Just Simone."

Shade's errand had been one she could carry out in mere seconds, and she vibrated to a stop and began to de-morph.

"Hi, I'm—"

"I know who you are," Shade said, in the kind of voice you might use on being introduced to your sports hero or a saint. "I'm Shade Darby."

"Edilio," Dekka said, "we need more flamethrowers; they're all that works. Sam. Oh, God, Sam, am I glad to see you."

"Can you bring me up to speed?"

They were in the middle of the great hall of the armory, a space that seemed almost cozy now compared to Grand Central. All the chairs were against a wall, so they sat down on the floor, cross-legged, in a circle.

And Dekka narrated. She told Sam about Vector. About the New Jersey killing field. About their first failed effort to take him down. And with bitter words she detailed her own failure to prevail at Grand Central.

Sam waited quietly through it all. From time to time, he nodded or raised an eyebrow, but he seemed to understand that Dekka needed to make this public confession.

When Dekka was done, no one spoke for a while. Even Shade had nothing to say, quiet for once in the presence of the boy, the man, who she had studied for years.

Finally, Sam said, "Tell me something, Dekka. How dangerous is Vector compared to Caine?"

Dekka frowned, confused. Was Sam so out of it he still thought this was the FAYZ? "Caine was a bastard, but his power was limited. He could never have done what Vector did at City Hall. Have you seen any of the video? He—"

"Right," Sam interrupted. "That wasn't just terrible, it was sadistic, cruel. It was meant to terrorize. Caine was a bad person, a very bad person, but no, he would not be capable of that, even if he'd had the power. But Drake? Drake would be every bit as vicious."

Dekka nodded, still confused and even worried that Sam was making a fool of himself.

"Yes, Drake was evil. Sadistic and cruel. As morally sick as Vector, but with far less power."

"So?" Dekka cried, unable to contain herself any longer.

"So," Sam said. "Did I stop Caine?"

"What?"

"I battled Caine many times. Did I take him down?"

"Not in the end, but—"

"And Drake. Did I stop Drake?"

"You tried. It wasn't your fault that—"

Sam held up a hand, silencing her. "I failed, Dekka. Again and again and again, I failed. I tried. I tried like hell—you *know* I tried; of all people you know that. But I failed." Dekka was looking down, so Sam leaned forward and raised her chin. "Hey, Dekka: I failed. The big hero of the FAYZ? I failed."

"But you . . ." Dekka's lower lip quivered. "You . . ."

Sam nodded. "Yeah, I tried. Just like you're trying. But, Dekka, my love, you are up against so much more. The stakes are so much higher. The people fighting you are so much more powerful."

Five minutes earlier, Dekka would have sworn she wouldn't cry. She'd have said she was way past that kind of emotion. But now she felt her throat convulsing with sobs and knew tears were rolling down her cheeks.

"What you've done is amazing, Dekka. If you were a soldier they'd be pinning medals on you. Listen to me. If this is you measuring yourself against me, stop it. Just stop it right now." He swept his arm around, indicating the group, the six scared, defeated faces. "The only thing you're failing at is not pushing everything aside and remembering that you are still the leader of the Rockborn Gang."

Dekka's eyes widened in alarm. "But you're here now!"

"Yes, I am," Sam said. "And I am offering you my services, such as they are." He leaned in close again to make eye contact, though Dekka was again looking at the floor. "Now, I'm going to do for you what you so often did for me. I'm going to tell you to drop the self-pity right the hell now, because people need you. So you are going to turn off the waterworks, and you are going to pick your head up, and you're going to show me that defiant, screw-all-of-you, scary Dekka look I know so well."

Dekka wiped her tears again. She stifled the sobs, and the constrictions in her throat came once, and once again, and stopped. She took a deep, shaky breath that was steadier when she let it go.

It's not because I owe these people, though I do, Dekka thought. *But I'll be damned if I'll sit here and cry in front of Sam.*

After a long minute, Dekka said, "Is Astrid here with you?"

"No, she had other things to do."

Dekka was alarmed. "But, Drake!"

Sam fished out his phone, unlocked it, and swiped a few times. Then he turned the phone around to show Dekka his texts. The most recent was from Astrid.

All taken care of. Love you.

"Yeah, see the thing is, someone mailed Astrid a dose of the rock." He arched a brow. "I can't imagine who'd have done something like that."

"Is she . . ."

"Oh, Astrid is very scary now."

Dekka managed a smile. "Astrid was always scary." She met his gaze, unflinching now. "I don't suppose the anonymous person who FedExed you one dose of the rock may have included two doses?"

"Interesting that you'd mention FedEx, because I don't believe I mentioned how the rock got to us." He winked. "How the *two* doses of rock got to us."

"I wanted so much to keep you out of this," Dekka said.

"And yet, here I am." He looked around at the others. "Here we all are."

A line from Tolkien came to Dekka. *I am glad you are here with me. Here at the end of all things, Sam.* But she did not say it aloud.

"Now, if you'll have me, I will be the newest recruit to the Rockborn Gang."

Dekka laughed. "Well, depends on what you have to offer, young man."

A slow grin spread across Sam's face. "Oh, you're going to like this. It was a strangely fitting gift from the rock."

CHAPTER 32

Domes

DOMES HAD PLAYED an outsized role in four of the lives of the newly enlarged Rockborn Gang.

Shade Darby had been sitting next to the PBA dome, the FAYZ. She'd been a kid of thirteen whose mother had been hired to add her own scientific expertise to the attempt to understand the dome.

Shade could still remember the first time she'd seen it on the news. On video the dome looked like a nothingness, an opaque, nonreflective, vaguely gray-colored dome, a perfect half of a sphere twenty miles in diameter. There had been ground-level video and helicopter video and drone video up on YouTube, and she had seen as much of it as her Google-fu would bring her.

Then she had seen it in person. No video could begin to convey the sheer size of the thing. Up close it wasn't a dome; it was a gray wall, a gray wall that went up and up until it curved away many miles in the air, reaching so high that airliners had to divert to avoid smashing into it. It extended from horizon to horizon, incredibly large, dwarfing anything ever built by *Homo sapiens.*

The only way to show just how big it was on a video was to go to satellite imagery. From near-Earth orbit, it was a giant gray punctuation mark. It lay over land and sea, unperturbed by either. It was unnatural in every way, in the sense of something unfamiliar, in the sense of something too perfectly shaped to be a part of any natural landscape. Unnatural in that its existence defied the laws of physics. It was impossible; that was the unique thing about the dome, the thing that made it different and, yes, more interesting than anything anywhere, anytime, ever.

It was impossible.

And yet . . .

Shade had spent a couple of weeks with her mother in the army-slash-CHP-slash-media tent city that grew up where the northbound 101 came to an abrupt stop. Another few seconds on the 101 would have taken you to Perdido Beach, but Perdido Beach had lived up to its name. It was lost. It was gone. It had been covered by the dome.

Shade had gone back to Chicago for a while to attend a math camp that had entirely lost her interest. Then, back to the tent, truck, and trailer village to find everything changed. The dome had become transparent, completely invisible, and yet, just as impenetrable. What had been a blank wall became a sort of aquarium, or living diorama. And for the first time the world's questions about the mystery, some of them at least, were beginning to be answered.

No, the dome was not solid like a big ball bearing.

Yes, there were people inside. Children, teenagers, all younger than fifteen at the start, 332 of them—minus some deaths.

Minus quite a few deaths.

Shade had never told Dekka, but she had seen Brianna, in person. The Breeze had been within ten feet of her. Brianna was in some ways Shade's counterpart, another girl with extraordinary speed, but within the dome the rules had been different. Brianna had run as Brianna. No Watchers in her head. No protective insectoid morph. Brianna came to the edge of the FAYZ, to stand almost within arm's reach. She would take questions written for her on posters and iPads and scrawl the answers on pieces of wallboard or in one case the white shell of a clothes dryer. Paper, obviously, was in short supply in the FAYZ.

So was soap. Clothing. Food. The kids huddled against their side of the barrier looked like abused puppies in a shelter: scared, wary, alert. Damaged.

The only thing not in short supply were weapons. So many weapons. Crowbars, sledgehammers, baseball bats with spikes driven through them, the steel bars of hand weights, maple table legs, knives, machetes, and guns. Far too many guns.

Shade had seen Brianna, and she had seen Caine, the infamous Caine, the self-proclaimed king of the FAYZ. He was a handsome devil, made more handsome in memory because he'd been played in the movie by an actor who was full-on Hollywood handsome.

She'd seen Gaia, too. Gaia who had every power. Gaia, the mad child, the creature from videos with hundreds of millions of hits, especially the one where she had ripped a person's arm off and . . .

"They found a way to stop her," Shade muttered. "Is Vector that much more dangerous?"

It had been meant as a rhetorical question, but now she considered it seriously. Gaia had been a murderous, monstrous creature, but though she'd had designs on a life outside of the FAYZ, she had been taken down with the dome.

Level One, some part of Shade's mind said.

We are now on Level Two of this insane game. With how many more levels to go? And no spare lives?

"I'm tired of this game," Shade said to no one.

Dekka had first seen the dome when she stepped out of Coates Academy and snuck into the gloomy pine forest to smoke a joint.

Coates was a school, but not a normal one. Coates was for the disappointing children of people who had means. Dekka's family didn't have money, but Coates had a scholarship for diversity, and Dekka—black and LGBTQ—was a twofer.

The way she had disappointed her parents had been by being herself. She had come out and made a mess of it, saying things wrong, words that did not form the way she'd have liked. Dekka had been arguing with her parents about something unrelated when she had blurted out the truth. Her mother had been going on about Dekka's obligation to be able to make her own way in the world, to find a husband who would love her and with whom she would have babies. And Dekka—who had never been the most tolerant of human beings, by her own admission—said, "If I marry anyone, it'll be a girl, Mom, and if there's a grandchild in your future it'll be adopted."

Not, perhaps, her most diplomatic moment. She'd been just about to turn fourteen, an age when parents still harbor the illusion that their child is malleable, shapeable. Her parents dismissed the whole "lesbian thing," and from there things went right downhill, her parents being stiff-necked evangelical Christians and Dekka being rebellious, sullen, increasingly irreligious, and above all, worst of all, though her parents would never quite admit it, a lesbian.

So much anger and pain, and I wasn't even getting laid. Boy or girl.

They'd found out about the diversity scholarship at Coates, and Coates had found they had an honest-to-God black lesbian (ding-ding-ding!) and Dekka had been packed off, not even very upset, because after all, could it really be worse than home?

It could be.

It was clear from the start that Coates was not run by the administrators or the teachers, but by an intelligent, attractive, charismatic boy named Caine Soren. Caine ruled Coates like a gang boss. His chief enforcer was a boy who was also attractive, but the kind of attraction you might feel for a cobra. Drake was mesmerizing. It was hard to look away from him, and when you did you could feel his eyes following you.

Caine was a rotten bastard. Drake was evil. And between them they ruled Coates and made Dekka's life a misery.

And then had come the dome.

Dekka had been rescued from Coates, that's the way she saw it. Rescued by Sam Temple, and not just rescued but raised to high status, made over as Sam's strong right arm.

Dekka had suffered, but she had suffered for a cause. Sam had never cared whether she liked boys or girls; he'd cared whether he could count on her in a fight. And he could, her and Breeze and Edilio. And yes, Astrid, though Astrid always played games within games. And every nasty fight, every vicious battle, had been fought to keep the kids in the FAYZ alive and as free as they could be. Dekka had been given responsibility . . . no, she corrected mentally, she had *taken* responsibility. She had picked a side and done what needed to be done.

Isn't that what you're doing now?

Yes, she had taken this responsibility on, but she would have gladly given way for Sam, once he appeared in New York. Dekka had been happier as his lieutenant than as a general.

It's what these stars on my shoulders are about—sending good young people into harm's way.

And losing. Getting beaten. Feeling helpless and inadequate and overwhelmed. Watching people die or live in agony and being able to do nothing about it. All of that.

In a million years it never would have occurred to Dekka that she'd end up feeling sympathy for a four-star general. Or that she would try to step aside to make room for a white boy. The truth was that Peter Parker's uncle was only half right. With great power came great responsibility; and with great responsibility came a weight so massive it threatened to crush you.

But I'm not crushed. Not quite.

Not yet.

Sam Temple's life had also been shaped by a dome. He'd been an average student in a mediocre school whose only real passion in life involved getting up at four thirty in the morning, carrying his board down to the beach, stuffing himself into a clammy wet suit, and paddling out into freezing water to wait and wait for the opportunity to ride a wave for thirty seconds.

He'd had no plans. He'd had no real goals aside from the vague notion of a career that would leave him plenty of time to surf. He'd had no girlfriend and only one real male friend, Quinn Gaither.

When the FAYZ had come, Sam had tried to avoid taking any sort of leadership role. But Sam had an event in his past that had been largely forgotten but that took on new saliency when every single adult, every parent, teacher, shopkeeper, doctor, and cop was suddenly . . . *poof!* Gone. Sam had once saved a school bus full of kids when the driver had suffered a heart attack. He'd never thought it was a big deal, and neither did anyone else once the excitement of the moment wore off.

But in a world suddenly without responsible leaders of any sort, a world falling under the sway of a sociopath and his psychopath enforcer, people had looked to Sam.

Slowly, reluctantly, Sam had become a leader. He'd made life-or-death decisions on an almost daily basis. He had been attacked, hurt, hated, mistrusted. But also admired and relied upon and even loved. And he had stored up enough nightmares to last ten men ten lifetimes each.

Then, suddenly: no dome. Sam the reluctant hero had been transformed into Sam the fall guy and then Sam the media hero, and Sam the guy in a book his wife wrote, and Sam the actor who played Sam in the movie. He still had no goals and no plans. He intended to go to college eventually. He intended to get a job and a career and live the rest of his life—yes, in the shadow of his past, but hopefully with a brighter path ahead.

He had started drinking. He was a happy drunk, never a bully or a bore, but when he drank, the darkness he'd experienced came seeping out of the mental box he'd stuffed it all in. He cried when he got drunk, then got drunker to numb the memories.

With the help of therapy and Astrid, his rock, he'd gotten the drinking under control. For now. No alcoholic—and he admitted that's what he was—could ever be completely safe from a sudden stumble and a long, long fall.

But not today.

Now everything he'd escaped four years earlier was back. The threat was bigger. The horror even deeper. The possibility of survival even lower.

And the thing was, he was happier than he'd been in a long while. Especially knowing—though with a twinge of guilt—that the bulk of the weight was on Dekka's shoulders now.

He was back! School Bus Sam, who became Sam Temple, the hero of the FAYZ, had acquired a new power, and surfing would once again be delayed.

Sam Temple 3.0.

Was a part of him itching to be in charge? Yes, but it was a very, very small part. It was someone else's turn.

He looked down at hands that once had fired killing beams of light. He'd half expected the rock to regift him that same power, but, as always, the rock seemed to have its own agenda.

Now, sitting apart from the others in a dark corner of the armory, Sam began to change, subtly. He became shiny, like he'd been run through a car wash and opted for the clearcoat. Shiny, and slick, and hard to the touch. He had taken a selfie and studied the effect. He looked like himself, yes, but himself dipped in clear plastic.

He raised his right hand, palm facing up. And a transparent sphere appeared, just six inches across and hovering like a soap bubble waiting for a breeze. With his left hand he flicked the sphere and felt its solidity.

Not a soap bubble.

A dome.

"Twitter is going to call me Bubble Boy," Sam muttered. "Well. There are worse things."

Edilio was the fourth person whose life had been shaped by a dome. He'd been a nobody at school, an undocumented Honduran immigrant—an illegal, many people would say. He'd come to America as a small child with his parents. He had only vague memories of an interminable trip, most of it on foot, walking and walking by the sides of dusty roads, hot, thirsty, and boring, the whole length of Mexico. Weeks of sleeping in fields and under bridges.

He had no memory at all of being taken across the border from Mexico to the US because he'd been delirious with a fever at the time, most likely, his mother said, some kind of waterborne disease.

They had moved around various migrant labor camps, young Edilio sitting at the edge of a field under a wide hat, or sometimes under a sun shade or umbrella. He'd sat for hours watching stooped figures, including those of his mother and father, picking strawberries within sight of million-dollar homes. Later, when he was able, he had helped with the work. Mostly the Escobar family picked strawberries and grapes, occasionally pitching in on other physical labor, helping to move the mountains of oak barrels at a winery, or hauling bales of hay down out of lofts.

But then his father had gotten lucky. One of the farmers he had worked for had a smaller plot of land, farther up the coast, mostly table grapes but some sauvignon blanc as well, from which they made a good white wine. The farmer needed a foreman to handle the seasonal labor, men and women, families like the Escobars. And from that had come a degree of stability. Edilio had been able to enroll in an actual school, not one of the traveling camp schools.

He had not been happy at Perdido Beach High School, but neither had he been unhappy. He'd done enough miserable work by then that homework didn't seem like much of a burden. His mother did piecework, mending or tailoring clothing. And she had a dull job handmaking tortillas for a local Mexican restaurant looking for authenticity, never mind that his mother was Honduran, not Mexican.

As for Edilio, he'd picked up work on the side, day-labor jobs, the kind that involved standing in the parking lot of Home Depot waiting for some person in a pickup truck to point a finger.

When the FAYZ came, Edilio had been a nobody, an outsider, a poor kid in a middle-class school, an undocumented immigrant in a country turning hostile to his kind. Then he had been swept into Sam Temple's orbit, and from that point on, they had been inseparable, even as Quinn became jealous and tried to undermine Edilio's friendship with Sam. They'd stuck together because Edilio was used to being told what to do, and at first that had been what Sam needed. But things had begun to change quickly, and the relationship that had been one of white local boy and brown-faced outsider, a relationship where Sam had a certain unspoken ascendancy, had evolved. Sam had come to rely more and more on Edilio. Edilio was consulted on everything, and increasingly, he spoke up. And almost to his own surprise, he had useful things to say.

Then, as things grew ever more dire, Sam had given Edilio the job of training recruits to serve as a security force, a tiny army. But a tiny army with real guns and real responsibilities. Edilio had been in firefights like something from a war or maybe the streets of Baltimore. Except that Edilio's firefights might or might not involve guns, but almost always involved Sam's blinding laser light and Caine's telekinetic whirlwind.

Edilio had come to see himself as a professional, almost. A soldier of sorts. An advisor. An organizer. In the end Astrid had said, "Edilio, you may be the one person to get out of here with your soul intact." Astrid had lost her faith; Edilio had not.

In the movie Edilio's role was smaller than it had been in real life. For a while he'd been famous, but he was still undocumented, and fame did not work well for people who could not produce a green card. Many promises had been made, but in the end nothing had come of it. ICE had picked up his mother. His father had passed a year earlier from lung cancer.

Rest in peace, you good man and wonderful father.

Edilio couldn't let his mother be hauled off alone to a country she hadn't seen in more than a decade, so he went with her. With financial support from Albert, Edilio settled her in, rented her a small apartment where she spent her days playing cards with an elderly couple who lived next door.

Edilio had gone off on his own, finding the job as a desk clerk in La Ceiba. He was on the management track, or so they assured him. He even had a boyfriend named Alfredo, although he preferred to be called Al. Edilio did not expect he would ever see him again.

He'd known as soon as the earliest word of the rock came down from the States that the peaceful interlude of his life was coming to an end. While the world wondered what could possibly have caused monsters to emerge, Edilio had known. The gaiaphage, they'd called it in the FAYZ: the malicious alien will that rose from the first ASO, the one that had taken the shorter orbital path to intersect with Earth. Edilio had known that terror was coming, a terror no radical group could begin to equal. The FAYZ had escaped the dome. The FAYZ was the whole planet now. He hadn't even been very surprised when the National Police had given him five minutes to pack a bag before hustling him off to a waiting plane.

And now, it was all back. The fear. The unsettling weirdness. The sense of creeping evil, of doom waiting just out of sight. And on this night, in a dark rail yard in New Jersey, the evil felt very, very close.

"I need some signatures from you," the Marine Corps captain said, turning his clipboard toward Edilio.

Edilio signed.

The captain looked apologetic. "And there's this. It's a confidentiality agreement. Basically if you ever tell anyone about what we're doing, you could be arrested and go to prison for a long time."

Edilio laughed. "Or you could just deport me again."

The captain let that pass. "It's loaded in your truck. It's crated and padded and strapped down, but I'm sure I don't need to tell you to drive carefully. Sarin is . . . well, you know,

it's very nasty stuff. If you are exposed you should immediately administer the atropine pen. You'll have muscle spasms
and feel like shit, but you won't die. Without atropine, you're
a dead man."

Edilio glanced at the pickup truck he had "liberated."
Malik was in the driver's seat. He'd come along for protection and company, and Edilio was grateful. This dark deed
on this dark night was made a bit easier by having someone
else with him.

"Don't worry, we will be all kinds of careful," Edilio said
to the captain. He finished signing and handed the clipboard
back.

"Listen, I uh . . ." The soldier looked down at the oily gravel
under his feet. "I've been in the shit. Two tours. I've seen the
video of Vector's victims. And I just wanted to say that you're
about the bravest son of a bitch I've ever met. I just wanted
to say what many people have said to me: thank you for your
service."

Despite himself, Edilio was touched. "Captain, I'm just
hoping not to screw up."

The captain grinned ruefully. "Mr. Escobar, that is the
fondest hope of every poor son of a bitch who has ever walked
toward the sound of guns: 'Please, God, just don't let me
screw up.'"

CHAPTER 33
Plans and Plots and Stolen Kisses

THEY HAD ABANDONED the armory and the brownstone. Both would be known to Vector, if not already, then soon enough.

Edilio, with some assistance from Simone, found them an empty apartment ten blocks away. It wasn't hard finding abandoned property; the city was half-empty already, and the only traffic still on the streets was heading away. Video of the horrors at City Hall and One Police Plaza and the Federal Building had broken the city's courage. It was one thing to face a Knightmare or a Napalm; they could be fought, and the worst consequence of losing was death.

Death was far better than what Vector threatened.

The memory of the pus-draining, rot-reeking, diseased, agonized Williams was fresh in Dekka's mind. The memory of reducing him to hamburger . . . that was fresh, too.

The new apartment faced Central Park, just a few blocks from the Markovic home, though somewhat less luxurious.

It was an anonymous location, a well-furnished apartment that had belonged to an elderly couple who, should they suddenly decide to come home, would be rather shocked by what they saw.

Everyone was in morph. No one was human. They thought, hoped, *prayed* that Vector's disease-bearing minions couldn't infect a morph. And they were very damned sure they didn't want to take the chance of remaining vulnerably human.

The Watchers were having a field day, access to all of them, all the time, eight little nodes through which they could watch. Eight minds for them to occupy.

Edilio did not have a morph and refused any suggestion that he consider taking the rock. He did, however, insist on what they each had agreed to: if any one of them was taken by Vector, the others would end their suffering in the only way possible: they would be killed. Killed, Dekka knew, by *her* if she was uninfested herself. A suicide pact. Or was it a murder-suicide pact? Yes, she supposed that's what it was.

That at least is not something Sam ever had to face.

Simone and Shade had made regular scouting trips to Grand Central to see whether Vector would emerge to hunt them down. But Vector showed no signs of launching his insect army for the final blow. Yet. Possibly their move had left him with a cold trail, and he didn't know where they were. Or possibly he no longer considered them a threat.

Yet.

"I've restocked with flamethrowers, but these are even more primitive than the first round," Edilio said. "I piled them in that closet there. But the real weapon we have is in the truck down in the parking garage."

"That's a hell of an object to have stuck in the back of a pickup truck," Simone said.

"Better than bringing it in here," Sam pointed out.

They were in the unfamiliar living room, Dekka feeling like a burglar. *Just another felony—what else is new?* Two sofas faced each other across a dark carved Moroccan-style coffee table piled with food. They sat looking like costumed extras from a *Star Wars* movie taking a lunch break on the set.

Cruz and Armo were off raiding adjacent unoccupied apartments and had already rounded up an impressive larder of cookies, crackers, cheese, hummus, canned beans, and soup before deciding to continue their explorations rather than sit in on yet another planning session.

So the plan for round three with Vector was hatched between Dekka, Shade, Malik, Simone, and Sam, with Edilio confining himself to questions of logistics. Francis napped in one of the bedrooms.

"Vector hasn't moved yet," Shade said, forcing herself to slow her speech to be understood. "We have to hit him fast, before he makes plans."

Dekka felt a rush of wind, and Shade was gone. Seconds later a sandwich appeared on the table, minus one bite.

"We're relying a lot on Francis," Malik pointed out. He was the one most used to the irritant of the Watchers and was the least agitated now. Everyone else who had morphed, especially Sam, for whom this was a new feature of life, seemed distracted and on edge.

"Yes, we are relying a lot on Francis," Dekka agreed. "You have a better way?"

Malik thought hard, then admitted, "No. I don't. Not yet, anyway."

Sam said, "I'm new to this Watcher thing. Are we sure they don't pass information along to Vector?"

"They may," Malik said. "We don't see any evidence of it yet, but it could happen. They seem more like lurkers watching a game rather than active players."

"I worry about that Mirror person," Shade said too rapidly. "He says he can mimic any Rockborn, which would mean he could be me, or Malik, or you, Dekka."

"Who's going to jump in the bubble?" Malik asked. "I would, but I'm not strong enough. It will have to be Armo or you, Dekka."

"I'll do it," Dekka said.

"Maybe you shouldn't be the one," Sam suggested. "You're the general; you should be out of the action."

"Oh? Like you always were?" Dekka retorted drolly.

"You're strong in morph, Dekka, but that gas shell is more than two and a half feet long and weighs just about a hundred pounds," Sam interjected. "Is Armo stronger than you?"

"This could be a suicide mission," Dekka said. "I'm not sending Armo. I'll manage." She ended with a hand chop signaling the matter was decided. No one argued further.

"So, let's walk through it again," Malik said. "I do my

thing, just a one-second blast, just enough to scare the hell out of any unmorphed humans with Vector. Shade zooms in and issues the warning. Hopefully any humans in there make a run for it. Then Sam does his thing. Francis takes Dekka and our new toy. In and out. The timer is set for six minutes. Bang."

Dekka nodded. Vector Plan #3. Maybe the third time would be the charm.

Or maybe this was the last round. She closed her eyes and saw Williams, except now it was her, Dekka, her flesh erupting . . . her tongue swelling . . . her throat torn by screams of pain.

Dekka. Herself. Begging for death.

Two defeats. A third would very likely be the end of the Rockborn Gang.

"Oh, my God. That's an entire red velvet cake." Cruz stared at the object, all covered in white frosting, kept fresh beneath a glass bell jar. Untouched perfection.

"We should bring that back for everyone to share," Armo said doubtfully. "Right?"

"Well," Cruz said, "I am a little worried that it might be stale or taste bad. So we should probably sample it first."

They were an extremely unlikely pair of burglars. A seven-foot-tall mass of muscle and white fur, and Jennifer Lawrence, Cruz's morph of choice at the moment. JLaw seemed like a good choice; after all, what red-blooded male didn't like her? But Armo had not seemed terribly impressed, and of course why would he? He knew who Cruz really was, and she was not Jennifer Lawrence.

"Let me get plates and forks."

"I can't eat with a fork," Armo admitted, holding up one of his big claw-tipped paws. He grinned and gleefully stuck his rail-spike black claws into the cake at roughly the middle and scooped a huge piece into his other paw and began eating.

"Yeah, okay, I can do that, too, if we're going all barbarian." Cruz dug JLaw's hand into the cake and scooped out a smaller piece, red crumbs falling to the floor, icing smearing her fingers. She licked the icing one finger at a time and looked up to see Armo watching her. Then she laughed because a cupcake-sized chunk had fallen to his chest and was now sliding down his white fur.

Cruz snagged the escaping piece, and without thinking about it, really thinking only that Armo's claws were not much good for delicate work, she fed the cake into his muzzle.

He looked at her through big gold-and-black eyes and licked her hand with his bluish-pink bear tongue. And then, time just seemed to stop. Cruz knew time had stopped because she was no longer breathing. He towered over her and she looked up at him.

Then he said, "I would kind of like to kiss you someday."

And that did not help Cruz's breathing issue at all.

"I mean, not now because, you know: bear." Armo sounded flustered, as if thinking he'd embarrassed her. "I don't quite have lips right now. Also you're not you."

A squeaky laugh came from her. "I should be JLaw all the time. I get the nicest compliments."

"What's JLaw?"

"Jennifer Lawrence. JLaw. The actor. You know. She was in *Silver Linings Playbook*." Nothing. "Or *American Hustle*." Still nothing. "She was in *The Hunger Games*."

"Oh, yeah, I saw that." He nodded his big shaggy head. "That girl. She had a bow and arrow."

"That's her. I thought maybe you'd . . ." She shrugged, not quite sure how to finish that thought. She'd thought what, exactly? That he would be attracted to a movie star and forget that she was really just Cruz? She finished lamely. "She's gorgeous. You know, like you."

Dark eyes fringed in white fur contemplated her. "I don't like when you do that."

"Do what?"

"Act like you have to hide, or be some famous movie star."

Cruz sighed shakily and looked away. "It's just, I know what I look like to people. I look like a guy trying to pass himself off as a girl. I mean, in my head . . . But what's in my head isn't what people see."

"I'm not people."

"I mean, when this is all over I can start on the hormones and then, you know, maybe, if I have the money, I can do reassignment surgery. Then I'll look more like how I feel inside my head."

He waved all that away. "Whatever, that's up to you. I

don't tell anyone what to do."

"But what if you could?" Cruz blurted. "I mean, if somehow it was up to you?"

"Up to me?" He scooped up what was left of the cake—no one else was getting any part of it—and thought about it. "Look, you're Cruz. Right? I mean, that's who I know, I don't know some other person you might be, or I don't know ... it's all confusing."

Cruz grinned. "Yeah, I know. It's confusing for me too."

They fell silent for a while as Armo licked up icing. Then he said, "We could try."

"Try what?"

"There are no Bug Man bugs here. We could stop being Berserker Bear and Transit. Just for a minute, but you can't tell Dekka because she'd give me that look of hers."

"You want to de-morph."

"For a minute." And already Cruz saw the changes begin. The face that had been an uneasy melding of the human and the ursine became more human. The fur that covered him seemed to be sucked into him like a million strands of spaghetti. He shrank from *absurdly* large to merely *very* large.

And then, there he was. And there she was, still hiding behind her false face.

This could go so wrong.

Yes, it could. But we could both be dead an hour from now. What the hell are you scared of?

She dropped the mask, resuming her normal appearance.

"So," she said with forced nonchalance, "are we going to do this kiss thing?"

They were.

And nothing went wrong.

Many blocks south, Markovic waited and expanded. He had no way of counting his individual parts, but he definitely felt the damage the Rockborn Gang had done. He'd played it cool and confident, but the truth was their attack had shocked him.

He'd overlooked the fact that all his human supporters would be knocked out of the action right from the start by Malik. He hadn't imagined the gang would have flamethrowers. He'd underestimated just how hard it was to cope with Shade Darby's speed. In fact he was fairly sure the speed demon had been in and out of Grand Central at least once more and no one had even seen her, let alone been able to stop her.

And the skinny little girl, the one who looked like she was twelve, what she had done to one of Markovic's few useful mutant recruits, the guy who'd called himself Bengal Tiger, had been scary. Tiger had not returned, and Vector had no idea what she had done with him. Another of his recruits, Knightmare, had gone to the bathroom just before the battle and had not returned, and Markovic suspected that little girl had somehow taken him out of the game, just as she'd done with Tiger.

What was it she was doing? She'd grabbed a handful of Tiger's fur and he'd disappeared. A second later the girl was back. And nothing more was seen or heard of Tiger or Knightmare.

The little girl has big powers.

Markovic did not like making mistakes. Mistakes rattled his self-confidence. He knew, deep down in his bones—well, his figurative bones—that he should attack now and take out the Rockborn Gang. But unless they were damned fools, they'd have relocated, and he didn't yet know where they were.

Worst of all, Markovic had one great mystery hanging over him like his own personal sword of Damocles: he did not know *where he was,* him, the mind, the thinking part, the identity. Was he equally present in each of his thousands of parts? Would the gang have to kill all of his insect cells in order to kill him? Or was there some critical number beyond which he would not survive?

"We're not going after them?" The middle-aged black man who called himself Mirror was now Markovic's most powerful remaining ally. But he, too, had a problem: he could only become—mirror—a mutant when in their physical presence. He'd gotten lucky being able to morph Shade Darby, but she would be unlikely to give him a second chance to catch her moving slowly enough.

"Don't like it here?" Markovic asked in his sinister, reedy voice.

"I don't like waiting for them to come back," Mirror, whose real name was Frank Poole, said. He was standing on the top level of the balcony beside Vector. He assumed he had a right to that position, and the truth was that Markovic couldn't afford to alienate him—he was a bit short of effective allies. Flying Fish might be of some use if she'd carry a gun, but she had refused thus far. Which left Batwing, who, as far as Markovic could tell, was capable of nothing but growing awkwardly large wings.

My gang sucks.

"I like it just fine," Mirror said. "But I want more opportunities. I want to morph Lesbokitty. I want to see what that's like."

"Yes, well, I have greater ambitions," Markovic said, unable or unwilling to disguise his condescension. "Do something useful: go out in the streets and find me hostages."

"How am I going to do that?"

"I don't give a damn!" Markovic snapped. "Just get me some warm bodies. Children, if you can find any."

With Mirror gone, Markovic returned to his thoughts. This was just like any business expansion. He had to think it through to understand the perils and the possibilities. He owned New York City, aside from the Rockborn Gang. He could consolidate his control here and then move against nearby targets—New Jersey, Philadelphia. But that was a mere geographical proximity model. The real target, if he wanted to really take control, had to be Washington, DC.

"Problem," he muttered, thinking aloud. "How far does my reach extend? Can I have parts of me at long distances?" He had sent small swarms around the immediate vicinity and had maintained contact, seeing through their eyes, hearing what their antennae picked up. Had it been a degraded signal, though? He searched his memory and said, "How about you, Watchers? Any suggestions, oh silent ones?"

But of course the Watchers offered nothing. He'd not quite gotten used to these unseen and maybe unreal observers constantly looking over his shoulder, but he had experience being watched: government regulators from Washington and Albany had been in his face for a long time. Then, too, local media every now and then got the clever idea of attacking him, and he'd heard through the grapevine that *60 Minutes* was preparing a piece on Markovic's Money Machine. He was used to being watched.

Still, damned if they weren't distracting. And worse, they were vaguely humiliating. He wasn't some plaything; he was Vector. Vector, Ruler of the Big Apple.

There will be a reckoning with you, too, Watchers. Mark my word.

Had there been a signal loss when his parts were farther away or not? He wasn't sure. Even a small degradation would mean that he had geographical limits, and that made the prospect of aiming for Washington problematic. Expanding too quickly was a common mistake of businesses. He knew this from personal experience. When he'd tried to expand Markovic's Money Machine into California, state regulators had made life impossible, and he'd had to retrench, losing half a billion dollars in the process and watching his stock price drop 8 percent.

And yet, if he didn't take Washington, some politician or

general was sure to get the bright idea to nuke New York. They'd be nowhere near such a drastic move, not yet, not while they still had the Rockborn Gang.

And that realization was the deciding reason for his hesitation: as long as the gang was in business, the government had hope. If he destroyed the gang, he might be looking at a mushroom cloud sooner rather than later. The thing was, New York was paralyzed. He could slip out of town, make his way to Washington, and take the national government down. He could infest every congressperson, every senator, the president and his cabinet. But he would keep enough alive and well to be useful hostages.

And then?

The "and then" part had him baffled. He had never played this game before, and he wasn't entirely sure what a victory would look like.

"I'll figure it out. I always do."

In the meantime, he needed transportation, and in a small irony he was actually in a train station that had no trains running. The Acela Express that ran from Boston to Washington no longer stopped in New York. It was running from Stamford, Connecticut, to Boston, and from Newark south to Washington. The middle of the route—New York—had been cut off, isolated.

Rather like the PBA, the so-called FAYZ that had isolated the far smaller Perdido Beach. But unlike the prisoners in that dome, there was nothing stopping Vector. Newark was just over the river.

Yes, he decided, that was the plan. Attack, but not where the enemy expected it. His numbers were vast. His power terrible. The fear he represented broke even the strongest wills.

This expansion would not be shut down.

From the Purple Moleskine

My candle burns at both ends;
It will not last the night;
But ah, my foes, and oh, my friends—
It gives a lovely light!

That's from Edna St. Vincent Millay, who wrote it in 1922 if you believe the internet. That was during the Roaring Twenties, America's wild spring break party when everything was new: jazz and radio and planes. All the roaring stopped when the stock market fell and the Great Depression came.

Did Edna sense that the big party was coming to an end in less than a decade? Do people have that power, some at least, to sense the temporary nature of their reality? I don't know, and honestly it's not something I've ever thought about much. Until now.

There are lots of things I think about now that I never had to think about before. Like the fact that I sense candles going out and darkness ahead.

Hope tortures you. And suddenly, lately, I've had this pathetic hope that Armo actually liked me. And the thing is, he *does. Shouldn't that make me happy? But when you feed hope, it grows and demands more—like a child, I suppose. That he wasn't repulsed by me, that he actually likes me just makes me wish he loved me. I know how pathetic and needy I must seem. How pathetic and needy I am. It's just that growing up, I was loved, at least a little, and then, when I revealed who I am, that love stopped. Probably it would have been better if the whole "L" thing was unknown, something I had never experienced, then I wouldn't miss it. I think a person blind from birth doesn't miss color like a person who goes blind later.*

I see the way Shade and Dekka both look at me. They think I don't notice, but I do, and I know they see how pathetic— there's that word again—I am. They want to warn me off. They want to say, "Cruz, don't get yourself turned inside out over some guy." I know because that's what I would say to me, what I do say.

Everything is coming apart. What am I supposed to do, tell myself he's not the only guy, there are lots of fish in the sea? But time is short for all of us. I can feel it. My candle is burning at both ends, but night is coming, and sooner not later, my little candle will be snuffed out.

I'm not strong like Dekka, or brilliant and strong like Shade and Malik. I don't want to be some superhero. I want to go to college, or maybe have a nice job that I don't hate. Some day I may want to adopt kids. And I want to do all those boring, safe things with a big, sweet, impossible-to-push-around white boy with a silly name.

Is that asking too much? Of course it is. Because the big, sweet white boy sometimes turns into a bear and I sometimes turn into Beyoncé, and the whole world is teetering on the edge of a cliff and even if we somehow survive, the world I know will never return.

Maybe that's why that poem that I memorized in, like, fifth grade suddenly came back to me. Because it's not just my own candle that will not last the night.

CHAPTER 34
Speed, Nothing but Speed

IT WAS LUCK. Luck and Sam's instincts.

"I don't like that he hasn't come after us," Sam said, speaking privately to Dekka. They were in the backyard of their temporary headquarters. Sam had not wanted to say anything challenging in front of the others, anything that might shift focus to himself. This was Dekka's command, not his, and he was happy to have it stay that way.

But there was a nagging voice in the back of his head, and even though he was in morph, it was not the Watchers this time.

"What are you thinking?" Dekka asked.

Sam shrugged. "From all you say, this Markovic character is smart and experienced. So he's not like Knightmare or even the Charmer. He's not just some thug; he's a smart thug."

Dekka nodded. "You think he's up to something?"

Sam nodded. "Smart guys think. He's got to know that the government will be sending in tanks at the least, and possibly something much worse for him. He won't just wait around. So, I ask myself: WWCD?"

"WWCD?"

"What would Caine do? He was a smart thug, too. He wouldn't have waited for me to come after him again. He'd attack in some new direction, somewhere I wasn't looking."

"It's been bugging me too," Dekka admitted. "No pun intended. He laid a trap for us, but it ended in a draw. So what's he doing? Trying to rerun the earlier game, hoping to win this time? Shade says he hasn't added recruits. It's him and that fish girl and Mirror and a few hangers-on."

"Maybe have Shade take another look? Once more before we go in and set off explosions?"

Dekka led the way back inside the house. Shade was talking to Cruz about something in clipped, high-speed, barely comprehensible speech.

"Shade. How would you feel about taking another run through Grand Central?"

"Bzzt," Shade replied, and was gone. A door slammed.

"Good timing," Cruz snarked. "We were talking about emotional things earlier, and you know Shade."

Shade, for her part, was not happy hearing about Cruz's encounter with Armo. Not because she wasn't happy for Cruz, but because she still did not think it would work out in the end, and she couldn't bear to see Cruz have her heart broken on top of everything else.

She'd suggested to Cruz that maybe this was not the time

to consider romantic entanglements.

To which Cruz had replied, "Like you and Malik?"

That had just forced Shade to start really thinking about what exactly she was doing with Malik. Was it pity, was that why she had gone to him? That didn't feel quite right. No, if she was honest with herself—and she tried to be—she had needed him. She had felt afraid and isolated, and maybe that's what it took to get her to admit she needed someone.

Now she was relieved to be out the door and racing down the avenues toward Grand Central. The last time she'd passed through she'd seen a pair of Vector's human minions, looking haunted and terrified, perhaps afraid of Vector, or just as likely, nowhere near getting over the shattering experience of Malik's blast. The two of them were trying to string wire across the doorways, driving nails into marble with difficulty. And all of it pointless—with her momentum and chitin covering, she could blow right through wires.

It was a run of only a few seconds, so Shade took a few extra seconds to play a game of Mach-1 parkour, leaping from car roof to car roof, bouncing off walls, swinging around light poles, and her favorite new pastime: going around and around in revolving doorways until the bearings smoked and the glass started to crack.

I'm entitled to have a little fun, aren't I?

At the station, she found the wires had not been successfully strung, and she had no difficulty blowing in past . . . past no one. Vector had posted no guards.

She ran at half speed, which was still twice as fast as a

race car, around the main concourse, running up walls and over ticket booths. Grand Central was empty. No Vector. No flying-fish girl. No Mirror in or out of morph.

Suspecting a trick, she blew down through the dining level, raced through kitchens, ran through the subway station; in all, she spent an interminable five minutes carefully searching the place at hyperspeed.

Of course, it's easy to hide bugs. Just because you don't see them . . .

She ran back to the main concourse and saw that there was only one living thing left behind. She dashed back to the dining level, retrieved a twelve-inch chef's knife to cut through duct tape, returned, and leaped the dozen feet to land atop the information booth.

The stink that came from the tortured man was stomach-churning. He was like a corpse exhumed from a grave, his body a breeding ground of diseases known and unknown. One bicep showed bare bone poking through rotting hamburger. His abdomen had been hollowed out, his stomach and intestines gone, and in their place a black pit oozing pus and blood.

He did not know Shade was there. His face was still covered by the cushion that muffled his screams. Shade dreaded removing the cushion and seeing his face, but this was not about her delicate sensibilities. The man was writhing in hell.

She sliced through the duct tape and tossed the cushion away.

"Please God, please God, please God!" the man cried, his

voice faint and ragged from too many such screams and cries.

"Listen to me," Shade said. She squatted on the slanted top of the booth, and looked at the place where his eyes should be, but his eyes were gone, consumed by voracious bacteria and viruses that had eaten so far through his left eye that Shade saw pink brain tissue.

He should be dead. If there was any pity left in this new world, he would be dead.

Shade leaped clear of the booth and made it to a place out of sight behind a pillar and vomited. She was back before the tortured man could have noticed her absence. Then again, he hadn't noticed her presence.

Shade slowed her voice till to her own ears it sounded like molasses. "I'm here to help you. Where is Vector?"

"Kill me, please, please, please have mercy!"

"I need you to answer me! Where is Vector?"

Shade felt exposed and vulnerable standing still for so long, but the man was in no state to be answering questions, and she had to take her time with him.

"Vector. Where is he?"

"He's everywhere! He's inside me! Oh, God, help me!"

Nothing was going to penetrate this brutalized mind. Nothing. With one possible exception.

Dekka did it when she had to.

Still, Shade hesitated. It was one thing to be in a fight, and to try to not take a life, but do so nevertheless. This wasn't a fight.

No, but it is a war.

"Answer my questions and I'll help you."

"Kill me, please, please, God, oh please." The words came so very slowly to Shade, and she could hear desperation in every single syllable. Utter despair.

"All right," Shade said. "I'll end it for you. But you have to tell me: Where is Vector?"

"I-I-I—don't lie to me. You have to swear!"

"I swear."

"Washington. I heard him say Washington. Now do it! Please, I'm begging . . ."

"How would Vector get to Washington?" Shade wondered, picturing a massive insect cloud flying south.

"Train. Train in Jersey. Now! Do it now!"

"Do you want to pray or anything?" *Those words coming out my mouth!* "Before I . . . do it . . . would you like to say a prayer or something?"

"Prayer?" He lolled his horrifying face toward her. "Do you think I haven't prayed? Do you think I haven't begged God to let me die?" His voice was raw, savage, a voice rising up from the pit.

Shade tightened her grip on the knife, and with one swift sideways swipe, she cut through his throat till the blade scraped spine. Then she reversed direction, severing the spinal cord completely.

The man's head fell, bounced down the slanted roof, hit the marble floor, and rolled once, heavily. It came to rest with its face blessedly pointed away.

I've just killed a man.

She felt the enormity of her deed gathering force like a tidal wave far out at sea, knowing it was rushing toward her, building size and speed. Sooner or later it would sweep over and through her. Sooner or later there would be a reckoning. But now was not the time.

Shade raced out of the station, thumbing her phone so fast that the software could not keep up. First to Google Maps to find out where the Newark train station was. Then a text to Dekka.

D. Vector poss en route DC train out of Newark. OMW.

With that out of the way, it was time for sheer, unrestricted, all-out *speed*.

Forty-Second Street was a half-second's blur. Left on Park Avenue, a left so sharp that she ran up the side of a building, feet smashing third-floor windows as she executed her turn. Right onto Thirty-Ninth Street, and the world was a blur of banks and sandwich shops and phone stores. Almost instantly she ran into the mass of cars still trying to escape the city. But the sidewalks were clear, and she tore along, leaping piles of bagged trash, running through mostly empty intersections. She was going so much faster than her Google Maps app that she missed a turn and had to skid to a stop and back up.

Down a winding ramp with concrete walls high on both sides, beneath an overpass, and she took a sudden plunge into the nicotine-tiled Lincoln Tunnel, which was wall-to-wall cars moving at three miles an hour. The walkways that ran along the sides of the claustrophobic tunnel were too narrow for her to stay on them and keep up her speed. She had to slow so much that a man squeezing around cars on a motorcycle actually passed her.

Shade hopped onto the nearest car roof. Cars are generally under five feet tall, and the tunnel was just over thirteen feet. Plenty of clearance. She was going to dent some roofs, probably break a few windshields, and almost certainly scare the hell out of some motorists, but she'd just killed a man, and none of that minor mayhem was worth worrying about. She ran in great, bounding steps, roof to roof, bouncing across lanes to bypass trucks and buses.

All at once she was in the open air. She leaped down onto solid ground, moving like a compact hurricane beneath a dozen overpasses, then skidded to a stop, realizing she'd taken an off-ramp by mistake. She backtracked, slowing to allow the maps app to catch up. She crossed a river, crossed a marsh, crossed another river, and was suddenly in downtown Newark with nice, wide, uncluttered sidewalks.

Turn coming up.

Shade skidded into a sharp left turn, and there it was, an ugly concrete building that bridged over the road, marked with tall gold letters. *Newark Penn Station.*

It was smaller inside and nothing like as grand as its Manhattan counterpart. She stopped in the midst of a crowd on its way here or there, seeming to materialize out of nowhere, unless you'd noticed coats suddenly flapping, hats flying off, shopping bags almost torn from hands by the wind of her arrival.

Take the time to ask questions in slo-speech? Or check the signage? The signs were quicker. One pointed the way clearly to the Acela, the fast bullet train that ran up and down the East Coast. She shot down a ramp—amusingly marked with Do Not Run signs—and came to a stop again on the Acela platform.

There was a crowd of people, many with suitcases, all milling around and looking scared and angry.

But there was no train in sight.

"Train's gone," Dekka snapped, reading Shade's text. "Dammit! If Vector's on that train, he can be in DC in just over three hours!"

"Faster," Simone said. "There are half a dozen Acela stops between Newark and DC, and I doubt the engineer is going to argue with my fa . . . with Vector. They'll blow right through those stops and ignore speed limits."

Edilio had been tapping his phone. "It's about two hundred miles, and the Acela's top speed is one fifty." He looked up at them, at the entire Rockborn Gang, all in morph, all crowded into the living room. "It won't be able to do one fifty the whole way without derailing, but we aren't going to catch it."

"Oh ye of little faith," Dekka said. "I talked to my friend the general as soon as I realized we might be racing a train. A chopper will land in the park in five minutes. Let's go. Armo?"

"Yeah?"

"Grab the . . . Um, your strength would be much

appreciated. Would you be willing to grab our new toy?"

The artillery shell Edilio had obtained from the army currently occupied a couch. It was painted dark green, gray at the tip, with red warnings all scratched and rendered almost illegible by time. The shell, and the poison gas within it, were older than any two of them combined. The Marine captain had emphasized that it was dangerous even unexploded, capable of leaking and killing anyone nearby.

The shell had been modified. It now had a small digital timer literally duct-taped on, with wires running to the detonator.

They ran—or in Simone's case, flew—the few blocks to the park just as an olive drab military helicopter with a strange triple tail swept over them, beating the air and flattening the grass. Armo, never fast in bear morph unless he dropped to all fours, struggled to keep up while running with a shell that could kill everyone within a several-block radius, very much including Armo himself.

Once again, a battle plan had come to nothing. Dekka had intended to set the nerve gas off in Grand Central, with Shade and Francis running as many nonmutant humans to safety as possible. But Grand Central was irrelevant now, and there was no way to plan for what was coming.

Dekka waved them all into the helicopter's open door, assisted by a helmeted crewman. Armo barely avoided having the top of his bear head lopped off by the whirling blades as Cruz grabbed him and yelled, "Duck!" He shoved the shell into the helicopter and climbed in after it.

The loadmaster yelled, "What the hell is that?"

"Nerve gas," Sam said, projecting a calm even he could not possibly feel.

"Jesus H.!" the crewman yelped.

"Yeah, welcome to our lives," Cruz muttered.

In the helicopter there were eight seats, five facing each other with a row of three stacked behind the row of two. Nothing about this configuration was good for Armo or Dekka since they left little room for anyone else to sit beside them, so they de-morphed as Dekka yelled, "Go, go, go! Don't wait!"

The helicopter lifted off and veered away, skimming over trees, rising to clear the apartment buildings that lined the park and racing above the Hudson River, heading west.

Dekka, human once more, squirmed forward to the cockpit and tapped on the pilot's shoulders. She started to tell him something but the noise of the turbines and blades obliterated speech. The pilot tapped his headphones, and at that moment the loadmaster squeezed beside her and clapped a pair over Dekka's ears.

"Do you know where you're going?"

The pilot shrugged. "Newark train station."

Dekka shook her head. "No, the train's left already, heading south. You need to plot an intercept course. The train goes one-fifty, top speed."

There was a low curse from the pilot, who keyed his microphone to ask his controller at the base to plot an intercept with a train moving south. He preemptively banked the helicopter from almost due west to south-west.

After a few minutes the pilot was in Dekka's headphones again. "Intercept is a no-go unless someone slows that train down. We do a hundred forty-five knots, which is about a hundred seventy miles an hour. If the train's going one fifty with a head start, it'll take a hell of a long time to catch him."

"I'm pretty sure someone's trying to slow it down," Dekka said. "Listen, I know this'll sound crazy, but can you get me through to General Eliopoulos on the radio?"

The pilot turned all the way around and raised the visor on his helmet to favor her with a look that suggested she was crazy.

"Lieutenant, the worst person on earth is on that train heading to DC. If he gets there and escapes us, he'll destroy the entire US government. So make the call!"

The door of the helicopter was open, and the wind whipped clothing and hair as Dekka made her way back to the canvas jump seat between Sam and Malik.

"He says—"

"We heard," Sam interrupted, tapping his own headphones by way of explanation. "I guess we have to hope Shade can slow the train down."

Dekka clenched her jaw. So close! If she'd been quicker. If she'd thought of it instead of needing Sam to spot Vector's likely next move. If, if, if.

If when Tom Peaks first rolled up in the parking of the Safeway you'd just told him to go . . .

But that wasn't true. Not really. This disaster was not her fault; she accepted that.

"General Eliopoulos," the pilot announced in an awed

tone. Lieutenant chopper pilots did not speak to chairmen of the Joint Chiefs unless they'd just earned the Medal of Honor or been the cause of some truly spectacular screwup.

"General, Dekka Talent," the pilot said, and handed the microphone to her.

"I suspect this is not good news," Eliopoulos said, voice stretched and grainy in the radio.

"We are pretty sure Vector is aboard an Acela train heading for DC. Could get there in as little as an hour. We're chasing him, but it doesn't look good."

The general then showed why he'd risen to become the top soldier. He went right to the point. "What kills him?"

"Fire and nerve gas, we hope. Fire for sure."

"Got it. I'll get some planes armed with napalm in the air."

No goodbye, just a dead line. Okay then. "Hey, Mr. Pilot: I like your general. The man does not screw around."

The pilot shot her a thumbs-up and the helicopter flew on, barely above the roofs and treetops.

Dekka, not wishing to broadcast her conversation with Sam, lifted one side of his headphones and spoke into his ear. "I know you had doubts about Grand Central. Do you think you can do your thing with a fast-moving train?"

Sam tilted his head back and forth, then said, "I'm not sure, Dekka. It will sure as hell wreck the train."

Dekka nodded and replaced her headphones.

Kill a policeman, wreck a train. A day in the life . . .

CHAPTER 35
Stop That Train! I Want to Get On!

SHADE HAD NEVER run this long, this far. It was, she knew, impossible. Every part of it was impossible. Impossible that she could generate the energy required. Impossible that her brain could seamlessly adapt to a world that should be nothing but a blur.

At top speed she could run faster than a 787 jet; in fact, right now she was moving just below cruising speed for an airliner. Impossible that she could still hear in what amounted to a wind tunnel cranked up to maximum, not to mention the Doppler effect, which should have reduced anything she heard to a whine. Impossible that she could even keep her eyes open, let alone actually be able to see the railroad ties flying away beneath feet moving so fast they should have caught fire.

Malik is right. The laws of physics have been hacked.

Not time to think about that. Maybe I'm a real person; maybe I'm a sim. It doesn't matter because life is what it is, no matter how strange or impossible it seems. Maybe it was all a game invented by some alien species, maybe, but Vector was still en route to Washington, DC, and people, whether biologically evolved or created on some futuristic keyboard, would suffer terribly.

Is that right, Watchers? Maybe give me a little wink if I'm right?

She remembered once diving into Wikipedia's philosophy page and following links through all sorts of speculation about the nature of humanity. The problem of free will had been debated and written about endlessly, but in the end it came to a dead end because the fact was that humans were simply not capable of pretending as if free will did not exist. The human mind had limitations.

It was not easy running on a train track, not easy at all. The spacing of the ties was awkward, and if she missed a step and landed on gravel, it slowed her down so that she missed her next step. As a result Shade was moving at half speed, probably no more than four hundred miles an hour.

Which seemed poky.

She actually had time to notice how very slowly the planes landing at Newark airport were moving. It made her laugh; they looked as if they had to fall, but just kept gliding along at what to Shade looked no faster than a car pulling out of a suburban driveway.

Shade had no idea how far ahead the Acela was and berated herself for not asking one of the passengers who'd been forced off. In the back of her mind, she ran the algebraic equations, trying to calculate how long it would take a person moving at four hundred miles an hour to overtake a train moving at one fifty.

Another part of her mind wondered just what she thought she would do if she caught up to the train. Run ahead and drive a truck onto the tracks? That could work. Or she could race ahead and throw one of the switches that would shunt the train off onto a side track.

The problem with both of those solutions—aside from not having any idea how train switches worked—was that the train would likely go off the rails at a hundred fifty miles an hour and rip through some residential neighborhood like a meteorite—a meteorite filled with a swarm of disease-causing insects that would undoubtedly survive a wreck just fine.

The best way was to get aboard the train—a train moving at NASCAR speeds—with locked doors and shatterproof windows. That would not be easy.

Then, in the distance, intermittently visible between trees as it took a curve, she saw it, a silvery snake. It was just going into a turn, and Shade counted six passenger cars, wedged between two "energy cars," which were the electric version of locomotives. Hopefully all empty.

She could catch up to the train in under a minute. Then what?

Excellent question, Shade. Got any answers?

She had the clean phone Edilio had provided, and slowed slightly to be able to focus on texting. Texting was odd in that her fingers moved faster than the software could generate a letter, so that there was a lag. She had finished her message before the third word appeared on her phone.

Caught train. Residential area. Somewhere safer ahead?

She knew what Edilio would do: open a maps app and search ahead on the track for a more open spot where whatever she did wouldn't involve derailing a train right into a subdivision or an elementary school. It would take forever by her calculations, minutes at least.

So as she waited for Edilio's reply, she kept racing ahead until she was in the train's slipstream, trotting along just a few yards behind it, slowing to match its speed, a crawling hundred and fifty miles an hour.

The last car, the one she could almost reach out and touch, was an energy car, an engine, identical to the one at the front of the train, bullet-headed and streamlined. There were no evident handholds, so if she was to leap atop it, it'd be a mad scramble not to slide right back off.

They were coming up to the Metropark station where the train was to stop, though Shade really doubted it would.

She checked her phone. A text was just popping up.

Abt 7 miles south of Metropark sta see Costco/Target on rt. 2 m after. Trees sparse houses.

"All right, Edilio," Shade said. Pretty quick for a mere human.

The train instead blew past crowded platforms. The draft from the swift train pulled a baby stroller toward the tracks, but Shade saw it, saw the mother in slow motion rushing to grab it, knew the woman was too slow, and skidded to a stop just as the stroller tipped over the edge of the platform. Shade pushed it back before taking off again.

My superhero good deed.

No, she corrected herself mentally, *my second superhero good deed. Save a baby, kill a man.*

Not now!

Now she had to accelerate to pass the train. She moved onto a parallel track and ran beside the train, hoping she wasn't running into a train coming north—her armored body was strong, but she was pretty sure hitting a train at hundreds of miles an hour would crush her like a bug on a car windshield.

The last passenger car looked empty, a relief. The next car and the one after that were empty as well. Then she reached the first-class car, the one just behind the front energy car. There Shade got a shock: passengers! She'd assumed Vector had forced everyone off the train before seizing it, but of course he'd kept hostages. *Of course!* At least two dozen of them, it seemed, all sitting with frightened, desperate looks on their faces.

So much for derailing the train by any of the means she'd considered. It might come to that, but not yet, not with people aboard the train.

Now, unfortunately, she had another problem: keeping pace with the train, her speed zero relative to the train, she was perfectly visible to anyone on board, including Vector's insect eyes.

Shade dropped back past the rows of windows, to the back of the train. She took a breath and leaped up to the sloped windshield, and had to motor her legs like Road Runner to keep from slipping off. She clawed and clambered up onto the roof to discover her way impeded by the raised framework called a pantograph that scraped along the bottom of a live electrical line running very high current. She gave as wide a berth as possible to the pantograph then trotted forward, easily leaping the gaps between cars, indifferent to the gale-force wind that would have knocked any normal person flat, and flashing on movie scenes she'd seen of people doing just this. Hadn't Tom Cruise done this in at least one movie?

Ahead on the right was a big shopping center with, yes (thank you, Edilio!), a Target and a Costco. She ran to the front of the train, scooted past another pantograph, and threw herself flat. She edged forward on her belly to peek down through the tinted front windows. She was quite suddenly face-to-face with a dark-skinned woman—a woman with a dusting of strange insects on her shoulders and head. The woman had not been infected, not yet, but the threat was unmistakable.

Shade sat up, swung her legs around, and with the power that allowed her to move at jet speed, she smashed the window with her heels, then slid down into the train's cockpit to find that the engineer had been knocked back against the bulkhead by the sudden wind. And, as Shade had hoped, most if not all of Vector's bugs had been knocked loose.

They were quick, the insects, but Shade was quicker, snatching them out of the air and crushing them in her fists or stomping them underfoot.

Slowing her voice, Shade said, "Stop the train."

"He'll kill me!"

"Don't worry about Vector. The Rockborn Gang is here."

It sounded ludicrous in Shade's ears, like yelling "The cavalry is coming!" but the engineer, seeing dead bugs littering the floor, complied, and the train began to slow.

"Now hold on!" Shade yelled.

"What are y—"

Shade grabbed the engineer, dragged her to the side door, slid it open, and leaped. Shade and the engineer flew through the air at shocking speed. Shade's legs were moving before she hit the ground and she matched speed before slowing enough to deposit the engineer well off the tracks in a soggy ditch. She muttered an apology the woman could not hear, and raced after the train again, catching it effortlessly as it slowed to freeway speeds.

Did Vector know what she'd done? If he did, he would threaten the passengers to stop her, and the extortion would work. So thing one: in and out before Vector could react. You can't threaten if no one hears the threat.

She ran ahead of the train, spun, leaped, and flew backward through the air, as the train caught her at a relative speed of just a few miles an hour. Back through the windshield she'd broken, a stagger-step that smacked her into the bulkhead with just enough force to make her yell, "Ow!"

The speedometer showed seventy-four and dropping.

How long until Dekka and the others in the helicopter caught up?

Shade made sure the door to the cockpit was locked, then climbed back out of the window and onto the roof to scan the sky for approaching helicopters.

Markovic had indeed seen the shattering of the windshield, followed by the blur that had resolved briefly into Shade Darby, speaking in a weird, clipped, distorted speech.

He had felt the braking, the loss of speed, the sudden disappearance from sight of both Shade and the engineer.

"Oh, clever, clever girl," Markovic said. "If only she would join me!"

He regretted now not bringing Mirror, but that mutant, though possessed of a useful power, was a difficult man, an unpredictable man, and Vector had left him behind, left all his hangers-on behind. Why should he need followers? He was Vector; his own power was all that was necessary.

Still, Mirror would have been useful now that the speed demon had shown up unexpectedly. A mistake. Bob Markovic did not like making mistakes, Vector still less.

But it was a minor matter. The Rockborn Gang might be on his tail, but he'd seen their pathetic efforts to take him down and was not overly impressed.

The mass of Vector's tens of thousands of parts was in the first passenger car, first class, buzzing around terrified passengers. On the floor lay Vector's "demonstration," a woman writhing and crying out as disease organisms ate into her flesh.

Vector had no idea what Shade had planned, but one thing

was certain: he had to get the train moving again and quickly. The damnable thing was that the door from the passenger car into the energy car was a secure door, and no amount of battering was likely to bring it down. Which meant he would have to send his swarm outside and enter the cockpit through the shattered windshield.

Two problems: One, his swarm moved at no more than about thirty-five miles an hour, and the train, while slowing, was still going faster than that. If he swarmed outside, the wind would blow him clear away from the train.

The other problem was that he had no hands, which meant he could not manipulate the instruments, could neither step on a pedal nor throw a switch.

Definite downsides.

He looked through his many eyes, searching for a hostage young enough and fit enough for what he had in mind. He settled on a young Hispanic man wearing sneakers.

"You!" Vector said. "Break that window."

"Break it?"

"Use that fire extinguisher. Bash it out!"

The young man complied. It was neither quick nor easy; the glass had to be hit again and again until enough glass was pushed out to allow the man to writhe through the open window. At that point the train was moving at perhaps twenty-five miles an hour. So the man hit the ground, rolled like a stunt man, jumped up, and ran away across backyards, scrambling over fences.

Dammit!

Another mistake! Vector swarmed around a fit-looking woman with a toddler in tow. "You: climb out, make your way to the front of the train. If you disobey me, I will give your brat my own special treatment."

The woman did as ordered. She climbed out as her daughter cried and called to her, and she shouted back, "Don't be afraid!" in a voice guaranteed to have the opposite effect, and, "Carlita, you have to be quiet!"

The train was slow enough now that Vector could follow the woman out, watch her struggle to stand up on the windowsill and try to claw her way clumsily up onto the roof of the car. But she was too short to manage it, and Vector had to waste still more time getting two other hostages to grab her legs and boost her higher up.

By the time Vector's unwilling, impromptu engineer had made it to the roof, the train was nearly at a standstill.

And there stood Shade Darby atop the roof, in morph, looking quizzically at them. In slo-speech she said, "Well, hello there, Markovic. Bummer not having hands, huh?"

"If you try to stop us, I will take her child and its screams will fill your nightmares!"

"I see you've mastered the art of supervillain monologuing," Shade said.

"If you don't—" But Shade was gone. He cursed silently and raged at his hostage, "Get down there! Slide! Now!"

The hostage did, and Vector flowed after her. He was a quick study, and the train's controls were not difficult to grasp. He gave the hostage his orders, ignored her weak requests for reassurance about her child, and the train began moving once again.

It accelerated smoothly away, and Vector breathed a sigh— a figurative sigh, since he had no lungs—but realized he had a different problem now: neither he nor his captive knew what speed they should set. Vector knew vaguely that different sections of track were capable of sustaining different speeds, but decided to take the risk of going full speed. So what if the train derailed? It would slow him down, but only the humans aboard would die.

Shade had not tried to derail the train, though she probably could. She had only tried to delay it. Which meant the train was being pursued, probably by the rest of the Rockborn Gang. Could he destroy them without killing Simone? Did he care? You couldn't make a revolution without breaking some eggs, and this was a revolution, wasn't it? No more democracy with idiot voters making idiot decisions; he would rule directly. He was a businessman, not some bumbling politician. He knew how to get things done.

Yes: a revolution. The rise of the Vectorian Age. Hah!

That thought made him happy, an emotion that lasted for a full five seconds before he realized he had wasted too much time: a helicopter was passing overhead, and it was not a news chopper.

Vector flashed suddenly on *The Wizard of Oz*. On the Wicked Witch of the West dispatching her flying monkeys.

"Fly!" Vector wheezed. "Fly, my pretties, fly!"

CHAPTER 36
Too Late for Flying Lessons

"WE HAVE VISUAL on the train," the helicopter pilot said in the headphones. Dekka crouch-walked to the cockpit and leaned over the pilot's shoulder. And there it was, visible through the bubble canopy, just a mile ahead and, astonishingly, stopped.

"Someone's standing on the roof," the pilot said.

"That would be my girl Shade," Dekka said. "Land just ahead of it."

"No can do, miss: wires."

"Damn!"

"And now it's moving!" the pilot shouted.

"Keep pace with it and get as low as you can!" Dekka ordered. "We're about to get another passenger."

The helicopter swept in a tight circle and came back to hover just above the electrical wires, keeping pace with the train, which accelerated slowly, five miles an hour, ten, twenty . . .

Suddenly the helicopter lurched as it took on the weight of

a new arrival. Shade Darby had jumped from the roof of the train straight into the helicopter's passenger compartment.

"Talk to me, Shade," Dekka demanded.

Shade had far too much to say to be able to do it in buzz-speak and de-morphed quickly. "He's got people on that train. He's already 'Vectored' one person and the rest aren't going to argue with him."

"How many passengers?"

Shade shrugged. "Looks like a few dozen, maybe fifty people."

"We need to stop that train, no matter what," Simone said, surprising Dekka with her intensity. "If Vector reaches Washington, the US government will be over. Then there'll be no one but us. Just us."

No more "father," no more "Markovic." Simone had seen what her once-father had become and had begun to accept that Bob Markovic no longer existed. Dekka felt a wave of pity for the girl: she'd been through a hell of a lot in a very short period of time. It said something about her that she was still standing at all, let alone that she had adapted so quickly and . . . Dekka had been about to add "easily," but of course that was almost certainly not true. Dekka had known many kids in the FAYZ who seemed to be coping easily and ended up as psychiatric in-patients or suicides. Simone might be suppressing the pain for now, but it would come. Impulsively she reached and squeezed Simone's shoulder.

Malik said, "She's right, Dekka. This isn't a maybe-we-should-maybe-we-shouldn't thing. If Vector takes Washington, the eight of us will be dead within a month. He'll be able to turn military, FBI, everything against us."

"You think that many people in Washington will just go along with some unhinged lunatic?" Cruz wondered aloud.

"Obviously you don't pay much attention to politics," Malik snarked. "People are weak. They take the easy path. Wait until Vector has the president on a live feed, screaming in pain and begging for death. Not one person in ten thousand will stand up."

"He's right," Sam said. "And once people roll over for Vector they'll resent anyone who *doesn't*. It's human nature. They'll serve Vector and they'll easily be turned against us."

Dekka looked out through the open door, down at the train, wind blowing her snake-dreads straight back. The Acela was moving at maybe twenty miles an hour already. "Fifty or sixty people . . ."

"I can try to get some of them off the train," Shade said, "and maybe Francis can, too, but anyone we save may have Vector's bugs on them. We could save them and Vector simultaneously unless I take the extra time to de-bug each hostage."

No one was telling Dekka what to do. They all knew the decision she had to make, and Shade, while knowing what she would do herself, was glad not to have to make the call. The passenger compartment of the helicopter was a howling wind tunnel, and yet it seemed quiet as they waited for Dekka to decide their fate, and quite possibly the fate of the human race.

"Lieutenant," Dekka yelled to the pilot. "You're going to

have a sudden loss of weight." Then, with her heart in her throat, Dekka turned to Sam and Francis and Armo and said, "Let's do it."

The helicopter flew low, keeping pace with the accelerating train. Armo stood and hefted the heavy artillery shell. Francis gripped his furry arm tightly. Dekka took Francis's free hand.

"Wish us luck," Dekka said just as a swarm of copper and silver and red insects flew in through the open door. The bugs swirled around Dekka, invulnerable in morph, and went straight for their vulnerable targets.

"No!" Cruz cried. Cruz was not in morph.

In the cockpit the pilot and copilot slapped frantically at bugs aiming for their eyes, mouths, and ears.

Shade was already morphing fast, fast enough that Vector's beasts did not find her before chitin armor covered her.

"Cruz! Morph!" Malik cried in slo-mo speech.

But that would take too long. One of the bugs was inches from Cruz's face. Shade could see the beats of its penny-bright wings. She snatched it out of the air and crushed it. Then looked down at it in her hand, a broken toy, yellow insides oozing, antennae broken like twigs. She threw it out the door.

Then, the Whac-a-Mole game got serious. Hundreds of insects had found the pilots, but dozens had recognized Cruz and Sam as targets as well, neither being in morph. Shade's hands and arms were a blur, snatching and crushing, snatching and crushing. The bugs were not quick by Shade's standards, but there were a lot.

And Shade found she had help from an unexpected source. The living dreads on Dekka's head were almost as fast as Shade, snatching bugs out of the air and biting them in half.

But neither Shade nor Dekka could wedge into the cockpit and save the pilots flying the helicopter, which now veered wildly away.

Cruz had begun to morph, an amazing thing to watch with Shade's accelerated senses. And as Cruz's morph appeared, the bugs attacking her seemed to lose focus, as if they'd forgotten what they were doing. They turned in midair, and redoubled the assault on the cockpit.

"The pilots!" Dekka cried.

But Shade could see that it was too late. Far too late. The lieutenant pilot's face was already erupting in pus-filled boils, slow-motion corruption of the flesh.

No time to consult Dekka. No time to parse the moral pluses and minuses. Time only to see the solution, the bright, clear, ruthlessly drawn line from where Shade was to a solution. The faint, probably futile, but *only* solution.

Shade pushed Dekka aside, reached into the cockpit, grabbed the pilot by the shoulder of his uniform, reached around to smack the buckle of his safety harness, yanked him out of his seat, and hurled him out of the door.

She was back to repeat the same sequence with the copilot. Finally she grabbed Malik bodily and pushed him toward the cockpit. All of this within three seconds.

She had time to watch in horror as the two men fell so very slowly, arms windmilling, mouths open to scream. The pilot hit the ground. The copilot smashed into a tree. Two rag dolls.

Three. I've killed three men today.

It took seconds for the others to realize what she'd done. It took Malik seconds to realize he was in the pilot's seat. It took Dekka seconds to cry, "What have you done?"

"The only thing I could do," Shade said at a speed Dekka would never be able to interpret.

Sam was on his feet now, putting an arm around a furious Dekka. He said, "Not now!"

The helicopter banked sharply, so hard that Shade was certain it would roll completely over and hit the ground in a fiery explosion. But then the roll slowed and reversed. Cruz and Armo crashed together into a bulkhead, knocking Sam and Dekka to their knees on the steel floor.

Shade knew one of them, just one, had the power to escape unharmed.

"Francis!" she cried.

But it was a tenth-of-a-second chirp in a howling tornado of wind as the ground rushed at them.

Malik quickly saw what Shade had done, quickly saw that she was hoping he would somehow figure out how to fly a helicopter, and stared in blank panic at an array of unfamiliar instruments.

Through the windshield Malik saw tall, straight pine trees rising suddenly like arrows, then tilting away. He felt the helicopter accede to gravity and slide sideways toward the ground.

House roofs. Telephone poles. Grass. An aboveground backyard swimming pool. It was as if some giant had scooped the
ground up and flung it at them, so that it felt less like they
were falling and more like the ground was attacking them.

And yet, they were falling.

Malik understood Shade's thinking: Malik was a techie, a
gamer, a guy who'd spent thousands of hours driving virtual
tanks and flying virtual jets. He was the best choice to play
emergency pilot.

Just one thing: he'd never even flown a virtual helicopter.

To his side, right where the parking brake might be on a
sports car, was an ornate sort of yoke, but it was no simple
stick; it had various holds, things that needed to be pushed,
things that needed to be rotated, things that needed to be
pulled, and he had no idea, none, none, *none* what to do. But
in flying planes, pulling back on the yoke had always sent the
plane upward.

So Malik pulled up on the yoke. He heard the rising scream
of the turbines, felt a sudden surge of speed, saw a whirlwind
outside the bubble canopy . . .

The tip of a rotor caught a power line. There was a shower
of sparks; the helicopter shuddered and jerked wildly, rose
a few feet like a breaching whale, and spun madly. Malik
was pushed back in his seat by the centrifugal force, suddenly several times his own weight. Behind him the bodies
of his friends—those not buckled in—were hurled around,
smashed into bulkheads, and suddenly Dekka fell, back first,
feline hands clawing at the sky, out of the helicopter.

Shade moved, snatched Dekka's desperate hand, and held on, but she wasn't strong enough to pull Dekka in against the force of gravity and the delirious spinning, spinning . . .

The rotors hit again, and this time they bit into something solid, and tree branches and pine needles lashed the windshield. Trees. A fence. The helicopter's tail rose sharply, and the machine flipped over and smashed into the ground.

Even after impact the rotors churned on, tearing up grass and lawn toys and throwing steel chunks into the house whose backyard they had invaded.

Then . . . quiet, as the turbines whined and stopped. Malik was on his side. A tree branch had shattered the cockpit and now stuck there like a gnarled spear, having barely missed Malik's head.

Then . . . Malik smelled *smoke*!

To Shade the destruction of the helicopter was like watching a car crash on a slowed-down video. The rotors moved very fast, but she could see the individual blades making their individual contacts with trees and dirt. The helicopter had flipped onto its side so that Dekka was now above her and falling in toward the door.

Dekka, though, did not need Shade's help: with feline speed she landed with feet and hands on the open hatch.

Cruz had buckled up, but blood was pouring from a gash in her leg—or at least the leg of whatever morph she was in. Francis lay in a heap, her neck at a precarious angle.

If Francis dies, we're done.

Simone had been lucky enough to be thrown into Armo, who lay now on his back on the grass with Simone cradled in his arms.

Priorities: Francis.

Shade went to her, holding on with one hand and a leg pressed against the door to the cockpit. She knelt and saw a slow pulse throbbing in her throat. Her neck . . . her neck . . . it had to be broken!

But then Francis stirred and moved her hands in a wild, belated effort to protect herself. Shade caught her hands in midair, pushed them down, and looked up at Dekka, still stretched across the doorway. Dekka spit blood and yelled, "Smoke!"

Dekka jumped out of the way, and Shade blew past her, up and out through the sky-pointing door. She saw it: fire, spread out in a fan shape behind the helicopter, burning the wooden fence, burning random yard toys, burning the crumpled tail section and beginning to eat its way forward.

Shade dropped back inside and had to crawl to reach Malik, separated from him by a substantial tree branch. She pulled at the branch, but not even her morphed strength was enough.

"Bzt!" Shade yelled, then forced herself to slow down and yell, "Everyone off!"

"I'm trapped. Get out of here!" Malik said.

"The chopper's on fire," Shade said and tried to squeeze past the branch, but here speed was of no use. She needed a chain saw or the Jaws of Life.

The breeze caught the smoke and brought a dense cloud of choking, oily black smoke into the cockpit.

"I don't want to burn again!" Malik cried. "I don't want to burn again!"

"I've got you!" Shade said, but did she? Could she do . . . *anything*?

Now came the heat behind the smoke. A frantic glance showed orange flame licking its way along the fuselage as smoke filled the passenger compartment.

"Can you get out through the windshield?" Shade asked, but Malik, cool and calm Malik, was no longer able to comprehend. He was in full, flailing, screaming panic.

"Malik! Malik!" Shade cried as she saw the smoke being drawn into his nostrils.

"Don't let me burn! Don't let me burn!"

"Malik!"

The fire was so close now, so close, and Shade knew she would be able to escape, knew she could run through the flames before they could touch her and knew that if she did, Malik would burn and she would live to hear his desperate cries echoing in her mind forever and knew that she could never . . .

A hand reached through the broken windshield. The hand felt around, then found what it sought. Francis's fingers closed around Malik's knee, and all at once Shade was alone in the cockpit.

She crawled back to the passenger compartment and found Sam, groggy, fighting for consciousness, a gash down the side of his face. She pushed one arm beneath his back, her free hand grabbed a leg by the ankle, and she pushed him up, up and tipped him out of the sky-facing door.

Then Shade leaped clear, landing on a deep-green lawn that looked as if someone had attacked it with a massive hoe. A long piece of rotor stuck from the wood siding of a two-story house.

The Rockborn Gang was spread around a suburban lawn, standing or sitting back from the fire, upwind from the billowing smoke. And now Shade saw the damage done. Francis's leg wasn't just bleeding, white bone was protruding through the skin of her shin. Dekka had had to carry her to rescue Malik. Sam's gash was easily six inches long, gushing blood, and would require stitches. Simone had a sprained wrist. Cruz had sustained a head wound that bled down her face in rivulets, blood pooling in the hollows of her eyes and spilling like red tears. Malik lay coughing up smoke and gasping for breath.

Only Armo seemed to have survived unscathed, but his white fur was gray from the oily smoke. He lay on his back with the nerve gas shell beside him.

"We need an ambulance," Cruz said. She was out of morph and pressing her palm flat against the cut in her forehead.

Francis had caught the worst of it. She could not walk, and from the sheet-whiteness of her face and the sweat beads on her forehead, it was clear she was in great pain.

"We can't lose the train!" Shade cried twice, once at speed, then again in slo-mo.

"We can't ignore our own people, either," Dekka said firmly.

Shade nodded and started to call 911. Then she thought better of it. "How about I get you an ambulance and a paramedic and we keep going?"

Dekka pursed her lips and started to say yes, but by then Shade was gone. Her maps app showed an emergency room just two miles away, a matter of seconds. She was in luck and found an ambulance that had just unloaded a patient. She came to a sudden, startling stop in front of a paramedic just climbing out of the back of the red-and-white ambulance.

"I need you," Shade said, and without waiting pushed the woman back inside and slammed the door. She zoomed around to the driver, opened his door, yanked him out as gently as she could, which was not very gently. "You, I don't need."

Shade hopped up into the driver's seat.

"Hey! You can't—" the driver protested, but by that point Shade had thrown the vehicle into gear, executed a tire-squealing reverse out of the emergency room loading area, spun the wheel, and taken off.

"Hey! Hey!" the captive paramedic in the back yelled as she was tossed back and forth by maneuvers carried out at speeds no normal human driver could manage.

"Strap in!"

"You can't—"

"And yet, I did."

This was no sports car, and it was top-heavy and precarious

on corners. Coming around one sharp turn the vehicle started to tip, but its driver had extraordinary speed and felt the roll coming and shifted the wheel just enough to bounce violently onto a median and then careen back onto the street. It took longer to get back to the crash scene—easy to locate from the pillar of smoke—than it had to run to the hospital, but soon Shade crashed the ambulance right through the wooden fence and brought the vehicle to a halt in the destroyed backyard. On the way she blew past police cars no doubt heading to the scene and knew she would have just seconds to get away without a possible gun battle.

Shade leaped from the ambulance and practically threw Sam in the back, earning a shriek from the paramedic. Then she scooped up Francis and laid her as gently as she could on the stretcher inside the ambulance. She grabbed the paramedic, a twentysomething Latina, by the collar of her uniform and slowed her speech just enough to say, "Your patients. More coming."

The police cars were pulling up on the street, sirens dying, lights flashing, but by then Shade had everyone but Dekka loaded.

"Let's go!" Shade said. "I'm driving."

"I have shotgun," Dekka said.

"Yes you do, my friend," Shade said.

Shade drove back through the fence she'd flattened, between two police cars, past shouting police officers as Dekka stuck a hand out of the passenger-side window and carefully shredded the tires of the cop cars. Shade mashed the gas pedal and aimed south, toward the New Jersey Turnpike.

Dekka, beside her, was already on the phone with General Eliopoulos. "No, no, if you bomb it or derail it, Vector will escape into the countryside." A long listen. Then, "Delay, yes. Mess with the switches if you can." Another listen. "I understand, General. Okay. Yeah. Then, what we need is no cops on our tails and a faster ride. Okay. Okay." She glanced at Shade. "Yeah, that should work."

"So?" Shade demanded.

"So he's seeing about having Amtrak mess with the switches, but he can only do so much without derailing the train. Vector can force his hostages to climb out and manually change the switches, but that will eat up some time."

"He offered to bomb it?"

"He has F-16s in the air. But if he tries that, Vector will just buzz away."

"This ambulance's top speed seems to be a hundred twenty," Shade said, disgusted. "I thought ambulances were fast."

"Eliopoulos has another idea. Some new helicopter they have with a top speed of two fifty. Faster than the train."

"That would do it."

"He's having it meet us."

"Where?"

"In the middle of the New Jersey Turnpike just south of Philadelphia."

A police barricade waited at the on-ramp of the turnpike,

but as they neared, the police cars hastily reversed out of their way.

"Eliopoulos," Dekka said.

"Okay, then. Pedal to the metal."

"And?"

"And what?" Shade asked.

Dekka smiled. "Lights and siren, girl. Lights and siren."

"Hah!" Shade said. "Hell yes, lights and siren."

CHAPTER 37
Justifiable Homicide(s)

IN THE BACK of the speeding ambulance, Sam Temple winced as the paramedic went to work on him, shooting lidocaine into raw flesh to dull the pain of the sewing needle. It still hurt, especially since the ambulance continued to hurtle through traffic at ridiculous speeds, causing the paramedic to jab her needle repeatedly in the wrong places.

"Sorry to have to hijack you this way," Sam apologized.

The paramedic was intensely focused on her work. "You're the Rockborn Group, right?"

"Gang, but yeah, that's us."

"Are you after that bastard from New York?"

"We are."

The paramedic met his gaze. "Then no problem."

Francis lay on her back opposite Sam, behind the paramedic. The paramedic had eased her broken fibula back roughly into place and had cleaned and bandaged it. But Francis would not be walking any time soon.

Armo had de-morphed out of necessity—the ambulance was capacious, but not enough for a shaggy nine-hundred-pound beast. He sat on the corrugated steel floor with Cruz, holding gauze to her forehead. She was the next in line for the paramedic. Simone was squeezed in a corner, nursing her wrist, morphed, with her coat of tiny wings buzzing but not enough to cause her to lift off.

Sam itched to ask Dekka what she was doing, what the plan was, but A) he was being sewn up, and B) he was not in charge.

Serves me right. I didn't always explain myself to the troops, either.

He was feeling very much like a fifth wheel, lacking a useful power for combat, not really knowing most of the gang. He was painfully aware of his reputation as some kind of ten-foot-tall hero-demigod, but that had only been true, insofar as it was ever true, a long time ago. He was a passenger now, a hanger-on, an extra. He had one useful thing to offer, and it was looking increasingly unlikely to be helpful.

"How you doing, Simone?" he asked.

"The wrist hurts, but I'll live."

For how much longer? Sam did not say.

Suddenly the ambulance was fishtailing down the center lane of the turnpike as Shade stood on the brakes. Sam peered ahead through the windshield and saw a sleek, dangerous-looking helicopter landing right in the middle of the highway as traffic swerved past it or slammed on the brakes.

The ambulance doors flew open, and all of them—including

HERO   381

the paramedic and her medical kit—ran or were carried to the helicopter, which took off immediately, leaving an abandoned ambulance parked across two lanes.

It was immediately clear that this helicopter was to the first one what a Formula One racer was to a Prius. It tilted sharply, nose down, and roared away, rotors and turbines deafening, and soon there was railroad track two hundred feet below them.

Dekka unbuckled her seat belt and stood up, steadying herself with a hand pressed to the low ceiling. "Listen up. Eliopoulos is trying to slow the train. We are chasing it. It's going to be a very close call, even if the train is delayed a little. We may not have time to get any of the hostages off."

"If we're giving up on the hostages, why doesn't Eliopoulos just blow it up? He's got fighter jets and drones," Simone demanded.

"You don't kill bees by blowing up a hive," Malik said.

"Then how . . ." Simone let the question hang.

Dekka nodded at Sam. "We're hoping Sam can contain the swarm."

Malik frowned. "How exactly would you do that, Sam, if you don't mind me asking?"

The paramedic had finished stitching Sam's face— nineteen stitches—and was smearing antibiotic ointment preparatory to bandaging.

Sam said, "May I borrow this?" He slid a pen from her blouse pocket. "I've often suspected that whoever, whatever is behind this rock madness has an odd sense of humor. Ever since the dome came down, I've been sort of, you know, lost, I guess. So after I took the rock . . ."

Sam tossed the pen toward Malik.

The pen flew and suddenly stopped in midair. Stopped and bounced and rattled a little, rolling back and forth slightly, imprisoned in a transparent sphere less than a foot across. The sphere floated like a soap bubble as Malik and the others gaped in amazement.

Sam flicked a finger, the bubble disappeared, and the pen fell to the floor. "Inside the FAYZ dome, I was a big deal," Sam said, more wryly self-aware than self-pitying. "My fame came from a dome. And now, I can make domes."

Malik's eyes glittered beneath his sleepy lids. "How big can you make it?"

"That's the question, isn't it?" Sam said.

"Does it go through solid objects?"

Sam bent down, reeling with dizziness for a moment, picked up the pen, and tossed it again. This time there was a *snap!* as a small sphere appeared, containing just half of the pen. The other half fell to the floor.

"Cool," Malik said. "But anything trapped in one of your spheres would still have all its momentum?"

"Sorry?"

"I mean, if you threw a dome over the train, it would still be moving, right? It would smash into the inner side of the sphere?"

Sam shrugged and thought, *Oh, good, I get a day away from my brainy wife, and now I've got Shade and this dude to make me feel stupid.* "Seems so," he said. "I haven't exactly done a lot of testing yet."

Malik thought that over, nodded, and said, "Interesting. Have you ever heard of multiverse theory?"

"I have not," Sam said. In fact he had, but he was not interested in encouraging a long discussion. At times like these, visions of long white beaches and big, rolling waves came to mind, images of himself on his surfboard. . . . He wasn't giving that up just to listen to a science lecture.

Dekka came back from speaking with the pilot and said, "They think we'll intercept the train just as it reaches the Anacostia River, which is the edge of DC."

"Ow!" Cruz yelped as the paramedic got to work on her.

Shade had pulled it up on her phone. "It's a railroad bridge over a river, with what looks like marshes on both sides."

"Good," Dekka said, nodding. "That's the place, then. But it's just too close to the city to have any margin for error."

Sam locked eyes with her, and in the course of a few seconds much passed between them unspoken. Sam knew what she was asking of him, and so did she. Both knew what Sam had asked of Dekka in years gone by. Sam felt a blush of shame, shame at being relieved that the decision was hers and not his.

And yet, when you do it, it'll be you, not her, won't it?

How many innocent people on that train? And how many would survive? What share of the blame would fall on Sam? How would he deal with it?

First see if you survive, then worry about that.

"As soon as we drop in on the train, Vector will know something's up," Dekka said. "He could disperse, and then we're screwed. So as soon as Francis and I—"

"Francis can't walk," Armo said gruffly. "You still need one more person, and I'm it."

Dekka nodded as if she'd been expecting this. "Okay, yeah, one to carry the shell, one to carry Francis. The three of us."

Shade raised her hand. "Four. There's some time between when we get there and when Vector can react, right? Not much time, but enough that I can save a few hostages, even if I have to de-bug them."

"At risk to yourself?" Dekka's fist clenched by her side, and the next words she spoke seemed to be torn from her against her will. "No. No, Shade, as much as I honor your courage, no. We're risking Francis, Armo, and me. If something goes wrong, I need you, we *all* need you to survive."

"But she's saying she can save at least a few . . . ," Simone protested.

Dekka lost patience. She erupted in all the despair and fear and self-loathing she'd managed to suppress. "Hey, thanks for pointing that out, Simone," she snapped savagely. "I wasn't quite clear on it you know? I wasn't quite clear in my head"— she stabbed a finger at her own temple, startling her living dreads—"that I was condemning some innocent people to die. Maybe children. Yeah, never even occurred to me!"

Simone bristled at first, but then sat back, abashed.

"Listen," Dekka raged on. "If anyone else wants to take over and make the decisions, be my guest. Because I am happy to let someone else do this." She glared around, no doubt expecting an argument, but Sam saw around him only faces marked by pity.

"I'm so sorry," Simone said. "I wasn't thinking."

Dekka bit her lip and seemed to be heaving with every breath.

The pilot came on in their headphones. "Five minutes!"

Malik helped Francis to sit up, then stood back to let a morphed Armo lift her easily in his arms. Dekka squatted and hefted the artillery shell. "Malik, go ahead and set the timer. It can't be as long as we were planning on for Grand Central. Make it for . . . I guess one minute. Hit it right before we go."

Malik leaned forward and poked at the timer duct-taped to the shell.

"Sam? As soon as we jump back . . ."

"As soon as you're clear, Dekka."

"Francis?" Dekka asked. "Can you do this?"

Francis nodded. She was in obvious pain, held like a baby in Armo's arms, grimacing, her voice shuddering. "I can do it."

"Yep," Dekka said.

"We're passing the train," the pilot announced.

Cruz, her forehead bandaged gruesomely, came to lay her head briefly on Armo's bicep. "Don't get killed."

"You trying to tell *me* what to do?" Armo demanded archly.

Cruz smiled through tears. "Never."

Malik slid the helicopter door open and was almost knocked down by the stiff wind. The noise of the rotors rose from merely deafening to overwhelming. They had run ahead of the train and come to a stable hover. The Acela raced at them like a bullet.

Armo moved Francis to the door and stood there, fur flapping, as Francis looked down. It was always better when Francis knew where she was aiming. Francis reached and took hold of Dekka's hand.

"All right," Dekka said to Malik. "Hit it."

Malik leaned forward and pushed the button on the timer.

The helicopter hovered over the tracks.

The train rushed toward it.

Armo cradled Francis in his arms. Dekka held the nerve gas shell. 01:00 . . . 00:59 . . . 00:58 . . .

Sam leaned out the side door, face stretched back into a grimace by the wind, droplets of blood torn from his oozing wound.

"Ready?" Dekka's voice was flat.

00:55 . . . 00:54 . . .

Francis nodded.

"Do it."

"Wait!" Shade screamed, but it was a buzz that no one heard.

CHAPTER 38
Momentum

DEKKA HAD NEVER traveled through n-dimensional space, and despite Malik's warnings, the effect was absolutely disorienting and shocking. She had never seen Malik in his charred and livid natural state. She had never seen her own veins and arteries seeming to float outside of a hand that was hers, not the morph's.

And she had never seen inside Shade Darby's head, seen her actual brain, like a cauliflower Mandelbrot video.

"Shade?" Dekka said, blinking in confusion. And had just enough time to wonder why Shade was with them.

Shade had leaped at the last moment and grabbed hold of Francis because Shade had remembered what everyone had forgotten: momentum.

The train was moving now at just over a hundred miles an hour. When Dekka, Armo, Francis, and Shade popped back into three-dimensional space from the stationary helicopter, they were not moving, but they were inside a train that was moving very fast.

They emerged back into 3-D space toward the front of the second car. Shade appeared at the exact same moment, but a "moment" to Shade was not a "moment" to the others.

The rearmost wall of the train car was moving at a hundred miles an hour, or a hundred forty-seven feet per second. The distance between the nearest of the Rockborn Gang, Armo, and that door was seventy-five feet.

Shade had less than half a second. And that was not enough, not even for Shade. She might save one, but not the others. Unless . . .

The car ended in a door. The next car would also have a door. Eventually, they would slow down.

Eventually.

Shade leaped, spun in the air, so that she flew backward, facing Armo's back as the steel door rushed at her. She stuck out her hands and grabbed seat backs that tore away, row after row of blue upholstered seats, *bam, bam, bam bambam-bambam!*

Grabbing at seat backs had bled off only a little of their relative speed, and Shade hit the door at seventy miles an hour. She took the impact in her back and felt her chitin armor snap, crushed like a cockroach under a boot. Her head smashed into steel and the thick glass window, cracking her skull like a dropped cantaloupe.

The impact smashed the door open, and Shade plowed into the next door at a mere fifty miles an hour. Her hands were torn, some fingers ripped off and spraying blood, her back broken, her head caved in. She was reduced to a bloody mess of bone and chitin armor and blood.

The impact went: Shade, Armo, Francis, Dekka, and the shell.

Armo, Dekka, Francis, and the shell survived.

Shade looked like a lobster that had been cracked open and torn apart with a fork.

Armo knew only that he had flown through the air at fantastic speed, whooshing past blue seats before coming to a brutally sudden stop. The back of his head hit something hard and unyielding. His left arm had been snapped like a twig by impact with the bulge of the restroom bulkhead. He slammed into something crunchy behind him and took the momentum of Francis then Dekka in his gut, blowing the air from him.

And then he was out.

Dekka hit Armo, the best cushion possible, and her morphed body took a blow like being hit by a truck. Brutal, staggering, and fatal . . . had she been in human form.

Dekka saw stars, swirling lights, a blankness that came, then receded, came back again as she tried to move, then receded again, leaving her conscious and all too aware of pain throughout her body. She couldn't breathe. Couldn't make her lungs work, like they were empty balloons, flat and hard to inflate. Then a gasp. Another gasp. A sudden, deep breath that was like needles inside her. But pain was pain, while suffocation was death.

Her hands and feet would not work at first, hands seeming disconnected, reaching out toward targets like seat backs and missing. Legs all wobbly. She was like a drunk, a brain confused and lost and unable to . . . But at last with great focus she managed to get her fingers around a seat back and pulled herself up. She stood, swaying, trying to make sense of what she was seeing. There were no passengers here, just the clickety-clack of the track and a pile of bodies.

She stumbled back and stepped on something soft.

"Armo!" she cried. "Armo!" The aisle was too narrow to let her get beside him, so she clambered over the seats till she could kneel down on an aisle seat and look at his face. There was blood coming from his nose and ears. Blood coming from his eyes as well. But he was moving, random, unfocused, groggy but alive, though maybe not for long. A puddle of blood too large to have come from Armo's ears, nose, or eyes saturated the carpet.

"Armo! You have to de-morph! Now!"

"Urrhh?" He was groggy, barely conscious, and yet heard an order and instinctively thought, *No*.

"De-morph, now!"

He blinked bloody eyes and half raised a bloody paw. Dekka realized she was crying only when his face was blurred by her tears.

"Armo! Armo, you . . . I . . . Armo, maybe you should consider de-morphing!"

"Urr."

Slowly at first, then faster, Dekka saw the white fur receding and the bear man being replaced by the man.

And then she saw what lay beneath Armo.

"Oh, God! Shade! Shade!"

Shade Darby looked far too much like a huge grasshopper that had been stepped on. It was impossible even to make sense of the lower half of her body. Bones, strips of chitin cracked like lobster shell, pink flesh protruding, and ripped arteries that pumped blood far too fast.

Dekka shot a look forward. The shell lay in the aisle, rolling sluggishly back and forth. Red numbers read 00:24 . . . 00:23 . . .

Dekka had to climb over the last row of seats to get to Shade, and she knelt over her and yelled, as she had with Armo, "De-morph, Shade, de-morph!" Again and again.

She glanced back, looking for the shell and its timer. Red numbers swam in her tears. Fourteen seconds!

"Francis!" Dekka cried. She found the girl curled up under a seat, her broken leg bleeding freely, blood coming from her nose and trickling from one ear.

"Francis! Francis!"

00:09 . . . 00:08 . . .

"Unh?" Francis moaned.

"I need you. Right the hell now!" Dekka shouted. "Get Shade out of here!"

00:07 . . .

Seven seconds.

In the helicopter Sam turned his wind-whipped face to Malik, Simone, and Cruz. "Something's wrong. They should be back by now."

"Where's Shade?" Simone demanded suddenly.

"Dammit," Sam snapped. The plan was already falling apart. The train was still racing at speed, not its full one fifty, but very fast. The Anacostia River sparkled just ahead, their target area, the very last relatively unpopulated space before the city proper.

Looking ahead, Sam saw the dome of the Capitol building, and the white needle of the Washington Monument. He'd never been to Washington. This was a hell of a first visit.

"We have to stop that train!" Simone said.

Malik erupted. "Oh, God, Shade must have grabbed Francis as she was . . . No, no, no!"

"Why would she do that?" Simone cried.

"Momentum," Malik said grimly.

"If the train hits the inside of the dome, everyone aboard, including our friends, will die!" Cruz cried.

"If my father isn't stopped . . ."

And just like that, Sam was back in the business of making life-and-death decisions.

Francis's brain was a swirl of images and shouts and pain.

Get her out of here!

She fumbled for something to hold on to, felt her hand sink into flesh like hamburger studded with shards of glass.

"Now, now, now!" Dekka's voice cried from far, far away, and Francis knew Dekka meant her, meant that she . . .

In an instant Francis and the wreckage of Shade were back in the helicopter, which had blessedly turned to match speed with the train.

"Shade!" Malik cried. He and Cruz knelt beside the gruesome horror of Shade's barely alive body, yelling, "De-morph, de-morph, Shade!"

Sam was yelling something different. "Four seconds! Francis!"

"You have to do it, Sam!" Simone cried.

Sam staggered to the door and gripped a handhold, leaned out, and extended his free hand.

"Look!" Armo yelled, and tried to point with a hand that was not exactly obeying his brain's instructions but wavered like a drunk pointing the way to his car.

Dekka looked. And saw.

00:04 . . . 00:03 . . .

A dark swarm was rushing toward Dekka, and she thought, *If I have to die, I'm taking some of you bastards with me*, and fired her shredding beams into the mass.

She was still firing when she suddenly found herself back in the helicopter, narrowly missing Sam's head while shredding the sill of the helicopter's door.

The train was well past the open space of the wetlands by the river. They were not a mile from the station, and now the train's brakes were squealing.

A big freeway interchange to the right.

A college campus to the left.

Sam whispered, "Forgive me."

CHAPTER 39
Gas Will Expand to Fill Available Space

VECTOR LOOKED THROUGH many eyes at once and saw the Capitol dome rising in his field of view. He had ordered his hostage train driver to begin slowing, not that the fool knew what to do, but she had hands, and hands, it seemed, were useful.

Seeing the Capitol and the Washington Monument ahead filled Vector with grim excitement.

I'm taking over the United States government!

He felt the brakes beginning to bite. He would survive a headlong crash into the train station, but it would disrupt his swarm, and who knew, he might want to use the train again someday. It changed your perspective, Vector realized, when you started to understand that everything belonged to you now. *Everything!* New York was his. Washington would soon be his. And then what of the Rockborn Gang's resistance? Where would they go? Where would they hide when the US military and the National Guard and the Secret Service and

FBI were all working for him?

President Vector? Or President Markovic?

Not that he would reside in the White House, that run-down dump. No, he could have any place he wanted, and the beauty of it was he didn't really need a place at all. He could be anywhere or everywhere. The thought made him laugh from sheer glee.

He had seen the desperate efforts of the Rockborn Gang. It had been clever of Shade to remove the train's engineer, but not, in the end, effective. He'd watched as a pillar of smoke had receded behind him, the burning of the Rockborn Gang's last, faint hope.

Then to his shock he'd seen a newer, sleeker, and obviously faster helicopter come zooming overhead. It now hovered menacingly above the tracks. No question that it could fire missiles and derail the train, but he was so close to the city now that it would barely amount to a delay.

Blow up the train, fools, if you must: it will only kill the hostages.

Then a series of rapid-fire sounds, fast as a machine gun's fire, followed by an impact that sent a shudder through the train. He had turned part of his swarm to investigate and had come upon the startling spectacle of three bloodied, stunned members of the Rockborn Gang . . . and one who was well beyond stunned or bloodied.

Shade Darby is dead!

One down! Now for the black bitch.

His swarm raced back as an enraged Dekka ran forward.

So much the better. Let her come all the way to the passenger car, and there he would present her with a stark choice: surrender or watch helpless people writhe in undying agony.

Hah! That was the problem with virtuous, heroic types: they lacked ruthlessness. Rather than allow the passengers to come to harm, they would leave him to annihilate all opposition and rule the country. The world!

Wait . . . where was Shade Darby's body?

Dekka fired, and Vector registered dozens, hundreds of his eyes going dark, but no matter: he had hundreds of thousands of eyes to spare.

Then, still searching for the crumpled remains that had made him too happy, he spotted the curious object on the floor. Green. With scratched letters.

And a timer.

And the glowing, red number . . . 00:02 . . .

No!

Dekka and Armo disappeared. The shell . . . did not.

But no explosion would kill him. His swarm would be diminished, scattered, but not annihilated.

Unless . . .

NO!

Markovic ordered his swarm out, out through the shattered windshield of the energy car, out through the broken side window of the first-class car.

Then Vector's world came apart, as the hurtling train came to a sudden and total stop. His parts swirled in a tornado of crashing steel and flying hostages.

Sam Temple focused his mind, the same mind that had learned to manipulate light itself during the FAYZ. It felt like old times, but not in a good way.

The timer on his phone counted down. 00:03 . . . 00:02 . . .

Armo, Dekka, and Francis appeared, their weight causing the helicopter to yaw, nearly throwing Sam out through the door.

"Now!" Dekka yelled.

Sam focused, and a split second later, the Acela train, now moving at a relatively sedate fifty-five miles an hour, smashed into the interior wall of a transparent dome. This was not a derailment. This was not a sideswiping of another train. This was a collision like nothing any train had ever endured. This was train vs. brick wall. Irresistible force meeting unmovable object.

The deceleration was shocking to see. The energy car accordioned, swung left, breaking away from the first car, smashed sideways into the barrier, and bounced back. The second car, the one containing the hostages, plowed into the engine, T-boning it, and split open. Bodies flew from the jagged tear, one flying so fast it smashed into the dome's interior, splitting the body open like it had just been autopsied.

The remaining cars cascaded in a jumbled pile, like some terrifying game of pickup sticks.

Malik was yelling something that Sam barely understood at first.

"Shade! De-morph!"

Sam heard but could not take his eyes off the destruction he had just caused. He could imagine all too easily the carnage inside, the bodies suddenly hurled around a steel tube, smashed, broken, split open, spilling their intestines . . . He could not stop looking because to stop looking was to avoid taking on all the pain he knew he deserved. He owed it to the people—*the people he had just killed*—to look, to acknowledge.

And he thought, as the helicopter swerved away to avoid hitting the exterior of the dome, that it would be a sort of justice if he simply let go and fell to his death. The alternative was living this moment over and over again in his mind. And he already had so many terrible moments that his nights would never be safe from nightmares.

It was Dekka who pulled him back inside and pushed him gently into a seat. Sam now saw the nearer horror, right at his feet: Shade, a gory mess, and Malik and Cruz shouting and Simone crying and he was back in it all, back in all that he had escaped.

The helicopter made a wide turn, having run past the dome, which was little more than an eighth of a mile in diameter. The dome that had appeared at Sam's command and had cut through buildings and cars and people.

How many dead? Oh, God, how many had he killed?

Vector had no warning. The dome was perfectly transparent. No warning. Just a catastrophically violent impact that sent bags, seats, glass, and bodies flying through the air.

An impact that twirled the cars like cheerleaders' batons. Through tens of thousands of eyes Vector witnessed the wild madness of annihilation.

Vector was not immune to the effects of the laws of physics, at least not the laws having to do with momentum, and thousands of his bugs were killed by smashing into walls at high speed or being struck by flying bodies and debris.

Bad. Infuriating! But not the end, not by a long shot. Only a few percent of his eyes went dark; the rest, including those outside the train, were intact.

Then, almost simultaneously, came the explosion.

The shell blew up, but it did not spray napalm or even shrapnel aside from the shell's casing.

Vector had just enough time to think, *Hah, you can't kill me with . . .* Then Vector's eyes started to go dark in waves. Not hundreds, but thousands. Not an easily replaced few percent, but masses, multitudes, a rapidly closing circle of darkness.

Gas, he thought. What he had feared.

Gas!

But the crash had created escape holes, too. Vector sent his surviving parts racing toward fresh air, escaping through broken windows and twisted doors and great gashes in the aluminum body of the cars.

He rose in a wave of millions, still alive, still able to spread disease and terror.

Still Vector!

A part of his mind looked for but did not find the solid object the train had clearly hit. No one had driven a tank

onto the tracks. No one had built a wall. The train had simply
hit . . . nothing . . . and stopped instantly with devastating
results.

Then the first of his insects banged into what felt like glass.

Impossible!

He sent his swarm higher, up and up, but the invisible barrier persisted. It seemed to be curved. Like a bowl. Like an
invisible bowl. Like . . .

Like a dome.

The lower edge of his swarm began to go dark now, and
his bugs fell in their hundreds and their thousands as the gas
slowly dispersed and filled the interior of the dome.

Vector flew his swarm as high as it would go. To the top of
the dome, the inescapable dome. From there he looked up, up
through his dwindling number of eyes and saw a face looking
down at him from the door of the helicopter.

It was a black feline face surrounded by writhing serpents.

The gas rose, and Vector's bits died.

He switched frantically between views, like a desperate
TV watcher whose cable has gone out, looking for active eyes,
and finding fewer and fewer and fewer

No! No! It doesn't end like this!

In the end he had only a handful left, just four. Four out
of his millions. Four insects whose eyes were on leaves and
homes . . . outside the dome.

He was not dead but . . . but his mind was . . . he could not
quite . . .

Shrinking, that's what it was like. Like shrinking, smaller

and smaller. Like he was a house and someone was walking through that house systematically turning off lights, so that room by room he went dark.

His focus wavered and fragmented, thoughts becoming random, irrational. He should . . . he could . . . He was . . . Lights going out . . . Confusion . . .

I am Vector . . . I am Markovic!

I know who I . . .

Somewhere a voice was shouting.

De-morph, de-morph, over and over again.

It was irritating. And Shade had other worries. Pain. Confusion. Blindness.

De-morph, de-morph. Shade, de-morph now!

Okay, if it will shut you up.

Watchers in her head. Was it them yelling?

Her mind was on the very edge of a cliff, a cliff a thousand feet high over jagged rocks, and if she slipped . . .

De-morph, goddammit, Shade!

Malik?

Shade formed a thought, a tenuous, slick, impossible-to-hold-on-to thought . . . and slipped over the edge of the cliff and fell and fell and fell.

CHAPTER 40
A Lair of Their Own

FORTY-TWO PEOPLE, INCLUDING seven children, were on the train. Twenty-six died instantly on impact. The rest died from nerve gas, their bodies racked by violent spasms.

There were no survivors.

As ambulances and police cars swarmed the crash site, helpless to penetrate the dome, the helicopter flew the short distance to the Pentagon, the massive, five-sided, seven-story headquarters of the American military in Virginia, just outside of the District of Columbia. It landed on the helipad on the north side of the building and was met by the inevitable dark SUVs, three of them.

As the turbines powered down and the rotors slowed, Malik saw a sort of honor guard waiting, a half dozen older, bemedaled soldiers and dark-suited civilians.

There were also two ambulances parked at a discreet

distance, awaiting the badly injured members of the Rock-born Gang. A group that did not include Shade Darby.

Shade had de-morphed, returned to her human form, alive and uninjured—harm suffered in morph was repaired by de-morphing, so long as the human form had not been injured. Malik did not like the look of shock on her face, the closed-down, unresponsive, Shade-running-in-safe-mode expression on her face. Malik knew her near-death experience would leave deep scars on her mind. He'd been there.

We all have scars. Some will be mended with stitches. Others will never be healed.

"There's a welcome committee," Dekka observed with a bit of an eye roll.

"At least it's not a firing squad," Simone muttered. She stood beside Dekka, and Malik sensed that something had changed between the two women. A connection had been made, perhaps nothing more than the fact that Simone had now become a full member of their strange little tribe.

Simone had lost her father. At least they all hoped she had lost her father, which was a terribly complicated set of emotions to make sense of. They all liked Simone well enough not to wish her the pain of losing a parent. But to Simone, Malik imagined, her father's death had occurred days earlier when Vector was born.

More business for some future therapist.

Francis would be going straight to the ambulance. She was in pain, her face a bleached white, hair matted with sweat. Francis, without whom their victory, if you could call it that, would not have been possible. Malik leaned forward, put his hand on her shoulder, and said, "You did good, Francis. You're a hero."

Armo had de-morphed and—astonishingly—had to be wakened from a nap when they landed, having managed to actually fall asleep on the flight from the train wreck to the Pentagon. Cruz, herself once more, was beside him. Malik was certain something was going on that was not strictly to do with battles or morphs or n-dimensional universes.

Malik felt almost sorry for the big dude. Everyone liked Armo, but at the same time, everyone had the same thought: *If you break Cruz's heart, we will make your life miserable.* Any normal person might have been intimidated at having the likes of Dekka, Shade, and Malik watching them like a hawk, but then, Malik admitted with a private smile, Armo was not normal.

Malik was most interested by Sam Temple, about whom he knew the least. Sam had come with a reputation. He'd been called everything from the Winston Churchill of the FAYZ to the Ulysses S. Grant of the FAYZ. But Malik had found him humble and devoid of ego. Sam had managed to remain immune to the lavish praise as well as the uninformed criticisms.

Now Sam sat among the shell-shocked Rockborn Gang, waiting for the door to be opened, drawn into himself, contemplative, and, Malik thought, sad. Sam, Malik suspected, would torture himself over the people on the train, the same way Malik tortured himself over the things he'd done at the Ranch.

You carry a heavy load on your shoulders, surfer dude.

A soldier slid the helicopter door open. Dekka was the first one off, followed by Shade. Armo gently lifted Francis in his arms and climbed down carefully. A gurney appeared, and Armo laid her on it, patted her on the head, and whispered something that earned a weak smile from Francis.

Malik was the last off the chopper, lingering behind for just a moment to collect his thoughts. The others were all de-morphed. He alone remained trapped in the world of the Watchers.

Did you enjoy that, Watchers? Was it all entertaining enough for you?

He planned to deal with them, just as soon as Francis was cared for and ready. The gang had scored a win, but it was a close call, and Vector might still survive in some form. And even if Vector was gone, what horror might rise tomorrow or next week? How many more times could the gang get lucky?

This has to end, Malik thought grimly. *This has to end.*

"General Eliopoulos, it's good to meet you in the flesh," Dekka said, and shook the general's hand. She was pretty sure that the nation's top soldier did not make a habit of greeting every arriving helicopter: he was paying them respect.

"Ms. Talent, it is my honor," Eliopoulos said.

Introductions and handshakes followed, then they boarded the SUVs for the short drive to a side entrance and trooped wearily down long hallways to a conference room. The general's staff had laid out an impressive buffet, and Armo was already snatching cold shrimp and quaffing cold juice. The mad chase and the sound of helicopter rotors had given way to this quiet, stuffy, banal conference room.

"We have a great deal to discuss," Eliopoulos said after the gang had massacred much of the food—no one could remember the last time they'd had anything to eat.

"Okay," Dekka said cautiously.

Eliopoulos sat at the head of a long, oval, dark wood table. Dekka sat at his right hand, feeling out of place and a bit ridiculous. Safeway cashiers did not as a rule sit next to four-star generals in the heart of the Pentagon. She was acutely aware that she and the rest of the gang were indifferently dressed, bloody, sweat-stained, torn, and smeared with oily grease among spotless uniforms. And she was aware as well of how young the gang all were compared to the general and his people.

On the other hand, we did save Washington, DC. For now.

"Let me lay it out in plain English," Eliopoulos said. "It is a simple fact that you saved this government, and the country as well. If you were soldiers in uniform, we'd be putting in for Medals of Honor. I have never witnessed greater courage."

"But?" Shade said.

"But," Eliopoulos said with a disgusted sigh, "there's reality, and then there's the law. And you were acting outside the law."

Malik cleared his throat and said, "General, we were all deputized by the mayor of New York City. She was worried as well about the law."

"Were you indeed?" Eliopoulos said, nodding. "Excellent.

A legal argument could be made that you were in hot pursuit of a criminal. . . . Yes, that is helpful."

Dekka felt another "but" coming, and it came.

"But," Eliopoulos said, "we have a problem going forward. The fact is we need you. You exposed the Ranch. You stopped Dillon Poe in Las Vegas, and, well, this entire thing in New York . . . Nevertheless, there is no legal way for you to go on doing what we clearly need you to do."

Sam said, "Yeah—I mean, yes, General, we went through this after the end of the FAYZ."

"Indeed. The laws of this country do not allow for superpowered vigilantes, however necessary, however self-sacrificing and heroic. And let me repeat: if *you* aren't heroes, the word has no meaning."

The other officers nodded agreement. Dekka had the startling realization that these senior officers were looking at them with something like awe. Awe and a bit of jealousy.

"So . . . ," Dekka prompted. Weariness was following the retreat of adrenaline-fueled energy, and she felt as if she could all too easily slide out of her chair and sleep under the table.

"So. I have a proposal. It does not solve the problem of your legal status. It does, however, give you a safe place to operate from. And certain resources could be made available."

"What if we don't want to keep doing this?" Shade asked. "What if we're done? What if we just want to go back to our old lives?"

It was Malik who answered. "Shade, there is no going back. We took down Poe, and we took down Markovic. The next Rockborn lunatic with delusions of godhood will know he has to deal with us. The Rockborn Gang is Target Number One for ambitious bad guys."

Eliopoulos nodded. "You have every right to expect to be able to return to your old lives. But Mr. Tenerife is correct: you are targets, and anyone near you is likely to end up as collateral damage."

Dekka expected this, knew this, and yet felt her stomach sink. She hadn't even liked her old life, but being told she could never go back to it had the unsettling sound of a death sentence.

"Hold up," Armo said. "Are you telling us we have to go to this place of yours?"

Dekka jumped in quickly. "I'm sure the general is just offering a suggestion."

"Hmph," Armo commented, and glared slit-eyed at Eliopoulos.

"There is a secret facility, a leftover from the Cold War. It's in the Maryland hills, not far from a town named Thurmont. It's very secure. There are living quarters and even a swimming pool, though it will need some work. The perimeter will be guarded by MPs with high-level security clearances."

"Dude," Armo said, "sounds like a nice prison. Kind of sounds like the Ranch, too."

Dekka's eyes had gone wide on hearing Eliopoulos addressed as "dude," but she kept quiet.

Eliopoulos shrugged and nodded and said, "In a way it is a bit like a prison, Mr. . . . um, Armo. But the fences and gates are there to keep people out, not in."

"We come and go as we choose?" Cruz asked, clarifying for Armo's benefit.

"Of course. I'll repeat, because it bears repeating: we need you. And"—he dipped his head in wry acknowledgment—"we've seen what you do to government facilities you don't like."

"Okay," Dekka said. "What else, General?"

"You would have a private jet and pilots at your disposal, twenty-four/seven/three sixty-five. If you need funds, we'll take care of it. The Pentagon budget is large, more than large enough to conceal money spent on you."

"You're saying the rest of the government wouldn't know about this facility?" Shade asked.

"Exactly. We'd be hiding it from Congress, from the Justice Department, from anyone with a, um, different view of things. I have broad powers when it comes to national security."

Dekka glanced at Shade and saw a resentful acceptance. She looked next to Malik, who nodded slightly. Then she turned to the person she still trusted more than any other.

"Sam?"

"It would leave us vulnerable to the military. No offense, General, but you won't always have this job." Sam blew out his cheeks and winced at being reminded by a sharp stab of pain that his face had been barely sewn together. "But as it is, we are not just the targets of bad guys, we're the targets of paparazzi and hustlers and con men and crazy people. Our faces are everywhere in the media, in social media. The only one of us who could walk down a street right now is Cruz, and that's only because she can change her appearance."

"Armo?" Dekka asked.

"If they fix the pool," Armo said. "Also they better have decent Wi-Fi."

One of the officers opened a folder, glanced down, and said, "There is a dedicated fiber-optic line that delivers five hundred megabits per second."

Armo looked to Malik, who said, "Yeah, that's about as fast as it gets."

Armo shrugged. "Okay, but free Netflix, too."

"That can be arranged," said the most senior military officer in the country. "Free Netflix."

"One more thing," Sam said. "I'm married."

Eliopoulos smiled a little ruefully. "We have already arranged for Ms. Ellison to join us. As a matter of fact, she should be landing at Andrews in just a few minutes. She is . . ." He let it trail off and seemed embarrassed.

"Were you about to say intimidating, even a little scary?" Sam laughed.

"I was going to say impressive and not easily convinced." Eliopoulos grinned. "But yes, a bit . . ."

"Mmm," Sam said. "And now she's not just a genius; she's got super-strength. I will no longer be throwing my laundry on the floor or leaving dishes in the sink. Or, you know, arguing with her. About anything." He brightened. "Oh, and I should mention that Astrid has a steel box she would like to have dropped into the Marianas Trench."

"She mentioned that, yes," the general said. "That box is currently being loaded aboard a C-17 in California. The box in question will be rolled out of the cargo door and dropped into the deepest spot in the Pacific Ocean."

"That ought to do it," Sam said. And thought, *Maybe.*

The facility was named Site L. It encompassed more than a square mile of forested land with a scattering of uninteresting buildings aboveground. But belowground it was a great deal more, a vast complex of tunnels, empty, echoing chambers, storerooms filled with neatly organized canned food and swimming pool–sized fuel tanks. It had its own water supply, its own power generator, and could in theory survive a direct hit from a nuclear weapon.

We are ten now, Malik thought. *Will we be more or fewer a month from now?*

Dekka, Shade, Cruz, Armo, Francis, Sam, Astrid, Simone, Edilio, and Malik himself. Ten against how many? How many more Vectors were out there? How many enemies did they have within the government itself? How long would this lair of theirs remain secret?

The Military Police security was all outside, monitoring the cameras and sensors that augmented the razor wire–topped hurricane fence. Within the underground facility lived a small maintenance and housecleaning staff of enlisted men and women who did unglamorous work despite having security clearances higher than the captain of a nuclear submarine.

And at the center of the web of hallways and tunnels, defended by steel vault doors a tank could not dent, was a command center like something out of a movie, with video monitors on the walls and desks and wheeled chairs and the stuffy atmosphere of a place long disused. The monitors were all blank. Dust rings showed where computers had been removed. At the very middle was a ring of chairs around a rectangular table.

Edilio spoke to the lieutenant assigned to escort them through the facility. "I don't mean to make work for you, but could you please see if you can get us a different table? Round, not rectangular."

"Yes, sir."

Sam nodded and said, "You're thinking Knights of the Round Table?"

"Something like that," Edilio said. "I thought we should sit as equals, at least the nine of you."

"Good idea," Dekka said. "But there's no nine plus, Edilio, there are ten."

"The Ten Musketeers," Simone suggested.

Food was carried to them and coffee poured, and at last they sat around the rectangular table, exhausted, drained, and devoid of any ambition but to sleep for a very long time.

"So this is our lair," Cruz said, looking around at what had once been a very different lair.

"Yep," Dekka said.

They sat swiveling idly in their chairs and looking around, all feeling lost and disoriented. No one knowing what they should do next.

The end of battle, and the troops sit quietly awaiting the next round.

But Malik had already decided on the next round.

"I have a plan," Malik said. "We all know how this ends. The ten of us have power, but there are too many possible dangers, not just to us, but to the whole human race."

Shade sighed. "I had a feeling this was coming."

"What?" Dekka asked.

"Malik wants to go Over There."

"If Francis is willing. Maybe, just maybe, I can make contact with the Watchers."

Edilio spoke up again, and Malik was relieved to see him taking up the role of organizer. Someone had to do it. "I think," Edilio said, "that when we are in a battle we need one person in charge. But if we're going to hang together as a group for months, possibly years, I think we should vote on the big things. And this sounds like a big thing."

The vote was unanimous. Malik had known it would be.

CHAPTER 41
Meet Your Maker

SITE L WAS even stranger seen from the other side. It was fascinating to see the n-dimensional deconstruction of the massive steel doors. Fascinating to see the forest of wire and fiber-optic cable all surging with clouds of photons. Fascinating to see through subterranean walls into the surrounding earth, with tree roots visibly sucking water and nutrients, earthworms eating and excreting, insects crawling on legs that seemed to move apart from the body they were connected to.

All fascinating. And in another time and place Malik might have simply reveled in observing and taking mental notes and formulating hypotheses. . . . Malik had always been one of the smart kids, the ones who barely bothered to crack a textbook because school was just that easy. He'd imagined a future life working at MIT or CERN or NASA. A future of intellectual adventure, of searching for answers.

On many occasions those happy daydreams had included

Shade, working beside him, or perhaps teaching at a university, the two of them with a neat little home in a nice neighborhood. Maybe kids. Sure, why not? Any child borne by Shade would be brilliant and beautiful. And as to their moral and ethical upbringing, well, Malik figured he'd better take a hand in that.

And none of those fantasies mattered anymore. All of that was dead. Dead and buried.

Malik was trapped in a life where his only escape from mental invasion by the Watchers was to de-morph back to a body that would die within an hour in agony. That was his reality.

His reality also included having seen a morphed Shade lying on the steel floor of a helicopter so mangled that he had needed no extra dimensions to see her bones and arteries and intestines. She had looked like a crab run over by a truck. He had begged her to de-morph. How many times? A hundred? With tears streaming down his face, he had begged her, and he had to his shame prayed—yes, prayed—to the Watchers.

Don't let her die. Without her I have nothing.

The Watchers had merely watched. Malik had sensed no pity, no concern, just curiosity. Like they were scientists peering down through a microscope at amoebas.

Malik was, had always been, a controlled person. He was not hasty or careless. He monitored his own mind and thoughts the way he would monitor any other complex computer, calibrating his mental speed, guarding against false data. He felt emotion, strong emotion at times, but that had been all the more reason to control himself.

But a rage had been building within him, and to Malik that rage felt like a fire he could not fully extinguish but which he had to contain lest it burn him up inside as surely as fire had burned his body. Each time he felt the Watchers, he raged and told himself sternly that he should accept. Each time he'd witnessed some new horror he had felt like someone had thrown gasoline on that fire, and he was the fire department, limiting, containing.

Then he had nearly been burned again and had, for the first time in his life, panicked. Panicked! Screaming, flailing, unreasoning panic.

And then had found himself on his knees on the steel deck of a helicopter, begging for Shade's life. And almost miraculously, she had done it. With the last of the dying light in her mind she had found the way to escape death.

This time.

Now Malik floated in n-dimensional space with Francis's hand in his. The scientist within Malik still observed, but he observed through the wild flames of his own fury.

"Come out and talk to me!" he raged, his words becoming multicolored swirls that floated away like the smoke of a cigarette.

He searched for and soon found the flat, blank, featureless circle he believed to be a connection to the Watchers. He impatiently fought off the slug-like defenses and moved closer to the circle, which receded with each forward step and yet drew slowly, slowly nearer, as though it took ten of his steps to equal one.

"Talk to me, you cowards!"

The circle of nothingness grew larger, fractionally at first, almost imperceptibly, then it grew faster, expanding until he at last reached out a hand toward it, a burned hand, his true hand.

And suddenly he was no longer in the weird vortex of disconnected bits of his 3-D world. He stood now in a space that was white, nothing but white above and below and to every side. Like he'd been dropped into a bucket of white paint, or a box of cotton balls.

He glanced down and with relief saw that Francis was still there, still holding his hand.

"Come out and talk to me!" Malik cried, and this time his words were not vapor but just sound, flat, dying quickly without echo or resonance.

"Impressive," a voice said. A human voice. A human voice with something familiar about it.

A distant dot of color appeared on the white nothingness, a human shape it seemed, but far away, though its voice was close and intimate in Malik's ears.

"Who are you? What are you?" Malik demanded.

"No one thought it possible, but I suspected you might just be able to manage it . . . Malik."

Malik was not surprised that the distant creature knew his name, but hearing it aloud in this place was disturbing.

"Are you still okay?" Malik asked Francis.

Her eyes were wide, her face pale. She stood beside him on one good leg, a rigid cast holding her broken bones in place. "Yes," she whispered.

"Do you see that . . . person? Are you hearing him speak?"

"Yes," she acknowledged.

So at least if this was some hallucination it was one they were both experiencing. Malik began moving toward the distant creature, but like the gray circle, the creature seemed to recede almost—almost as fast as Malik advanced.

"What is it you want, Malik?"

"I want you to stop torturing me and the people I love. Do you have any idea the horror you've caused?"

The figure seemed to nod; he was still too far distant for Malik to be sure. When he spoke, his voice was so close he might almost have been whispering into Malik's ear. "Strictly speaking, I did not cause any of this. Though, yes, I admit to guilt. I admit to hubris. But I have done nothing that you would not do, Malik."

"I know my universe is a simulation," Malik said. "And you are its creator."

This time the head shake was near enough that Malik could be sure of it. The creature definitely had the shape of a man, a fit man of perhaps middle age. A black man, Malik thought, though what did such distinctions mean when dealing with aliens?

"Twice, just twice has any creature within the sim become aware enough to escape the simulation. You, Malik, are the second. The first was an impressive little boy named Pete

Ellison. You've heard the name."

Malik nodded, curiosity distracting him from simple anger. "Little Pete. Of the FAYZ?"

"Yes. Of course he was an unusual boy, too young and too limited in his comprehension to be able to explain what he felt. But now: you. And you, Malik, are quite capable of understanding."

"Am I supposed to be flattered?"

"His voice . . . ," Francis whispered. Her hand was sweaty in Malik's grip.

"I am simply describing reality," the creature said. "You and Francis have done the impossible. And I am left to wonder about intentions."

"My intentions?" Malik asked.

"No, the intentions of your creator."

"Are you not . . . you admitted guilt!"

"And I am guilty, but not of creating you, Malik, or the world you inhabit. You see, computational power has made astounding leaps, but still no computer, still less any number of programmers, can create a simulation as complete, as intricately detailed as the one you inhabit."

"Then how . . ."

"No *human* programmer, I should have said. But an advanced AI, a powerful artificial intelligence? An AI fed a dataset extracted from living, human brains? An AI tasked with inventing a complete alternate reality using the memories of . . . of volunteers?"

The distance between them now closed more rapidly. The

figure was a man. A black man in middle age, bald, still fit but with the hard-to-define caution in movement of a mature man.

"Yes, volunteers. We have learned to digitize most of the contents of the human brain. We copied those memories, Malik, and fed them to my AI. Yes, my AI, because although I did not create the sim, I did create the sim's creator."

"Your AI is a monster!" Malik cried, stabbing an accusing finger.

Malik could see the man's features now. The mouth. The nose. The heavy-lidded, sleepy-looking eyes.

Chills swept across Malik's flesh, and a new dread, a new and terrible dread hovered just at the edge of his understanding.

"Yes, it is," the man agreed. "It has created a savage, brutal world full of unpredictability. It has rewritten the assumptions of physics to make its own physics. It's a monster, yes, but a brilliant one."

The man actually sounded proud, which just fed Malik's rekindling anger. "How dare you be proud of this? The pain you've caused, the horror—what kind of creature are you?"

"The human kind, Malik. The very human kind. But a human from your own future. My time, in my universe, is twenty-six years ahead of your perceived time."

Now Malik stopped moving, but the creature advanced, walking on two normal legs, two normal human arms by his side. Speaking in a voice . . .

. . . the voice.

"Do you wonder whose memories were harvested to program my AI, Malik?"

Malik took a step back.

Francis, in a pleading voice, said, "Malik . . ."

"No," Malik said.

"You're beginning to understand, Malik. You don't want to understand, but already your mind knows."

"No," Malik said, a faint whimper.

"The memories we harvested are those belonging to a woman named Dr. Shade Darby. . . ."

"No, no . . ."

"And ours, Malik. Yours and mine. I created the AI, and I thought: who better to provide the foundational images and ideas . . . I had an obligation, I thought, to use my own memories."

Malik wanted to turn and run away but felt his legs would not obey his commands, felt that they might buckle at any moment. He had stopped breathing. His heart thudded in his chest.

Now the man, not alien, but *man*, stood an arm's length away. And Malik saw.

"Yes, Malik. I am Dr. Malik Tenerife, of MIT. I am you."

CHAPTER 42
To Be or Not to Be

"THERE IS NO escape," Malik said bleakly.

They sat in the control room, a platter of fruits and snacks untouched in the center of the table. Armo had dragged a sofa into the room, and he lay spread out there with Cruz perched on one of the sofa's arms. The others all sat around the table.

Dekka frowned and said, "Hold up a minute there, Malik. You're saying all of this, the FAYZ and this new reality, all of this, really is a simulation?"

Malik nodded.

"And the one who created it . . . is you?"

"Me. Yes. A future me, a me twenty-six years from now, from *our* now. Yes, terribly smart Malik, doing terribly smart things in the future. Playing around in a lab. Coming up with a never-before-seen use of an AI to create a sim."

"Well, get back over there and tell future you to cut it out!" Armo said.

Malik shook his head. "It doesn't work like that. AIs aren't computers; you can't reprogram them. He . . . future me . . . cannot change anything about this reality. He can only watch. He and his grad students and scientists around the world, they are the Watchers."

"What the hell do you mean he can't change it?" Simone said. "He *made* it!"

Shade said, "No, Simone, he's right. We can create AIs, we can feed them sets of data, but what they do with that data, the processes inside—"

"This is insane!" Cruz interrupted, jumping to her feet. "We're in hell and the god who made us can't save us?"

Malik said nothing, just looked down at the dusty, unused carpet of their "command center."

"He can do *something*," Francis said quietly.

"What?" Astrid snapped, shooting a suspicious look at Malik.

"He can . . ." Francis turned pleading eyes to Malik.

Malik, sounding like he was straining for every word, said, "He can turn us off."

Every eye was on Malik. Dekka felt a wave of panic inside herself and reminded herself sternly that she was supposed to set a good example, supposed to be the leader, but what she felt was suffocation, like all the air had been sucked from the room.

"Tell us," Dekka said.

Malik looked up, his face glistening with tears. "He cannot alter our world. He can only pull the plug. We would cease to exist."

"That's our choice?" Cruz asked, almost sobbing the question. "We can go on living in hell? Us and everyone? Or we can die? That's the choice?"

"Yes," Malik said. "I told him . . . told myself . . . that I could not make that decision alone. I know the way back now. I can give him our answer."

"What is our answer?" Cruz asked, looking to Dekka.

"Edilio said on big stuff we vote," Dekka said. "There's nothing bigger than this."

They found paper and pencils.

They found an empty wastebasket.

"It's 11:26 p.m.," Dekka said. "We should think, and we should talk to each other, and for me at least, I will pray. At midnight we vote."

From the Purple Moleskine

WE ARE VOTING. It's taking a while; we aren't exactly voting on class president. We're voting on existence. On life.

Shade and Malik are in each other's arms, whispering into each other's ears. Dekka, Simone, Francis, and Edilio sit together, murmuring in low voices, their eyes cast down. Sam and Astrid are silent, side by side in their chairs, reaching across the gap between them to hold hands. I sense that they've made up their minds.

Armo is beside me. He's said nothing and I almost imagine that Armo, of all people, is leaving the decision to me.

The choice is brutal. To live in this universe as freaks, superpowered people under constant threat. To live with Malik never able to experience a single moment of privacy alone in his head. To live knowing that we are not alone in this world; each of the planet's seven billion people are as alive and as aware as we are. To live knowing that with that choice we keep alive Rockborn monsters, horrors like Vector, some already wreaking havoc, some yet to reveal themselves.

We know that the Ranch will not be the end of governments trying to use the rock for their own ends. We know that if we vote for existence, we condemn billions to unimaginable sadness, and loss, and pain.

But they don't get a vote, those billions. We have to vote for them.

I see Sam and Astrid stand up and walk together to the little wastebasket we're using as our life-and-death sorting hat. Each folds and drops their vote. The paper strikes an almost musical note as it lands.

Armo squeezes my hand gently.

We have decided that the vote must be unanimous. No one is trying to persuade anyone else. Those who are talking are questioning, not dictating. No one knows the right answer.

Armo turns a sad smile to me and asks, "So?"

I don't know the right answer. There is no hope that the horror will end. None.

Armo's hand encloses mine.

I don't know what to do. I don't know what's right.

I don't know.

And yet, I vote.

Author's Note

Dear Readers:

I wrote this three-book spin-off of the Gone series out of self-indulgence. I wanted to create my own superhero universe. I wanted to see if I could find original approaches to the idea of superpowerful individuals. It was a challenge, and I'll leave the judgment as to my degree of success or failure to you.

Though I tried to be completely original, even someone with my limited knowledge of comics recognizes that the *Monster, Villain,* and *Hero* trilogy owes a nod, at the very least, to Marvel's X-Men. But there are other influences incorporated as well. Gone readers will instantly feel at home, but there'a fair bit of Animorphs DNA in this trilogy as well. And the famous Victorian-era book by Edwin A. Abbott, *Flatland.* Published in 1888, and still blowing minds today.

You will have noticed that I didn't give this story a pat conclusion, and that's deliberate. Katherine (my wife and frequent coauthor, K. A. Applegate) and I were among the earliest authors to encounter fan fiction via the internet. We've embraced it from the start. And some part of me hopes that fanfic writers will carry this story forward. Don't ask me what happens to these characters next, because I don't know. Will Dekka find love, perhaps with Simone? Will Cruz and Armo? How will Sam and Astrid do in this terrifying extension of earlier trauma? Maybe you have some ideas. I built the sandbox; if you want to bring your pails and shovels and play in it, cool. It's one of the best things about writing for young people: you are my collaborators in imagination. If I leave blanks it's because I know you'll fill them.

Is our universe just a simulation? Maybe. So what? Does it make it easier to imagine a sim created by God as opposed to one created by some future artificial intelligence? Is there a difference?

Reality is what we can see, what we can measure, what we can verify through experimentation. And maybe in the future we will develop a test to discover whether we occupy the only universe, or just one among many. But our subjective reality, our fears and our hates and our loves, while not scientifically measurable, are genuine and cannot just be dismissed. We have no ability to treat the world as anything other than real. Maybe the brick wall is a sim, but if you try to walk through it you'll still get a bloody nose, and it will still hurt. And sim or not, a broken heart still aches.

Whether we occupy the only universe or one of many, whether we evolved or were invented by a supernatural being, or are just the creation of other creatures who've evolved a bit further than we have, we still have to behave as well as we are able. In this universe or in any other, I stand with Kurt Vonnegut, who wrote:

There's only one rule that I know of, babies: God damn it, you've got to be kind.

How great would it be to live in a universe, real or simulated, where that rule was obeyed?

As ever, I am deeply grateful to my readers, who have been very kind to me and embraced my worlds. Thank you for so much. You make it all fun.

Oh, and how did the vote go? Good question. Let me know what you decide.

—Michael Grant

Acknowledgments

During my decade and a half with Katherine Tegen Books, I've had the great luck to always have a strong team at my back. On this book, the team includes Katherine Tegen and Lerina Alvarez in editorial, Kathryn Silsand and Mark Rifkin in copyediting, David Curtis and Joel Tippie in design, Meghan Pettit and Allison Brown in production, Audrey Diestelkamp in marketing, and cover artist Matthew Griffin.

They have my gratitude.

Michael Grant